FOUNDATION

FOUNDATION

(Epic of Eden, Vol. 1)

Christopher Abernathy

CONTENTS

Prologue

Fire and earth rained from the sky. Men and women fought a losing battle against the heavens. Aside from the sounds of death and destruction, the air was thick with the voices of those who commanded power into being with a mastery few of the age could fathom. It mattered not. What was mortal authority to divinity?

In the citadel at the center of a falling city, a ruler walked the halls in the final moments of the kingdom she had built over the course of hundreds of years. The strands of fate were finally converging around her. So close, yet barely perceptible; one wrong move and they'd become a noose around her neck.

Her steps took her to the Hall of Remembrance where she slowed to appreciate the Hall's majesty. Lining each of the walls, alcoves lit by dream fire spilled over with divine treasures even the most powerful divine artists would covet. Some of the greatest minds she had ever known contributed their work to the Hall's treasures pushing their skills to the limit to create artifacts of immeasurable power. A shame that all of the power before her could not forestall the kingdom's grim destiny.

At the end of the Hall of Remembrance, a massive black iron door loomed like a harbinger of the unknown. The dream anima permeating the air folded away from the black iron as though it could feel the finality of it.

The dreams had stopped after the birth of her daughter. Her beautiful daughter that she had abandoned because she knew what was to come. Now, she walked her path blind to her place in the great tapestry of destiny. It was a strange feeling she'd long since forgotten— the fear of not knowing what would come next. She was acting out the events of her last dream that had granted her insight into her own fate. The black iron door. Truly, they were terrifying. Once she stepped past the dark gate, her fate would be unknown to her. She would be blind to her destiny.

Above, her champions fought in her defense. Tortured souls pulled from the darkness and given a home; a home they now defended. They fought against losing odds willingly despite knowing of her uncertainty and failures. All because of faith— faith in her. Titanic impacts shook the citadel eliciting trails of dust to fail around her as she placed her hand on the door's cold metallic surface.

It was time.

Although the door towered over her, she pushed it open with ease. In the center of the room beyond, a machine like none the world had ever seen rested atop a beautiful mosaic. Runes lined the machine's ahāzurite body in patterns so complex their formulation had taken the greatest runesmiths in the world over half a century to complete. Of its architects, only she remained to witness its activation and after she was done, none would ever know of its existence.

Her spiritual senses danced with sensation as she stepped inside. She felt the power contained within the runes and the vibrations rolling off the machine with her very soul. She heard the gentle song of the unending font of essence at the core of the machine.

She placed her hands on the crystal apparatus acting as the control center for the machine and summoned the purest manifestation of her soul. It settled over her gently offering comfort like an old friend, ever by her side. The device reacted to her power, only she could truly wield this instrument for its intended purpose.

She waited. The moment of truth would come soon. She did not know when but such was the nature of uncertainty. Would her plan work or would the sacrificed of those who had died to bring her to this moment be for naught?

A presence that could only be described as pure oblivion alighted at the edge of her senses. Even deep within the earth, she heard *him* speak. Everyone in the world would hear his Edict, an unyielding declaration of what was to come.

His proclamation sought her out, closing in with little heed for the world between her and it. She closed her eyes and activated the machine. For a brief moment, everything was still as the strength of limitless dreams bent to the will of her soul, ready to fate itself.

Then, ruin descended.

Chapter 1

A cool midsummer breeze swept across the Maro Province rustling the grass and pulling leaves from the oaks dotting the landscape. Around the largest tree, the Du clan village bustled with anticipation for the day's festival. The date marked the founding of the clan over a thousand years ago and every year they gathered to honor their ancestors on it. Throughout the preceding weeks, Du clan traders and hunters had traveled the plains to obtain all manner of goods in anticipation of the celebration. Spirits were especially high this year since it had been one of the clan's most prosperous in decades.

The Du village was on an upswing; all thanks to Enkai's father, Kai, who had successfully become the second divine artist in the Maro Province to reach the exalted rank of Silver within the last century. His breakthrough had garnered the attention of the great Lin clan who dwelled in the northmost region of the Maro Province.

Enkai thought of his father and the pride the clan held in the man as he ran to the training field. He dreamed of following in his father's footsteps and reaching Silver. Enkai wanted to become a warrior that his father could be proud of. Unfortunately, fulfilling his wish would be no easy task.

Cultivating world essence, the spiritual energy of the world, was incredibly difficult which meant people had trouble making any progress through Lead, the first rank of the divine arts, let alone breaking through to Bronze then Silver. Unlike the Lin clan which always produced at least one Silver divine artist each generation, the four other clans were lucky to be blessed with even one in a given century. Throughout the history of the Maro Province, the clans that had the most powerful divine artists enjoyed wealth, power, and comfort. Against all odds, Enkai's father had managed to awaken his spirit and reach Silver by the age of twenty-five which put him on the same level as the Lin Matriarch despite being half her age. As a result, the Du clan enjoyed the Lin clan's favor since Kai had negotiated an alliance with the Lin Matriarch. If Enkai wanted to be like his father, he would have to push beyond his limits. On the bright side, his father had shown that it was possible.

Most of the clan believed that Kai was an unparalleled talent that would eventually surpass the Lin Matriarch to reach the fabled rank of Gold. Everyone looked up to Kai and trusted the man to bring them prosperity. Anticipation was high for this year's festival since the Patriarch announced that Kai would be leading the Ritual of Waking.

The ritual was, by far, the most important event of the day as it would shape the destinies of the Du clan's next generation of divine artists. Each year during the festival, the Du clan children, ages six and up, underwent a special exercise to awaken their spirits. In order to cultivate the divine arts, an individual had to draw world essence into their body which ignited their anima and sparked the awakening of the spirit. During the Ritual of Waking, a divine artist, traditionally the clan leader, infused a small amount of their anima, their inner spiritual energy, into each child to help them awaken. Not everyone succeeded in awakening their spirit the first time and the older one became, the harder it was to awaken. Most eventually succeeded but having an early awakening often indicated innate talent so Enkai aimed to awaken on his first try like his father before him. If he pulled it off, he would be able to immediately start his training in the divine arts.

He finally arrived at the training field, slightly out of breath but excited. Nearly two dozen children, both girls and boys, stood in neatly organized lines facing the huge oak at the end of the field. There, the Du Patriarch waited patiently as members of the clan assembled behind the children.

The Patriarch wore magnificent layered red robes with golden embroidery along the flowing sleeves and the hem. Long gray hair fell down his back in intricate braids and a bronze circlet sat on his brow. His eyes swept over each child gleaming with delight and hope.

The children, including Enkai, wore similar, though less impressive, ceremonial clothing to commemorate the day's events. The boys were adorned in modest red robes with yellow sashes while the girls sported bright yellow tunics and pleated skirts tied together with a red sash. Boy or girl, they all had the Du clan emblem of a mighty brown oak framed by an orange sun emblazoned onto the back of their clothing. Enkai took his place next to Shana, the Patriarch's granddaughter.

"You're late. I knew you would be," she said frowning at him. Shana was the same age as him at six summers. The two had been friends since before Enkai could remember according to their parents.

"Sorry, my father wanted to talk to me before I left." Enkai said.

Shana's eyes widened a bit. "Ooh, that's rare. What'd he say?"

Enkai suppressed the urge to frown at her. She wasn't wrong; it was rare for Kai to talk to him at length about anything. In fact, most of their interactions were painfully brief. His father devoted most of his time to training while the remainder went to overseeing the clan warriors and delegating with the Lin clan. Since his mother had died in childbirth, Enkai passed the majority of his time under his grandfather's care though he did occasionally receive terse lessons from his father. He didn't blame Kai for the lack of attention and the distance. Everyone relied on his father. Kai was a hero to the clan, so Enkai couldn't selfishly expect his father to shirk his responsibilities to dote on him.

Still, he did often wish Kai would be less *cold*. Sometimes while observing how other kids in the clan interacted with their fathers, he wondered if he had done something wrong to earn his father's ire. Even with his grandfather, affection was a rare treasure in Enkai's life. Nevertheless, today had been different. Kai had spoken to him like a father would a son for the first time in years. The thought of their conversation brought a smile to his face.

"I'll tell you later," he said, winking at Shana. Her brow furrowed as her lips pursed into a slight pout though before she could protest, her grandfather began to speak.

"Dear family! We gather here today to honor the founding of our clan over a thousand years ago when the Fall of Heaven ravaged earth and sky. Our honored ancestor, Du, fought valiantly among the gods themselves wielding his divine arts against grave peril..." Enkai tuned out as the Patriarch retold the story of Du, the founder of the Du clan. The story wove an epic tale of a hero pitted against impossible odds in the midst of a conflict between divine powers. Each of the five clans that called the Maro Province home had a similar story. Du and his four companions, Lin, Garo, Hu, and Ma, fought in the Fall of Heaven until the conflict became so catastrophic that it almost destroyed the world and the founders were forced to shepherd their people to sanctuary. Their journey brought them to the land that would become the Maro Province.

While Enkai enjoyed the story, he had heard it countless times from his grandfather already. For the last year, he'd begged his grandfather to tell him Du's story as well as many others at every available opportunity in the hopes that they would give him hidden insight into the divine arts for when his day to undergo the Ritual of Waking finally came. Even in his earliest memories, he had dreamed of becoming a powerful divine artist like his father. They would fight off the clan's enemies as an unstoppable father-son duo bringing honor and glory to their family. His smile broadened as he thought of his plans after the awakening.

According to his grandfather, the first step after awakening his spirit would be to figure out his elemental affinities for essence and anima. His affinities would determine the nature of his divine arts more so than anything else. Like his grandfather, his father's elemental affinities were blade and wind which meant he could cultivate wind essence, blade essence, or some combination of the two into anima. Kai had chosen to cultivate Graywind anima, a hybrid of the wind and blade elements. Enkai suspected his affinities would be identical to his father's and grandfather's since they were often inherited from parent to child but he held out hope that he would have an affinity for water and earth anima like his mother. Aside from honoring his mother's memory, the elements had several properties that he could use to support the clan; earth was strong and enriching while water could impart flexibility and healing properties if wielded skillfully— at least that's what people said.

Once he had his affinities, he would need to learn techniques. Techniques were the bread and butter of a divine artist's power; the better one's techniques, the stronger the divine artist. Like his father, he would master the best techniques as quickly as possible. He would be a menace on the battlefield. His mind conjured a daydream of becoming a revered warrior whom the clan relied on as much as his father.

After a time, someone nudged him hard in his ribs. He winced and snapped back to reality to see Shana glaring at him. Her voice was sharp and low as she whispered, "Pay attention, En. *He's* coming."

By the sound of it, the Patriarch was wrapping up. Enkai looked around and noticed the electric buzz of excitement in the air, both from the children and the crowd assembled behind them. The adults whispered among themselves looking back beyond Enkai's sight and the children fidgeted while they waited. Their nervousness permeated the air making even Enkai's heart beat a bit faster. By the grand oak, he saw that his grandfather, Makai, had taken up his position with the other clan elders behind the Patriarch. Makai nodded to his grandson pointing behind the crowd before adopting a relaxed stance with his hands folded behind his back.

Perhaps by coincidence or maybe by his father's doing, the wind picked up blowing through the training ground where the clan had assembled. Enkai caught the familiar scent of lavender, his mother's favorite flower, which Kai always carried with him in honor of her memory. The Patriarch spoke up.

"By the grace of the ancestors, one of our own has been blessed with the talent and insight necessary to achieved the rank of Silver. He is surely a sign that the ancestors smile upon the future of our clan." The Du leader gestured to Kai who crossed into Enkai's vision at that moment. "Today, Kai will perform the Ritual of Waking and usher our youth into the world of the divine arts."

His father towered over all of the other men in the village both in stature and in the presence he exuded. The man was like a living monolith of the success one could achieve through devotion to the divine arts. According to his grandfather, Kai had trained day in and day out even as a child which Enkai believed since his father's entire body was corded with muscle and he moved with the grace of a true warrior.

The Du Patriarch welcomed Kai with open arms and the two embraced before Kai moved to address the clan.

The divine artist's gray eyes swept over each child lingering on each one for a moment. Only Enkai and Shana could actually look Kai in the eye. His presence was too intense. When he spoke, the entire assembly hushed to listen.

"Before we begin today's ceremony, I have an announcement," he said, pausing briefly to look over the assembly. "As some of you may know, Patriarch Ba Kou has asked me to succeed him as the next Patriarch of the Du clan. I plan to accept his offer."

Cheers exploded from the gathered members of the clan. People rejoiced in support of Kai's decision, hollering, hooting, and calling his father's name. Kai let the cheers go on for about a minute before holding up a hand to silence the crowd.

"Though I am not yet Patriarch, the elders have decided to commemorate the day of our clan's founding by giving me the privilege of performing the Ritual of Waking. I am grateful for the honor and trust they give me." Kai turned to the Patriarch and clan elders and bowed at the waist.

Another round of cheers broke out. The children exchanged eager glances and whispered amongst themselves. Kai waited for the applause to settle before continuing. After nearly a minute, he addressed the children.

"We will now begin."

Enkai's heart raced. He calmed his breathing as his father had once taught him. The deep breaths helped to steady his trembling hands. Next to him, he saw Shana was nervous as well so he gave her hand a slight squeeze and flashed her an encouraging smile. She squeezed his hand in return.

"The cultivation of the divine arts is a deeply personal affair. To be a divine artist is to be in tune with your very soul, to recognize yourself as no one else does, and to accept the truth of what you see so that you may grow," Kai began. Several people murmured in the crowd and the clan elders nodded sagely. Enkai understood the significance of his father's words even though many of his peers could only stare, wide-eyed, in confusion. Those had been the words Du himself had spoken to his sons and daughters when he first taught them in the ways of the divine arts. Enkai recognized them because of his grandfather's stories. "Today, I will help you all take the first step toward awakening your spirits." He raised his hand. "To do this, I will inject a very small amount of my anima into each of you to weaken the barrier between your dormant spirits and the world essence around you. Afterward, I will walk you all through a basic meditation exercise. As many of you know, drawing in world essence is difficult; however, do not let that be an excuse for lack of effort. Some of you may fail in this exercise but do not be discouraged! This is only the beginning of your journey!"

***

Enkai sat cross-legged on the grass; eyes closed. Every now and then, bits of noise drifted from the crowd of adults who watched as Kai walked up and down the lines of seated children. He had already infused each of them with a sliver of anima from his spirit. Enkai wasn't sure what effect the anima had on the other kids but he had experienced a sudden tingling sensation along his scalp and arms. He concentrated on his father's voice making sure he didn't miss a single word.

"First, take deep calming breaths. Breath is the first key to awakening the spirit." Enkai fell into the pattern with ease. He'd been taught to control his breathing by his grandfather and father since he could talk. "The next is the body. In order for world essence to access your untapped spirits, you must relax yourselves completely. Use your breath to excise the tension. Let your muscles and joints rest so that your body is at ease."

Enkai thought of the evenings he spent curled up by their fireplace listening to his grandfather's stories. He let the stress of the moment bleed from him while everything aside from his father's deep voice faded from his perception.

"The final key is your mind. To awaken your spirit, your *will* must draw in the essence that permeates the world around us. However, because the world essence is thin, your *will* must be strong and your determination unwavering. Though this process will take time, persistence is essential. Your will is like a muscle. If it is not strong enough now, you must press on until it is!" Kai's footsteps sounded on the grass as he paced back and forth. Strong wind howled across the field rustling clothing. Enkai ignored it. "To direct your will, think of why you want to, why you need to, practice the divine arts then focus on the sensation you felt when I infused anima into your body. Anima is nothing but refined world essence housed inside the body. It is the internal mirror of the external energy that is world essence. The two are linked to each other. Concentrate your mind on replicating that sensation and the essence will answer if your will is strong."

Kai repeated his instructions twice more before he went quiet. Quiet reigned on the field as the youth attempted to follow Kai's instructions. A quarter of an hour passed, and then, half an hour, but the calm continued. In the absence of sound, the expectations of the clan hung heavy over the heads of each child.

For Enkai, the very air seemed to press in around him like a thick blanket. The pressure steadily built against his flesh but he kept his breathing steady as his head throbbed painfully. Soon, his breathing became more difficult. His chest tightened with each breath until he could barely stand it.

More than anything, he truly wanted his father's approval. Enkai was no stranger to the clan's view of Kai as an idol to be adored and praised. However, Enkai saw his father as a goal more than anything. It was the simple desire of a son who wanted to be like his father.

A new sensation alighted on his arms and scalp. The feeling was like when Kai had infused anima into him; although, this time, it was more natural, more familiar. Enkai focused on it and the tingling spread through his entire body making his hairs stand on end. The sensation sharpened until it felt like thousands of tiny sparks were danced on his skin. Even still, Enkai maintained his concentration. Something reacted within his body. His stomach burned with red-hot pain like someone had driven a knife into his navel. Suddenly, the pain spread as though liquid fire had been poured into his veins. Like a man desperately clinging to a precipice over the void, he clung to his focus, but the pain intensified beyond his ability to handle. He screamed as darkness took him.

***

Enkai woke up to the sound of voices from the adjacent room. He couldn't hear what they were saying but he recognized the voices of his father and the Du Patriarch.

A quick look at his surroundings revealed that he was in a small room lit by ample daylight streaming in from the window above the bed in which he was laying. He recognized the décor. He was in Shana's room which meant that he must be at the Patriarch's house. The question was why He remembered trying to cultivate world essence at the festival along with the other Du clan children. He recalled the strange sensations that had assailed him during the process and the pain that had followed. *Did the ritual make me fall asleep?*

He climbed out of the bed wincing as he realized his entire body was sore. He felt like someone had beaten him in his sleep. He moved toward the door which was slightly ajar. In the other room, the two men continued to speak. Instead of leaving the room, curiosity drove Enkai to listen.

"… can you be sure the Lin Matriarch isn't mistaken?" the Du Patriarch said.

"I've seen it with my own spirit-sight, Ba Kou. If she was right about that, she is likely right about everything." The severity in his father's voice informed Enkai that whatever was being discussed had to be important.

"Yes, yes, I know but he's only a child newly awakened to his spirit. Perhaps, we can…" Enkai's heart skipped a beat. Were they talking about him? Had he managed to awaken his spirit? He excitedly closed his eyes and searched for the feeling of his spirit within. He felt something vague, definitely more than had been there before, but it lacked definition and his head began to throb as he tried to focus on it.

Disappointment doused the fresh fire of his excitement. There was something wrong. It was almost like a veil had been pulled over his soul obscuring its true nature from him.

Enkai's attention snapped back to the two men as he caught the mention of his name by his father. "Enough. I will take Enkai to her."

He heard the Patriarch sigh heavily. "You are right, I suppose. If Lin Chun is right, then the journals of the founders cannot be ignored. Poor boy." The sound of a bottle being uncorked followed by the telltale pour of liquid into a glass reached Enkai's ears before the Patriarch spoke again. "A Forsaken amongst our own… I wonder if we have angered the gods."

The two men moved farther into the room leaving Enkai stunned. He couldn't be Forsaken; they weren't real. The Forsaken only existed in stories that adults told young children who misbehaved. They were cursed by the gods with corrupted spirits. Hated abandoned by their clans, Forsaken were hunted by terrifying monsters who sought to consume their accursed souls. In a state of disbelief, he walked back to the bed and laid down curling into a ball.

There must be some kind of mistake, he thought. Then, he recalled the odd obfuscation in his spirit and a wave of anxiety crashed through his denial. Could he not sense his spirit correctly because he was Forsaken? Tears formed at the corners of his eyes as fear took hold. There had to be some kind of mistake. The gods only made selfish and troublesome children Forsaken; he hadn't been either of those things. Had he? He choked down a sob. The tears flowed freely down his face, but he didn't want his father to hear his crying. Kai always scolded him for it. He thought of his drams of practicing the divine arts which now seemed so distant and wept harder burying his face in the bed covers. He laid like that for some time until he heard footsteps approaching the room. Haphazardly, he wiped at his tear-streaked cheeks to dry his face as his father pushed the door open.

When Kai saw him fidgeting on the bed, father and son exchanged a long look. Kai's frown deepened telling Enkai that his father noticed his puffy eyes and red cheeks. Enkai lowered his gaze, ashamed. Instead of acknowledging Enkai's distress, Kai said. "Come, boy, we are going home."

The look in his father's eyes made Enkai swallow the question he wanted to ask. He got to his feet and slid on his shoes which were by the door. Together, they left the Patriarch's home in silence. Their walk wasn't very far since they lived relatively close to the Patriarch.

Once they were inside, Enkai found the courage and asked, "Father, am I a Forsaken?"

Kai paused while making his way toward his room and turned to Enkai. For a fleeting moment, Enkai hoped against hope that he had missed something in his eavesdropping, that it was just a misunderstanding. Several emotions too complex for Enkai to understand passed through his father's eyes in the few seconds before he answered.

"Yes. Yes, you are."

Enkai's stomach twisted itself into a knot and he nearly cried all over again. He spoke but his words came out as the pitiful sobs of a child unable to understand his circumstances. "But I-I awakened my spirit. Did I do something wrong?"

Kai knelt down in front of Enkai and placed a massive hand on his shoulder. Rather than scolding Enkai, his father inhaled deeply then exhaled and repeated the process; unconsciously, Enkai mirrored the pattern. He squeezed Enkai's shoulder, steadying his shaky composure. Their eyes met and Enkai enjoyed the faint hope that, just maybe, things would be alright.

"You've done nothing wrong, but we must act regardless. Pack a bag for the road as I have taught you and be ready to leave within the hour." Kai regarded him for a moment longer as if he were going to say more, but instead, he stood up and walked away.

Chapter 2

Father and son left around midday as the festival was just beginning. Any hopes Enkai held of going unnoticed were dashed by the numerous looks his father's hulking frame attracted as they made their way to the southeastern end of the settlement. A few clansmen called out to Kai as they passed, but one look from him was enough to prevent anything further. They briefly stopped at the corral, where all the clan's beasts of burden and mounts were kept, to retrieve his father's mount.

The steed lorded over the other creatures in the pen with a mighty form that matched Kai's own. It was a great beast called a red mare. Reddish-brown hair covered her body while a maroon mane cascaded down her powerful shoulders. Apparently, she could run twice as fast as any other horse though Enkai had never seen his father ride her. Intelligent eyes watched Kai as he approached to prepare the beast for the journey before they shifted to Enkai and caused him to shiver. Red mares were known for their cunning as well as their stamina and speed. As great beasts, their bodies were empowered by anima pushing them beyond any normal creature. Only Silver divine artists whose bodies were re-forged by anima could handle a red mare. For that reason, these powerful steeds served as symbols of status for the greatest of divine artists in the Maro Province throughout history. Kai had received the red mare from the Lin Matriarch along with several other gifts from other clans after his advancement. After all, he held the honor of being the youngest member of the five clans to reach Silver in living memory.

As Kai finished saddling the horse, he picked up Enkai and placed him in the saddle before climbing up himself. The beast gave an agitated grunt at the extra weight, but when Kai cracked the reigns, she moved obediently to the east. They quickly left the Du clan camp behind them as the noonday sun beat down upon their brows.

The plains of the Maro Province stretched on beyond the horizon. They traveled through a flat landscape that was broken by the occasional tree or two. Soon after their departure, Enkai found himself clutching his father's waist tightly as the horse gained speed until she moved so fast Enkai felt he would be blown out of the saddle by the rushing wind. For hours, the two traveled in silence as the great beast devoured the distance between them and their destination. Although his father hadn't told him anything, Enkai knew they were going to visit the Lin clan based on the conversation he'd overheard. He tried to enjoy the journey, but the more he thought about visiting the most powerful clan in the Maro Province, the more nervous he became.

At the beginning of the journey, his father directed the red mare toward the Sky Tooth Mountains which was the home of an enemy clan, the Hu. Enkai didn't know much about the feud since none of the clan warriors, including his father, would tell him about it; however, he imagined any conflict between divine artists had to be as serious as it was spectacular. He sorely hoped that he could one day join the skirmishes which occasionally broke out between the two clans. Once they reached the river that marked the border between Du and Hu clan territory, Kai followed the river north toward the Lin clan's stronghold.

When the sky began to darken, a new feature appeared on the horizon that stoked the fires of his curiosity and fear. It first appeared as a blurry line of green on the horizon before slowly forming into a massive tree line that stretched from Sky Tooth Mountains to the western cliffs that fell into the rolling sea. Enkai's young mind raced as they neared *that place.*

The Forbidden Forest acted as a physical barrier between the Maro Province and the rest of the world. Its massive trees hid terrible secrets and monstrous great beasts that warded off any who sought to venture through its depths. It was a terrifying place to tread for even Silver divine artists. Once, Ba Ren, Shana's father, told Enkai that the spirits of those who died during the Fall of Heaven swept into the Maro Province at night to kidnap young children. Thanks to that ghost story, Enkai had suffered from nightmares for weeks afterward. Fear gripped his heart as he imagined being abducted by an evil spirit from the Forbidden Forest, but the feeling only lasted a moment. His father would protect him from anything like that. Moreover, they'd be in the Lin clan's seat of power; there was no safer place in the Maro Province.

That aside, not all the tales of the Forbidden Forest instilled fear. Stories about the Lin clan, the guardians of the Forbidden Forest, told of great wonders.

As the most powerful clan and de facto rulers of the Maro Province, the Lin clan usually occupied a neutral position in the constant contests of power between the other four clans. The forest held great riches as well as dangerous great beasts, and all except for the most trusted Lin clansmen were prohibited from entering it— or so the stories claimed. The divine artists of the Lin clan were skilled healers and alchemists who sold special elixirs and medicines created from natural treasures found in the forest. The leaders of the other four clans occasionally sought the counsel of the Lin Matriarch and Lin elders who were known to offer great wisdom. As he recalled some of the stories other clansmen had told about the Lin clan, an idea began to slowly take root in his mind.

Even if I'm Forsaken, the Lin clan will be able to fix me! His spirits soared and his apprehension melted away. If anyone would know how to cure his, supposedly, cursed spirit, it would be the Lin clan. Surely, an elixir of some kind could solve the problem. He went over all the etiquette his grandfather had drilled into him over the years, so he would be prepared to pay respect to the Lin clan once they met.

Stars dotted the night sky by the time they came across the first of the Lin patrols. When they were spotted, one of the riders called out to them. Kai eased his red mare to a stop. He'd managed to stay awake through the journey, but exhaustion tugged at his consciousness even as four men on horseback were riding towards them. A quick glance at his father reassured him that there was no need for concern.

Each of the men wore green and silver robes distinguishing them in contrast to the red and yellow robes worn by Enkai and his father. Kai shifted in the saddle to face the men as they brought their horses to a stop. He exuded calm confidence that made Enkai feel at ease despite the weapons they carried.

"State your name and what business the Du clan have in Lin territory," said a balding man from the front of the group. Though he looked to be past his prime, Enkai could tell he commanded the unit based on the way the other men arranged themselves behind him. His eyes scanned both father and son and lingered the longest on the red mare. When he looked back at Kai, his gaze was less confident.

"I am Du Kai and this is my son, Enkai," Kai said smoothly. "I come to consult with Matriarch Lin Chun on an urgent matter."

The men behind the commander exchanged glances with each other while the commander rode forward squinting to get a better look at Kai. After a brief moment, his dour expression changed.

"Apologies for my rudeness. Honored Du Kai. My sight is waning in my old age and I did not recognize you in the darkness. I am Lin Feng. On behalf of the Lin clan, I welcome you to our territory." Enkai noticed the commander sounded much more respectful than when he had hailed them. It made sense, of course: his father was Silver which placed him on a par with the Lin Matriarch herself in rank regardless of the gap in station and experience. Based on what Enkai knew about clan patrols, these men were probably all Lead though since they were Lin clansmen, Bronze was also a possibility. Kai status as an active Head Warrior was an exception to the standard for a Silver divine artist. The rarity and strength of Silver rank meant any who reached it often held high positions as elders or clan heads and, thus, rarely went out on patrols or fought like Kai.

Feng ordered the other men to continue their patrol then addressed Kai again. "If you would do me the honor, I will escort you to Matriarch Chun."

Kai nodded and flicked the reigns. The red mare continued to their destination though slower than before since the commander's mount wouldn't have kept up. The tree line of the Forbidden Forest grew ever closer with ominous shadows extending from the massive trees in the moonlight. At some point, Enkai fell asleep, but he stirred when his father pulled him from the saddle. They'd stopped in what looked like an empty stable. An elderly man stepped forward to carefully accept the red mare's reigns from Kai while asking Kai if he had any specific instructions for the beast's care. While his father spoke to the man, Enkai wiped the sleep from his eyes and took a look around.

Soft purple light immediately caught his attention drawing his gaze to small globes that drifted lazily through the air about ten feet off the ground. Enkai's eyes widened at the floating lights. He began turning in a circle as he noticed more of them all around him. Feng who had also dismounted noticed Enkai's reaction and smiled.

"They are called wisp lanterns," he explained as he held his hand out and one drifted into his palm. "They hold harmless spirits called wisps that we seal within these rune globes. They never go out as long as you feed a little anima to them every day."

Kneeling down, he handed the globe to Enkai who turned it over in his hands, fascinated. The wisp looked like a fluffy purple cloud that steadily pulsed with light. On the orb itself, two rings of symbols had been etched parallel to each other creating a belt around it.

Getting to his feet, the commander beckoned for them to follow and they made their way towards the heart of the settlement. The wisp lanterns colored everything in a soft purple hue which gave the whole place a mysterious atmosphere. More than a few curious eyes followed their progress toward the center of the settlement where a squat two-story wooden building sat adorned with the Lin clan banners. Each banner was different from the last, but all bore two key features: the color green and a silver leaf.

When they arrived at the building, Feng rapped three times on the door. As they waited for a response, Feng looked up at the sky and said, "You are fortunate to arrive so early in the night. The Matriarch will likely not have started her meditation yet."

Enkai lifted his gaze from the wisp lantern he still held to peer at the sky. He thought it was strange that anyone, but the guards, was up so late. However, many Lin clansmen milled about under wisp light performing various tasks as if it were broad daylight. He wondered if it related to the Lin clan's divine arts. Unlike the Du clan who generally favored themselves as generalists with a wide array of affinities among their number, the other clans each specialized in cultivating one or two specific types of essence. He didn't know what essence the Lin clan used though. Just as he prepared to ask, the door opened.

A middle-aged woman with pretty red hair and an ugly scar across her face stood in the doorway. Her grey eyes roamed over each of them and settled finally on Kai. where they stayed. Without looking at him, she addressed Feng, "You may go. I will take our guests to the Matriarch. She is expecting them."

Lin Feng bowed to the woman and Kai before heading in the direction of the stable. Without a word, the woman turned and headed into the building. Kai followed with Enkai on his heels. The inside of the building smelled of earthen smoke and medicinal herbs. Following her, they passed more than a few rooms where men and women ground medicinal herbs or meditated amidst rings of burning incense. They ascended a flight of stairs to the second floor where the herbal smell became more potent. The entire floor was just one large open space occupied by a single woman sitting cross-legged on a large pallet of beast pelts.

Even with his limited experience of six summers, Enkai knew the woman had to be the Matriarch. She exuded an aura of authority more impressive than the Du Patriarch. They walked to the edge of the pallet before Kai and the red-haired woman bowed deeply with Enkai awkwardly following suit.

Lin Chun appeared much younger than Enkai had expected. Her crimson hair fell loosely along her shoulders and face as if she couldn't have been bothered to tidy it up; in contrast, the scarred woman who had her hair in a neat bun. Her features played tricks on Enkai with smooth skin and a full face, but eyes that spoke of old wisdom and cunning. Those eyes took in their group and settled on Enkai gleaming with mirth as though she was enjoying some joke that only she knew. Enkai stood a little straighter and inwardly reviewed all his etiquette lessons once more. He refused to shame his father by being rude, especially to the leader of the Lin clan. Raising her head, the scarred woman stepped forward and turned to face them.

"You stand before Lin Chun, Matriarch of the Lin clan and protector of the For—" she stated before the Matriarch cut her off.

"There is no need for such formality, Fa." She favored the scarred woman with a soft motherly expression and a smile. He accidentally met the Lin Matriarch's gaze and to his surprise, she winked at him.

Looking back to Fa, Lin Chun waved her hand in the direction of the stairs. "Go rest. You've done much for me today, but you neglect yourself. The two of you will sit."

Scowling, Fa bowed to the Matriarch, offered a passing nod to Kai, then made her way back down the stairs. Enkai suddenly wished the Matriarch would give him permission to rest too as his body reminded him of how tired he was. The entire day had been exhausting. When they sat on the soft fur pelts, Enkai fought the urge to curl up into a ball and sleep. It must have been obvious because the mirth in the

Matriarch's eyes brightened. His father adjusted the sword at his hip, so it would not trouble him in a sitting position. As Kai made to speak, the Lin Matriarch raised a hand.

"No need to say it, Du Kai. I know why you are here," she said, lifting a pipe from a silver tray beside her and drawing deeply on it. Exhaling sweet-smelling smoke, she continued, "It has not been a good day for either of you, I'm sure. After all, the Du clan produced the first Forsaken in the last several centuries and it was none other than the son of their most promising warrior. Truly an unfortunate turn of events."

For his part, Kai kept his expression impassive, but something dark passed through his gray eyes.

Enkai's gut twisted. A large part of him hadn't accepted the whole Forsaken thing, but hearing it said out loud by the Lin Matriarch of all people really hammered home the reality of his situation. Despair clawed at his heart but he held on to the hope that he had fostered on their long journey.

"Can you fix me?" His voice seemed small in the large room. He tried to fill it with resolve, but even to his ears, he sounded tired and on the verge of tears. Chun favored him with a gentle smile and glanced at Kai before responding.

"Young Enkai, do not worry. Your father and I will see an end to your worries. Of that, I can promise you." Kai grunted in affirmation. It was enough for Enkai. He believed his father could do anything, so he decided to heed her words. With that burden lifted from him, weariness redoubled its fight to rob him of consciousness.

The two adults continued to speak about the matter at hand, however, Enkai struggled to remain awake.

Chun who'd been watching him since the beginning of the conversation gestured for him to come to her. Enkai nervously glanced at his father who nodded. Crawling over to her, he made to sit down next to her but the Matriarch surprised him when she adjusted her sitting position, then pulled him down to lie in her lap. The smell of sweet smoke and fresh loam filled his nostrils as his head rested against her thighs. Chun and Kai continued their conversation as Enkai faded into unconsciousness.

***

Du Kai watched as Lin Chun tenderly ran her fingers through Enkai's hair as the boy slept. The Lin Matriarch had always perplexed him. Not only did she look much younger than what he knew her age to be, but she also acted with an unwelcome amount of informality for a clan leader. Before he reached Silver, he had heard stories about her from the Du Patriarch which led him to believe she would be difficult to understand. He had expected it to be due to her age and wisdom making her mysterious and sagely; however, more often than not, the woman was eccentric and flippant in her disregard for etiquette. Even now, he wondered what was going through her head as she smiled softly at Enkai like a mother holding her child. His son looked peaceful lying there clutching the wisp lantern like some sort of stuffed animal.

The entire scene made him think of his late wife as he often did when he looked at Enkai. She would have known what to do. After Enkai's awakening played out exactly how the Lin Matriarch foretold, Kai had found himself at a complete loss on how to handle his son especially knowing what had to be done. The entire situation seemed so *wrong*, but he was powerless to do anything, just as he had been when Liu died. He caught himself unconsciously reaching inside his robes for the fresh lavender he kept tucked away there and stopped clenching the offending hand.

"Was it really necessary for me to seal his spirit?" Kai asked as his distaste for the situation demanded that he speak. Despite awakening, his son hadn't even gotten the chance to experience the joy of his awakened spirit. He didn't bother with decorum when he addressed her. He lacked the energy to fight her insistence on informality anyway.

"As I told you when I dreamed of his awakening, Forsaken are as much a danger to themselves as they are to others. He may be weak, but the repercussions of him attempting to cultivate essence would be severe. You did well to follow my instructions as you did."

Kai scowled eyeing the area on Enkai's forehead where he'd traced the sealing rune. It was invisible to the naked eye though, in his spirit-sight, it shone with dull gray light.

"Do you know of any other way apart from the old traditions to solve—," he paused trying to find the right word and failing, "*this*? Surely, the Lin clan could create an elixir for to lift the Forsaken curse on his spirit?"

"There is no other way. My dreams have told me that fate demands we must walk the current path." As she spoke, her gaze shifted from Enkai to him, her eyes growing distant.

Kai placed his head in his hands and began to massage his temples in an attempt to fight off the throbbing headache that had plagued him since learning of Enkai's condition. For him, his duty to the Du clan came before all else, so he would not hesitate to do what was needed. However, he could not shake the memories of Liu, his late wife and Enkai's mother. Her face smiled back at him from the memories he always tried to bury. She had been so many things to him: wife, lover, partner, rival and much more. During his youth, only two things had mattered to him: the divine arts and Liu, yet that all ended when she passed away. After her death, all that remained was the divine arts.

For years, he'd neglected his son to train. It had never seemed to matter to Enkai. Eventually, he noticed Enkai mimicking his morning stretches and watching him train. The boy showed admirable diligence, so Kai started teaching him when he found the time. Before long, he began looking forward to the day his son could cultivate the divine arts. Would he catch up to Kai? Would Enkai surpass him? These questions had withered the moment he had seen Enkai's spirit after his awakening.

"Forsaken …," he said bitterly. "The heavens must be unjust to forsake a child."

"Your son plays such a great role in what is to come *because* he is Forsaken." She affectionately stroked Enkai's sleeping face with one hand while taking another deep draw on her pipe in the other. Leaning down, she exhaled a stream of white smoke onto Enkai. Much to Kai's surprise, he continued to sleep peacefully instead of waking up with lungs full of smoke. She repeated the process twice more before smiling. The smell of sweet smoke grew much stronger.

Perplexed, Kai asked, "What are you doing to him?"

"I am giving him lovely dreams," she whispered as though talking to herself. She looked up at him with warmth in her eyes. "Sometimes, the dream is the only hope we have."

"What do you mean?"

"You need not concern yourself with it, Du Kai," she answered dismissively. Kai grimaced. Since their first meeting, something had felt off about Lin Chun aside from her eccentric behavior. Her crimson hair marked her as a direct descendant of the founder of the Lin clan, but her eyes were something else altogether. Kai had never seen a member of the five clans with purple eyes other than the Matriarch. It was potentially a side effect of advancement to Silver because the Lin clan utilized dream essence in their divine arts yet Kai would've suspected them to be silver to reflect the Silver Leaf anima cultivated by the Lin. His own eyes were dark grey, the same color as his Graywind anima. More than the color was strange though. They also held something altogether strange that made Kai feel small and vulnerable, neither of which he'd felt since he was a child. Those alien eyes held him in place as she continued, "What we must discuss is the coming trial. You may be a prodigy, but the Forbidden Forest will claim your life all the same without Lin assistance."

Glad for the change in subject, Kai nodded and averted his gaze. He knew the journey into the Forbidden Forest would be perilous. Despite that, he welcomed the danger as a distraction from the problem at hand. Such a journey would be beyond dangerous while protecting Enkai. Thankfully, in the past when high-ranking members of other clans had needed to venture into the forest for matters of great import, the Lin clan required that the other clan be accompanied by an escort. He hoped he would have the opportunity to test his skills against a great beast of the Forbidden Forest. With a Lin escort there to watch over Enkai, he could battle any creature that crossed their path with all his might.

"I will heed your warning," he replied half-heartedly. Curious what kind of escort he would receive, he asked, "How many will you be able to spare for our escort?"

"Only one," she said, matter-of-factly. Kai grimaced. With only one, they would have to move very quickly and he probably wouldn't get the chance to do battle with one of the great beasts of the Forbidden Forest. The stories painted them as extremely dangerous and powerful. He was not foolish enough to think he could protect Enkai while fighting a beast that equaled his strength or more.

With a sigh, he looked to the Matriarch and asked. "Who will be our escort?"

"Me," she answered sweetly.

Kai inwardly groaned.

Chapter 3

Rain pounded against the earth creating a treacherous landscape of mud and slick rock. A crack issued through the night as four spikes of sharpened earth anima veered through the air toward Enkai. He dodged, barely keeping his feet beneath him. Mist trailed from his body as he initiated the Jade Rain Enhancement technique. Anima crafted from earth and water essence pulsed through his body causing the world to slow around him while his own movements grew faster. The Hu warrior launched another Emitter technique resulting in another crack as earth anima formed into spikes and whipped through the air. Each spike came from a different angle, each cutting off a potential route of escape. It mattered little. With his body Enhanced, he dashed forward low to the ground, so the spikes passed overheard and then launched his own attack.

Green droplets trailed down his arm in contrast with the droplets of rainwater that poured down his body. Flinging his arm forward, dozens of droplets shot toward the Hu warrior who rolled to the side avoiding the attack. Enkai had expected that. Before the man could recover, he fired the second attack he'd prepared from his other arm. The man barely registered the impact even as he was struck dozens of times.

He laughed at Enkai, "You call that an attack, boy? Perhaps, the Du have grown soft under Du Kai if this is the best their warriors can offer!"

Despite the taunt, Enkai smiled at the man. His Jade Rain techniques did not boast high attack power like his father's Graywind techniques, but they excelled in other areas. The warrior's eyes widened and his stance weakened as the Jade Rain technique sapped the strength from his limbs. Seeing the moment of weakness, Enkai lunged forward closing the distance between them. Panicked, the man struck out, but his attack was clumsy. Enkai sidestepped with barely a thought then smashed an uppercut into the man's chin sending him sailing backward. The Hu warrior hit the ground with a wet smack, unconscious. His smile widened in the manic rush of battle fever.

"You Hu always underestimate us. Maybe all that earth essence is making you too dense for your own good," he said to the unconscious man.

Hearing the sound of metal clashing in the distance, Enkai dashed off.

His father would need him.

***

Enkai woke up in a room furnished with only a table and chair apart from the bed on which he slept. It took him a few moments to escape the grasp of the deep sleep that had taken him almost immediately after lying down in the Matriarch's lap.

He could not remember the last time he'd fallen asleep so quickly, but given the previous day's events, he supposed it made sense. Regardless, he felt amazing. His dreams had been so vivid that he could remember every detail. The feeling of anima coursing through his body was still held fresh in his mind.

Jade Rain... It had been the anima cultivated by his mother according to his grandfather. The dream drudged up a phantom pain he'd learned to ignore— the ache of a life without a mother. *I just have to do what father tells me and I'll be ok.*

Wiping the sleep from his eyes, a curious thought came to mind. He concentrated on the feeling from his dream of rich anima cycling through him and strengthening his body. Carefully, he tried to replicate the sensation. He focused for several seconds on concentrating as hard as he could on feeling his spirit. Yet no matter how much he focused, he couldn't break through the vague sensation and received nothing but the beginnings of a headache for his trouble. Enkai chastised himself for getting his hopes up. He wouldn't be able to feel and control anima until his spirit was cured which plainly hadn't happened yet.

After swallowing his disappointment, he swung his legs off the side of the bed and glanced around. A plate of fruit, a glass of water, and a note rested atop the table. Enkai straightened the wrinkles in his robes before he made his way over to the table. Most of the fruits on the table were familiar, though a few were unknown to him. Picking up a star-shaped fruit, he sniffed it. He smelled nothing alarming, so he took a small bite. A rich sweetness filled his mouth followed quickly by a bitter aftertaste which was not altogether unpleasant. He took another bite and picked up the note. It was in his father's handwriting.

Enkai,

Eat and meet me downstairs. There is a washbasin in the room at the end of the hall on the left, make sure you are presentable.

He put the letter down and ate until he was full. Afterward, he went back to the bed to put on his shoes which had been taken off him while he slept. As he slipped them on, he noticed a purple glow from underneath the thin covers on the bed and reached for it. His hand closed around the wisp lantern from the previous night. The light from the lantern appeared a bit dimmer than he remembered which concerned him, so he decided he'd show it to the Matriarch when he saw her. He placed the orb in one of his robe pockets and left the room. There was a slightly open door at the end of the hallway to the left. To his right, there were several more doors before the hallway ended in a staircase that descended, so he walked toward the open door. Looking inside, he found a large basin full of warm water. After washing himself as best he could, Enkai made his way down the staircase at the opposite end of the hall.

Three people waited for him on the first floor, gathered around a table looking over a large sheet of parchment. Lin Chun looked up at him as he came down the stairs, which alerted Kai and the third person that Enkai didn't recognize. The Lin Matriarch smiled at him as if he was her favorite person. His father waved him over then turned his attention back to the table. The third individual wore the typical green and silver robes of a Lin clansman, but it was clear that he was no average member of the clan. The man was ancient. By looks alone, his age must have surpassed even that of the Du Patriarch. Additionally, he held himself with a regal demeanor that spoke of authority.

As Enkai came to the table, he realized the parchment was a map. It depicted what looked like a small portion of the Maro Province as well as an enormous expanse of green which he guessed was the Forbidden Forest. Dozens of markers of various colors had been placed within the area representing the Forbidden Forest though he had no idea what they meant.

"So, this is the boy in question?" asked the ancient man. He looked Enkai up and down before turning to Kai. "I see the problem though I must admit it's a bit shocking. I've never seen anything like it. With such a blackened spirit, it must unquestionably be a curse of the gods."

The elder scratched his head which was decorated with braids of long silver hair that hung down to his shoulders. A mildly unpleasant sensation crawled down Enkai's spine and he squirmed as the elder continued to study him with hawk-like interest before Kai interjected by saying, "Elder Win, please stop prodding my son's spirit. Your curiosity only serves to make him uncomfortable which he doesn't need right now."

Appreciating his father's words, Enkai bowed his head and made to take his place next to his father; however, the Matriarch reached out pulling him close to her. He thought to pull away from her but did not. Instead, he let her bring him close where she held him in an embrace from behind. The situation felt far too intimate for Enkai who had never received such treatment, so he could not stop his face from burning with embarrassment. Despite his misgivings, he began to feel better as soon as she embraced him. Without thinking, he leaned into her and she ruffled his hair. For some reason, he felt so comfortable around her, but his young mind didn't think to question it. If anything, he welcomed the comfort given the circumstances.

Both men reacted to the scene differently. Kai frowned giving Enkai a brief look that somehow made him feel guilty, while Elder Win shrugged and said, "Apologies, it was not my intention to offend. Now, back to the matter at hand."

He gestured to the map indicating a point far into the expanse of forestland as he continued, "Review of our maps and scouting reports show only one location appropriate to what is discussed in the ancestral Lin documents and it matches what honorable Du Kai has told us of his clan's records on Forsaken. Without a doubt, the journey will be perilous. It will take a little under a week with an experienced guide, but none of our clan has traveled so far into the Forbidden Forest since the time of the founders."

Elder Win paused before fixing Enkai's father with a severe look. "I am aware of your situation, but I would very much advise delaying your trip for a few weeks to allow our clan time to scout the area in question."

The idea of going into the Forbidden Forest filled Enkai with fear. Dangerous creatures prowled within the dense forest and malevolent spirits haunted the places the beasts did not go. More than one nightmare had been inspired by stories Enkai heard of the Forbidden Forest. But frankly, the idea of being Forsaken longer than necessary terrified him more than the Forbidden Forest. What if they waited and his spirit somehow got worse? He blurted out, "I don't want to wait!"

Kai scowled at his outburst, but Enkai glanced up at the Matriarch with a pleading look in his eyes. She flashed a smile at Enkai and said, "There will be no waiting. With me guiding and the prodigy of the Du clan to turn away any beasts, we should be able to make the journey with few issues."

After taking a moment to process the Matriarch's words, Elder Win replied, "My lady, please reconsider this foolishness. We have plenty of experienced warriors that can guide our guests to their destination if they insist on going, but you are too valuable. If something were to happen—."

"Enough, I have made my decision and it is final," the Matriarch interjected. She squeezed Enkai's shoulder reassuringly. Her gaze showed no room for argument which elicited a heavy sigh from the elder.

"At least allow me to assign a few of our veterans to ensure the journey goes smoothly," he responded wearily. His expression made it obvious he thought the Matriarch was being unreasonable. Enkai remembered seeing very similar looks aimed at overindulgent children who threw fits at the annual Du festivals.

"We would be honored if more men could be spared. We do not wish to endanger the Matriarch unnecessarily," Kai added, his deep voice standing out compared to the softer voices of the Lin elder and Matriarch. Even to Enkai, the request sounded reasonable. He definitely wanted the Matriarch to accompany them to the Forbidden Forest since he liked her and she had promised to help cure his spirit; however, having extra warriors in case they ran into monsters in the forest definitely couldn't hurt as far as he was concerned. He fully expected the Matriarch to accept the elder's proposal which made him all the more surprised when she waved her hand dismissively.

"Absolutely not. I can Shroud the three of us, but any more and the effectiveness of the Shroud will be compromised. We will continue as planned," she confirmed with a tone that made it clear that she was done discussing the matter. Both men were transparently unhappy with the abrupt end to the discussion but nonetheless bowed their heads in acquiescence. With the matter put to rest, she asked Elder Win, "Have you prepared the supplies I requested?"

Apparently, they had not been available, so their departure was delayed for a few hours while the missing items were acquired. Kai left Enkai with the Matriarch while he went to attend to his red mare as well as arrange care for her while he journeyed through the forest. Unfortunately, the beast's size would attract unwarranted attention and compromise the Matriarch's Shroud. Enkai accompanied Lin Chun to the large room where they'd met her the previous night. The two of them sat next to each other on the fur pallet.

Several individuals including Lin Feng and Lin Fa visited the Matriarch. Each came to her with issues that required her attention before she left. Sitting in on these discussions made Enkai feel very awkward, as he was listening in on conversations that he had no business hearing. Based on the strange looks he got from the Lin clansmen meeting with their Matriarch, he wasn't the only one who thought he was out of place. In contrast to the rest, Lin Fa completely ignored him. She entered the room in a rush and demanded Lin Chun see reason. The two women argued for the next hour about the Matriarch's decision to venture into the Forbidden Forest without an escort. The whole time Enkai desired nothing more than to hide under one of the furs. Despite Fa's completely sound arguments, Matriarch Chun would not budge.

After Lin Fa left, the Matriarch lit her pipe then took a light drag. She smiled down at Enkai ruffling his hair as she said, "You are indeed well behaved. I don't know many your age that could sit through so many meetings so quietly. You didn't even fidget! Did you learn how to be a statue from your father?"

She laughed making Enkai's cheeks blush fiercely since she wasn't too far off the mark. He had been trying very hard not to make any noise or move more than necessary, so he didn't disrupt her meetings. His father always stressed the importance of silence and stillness during his meditation exercises. At first, Kai refused to let Enkai meditate with him because he could not sit still. In order to spend more time with his father, Enkai spent weeks practicing being still and quiet.

"Apologies, I didn't want to be rude," he said. He recognized that she was only teasing him but he couldn't stop himself from apologizing. After all, the idea of being chided even playfully by the most powerful woman in the Maro Province made him nervous. More importantly, Enkai realized how strange her treatment of him was. He had been so caught up in the events of the last day that he hadn't questioned the Matriarch's behavior. In fact, he had embraced her affection as a much-needed respite from the unfair truth he had been forced to bear. However, sitting in the audience chamber at the side of the Lin Matriarch, as she saw to the members of her clan brought clarity to the situation. Such an honored position next to a clan leader should be reserved for only clan elders or direct heirs, not visiting children from another clan. He wondered if it was because she knew about his father's position as heir to the Du Patriarch. Truthfully though, he really didn't care why she showed him such kindness. She smelled nice and radiated a motherly warmth not unlike what he imagined in his occasional daydreams about his own mother whom he'd never got to meet.

Additionally, Enkai got the impression Matriarch Chun did what she wanted regardless of what other people thought based on her interactions with Elder Win and Lin Fa. Still, he asked, "How come you are so nice to me?"

"I sometimes forget how observant children are," she sighed, shifting so she faced Enkai. For a moment, she looked him over then leaning forward. She cupped his face in her hands and said, "Do you know the nature of the Lin clan's anima, young Enkai?"

He shook his head. His father had focused primarily on lessons that would prepare him for when he started his own journey as a divine artist, as well as some of the basics of formal etiquette. His grandfather sometimes told him stories, but they were specifically about the Du clan or only contained cursory information about the other clans.

"We cultivate a special type of anima created by Lin herself called Silver Leaf anima," Lin Chun explained, pinching his cheek before she released his face. Reaching into her robe, she pulled out a pouch that she handed to Enkai. Inside, he found a variety of strong-smelling leaves and powder. "We of the Lin clan gather a variety of natural treasures from the Forbidden Forest. By imbibing elixirs brewed from herbs rich in vital anima and cultivating dream essence, we create Silver Leaf anima. As dream artists, we gain a variety of benefits, though dream essence is hard to find which is why we use the dream wisps in our lanterns to produce it."

Remembering the wisp lantern in one of his robe pockets, he fished it out. The wisp had grown dimmer since earlier that morning. The Matriarch plucked it from his grasp before he could react. She held it up at eye level, then the runes on the orb began to glow. They continued to radiate bright light until she tossed the orb back to Enkai who barely caught it. His eyes filled with wonder as he turned it in his hands. He could feel the wisp pulsing with renewed vigor.

"Wisps are dream spirits. We use them to saturate our settlements with dream essence. It isn't much but it serves our purposes. The trade-off is they have to be recharged every day and the runes on the lantern must be carefully maintained," she said, resuming her explanation. "Silver Leaf anima grants us many unique techniques such as being able to read the latent intentions of others and dream-walking among other things, but there is one ability passed down by our clan founder that only the Matriarch of each generation can utilize."

Enkai listened, completely enthralled by her words. He couldn't help but get excited at the notion of a technique passed down from one of the five clan founders. Such an ability could only be extraordinary.

"When I dream, I sometimes see little pieces of things to come." She blew a cloud of smoke from her lips into the air which swirled into shapes and symbols some of which looked vaguely familiar. "In one of these dreams, I saw you, a wishful Forsaken boy. You would help me in a way no one else could. I know it doesn't make much sense, but something amazing is going to happen and it will all be thanks to you. That is why I can't help but care for you. You are my little savior."

As she finished, she tapped him playfully on the nose. Enkai didn't mind though he did blush. Her words stoked the fires of hope burning within his heart. He couldn't fathom what he could possibly do for the leader of the Lin clan of all people, but when he looked into the Matriarch's eyes, he saw her conviction.

"When I'm not Forsaken anymore, I promise I'll do my best to help you," he pledged, squaring his shoulders. The Matriarch had said she would guide them through the Forbidden Forest, so it was the least he could do to help her with whatever she needed.

Before Lin Chun could reply, heavy footfalls echoed up the stairway. Enkai hurried to his feet as his father crested the stairs. Kai had pulled his long hair into a ponytail and rolled up his sleeves which revealed thick arms covered in a thin layer of sweat that suggested recent exercise. Knowing his father, Enkai guessed that he had done his morning workout in addition to handling the red mare. Matriarch Chun remained seated and asked, "Have you seen to your affairs and prepared?"

"Yes, I am ready to depart," Kai answered, crossing his arms. "Elder Win also informed me that all your supplies have been acquired and everything has been packed for the journey."

"Wonderful! Then let us be off. We have quite a bit of ground to cover and I don't wish to delay any more than necessary." She hopped up spryly giving Enkai an encouraging pat on the back as she made her way to the stairs. Enkai ran to his father's side and they followed the Matriarch. With little fanfare, the three of them set off into the Forbidden Forest.

Chapter 4

Fear quaked through Enkai's body causing him to tremble violently. Howls echoed through the forest around him. In the hollow of a large tree, he hid. Panic mingled with the fear as a large wolf with black fur passed in front of the opening of the tree. A wide lupine eye stared directly at Enkai, with hunger and cunning clear in its gaze. At that moment, he almost lost to the terror raging through him, but soft arms wrapped around him while warm hands firmly squeezed his own.

"Be calm, little one," Matriarch Chun whispered in his ear. Her breath smelled of the sweet smoke from the pipe she always used. Her voice contained no fear or concern for the large great beast staring directly at them. Her firm grip and warmth protected him against his terror like bastions of light in the darkness. A few seconds later, the wolf moved on, seemingly oblivious to their presence. "See? I promised I would keep you safe, didn't I? No beast will find us while we are in my Shroud. Now let us watch closely, little one. I am eager to see if your father's skill matches his confidence."

Enkai was relieved by the reminder that his father was watching from the branches above them. Any vestiges of fear that remained bled away as he thought of his father peering down on the large wolves like a vengeful spirit. He would make short work of these beasts. Enkai knew his father would be fine. It did not even occur to him that Kai could be in danger. His father was a prodigy, perhaps even comparable to the clan founders. No man or creature could defeat the mighty Du Kai. He calmed his breathing to match the Matriarch's steady rhythm. Now calmed, he gave a nervous smile to the Matriarch who beamed at him. Outside the hollow, a sudden burst of motion caught their attention. Enkai leaned forward eyes sharp for the sight of his father.

***

High above the hollow where Enkai and Lin Chun hid from the prowling wolves, Kai surveyed the scene before him. Four large wolves painted the color of night crept in the area below his perch. Two of them had lingered beyond his sight within the multitude of long shadows that populated the dark forest. Glancing at the sky, he noted the limited light of the rising moon in the sky, obscured by the thick canopy of the Forbidden Forest.

Their group had started hearing the howls as the sun's light began to fade on their third day of traveling through the forest. The Lin Matriarch had informed them that they should find a place to hide as quickly as possible. Enkai became a nervous wreck from the stress caused by the constant howling. While they rushed for cover, the boy convinced himself on more than one occasion that they were moments from being ambushed. Kai took pride in the fact that his son had kept his wits about him during their flight, all things considered. He doubted any other child of his clan would have fared as well. Thankfully, the Matriarch had located a suitable spot for them to wait out the night before the wolves found them.

Although he had mixed feelings about the woman, her vast knowledge of the forest and skill as a guide became increasingly clear to him the farther that they journeyed within it. She called these great beasts "umbral wolves". They stalked their prey as the sun set, then pounced once darkness took hold below the canopy. As great beasts of shadow, they grew stronger as the night descended while also being incredibly difficult to track due to the blending ability of their fur when they moved in areas of darkness. Most importantly, the beasts had the approximate strength of a Bronze divine artist.

After learning this, Kai had asked if the Matriarch could hide herself and Enkai in her Shroud while he confronted them. Surprisingly, she made no attempt to dissuade him. Once she knew his plan, she ushered Enkai into the hollow of the tree and nodded to Kai once before hiding herself as well. Like a phantom, he ascended into the branches of the tree and waited for the predators to follow their scent.

His plan was simple: lie in wait for the wolves, assess their numbers, and ambush them when they least expected it. For many divine artists, such a plan might fail due to the wolves' keen sense of smell. However, Kai cultivated Graywind anima. Utilizing his advantage as a wind artist, he had taken control of the ambient wind essence to create a gentle barrier around his body that masked his scent.

A howl echoed in the distance. The two wolves prowling in the shadows revealed themselves to join the two stalking the area below the tree in which Kai hid. As one, the four wolves released their own howls. Another distant howl answered.

Interesting, Kai thought to himself. They were communicating. Based on the information the Matriarch had given him, Kai reasoned that the four he saw below were scouts from a large pack. Clearly, the pack had sent them to track Kai's group, but their scent trail had disappeared. The last howl probably summoned the four below back to the pack so other prey could be pursued. If he wanted to test his mettle, he'd have to act quickly.

Silently, he eased his blade from the sheath on his hip. Blade essence radiated from its smooth metallic surface with power that danced in the air like thousands of tiny knives. Making a mental note of the position of each wolf, Kai leapt from his perch.

Before his feet even hit the ground, he activated his Enhancement technique, the Graywind Cloak, to sharpen his reaction speed and increase his strength. With Graywind anima swirling through his body, he landed next to one of the wolves and brought his sword down on its unprotected neck. The beast died instantly, but Kai launched an attack on his next target before its body hit the ground. He brought his free hand down in a swift chopping motion toward one of the remaining three wolves channeling anima into his Graywind Emitter technique. Instantly, a blade of condensed Graywind anima blasted from his hand cleaving the umbral wolf's skull in two.

Two down, he counted. Unfortunately, he had little time to think much else before the last two wolves were upon him. Faster than he expected, they dashed toward him one at his left, the other at his right. However, the wolf on the left was faster. A mass of shadow and fangs slammed into his side nearly barreling over him. Instead of trying to bring his blade around to ward off the wolf's attack, he shifted to absorbing its impact on his shoulder by using the beast's momentum to roll backward, and simultaneously avoid the attack from the slower wolf. As he came to a stop, he barely got his sword up in time to block the follow-up attack from the first wolf catching its bite on the flat side of his blade. He shoved the shadow beast away from him and it yelped as his sword sliced into its tongue.

With a brief moment to breathe, he took stock of the situation. The umbral wolves circled him, the white of their teeth catching the thin slivers of moonlight overhead. Their black pelts shifted within the growing shadows reminding Kai that the deeper the night grew the more dangerous they'd become. These beasts were already stronger and faster than he'd expected. Despite the Matriarch's assertion that umbral wolves were roughly equivalent to a Bronze divine artist, he doubted anyone without a Silver body could keep up with them. Nonetheless, he never doubted his ability to win the fight. Doubt was the seed of defeat. Sensing one of the wolves behind him, he decided it was time to end the fight.

As one, the two umbral wolves pounced. Taking a calm breath, Kai initiated the Gray Maelstrom technique. Blade essence and wind essence harmonized into a vortex sharp fury that exploded outward from his blade. The two wolves cried out as dozens of razor-sharp blades of wind bit into their bodies knocking them from the air. Before either of them could recover, he sent a blade of condensed Graywwind anima at the one in front of him killing it. Whirling around, he faced the umbral wolf behind him. The beast was a bloody wreck struggling to stand. If Kai left it alone, it would more than likely die of its wounds before morning, but he was not a man to leave a job unfinished. Stepping forward, he thrust his sword into its skull, quick and painless. The entire fight had lasted less than a minute.

After using the fur of the first wolf he'd killed to clean his blade, he surveyed his work. All four wolves laid dead on the forest floor. For a few moments, he listened to the silence of the forest, senses keened for any sign of danger. Perceiving nothing, he released the Graywind Cloak and made his way back to the hollow where Enkai and Chun hid.

Despite his knowledge of the Matriarch's abilities, it unnerved him that even though he *knew* they hid within that hollow, all he saw was an empty space. After a moment, the darkness inside the hollow bled away revealing his son and Lin Chun tinged with purple light from the wisp lantern his son still carried.

"I assume the danger is clear?" the Matriarch asked, looking impressed. Kai nodded and stepped aside to allow the two of them to exit the hollow.

"Let's move. It's quiet now, but we need to leave before their Eidolons rise," Kai said as the Matriarch stood and brushed herself off. Even as he spoke, thin tendrils of shadow anima rose from the first of the slain wolves. In less than an hour, they would coalesce into an Eidolon, the remains of an awakened spirit that rose after death. Even though Eidolons were never as dangerous as the original creature, they might summon their pack once they were fully formed.

"Father, that was amazing!" Enkai exclaimed with barely restrained awe. He crawled out of the hollow, eyes wide with wonder.

"Quiet, boy. Do you mean to bring all the creatures of the night down upon us?" he said, his voice low but harsh.

Enkai's eyes widened even further as he realized his mistake. He clapped one hand over his mouth while glancing around fearfully. Chun leveled an admonishing look at Kai. Patting Enkai on the head, she said, "Don't be so harsh with the little one. Even I'm surprised you managed to kill four umbral wolves at night without suffering a single injury."

Ignoring the compliment, Kai reached into the hollow and pulled out two heavy packs. He slung one over one shoulder then unceremoniously tossed the other to the Matriarch. Over the last few days, Lin Chun's motherly fawning over Enkai had worn his patience thin. Even more grating was Enkai's reaction to the affection. Truthfully, the boy bore no fault; nevertheless, memories of his late wife continued surfacing every time he saw them together which only increased his ire. If Liu were alive, perhaps things might've turned out differently. He banished those thoughts from his mind. He had a duty and he would see it done.

Turning to look Lin Chun in the eye, he growled, "I do not coddle my son. If you must do so to reconcile with what is to come, then so be it, but, Matriarch or not, do not tell me how to handle my own child."

Not waiting for her reply, he walked away heading southeast. Although he expected a retort from the Matriarch, they passed the rest of the night in relative silence. For a quarter-hour, they traveled in the dark with only the light of Enkai's wisp lantern until they came up the rock outcropping that Lin Chun had designated as their resting place for the night. Following a quick sweep of the area to ensure it was safe, Lin Chun cast her Shroud over the site and they bedded down for the night.

***

Deep in the depths of a landscape unknown, he slept. Around him, a cloudy vastness extended beyond any measurable scope. Lights flickered on and off far in the distance, too far for him to touch. Some lights called out to him as they faded like the dying fragments of a memory long forgotten. Each one was unique, but all that called to him shared one trait: their light cut through the fog so he could see them clearly, no matter how far they were.

He lamented their distance. If only one were close enough, he could be free! With each light's call, he tasted the promise of possibility. However, his slumber extended each time one of them died.

How long had he slept?

Why had he gone to sleep?

Memories, half-remembered, in a fog of scattered dreams, flitted through his mind. For what seemed like an eternity, he pondered. His mind was seemingly endless in its ability to produce possible reasons. So mired in the mazes of his own thoughts was he that he almost missed his chance. A small light, fleeting and dim, suddenly flared with power and drifted closer to him. He heard its call and eagerly

responded. A faint connection formed between himself and the little light.

Uncoiling his will, he reached out ...

***

On the fourth day, their group stopped around midday to rest. The break was primarily for Enkai who in addition to being a child also lacked the benefit of having a Silver body. He tried his best not slow down the journey, but willpower only went so far when his body refused to cooperate. They rested beside a stream that cut through the forest before eventually flowing into a jagged fissure in a nearby rock face. Enkai splashed cool water over his head in an attempt to revitalize himself while the adults refilled their waterskins. It dripped down his face and hair back into the stream as he watched bits of sediment get carried away into the dark fissure, causing him to wonder where the water went after it fed into the earth. His grandfather had once told him that channeling wind anima felt like being everywhere at once, free and unbound. When he was no longer Forsaken, he still hoped to have affinities for earth and water. How would he feel if he channeled earth and water anima?

For longer than he intended, Enkai lost himself in the flow of the stream and the sounds of the forest. As they traveled through the vast woodland, the landscape awed him at every turn. The Maro Province contained beauty in their own right, but it paled in comparison to the Forbidden Forest. While the night drowned the forest in deep shadows and bestial cries that chilled the soul, the day revealed a wonderland of vibrant greens, browns, and reds.

Throughout their journey, Enkai had asked questions whenever he could. Matriarch Chun happily indulged his curiosity when possible. Unfortunately, her Shroud could not hide them completely unless they stayed in one location. While they traveled, the Shroud only prevented beasts from sensing their presence through spiritual means but did nothing to mask detection by mundane methods. The Shroud's flaws required Kai who had the sharpest senses to keep a constant vigil for any impending threats, which meant they usually traveled in silence. His reverie broke when a soft voice called out to him from some distance away.

"Little one, come here." Looking up, he saw Lin Chun beckoning him over to her. Instead of moving, he looked to his father. After Kai's words last night, Enkai felt conflicted about his budding relationship with the Lin Matriarch. He had grown to truly treasure her presence in the past few days, yet hearing his father disparage her affection for him had made him feel unexpectedly guilty. Out of respect for his father, he decided to act in a more reserved manner around her. Thankfully, she did not force the issue. Last night, he'd slept by himself, tossing and turning on the uneven ground without her warmth to dull the chill of night. He hoped whatever tension there was between the two adults would resolve itself quickly.

On a nearby fallen tree trunk, his father sat in a meditative position. He opened one eye to glance at Enkai and the Matriarch. After a few breaths where no one moved, Kai waved a hand for him to proceed though Enkai swore he saw the hint of a frown on his father's face. Making his way over, he saw she had started a small fire which produced almost no smoke. The Matriarch held a pot filled with clear bubbling water over the flames with one hand while the other placed dried leaves into a small cup sitting on a flat rock by her feet. He sat down next to her patiently waiting for her to finish. She poured the steaming hot water into the cup carefully then picked it up with both hands. She raised the cup to her lips and blew on it several times before handing it to Enkai.

"Drink as much as you can. It won't be pleasant, but it will ease the ache of the journey," she explained. Enkai accepted the cup. He hesitated briefly upon smelling the liquid's pungent odor then took a reluctant sip. Enkai almost spat the liquid back out because it tasted like wet dirt. The Matriarch's eyes sparkled with amusement at his reaction. Despite the disgusting taste, he steeled his resolve and drank the entire cup. Chun's approving smile made the experience worth it and he felt the effects of the liquid almost immediately as the aches from the days of hiking through the wilderness eased.

"Thank you for your kindness," he said evenly.

"So formal!" she laughed, arching one eyebrow. "You wouldn't think you were the same boy who asked me to tell him a story before he fell asleep in my lap just the other night."

"Apologies, Matriarch," he replied as his face flushed with embarrassment. Over the course of the journey, Enkai had found it easier than expected to ignore the fact that Lin Chun was the leader of the honored Lin clan. Based on an offhand comment by his father, he understood she was supposedly the same age as the Du Patriarch which Enkai found completely unbelievable. She looked to be closer in age to Ba Ren, the Patriarch's son. Additionally, she behaved completely unlike the Du Patriarch who always appeared wise and distant to Enkai. She exhibited little concern for propriety as was clear from the way she interacted with her clan members and Enkai. Appropriate or not, something about her behavior made Enkai feel at ease around her. Even as he sat across from her, her warm demeanor made him want to move closer to her. He did not really understand his father's issue with her, but his desire for Kai's approval outweighed his growing attachment to Lin Chun.

"I'm only teasing, little one," she said, gently pinching his cheek. "Your father will be cultivating his anima for a little while longer from the looks of it, so why don't you tell me about your dreams? Anything good last night?"

Enkai frowned thinking over his strange dream from the previous night. Since the day he'd met the Matriarch, his dreams had been incredibly vivid. Each morning, he had taken to telling her about them. "I don't know. Everything was all foggy and confusing."

"Really? You can't remember anything?" she asked. She raised an eyebrow again, this time with an honestly curious expression.

"No, I remember, but…," he paused, trying to think of a clear way to explain the dream. "It was like I was dreaming in my dream, but knew I was dreaming, but there was fog and everything was far away and—"

She put a finger on his lips to quiet his rambling and regarded him for a long while. Her expression changed from curious to distant then back to curious. Eventually, she said, "That sounds like a strange dream. If you have any more of those, let me know, alright, little one?"

"Okay," he agreed.

They talked until his father finished his meditation. The conversation mostly consisted of Chun answering his questions about the names of plants and how they were used. The Forbidden Forest contained a wealth of useful herbs for divine artists who knew their value. Apparently, even the dirt had its uses if you knew where to harvest it. When Kai finally finished cultivating, they continued their journey.

Despite the Matriarch's curiosity, Enkai had no more odd dreams. While they were still strikingly vivid, none of them held the same strangeness as the dream of fog and lights. Instead, he dreamt of epic battles fought alongside his father and clansmen against attacking enemies or rampaging great beasts.

While the tension between his father and the Matriarch never really went away, Kai allowed Enkai to act as he wished with her. Enkai still avoided getting too lax with his manners as a way of appeasing his father; however, the only good it seemed to do was to give the Matriarch a reason to tease him. On the fifth day, Chun declared they would reach the Sacred Vas tree soon. On the sixth day, both adults grew more muted. They arrived at their destination a few hours after nightfall on the sixth day.

The sight took his breath away. It was like visiting another world. They stepped into a large glade filled with starlight that hummed with power even Enkai could feel against his skin. In contrast to the darkness, silver-white wisps of light drifted lazily through the air casting their glow on everything. The wisps of light immediately reminded Enkai of the one within his lantern. Pulling the small globe from his pocket, he watched with wide eyes as the purple wisp grew visibly brighter until it shone as brightly as the silver-white lights around him.

Bright red and silver flowers covered the ground filling the air with an almost intoxicating sweetness. Where they did not grow, rich jade-colored grass flourished creating an interlacing tapestry of silver, red and green. In contrast, dull redwood roots snaked through the glade leading to a solitary tree in the center. Once Enkai saw the tree, he knew it had to be the Sacred Vas tree. Around its base, which was wide enough to take three men of his father's size to encircle it, the flowers and grass shone more vibrantly. The silver-white wisps congregated among the branches of the tree giving it an otherworldly presence. The tree's color changed as it extended from the ground starting as redwood at the roots then transitioning to maroon at the trunk until finally ending in white leaves that covered its branches.

"Kai and Enkai of the Du clan, I present to you, the Sacred Vas tree," the Matriarch said. Because they were so engrossed in the sight before them, both missed the deep note of sadness in her voice. Enkai looked at his father with barely contained anticipation. Kai stood mouth agape and eyes wide as he took in the sight of the glade causing Enkai to do a double-take. He had *never* seen his father express such awe. Kai was the type of man who'd always had everything under control. Enkai wondered what the glade felt like to his father since even he could feel the power in this place. His father took a few steps forward then dropped to his knees, eyes brimming with tears. Enkai could only stare at him, dumbfounded.

They sat in silence until his father bowed his head and began to pray. Unsure of what to do, he knelt beside his father and sent prayers to the ancestors. For the first time in recent memory, Enkai prayed to the spirit of his mother. He wished for her to watch over him and bless him with affinities for the elements she had once cultivated, so he could be a great warrior of the Du clan. The moment hung heavily in the air until he felt a rough hand squeeze his shoulder. His father favored him with a look he had never seen before on him. Regret. He had no idea what his father had to regret, but he knew better than to ask Kai about his feelings.

"Come, boy," his father said, his voice heavy with emotion that Enkai couldn't identify. "It is time to perform the ritual."

Oddly, sudden nervousness overtook Enkai's heart. During the entire journey, he'd looked forward to this moment, but now he felt like running away. He took a deep breath to steady his nerves the way his father had taught him. When he calmed down, he released the wisp lantern which simply floated aimlessly through the air and followed his father to the base of the Sacred Vas tree. The hum of power against Enkai's skin caused goosebumps all over his body. Glancing up at the mass of the silver-white wisps and white leaves, Enkai saw specks of red amongst the branches. Before he could identify them, his father spoke.

"Enkai, do you remember the first priority of a Du warrior?" Kai's words immediately drew his attention. His father almost never called him by name. Sensing the seriousness of his father's tone, Enkai stood straighter before answering.

"To serve the clan to the best of his ability," he replied. Kai nodded approvingly.

"And do you wish to become a warrior of the Du clan?"

His father's deep voice made the question vibrate through the air with a weight that pinned Enkai in place. Perhaps, it was just the power of the glade, but Enkai considered his next words carefully.

"Yes. I want to become a warrior of the Du clan. I want to serve like you do."

"Then repeat after me," Kai said.

Enkai repeated carefully after his father. The glade filled with the sound of their voices weaving together, one after the other. "Upon my spirit, I pledge my life in service to the Du clan. I shall be the roots that anchor them in times of turmoil. I shall be the bark that shields them from harsh winds. I shall be the branch that sustains them until I fall. I swear this by the ancestors."

When they finished, Enkai met his father's gaze, his heart heavy with emotion.

"As Head Warrior of the Du clan, I accept your oath and hereby recognize you as a warrior of our clan," Kai declared. Emotion filled Kai's eyes as he drew Enkai into a tight embrace.

A tight feeling built in Enkai's chest as emotion welled up within him. He couldn't remember the last time his father had hugged him. The tightness continued to grow until he felt like he was going to suffocate. His father was hugging him too hard: he couldn't breathe. He tried to pat his father on the shoulder, but his arms had no strength. In barely a whisper, Kai said, "May you serve well, my son."

The tightness grew so great that his mind began slipping out of consciousness. He tried to say something to his father, yet no words came, just rasping breath and more tightness. As blackness crept around the edges of his vision, he felt something rough against his back and looked up to see his father standing over him. Before darkness overtook him, his eyes drifted to his chest where a single blade with a red and yellow hilt sprouted from his chest surrounded by a rapidly growing blossom of blood-red.

Chapter 5

Kai watched the life pass from his son's eyes. In a pool of his own blood, Enkai died. An expression of confusion and fear frozen on his face. Kai knelt down and closed his son's unblinking eyes. As a father, his heart ached, yet his eyes held no trace of reservation. Not a man to wallow, he got to his feet. The journals of the founders had been clear about what was expected of him. He pulled the blade from his son's heart so the blood could flow freely.

Forsaken held no place in the world of the divine arts. Due to their curse, they brought grave misfortune down on those around them. Even if they were allowed to live, their corrupted spirits became twisted under the strain of the sacred energies a divine artist channeled. They were nothing more than liabilities. However, the clan founders had discovered one use for these piteous souls.

During the exodus through the Forbidden Forest, the clan founders had discovered the Sacred Vas tree. Each fruit carried immense amounts of vital anima gathered by the tree over its lifespan. Unlike most anima, any divine artist could absorb vital anima and strengthen his or her spirit. Legends told of great power granted to those who obtained a Sacred Vas fruit. According to clan records, Forsaken lifeblood fertilized the tree enough for it to bear a single fruit.

Kai allowed the sight before him to burn itself into his memory. The life of a divine artist was full of sacrifice, pain, and hardship. He accepted that; however, he would remember his son as more than just another stepping stone on his path to greatness. Enkai's death marked a turning point for him. He no longer held any ties aside from his service to the clan and the divine arts. Kai was aware of the expectations the clan held for him. The Patriarch had already begun molding Kai to succeed him. As he grew stronger, so too would the Du clan. He would shepherd the Maro Province into a new era with the power of the Sacred Vas fruit.

As if on cue, the tree emitted a clear chime that vibrated through his very soul. All at once, it radiated a piercing light while dozens of the silver-white wisps faded to a dull gray. The light grew until Kai could no longer bear to look at it. Power flared against his spirit; the tree's sheer spiritual pressure drove him to his knees nearly knocking him unconscious. After several oppressive moments, the light faded. Amongst the branches, a single speck of red swelled with vital anima growing until it took the form of a deep maroon pear. The branch snapped as the fruit fell from the tree. Twice the size of a normal pear, it shone as bright as a star in his spirit-sight.

Kai gawked at the fruit until he heard quiet footsteps approach from behind. Shakily, he stood turning to face the Lin Matriarch. As soon as he saw her, his instincts told him something was amiss. Her features showed a mask of impassivity completely unlike what he'd expected to see from her. In a voice as cold as the winter, she said, "You were right. I told myself that giving the little one my affection to ensure his final days were full of warmth and care was the right thing to do. But truthfully, I was deluding myself to alleviate my guilt about what was to come."

Her words caught Kai off guard. Her demeanor was strange, but he had not expected such a candid confession. Evidently, his outburst a few nights ago had struck a chord with the woman.

Still wary, he responded, "I spoke in frustration and anger. It was unbecoming of me. For that, I apologize."

Then Kai continued, "Do not burden yourself with guilt over this matter. As his father, I bear full responsibility. His sacrifice does much for the Maro Province so let us not dwell on this unfortunate business and instead look to the future." Regardless of his feelings about the Lin Chun, she had shown kindness and compassion to his son while he, the boy's own father, had distanced himself. The least he could do was try to alleviate her pain. He turned away from her to make his way to the Sacred Vas fruit.

"You understand nothing of my guilt, young Du warrior."

A spark of ire lit within him, yet the hairs on the back of his neck stood on end at the sound of her voice. It had changed. Frowning, he turned to face her with a retort fresh in his mind, but when he met her eyes, the words died before they reached his lips. Instead of the eyes of a mortal woman, he stared into wells of purple light. Something foreign in those eyes made his instincts scream to get away from her.

Then, she disappeared.

Kai whirled around, eyes darting from side to side. It did not take long. Standing several feet away, the Matriarch stood with the fruit in her hands. He placed a hand on the hilt of his sword, ready to draw it at a moment's notice.

"What are you doing?" he demanded. Her odd behavior and his paranoia convinced him that something was amiss. She said nothing. She didn't even look at him. Instead, she raised the fruit up to her radiant purple eyes and turned it slowly in her fingers. His scowl grew deeper. Against the warnings of his instinct, he took a step forward, and when he spoke, it was with thick with suspicion. "Give me the fruit. Du blood was sacrificed, so it belongs to the Du clan. As we discussed, the Lin clan will receive their share."

Still, she said nothing. In truth, the planned alliance between the Lin and Du made the talk of possession somewhat moot; however, Kai wasn't fool enough to ignore the possibility of betrayal. The Sacred Vas fruit contained immense power and enough power for the Lin clan to disregard the alliance so they could have it all to themselves. He placed a cautious hand on his sword ready to draw at a moment's notice.

Finally, she looked in his direction frowning. One of her hands pulled away from the fruit and gestured in his direction. The barest hint of a warning echoed across his mind causing him to activate the Graywind Cloak, draw his blade, and leap skyward to avoid any incoming attacks, all in one smooth motion. The inherent wind aspect of his Enhancement technique carried him swiftly through the air in a perfect arc, so he landed directly behind her with his blade at the ready.

"What are you playing at?" he growled. He had no intention of actually harming her; she was too important for that and he had no intention of being the one to violate the terms of their agreement. All the same, his instincts had never failed him. She was acting like a completely different person and he was almost certain she'd just launched an attack on him, even though he hadn't seen anything. Despite his advantageous position, he stayed on high alert, as warriors of the Lin clan were notoriously slippery combatants. She continued looking at the spot where he had been, ignoring his draw weapon behind her.

"Did you try to dodge my attack?" she asked, surprise clear in her voice. The shiver of something foreign brushing against his spirit ran through him. Her surprise grew as she continued, "How interesting. You were no more than a half-step from Gold."

The muscles in Kai's arm trembled as she spoke. For the last few months he had known he was close to making some kind of breakthrough, but a half-step from Gold? He'd only reached Silver roughly a year ago. As he considered her words, alarm bells sounded in his mind. What did she mean he'd *tried* to dodge her attack?

The moment the question passed through his mind; reality fell apart. A flash of purple filled his vision and the world slammed back into focus as if he had abruptly woken from a deep sleep. All of a sudden, he was several feet away from the

Matriarch who stood with one hand grasping the Vas fruit and the other resting at her side. Purple wells of untold wisdom looked down on him. For some reason, he was on the ground. He no longer felt the Graywind Cloak around him. Confused, he realized he could barely sense his own spirit let alone channel anima. In fact, he couldn't feel his body at all. Dread took hold of his thoughts as the Matriarch's chilling voice spoke.

"Had you been born in the outside of my little sanctuary, you undoubtedly would have gone far. A pity," she said matter-of-factly before biting into the fruit.

Rage swept away his fear as her teeth sank into the maroon flesh. He had offered up the life of his only son for that fruit and yet, she reaped the reward of his sacrifice before his eyes. He desperately called out to the faint whispers of his spirit, but neither anima nor essence answered. He drew a steadying breath in an attempt to focus, but no breath came. Panic banished his rage causing his thoughts to begin blending together. Frantically, his eyes darted left and right searching for answers as his consciousness began to slip away.

Then, he saw it.

Lying so close that he'd almost missed it among the bed of silver and red flowers, there was a body. His body. Sword half out the scabbard, it rested still. Only one feature was absent. Where his head should have been, only a blood-soaked neck stump remained. Recognition pushed through the fog of confusion and panic. As the darkness took him, emotion and thought faded. All that endured was a sense of profound loss.

***

Turning away from the beheaded corpse of Du Kai, she ate the Sacred Vas fruit. Concentrated vital anima surged through her rekindling the embers of her faded spirit. She had waited so long for this moment, yet she did not let her anticipation lead to carelessness. Although the sheer magnitude of power coursing through her could crumble mountains, her spirit was quiet. Effortlessly, she guided the vital anima through her body and mixed it with her spirit. The stream of power flowed through her, growing and expanding until it became an unfathomably deep ocean. After over a millennium in hiding, Evaniel was reborn.

The features that had once belonged to Lin Chun morphed. Her skin became as smooth and pale as alabaster. Crimson hair grew so lustrous it shone in the silver light of the glade. Once mortal features refined to the point of alien beauty. The radiance of her purple eyes intensified as she summoned her Semblance. She shed the green and silver robes as indigo anima wrapped against her body until it formed a skintight suit. A portion of the energy trailed behind her like a bridal veil. When the process concluded, her only resemblance to the Lin Matriarch was her crimson hair.

Taking a deep breath, she reveled in the feeling of once again being in her true form. Unbound, her spirit extended for thousands of miles, subtly touching the minds of every creature within its reach. She felt their memories and dreams as if they were just below the surface of her own mind. A single thought was all it would take for her to know all.

Far from the glade on the Maro Province, she brushed the minds of her children, the Lin clan. Even as a clan of dream artists, none detected her. She was too far beyond them. Within her mind, a voice spoke tinged with fear and awe.

Mother? Evaniel turned her sight inward, locating the source of the voice and then pulling it forth into being. A piece of her Semblance broke away dispersing into purple smoke, which took the shape of a woman and thickened as the figure became more real and defined. Smoke became bone, blood, and flesh brought to life by her will. In moments, Lin Chun stood before her.

"How is this possible?" Chun asked as she felt her face, incredulous. Evaniel waited patiently as Chun inspected her entire body from head to toe. "Am I really here with you? But you're inside my body, aren't you?"

"A dream is not so dissimilar from reality for those with the will to shape it, dear daughter," Evaniel answered. She stepped forward extending a hand to brush the hair hanging in front of Chun's eyes behind her ear. "You may have given me your body, but your spirit still lingers within. I simply created a vessel to house it."

Chun nodded, lips slightly parted and eyes wide. She looked around wincing as she glimpsed the corpse of Du Kai. When her eyes fell on the body of Du Enkai, her expression strained with sorrow and tears streamed down her face. Evaniel had expected as much.

Since the Fall of Heaven, Evaniel had hidden in the minds of the women among the Lin clan in whom her bloodline ran the strongest. In exchange for their service, she gave them wisdom, knowledge, and most of all, love. Each woman in the generation she inhabited achieved greatness with many becoming Matriarchs of the Lin clan. For that reason, the clan soon began to see women born with red hair as good omens. Yet of the daughters she'd inhabited since founding the Lin clan, Chun was by far the most sentimental. As a child, the girl had wept when the plants she forgot to water died. Only after Evaniel explained that dead plants could be used to feed new life had she stopped crying. In a way, Evaniel treasured that sentimentality so much so that she fostered and supported it over the course of Lin Chun's life. Stepping forward, she pulled Chun into an embrace stroking her hair while her body trembled with sobs.

While holding her daughter, she contemplated the Enkai's fate. Over a thousand years ago before the Fall of Heaven, children born with Primal cores were almost as common as children with Exalted cores. Primals were even prized in some cultures because of the unique brand of divine arts they could cultivate. Only after her failure had they been marked as undesirables – Forsaken. Her enemy had crafted a history wherein Primals were the villains. In the modern age, those with Exalted cores comprised the near whole of divine artists in the modern age.

Ironically, the only thing that had prevented Enkai from cultivating the divine arts was an obstacle devised by Evaniel. It had been she who'd ordered the seal placed on Enkai's spirit; just as she had allowed the spread of her enemy's propaganda about the danger of Forsaken within the Maro Province. Lamentable but necessary steps given her situation.

Unfortunately, powers beyond mortal comprehension twisted the fabric of reality, so fewer divine artists with Primal cores were born each year, while those who'd survived the Fall of Heaven were hunted down and killed. When Evaniel had finally felt the time had come to resurface and resume her mission, it was too late. Year after year, she had waited for a child with a Primal core to be born so she could obtain the Sacred Vas fruit and restore her power. Yet each year, she was dismayed. As time went on, her chances of ever correcting her failures in the Fall of Heaven grew fewer and fewer. She'd nearly given up hope until she dreamed of Enkai's birth nearly a half a century ago. Thanks to the knowledge of Forsaken she gave the various clan founders, the legends she'd propagated about the power of the Sacred Vas tree, and the carefully orchestrated position of the Lin clan as the strongest clan of the Maro Province and guardians of the Forbidden Forest, the child was destined to come to her eventually. A small part of her mourned the death of such an innocent, but his life only added to the plethora of sacrifices she'd been forced to make. Nevertheless, her determination to realize the dream she had fought so hard to preserve did not waver.

Still, one thing did bother her about the boy. In the days traveling to the Sacred Vas tree, Enkai had claimed to have had a dream set in a world of fog. Based on his description, the experience sounded exactly as if the boy had visited the Sphere of Dreams. While she had allowed Chun to enhance the boy's subconscious to allow for more vivid dreams, a visit to the Sphere of Dreams could only be undertaken by powerful dream artists, or if a dreamer with a strong will had established a connection to one of the many powerful residents of the Sphere. Given that Enkai had been newly awakened, the only explanation was that the boy had connected with something. She knew he'd developed a bond with the dream wisp; however, a mere wisp didn't have the power to allow him to visit the Sphere of Dreams. Sadly, despite her curiosity, his necessary death rendered any further exploration into the matter moot.

Chun calmed in her arms. She grasped her daughter's chin tilting it up so that their eyes met. "Wipe away your tears, dear daughter. As the heir that bore my spirit to rebirth, you have done me a great service. I lament the pain you feel in your heart, but your grief will not change fate. Instead, look forward. If you feel sorrow in your heart, help me put right the wrongs of old."

Chun met her eyes. Briefly, awe crossed her daughter's eyes again as their spirits brushed each other. Though Evaniel was currently Shrouding her spirit from all, her connection with Chun meant she could not hide the true extent of her power from her daughter. Her voice trembling, Chun said, "I gave you my body because I believe in you, Mother. But how could I help someone like you?"

Smiling, she extended her will to flow which permeated all things. Like an old friend, it responded eagerly. Space folded around them shifting the landscape in an instant. No longer did they stand under the silver-white glow of the Sacred Vas tree. Instead, an abyss of darkness lit by countless lights stretched beyond even Evaniel's senses. Below them, their world loomed, massive and clear. Chun gasped from beside her.

"Genesis, the world you know, is only one of many," Evaniel said. Many times, reality shifted to show dozens of worlds each different from the last. "Those that oversee these worlds have chosen to twist the natural order to their whim. Their arrogance will doom all things. I cannot stop them alone. Of this, I am certain."

"But what can I do that you can't?" Chun looked overwhelmed.

Tenderly, Evaniel reached out through her connection with her daughter's spirit and spoke from within. *Our souls are intertwined. You can aid me in ways no one else can, dear daughter. Will you help me?*

Chun took into the vast expanse of space. She marveled in the stars, the worlds, and the emptiness before quietly replying with the whisper of a thought. *I will*.

Evaniel brushed away a strand of hair behind Chun's ear and smiled. *Then let us begin.*

***

Sethara was having a bad day. Before her, a world had died. Holes all over its surface birthed twisted monstrosities that spread across the world like a plague of locust. Strange tendrils extended from the holes tearing at the fabric of reality. The entire process had happened far too quickly. Only a few minutes had passed between her detection of the anomaly and the world's destruction.

She commanded the Emanation, the governing flow of all things, to stop time in her localized area. Her Providence, a white disk flanked by two pillars, materialized behind her then activated the stasis. Instantly, all activity stopped. The prowling monstrosities and reaching tendrils froze. Stepping through space, she appeared on the surface of the world. Around her, ruin dominated the landscape. Nearby, a particularly large breach attracted her attention. It had formed in a canyon and then had expanded from within leading to a massive hole in the world's crust at least a mile wide and several times as deep. The tendrils coming from this breach towered hundreds of feet into the air. They'd carved swathes from the ground leaving only emptiness in their wake. Several were frozen in mid-strike as they were stabbing into the surfaces around them. She frowned at the size of the breach. It was one of the largest she had ever seen. Concern growing, she sent her Providence into the Emanation.

Report the status of this anomaly and world. Additionally, send a message to the Primarch requesting his attention in Sector 6. Convey urgency.

Within seconds, tendrils of vibrant gold flowed from the center of her Providence delivering information directly into her mind.

[COMMENCING REPORT: TOPIC Status of Local Anomaly and World DCLXVI within Sector 6]

Anomaly has consumed approximately 43% of the world. An additional 20% has been damaged beyond repair. The world's core has also been irreparably damaged. World collapse is imminent.

Sensing 0 signs of surviving life.

Anomaly measured at 7 th Magnitude: Immediate action required.

Number of breaches: 108

Recommended action: Destruction of World DCLXVI and complete stasis of anomaly

[REPORT COMPLETE: Would you like a more comprehensive report?]

Sethara immediately dismissed her connection to the Emanation. The utter shock nearly paralyzed her. A 7th Magnitude anomaly was ridiculous even in one of the outer Sectors. Shaking away her surprise, she leapt into the sky. Her jump carried her outside of the world in one go. The only silver lining to the situation was the lack of surviving life. She could act swiftly without worrying about evacuating any survivors. With power flaring through her, she channeled the force of her being into one word.

"Obliterate"

The white disk of her Providence released a whirling screech as it began to rotate at an incredible speed. The pillars flared to life emitting enough light to rival that of a small star. As the power reached its apex, several layered rings appeared in front of Sethara releasing a blast of energy that struck the world below. Light erupted as the blast hit and enveloped the entire area. Seconds later, the light faded revealing empty space where the world had once been.

Unfortunately, even without the world, the breaches remained. There were no longer monstrosities or tendrils emerging from them, but it would only be a matter of time if the anomaly was left alone. Sethara reached out to resume her connection with the Emanation when another's Providence touched her own. Already aware of who it was, she allowed the connection to pass through to her.

Sethara, what have you to report? The Primarch's calm monotone voice echoed in her mind as soon as their spirits connected.

I just encountered a 7ᵗʰ Magnitude Anomaly within Sector 6.

Silence settled upon their connection for several seconds.

Explain.

I sensed the anomaly while handling other business, however, by the time I arrived, the anomaly had already consumed World DCLXVI beyond recovery. I was nearby when I sensed it. Only a few minutes passed before I arrived, but the world's core had already been destroyed. Given the speed of the anomaly's growth and the core's destruction, I suspected that it was seeded from within the core.

I assume you have already destroyed the world?

Yes. Thankfully, there was no surviving life, so the anomaly did not have a chance to recover from temporary stasis before I destroyed the world. I was in the process of creating a permanent stasis when I sensed you.

Good. Finish there and then return to The Garden. He will wish to know about this. The connection broke off abruptly jarring Sethara's mind. Annoyance flared within her. She had no desire to report such bad news to her father. Scowling, she resumed her connection to the Emanation and prepared to seal the anomaly in permanent stasis.

***

As the lifeblood bled out of his body. Enkai fell into oblivion. When all that he was began to drift away, something seized his spirit and dragged it away from the brink. He felt his spirit pulled from his body and thrust into a place filled with fog and flickering lights. For what felt like an eternity, he fell endlessly through the fog. Clouded visions of his life flashed through his mind. One memory, in particular, lingered; one of his earliest from around his fourth summer.

Enkai sat cross-legged on the floor, carefully inspecting the grain of the wooden table a few feet away. He was supposed to be meditating, but his young mind found it hard to understand the idea of sitting still in contemplation for longer than a few seconds. His grandfather sat in a similar position nearby.

"Grandfather, it's not working."

One of his grandfather's eyes opened to look at him sidelong. Seeing Enkai's obviously unfocused demeanor, he sighed. Uncrossing his legs, the old man stretched languidly and chuckled. "Of course, it isn't working, boy. That son of mine must have wood in that skull of his if he's thinking meditating will do any good for you at your age."

Enkai fiddled with his fingers considering whether or not he should ask his grandfather the question burning in his mind. He started chewing on his bottom lip while he thought, which earned him a cuff across the back of the head.

"Spit it out, boy. I don't have the patience for you to fiddle about trying to decide whether or not you're gonna waste my time."

After a few more moments of contemplation in which his grandfather's left eye began to twitch, Enkai quietly asked, "Does father not like me?"

His grandfather's expression changed from one of annoyance to one of sympathy. He considered the question for a few seconds, long enough to make Enkai anxious. When he spoke, his voice was weary and the words came out like a sigh. "He loves you, En. Just as I do. But my block-headed son's got a poor way of showing it. Make no mistake though. He cares for you in his own way."

The memory faded. Enkai continued to fall through the endless foggy depths. At the edges of his vision, multicolored lights flickered in and out. More memories came, though each passed like half-formed thought barely discernible amidst his clouded mind. Some appeared clearer than others as they twisted with nightmarish clarity.

He tried to say something ... no words came ... blackness ... looked up to see his father standing over him ... a single blade with a red and yellow hilt sprouted from his chest surrounded by a blossom of crimson.

"... do not worry. Your father and I will see an end to your worries ..."

"Father, am I a Forsaken?"

"... A Forsaken... I wonder if we have angered the gods."

It seems you've met with a terrible fate.

As if being jarred from a waking dream, his mind recoiled as a voice slid through his thoughts. Briefly, he sensed a presence brush his consciousness. It barely touched him, yet even that slight contact sent warnings of danger through his clouded mind. However, he also felt an intense curiosity build within him.

Hesitantly, he responded. *I don't know what happened. Where am I?*

A hiss echoed all around him making his spirit shiver. Once again, the voice slithered into his thoughts, but this time it did not leave. ***You are dying, little light. You were betrayed.***

Betrayed? As the question ran through his mind. The presence brushed his consciousness again flooding it with images. He watched himself walk with his father to the base of the tree. His father kneeled down and began to talk, but the words were inaudible whispers in the fog. When his father drew him into a hug, he drew the dagger from his boot and drove it into Enkai's rib cage. He watched himself fall from his father's arms and land against the base of the tree. As soon as Kai stabbed him, Enkai began to reject what he was seeing. It was impossible. His father wouldn't do something so horrible. Sadly, the visions did not stop there.

He saw the amazing bloom of the Sacred Vas fruit. Then, the Matriarch confronted his father. In horror, he watched her gesture with her hand sending a blade of purple energy that looked suspiciously like the Graywind Emitter technique at his father. Kai activated the Graywind Cloak, but the blade was too fast. The images faded as his father's head and body fell to the ground.

No! The cry poured from him with the force of his entire spirit. Despair flooded his thoughts, yet he refused to believe what he had seen. His father could never be killed so easily. *Stop lying! Father would never betray me. He can't lose, either! Your wrong! He wouldn't...*

Are you sure, little light? Another stream of fragmented memories flowed through his mind overtaking him.

... a tight feeling ... couldn't breathe ... "May you serve well, my son."

Tightness ... slipping out of consciousness ... a red and yellow hilt ... a blossom of crimson

Uncertainty filled his mind mingling with his despair. Some part of him knew these images were the truth, but he just couldn't accept it. Kai was his hero. Kai protected the clan and inspired others. He was their champion. No one doubted him because he lived to serve the clan. Kai's last words echoed through his thoughts. Would his father sacrifice even his own son for the clan? Uncertainty turned to fear. The fear brought another question into being.

I'm dying ...?

Silence prevailed in the fog as the question faded into the emptiness. Fear gave birth to terror. Terror of the unknown overwhelmed his thoughts drowning everything out. Visions of his life blurred through his mind in a jumbled mess, too broken to make any sense. At the point when his mind felt it would snap, the presence coiled around his spirit.

Do you want to live?

I don't want to die! He cried out with all the force his will could muster.

I can help... Are you sure you want my help, little light? It comes at a cost.

Enkai couldn't even begin to understand what the voice was implying. Beneath the panic and terror that ruled his consciousness, a feeling of primal foreboding rose from his spirit. At the same time, he could feel himself slipping away like the remnants of a forgotten dream. Enkai struggled to keep hold of himself. To not forget. Somehow, he understood he had been asked a question though what it was he couldn't say. Nonetheless, he answered. He wrestled one coherent thought from the madness, more a wish born of desperation as he felt himself fading. *I want to live.*

Then, we have a deal. A hiss sounded through the vastness as the presence struck his spirit. Like a drill, it pierced the core of his being.

He screamed then fell into darkness.

***

Deep within a world of redwood trees and silver light, an ancient being woke. Lying on a bed of leaves and grass, the creature raised its head to gaze into the distance. A tremor pulsed through the Spheres calling to it like a parent calling a child. Amongst its antlers, silver-white wisps danced eagerly. It lightly rose to its feet shaking loose the leaves sticking to its scales and hair. Around its bed, various creatures stirred from rest. They looked upon the creature and bowed their heads as it passed. Where its cloven hooves fell, flowers bloomed and grass sprouted. Space folded as it walked through the fabric of reality toward the source of the tremor. In only three steps, it stood before the Sacred Vas tree deep within the Forbidden Forest. Three things caught its attention within the glade: a spirit without a vessel, a disturbance in fabric of space and time, and a dying boy.

An Eidolon comprised of wind and swords wandered the glade. When the Eidolon saw the creature, it froze. The creature walked towards the Eidolon and while crossing the glade, it stepped over a beheaded corpse and when it passed, naught of the corpse remained but a mound of fresh grass and flowers. The Eidolon howled at the sky as the creature drew closer, but the creature only smiled. It sensed the lingering spirit's profound loss. The remorse of a life unfulfilled. Of regret. The vestiges of the individual had been lost in the mire of its last moments. If left to its own devices, the Eidolon would either be hunted and consumed by the beasts of the forest or wallow in its own suffering until the anima that composed its form faded into essence. Extending its scaled neck, the creature exhaled onto the Eidolon scattering it to the wind so that it could rest in peace.

Next, it turned to the Sacred Vas tree. Reaching its will out to the wisps within its branches, it extracted the events they had witnessed. It saw three enter the glade and two leave. Dimming its will, the creature immersed itself in the flow of time, experiencing the events that had taken place within the glade. The creature witnessed the rebirth of Evaniel and her escape into the Transcendent Realm. None would be able to sense her except for the creature and its kin. If she sought to continue her campaign of old, it would undoubtedly cross her path once again.

Lastly, the creature turned its attention to the dying boy. Cords of volatile scarlet energy slithered around his body. Lying in the center of the boy's chest next to a raw patch of mottled skin was a single wisp. The creature's smile widened as it nodded in greeting. Rising into the air, the wisp bobbed its own greeting then flew into a pocket of the boy's robes.

As the creature approached, the scarlet cords writhed violently. As one they flowed into the patch of mottled skin directly over the boy's heart. On the ground next to the boy, there was a bloodstained dagger with a hilt wrapped in red and yellow and a cracked glass globe. Looking within the boy, the creature saw that his spirit was whole though not unsullied. The scarlet energy ran through his spirit reinforcing it while the body healed. However, around his heart, a cluster of red energy tangled like a nest of vipers waiting to strike. The creature was familiar with this particular type of energy. If left to its own devices, the energy would heal the body by twisting and mutating it. The boy's mind would doubtlessly not survive the process, nor would his body live for long in the resulting unstable form. Briefly, it touched the boy's spirit bringing forth his memories, wishes, and fear of death. There was no guilt within him. He had been used as a pawn in a much larger game. Such things were not uncommon to the creature, yet it would not turn away from an innocent child robbed of his chance at life.

Around its antlers and shoulders, a mane of silver-white light flared to life. The wisps in the glade all chimed in unison and resonated with its power. Vital essence flooded the glade washing over everything.

First, the creature sent its spiritual perception deep into the boy's spirit. Closer inspection confirmed the creature's suspicions. The boy had a Primal core which explained why the other humans had sacrificed him. Such fates had been common for Primals since the Fall of Heaven.

Before the Fall, divine artists with Primal cores had been left to pursue their divine arts as freely as any other. In the current age, only great beasts walked freely Primal cores. For all his power, the Usurper had no sway over the fate of beasts.

Unfortunately, as he was, the boy would assuredly die, if not now, then later at the hands of other humans who realized what he was. It could not protect the boy from those dangers.

There was one thing it could do. Leaning down, it touched its nose to his flesh just below his navel. A small part of its mane broke off taking the form of a seed and sinking into the boy's skin. With practiced care, it guided the seed to take root within the boy's core. Next, it healed the damage inflicted on his body. The raw patch of skin grew dull as the body recovered. The heart mended. The lungs drew breath. The fractured ribs nicked by the blade repaired themselves. Lastly, the creature leaned down and picked the boy up between its teeth. Even with a healed body, he would need care until he was powerful enough to fend for himself. Thankfully, it knew of a candidate that would raise the boy as her own.

Space folded around the creature. In two steps, it was gone.

Chapter 6

Thousands of miles from the Maro Province amidst a sea of green, Old Omen slept. During the Fall of Heaven, the volcano had spewed fire and ash and covered the landscape in ruin. Yet for the past millennium, it had lain dormant. Within the mouth of the slumbering mountain, Nin toiled over a stone basin under the light of the moon. She was in her humanoid form as usual because it made handling her work easier and she preferred it to her original shape. In her hands, she held a long staff carved from ironwood. The mixture within the basin bubbled as she slowly stirred it with the staff. Even though her nose twitched incessantly from the acrid smell rising from the basin, she kept her eyes trained on the liquid, carefully watching for the right moment.

A few feet away from her, a tiny fox trembled in pain on a blanket of woven leaves. The cub released a tormented whine drawing Nin's eyes to her. She gave Nin a pleading look through moist eyes.

"Hang in there, Brem. Mama will make it better soon," Nin called, turning her gaze back to the basin though she kept an eye on Brem who was curled into a tiny ball of black fur. She wanted to go to her and offer comfort, but if she missed her chance, she wouldn't live through the night. The best thing she could do for her was focus on the task at hand. Another minute passed stretching into eternity, and then the moment she'd been waiting for arrived. As the bubbling reached its peak, the liquid began to release thick vapors. Summoning the energy of her spirit, Nin threaded it into the mixture through the staff while continuing to stir carefully. After another minute, the liquid changed colors from an angry green to a pale blue. Nin continued to refine the mixture with the power of her spirit. The process took another agonizing five minutes. When she'd finished, the amount of liquid in the cauldron had diminished significantly, but the remnants radiated a vibrant silvery-blue light.

Quickly, she extracted her staff laying it to the side of the basin to grab a small bowl from her collection of tools. Careful not to spill a single drop, Nin scooped the finished elixir into the bowl and rushed over to Brem. With one arm, she scooped up the fox. With the other, she gently tilted the bowl in front of the fox so she could to lap up the elixir. "Drink as much as you can, Brem. There you go, it'll be alright."

As Brem drank, her body calmed. Opening her spiritual awareness, Nin saw Brem's spirit fighting back the venom. She sighed with relief then wrapped the little fox up in the woven leaf blanket. Using straps on the blanket she'd fashioned specifically for such an occasion, she hoisted the bundle onto her back where Brem promptly fell asleep. Nin turned on her heel toward the basin to clean up when she felt another presence appear near the edge of the crater. Both her ears popped up listening intently as she shifted in the direction of the new arrival.

At the edge of the crater where the ground curved up to the lip, a curtain of moonlight rippled. Like a phantom fading into existence, a creature appeared. It had the body of a massive elk with scales instead of hair running down its neck and chest. Crowned by a forest of antlers, a human-esque face stared at her framed by a mane of vital anima. Within its teeth, the creature held another creature clothed in a red and yellow robe.

Nin's heart stuttered as her eyes fell upon the newcomer. She had never seen such a creature before, yet her spirit echoed with a deep sense of familiarity. Like a child recognizing its parent, she *knew* this creature. Time seemed to stop as it moved toward her. Fresh grass and flora sprouted from the hard earth where it stepped leaving a trail of life in its wake. At some point, Nin realized that she was crying. She couldn't understand her tears, but a wholesome joy swelled within her spirit as the creature stopped in front of her. For several moments, she gazed up into its eternal eyes. Somehow, she knew exactly what it wanted as it placed the robed creature at her feet.

Unsure of what to do, Nin bowed her head and said hesitantly, "Forgive me for my ignorance, ancestor, but I don't know what type of beast this creature is. How will I care for it?"

Instead of responding to her, it smiled. Immediately, images streamed into her mind. She didn't understand most of it, however, she understood that the boy needed her. He was human. A human who lacked the ability to care or fend for himself because he was still a child much like Brem and her son, Jak. Recognition shone in her eyes

The creature's smile widened. It turned away and walked off disappearing in a shimmer of moonlight. For several minutes, Nin stared at the space where the creature had vanished. Her mind struggled to comprehend what had just happened. She looked down at the boy to reassure herself that she had not imagined the entire scenario. He rested on the hard earth seemingly oblivious to the world. Truthfully, she had never seen a human, so she was genuinely curious about the child. Elder Onki who ruled over the region of the forest where Nin lived had told her stories about humans when she was young, but she'd never met one.

Looking over the boy, she noted his features. He had bronze skin which matched his short chestnut hair. She let her awareness inspect the child's spirit, but she recoiled when she sensed hostile energy lying dormant within it. He was a Deviant. Her curiosity gave way to a bit of concern as she wondered where that mysterious creature had gotten him. Whatever his origins, Nin knew Deviants were dangerous, so she needed to proceed with caution. The entire situation was bizarre in the extreme; she would need to ask Onki how to proceed.

She picked the boy up though it was a bit awkward since he was about the same size as her. On her back, Brem stirred as she was jostled but thankfully remained unconscious. Nin made her way down the mountain slowly having to take extra care on the treacherous slopes with the burden of the human child weighing her down.

The journey to Elder Onki's cave took her a few hours with only the light of the night sky to guide her. Several times, she rerouted to avoid obstacles and sudden drops in terrain, but she knew this mountain well enough that she never truly felt in danger.

At the base, she stopped in front of a massive hole in the mountainside. From end to end and top to bottom, it spanned several dozen feet. As always, Nin felt incredibly small when she walked into Elder Onki's cave, which wasn't unreasonable considering she was, in fact, tiny compared to him. The hole led into a tunnel that extended deep into the earth under the mountain. Because her eyes weren't suited to the dark, Nin had a hard time making out anything in the cave, so she called forward a tiny piece of her spirit. A mote of moonlight emerged from her hand and illuminated the rough walls.

Onki's lair opened up at the end of the tunnel. The antechamber made Nin feel even smaller than the tunnel and entrance. The entire lair was massive with boulders covering the ground like a forest of stone, each one standing at her height at least. Easily hopping onto twice her size for a better view, she searched for Onki among his maze of rocks. She spotted him almost immediately due to his large size. Adjusting her hold on the human and Brem to ensure they wouldn't fall, Nin rapidly made her way across the antechamber hopping from boulder to boulder. When she reached one near her destination, she laid the boy and Brem down on the mostly flat portion of the rock. Next, she turned her attention to the largest stone in the cavern.

"Onki, wake up! You'll never believe what's happened!" she called. Her words echoed through the chamber traveling through the dozens of tunnels along its walls. Several moments passed, but the *boulder* remained still which annoyed her. Onki would have known as soon as she entered his lair, which meant he'd probably chosen to remain sleeping even after she'd entered.

Nin hopped down from her perch. Facing away from the boulder on which she'd laid the children, she found her target, an opening. Mischief twinkling in her eyes, she conjured a ball of blue light, then sent it inside Onki's shell.

Wake up!" she shouted shortly before detonating the ball of light within the shell. Sparks erupted from the hole along with a booming pop as the condensed anima exploded. All at once, the mass shifted and a reptilian head slithered out of the hole.

"What's with all the racket?!" Onki cried as he emerged from his shell. He pushed himself into a sitting position as he woke. His leathery black skin stretched across his massive head and neck which were lined with rock-like growths, one of which was forming a stony beard on his chin. The mossy boulder which was really Onki's shell shifted as he moved. Every movement caused tremors in the cave and shook loose several layers of debris and dust. Nin found the whole display comical as she watched from the safety of her perch where she'd jumped after waking the elder. His snakehead swiveled towards her. Their eyes met and she couldn't help but laugh at his agitated expression. Technically, the ball of light she'd used to wake him up was a powerful Emitter technique, but she wasn't worried. Honestly, she wasn't sure there *was* a way to harm Onki. The ancient tortoise seemed nearly invincible to Nin.

"My discomfort amuses you, little rabbit?" he said with an accusatory tone. He adjusted his position, so he faced her directly then gave her the look of a parent ready to scold a child. His rumbling voice carried a hint of indignation as he continued, "What a horrible world it is when youngsters enjoy harassing their elders. Where did I go wrong in raising you? When I was young ..."

Nin listened to his overdramatic ramble with a smile on her face. Despite his occasional ornery nature, she enjoyed visiting him when she could. Onki had watched over her when she was younger giving her guidance as well as protection when necessary. She owed him a great deal though that didn't stop her from having fun at his expense from time to time. After a minute or so, she decided to interrupt his rant which she knew from experience could go on for hours.

"But Elder Onki, I had something really important to tell you and you were sleeping," she said donning a pout while casting her eyes downwards. She also lowered her ears so they hung down the side of her head and put on a pout. Sadly, a furtive glance at the tortoise told her he wasn't buying her feigned remorse.

"So, you set off an explosion in my face because I didn't want to wake up?" He shook his head, positively disgruntled. Nin, however, couldn't hold back a snicker which only increased the intensity of his glare.

"Well, it's not like I could literally hurt you! Besides, now you're up and I can tell you about what happened," she said with a wave of her hand. Onki huffed in dissatisfaction, still upset that Nin had disturbed his slumber but her words drew his attention to Brem and the young human resting behind her. He barely glanced over the two of them before he turned his eyes back to Nin.

"I see the antidote turned out well for the brat," Onki said referring to Brem. Then, his demeanor became serious. He lowered his head to look Nin directly in the eye before asking, "Now, why is there a Deviant, a human with a Primal core no less, in my territory?"

Making sure to leave nothing out, Nin described her encounter with the mysterious creature along with the strange feeling that had overcome her and how it had appeared from nowhere. He listened quietly, only asking a few questions about the creature. By the end of the explanation, Onki seemed troubled. For several moments, he said nothing while staring at the human boy. Nin knew he must be deep in contemplation.

Unsure what to do as the silence stretched on, Nin voiced her concerns about the boy. "I'm certain it wanted me to care for him, but I don't know what to do. I'm not sure I can take care of a human. And aren't Deviants dangerous? He might endanger Brem and Jak. Not to mention, he's barely more than a newborn. He is so fragile! If he dies, I'll feel horrible! I don't know what—"

"Enough, little rabbit," Onki commanded putting a stop to her nervous spiral. He extended his neck toward the boy then inhaled deeply through his nostrils. Grunting, he said, "He is less volatile than most Deviants, which doesn't surprise me given the circumstances of his arrival."

"Do you mean him being given to me by that ancestor creature?" she asked, curious. Onki withdrew his head slightly, then nodded to her.

"Yes, it's understandable that you'd use the word *ancestor*," Onki said. He looked away from her, eyes distant as if he were recalling a long-forgotten memory. "We call him the Silent Father. If he truly delivered this human to you, then the boy must have some significance."

Nin's apprehension grew as Onki spoke, the severity in his tone sending shivers down her spine. Even when dealing with matters related to ruling over his territory, Onki rarely looked as dire as he did now. Her nose started twitching.

"Is this Silent Father something we should worry about?" she asked, her voice rising a few octaves. Onki took another pensive moment then sighed. She had a feeling she wasn't going to like his answer.

"He is one of the Primordials. The last time one of their kind appeared to mortals the heavens fell. Something is coming, little rabbit."

For several long minutes, they sat in silence. Nin hadn't been alive during the Fall of Heaven, but Onki had been. When she was growing up, he had told her stories about all kinds of things, but the Fall of Heaven had always given her nightmares. She was naturally very prone to anxiety, so a story about the world almost ending didn't sit well with her. Nin nearly fainted when she heard that the creature she'd met was one of the Primordials. In Onki's stories, the Primordials helped the gods create the world when the heavens were still young. Truthfully, she hadn't even believed such creatures existed. She'd lived her entire life on Old Omen in relative peace, and she couldn't imagine beings with such unbelievable power. Elder Onki was the most powerful creature she knew, but other than his apparent invulnerability, he never demonstrated his strength in any tangible manner.

"What should we do?" It was the only question in her mind at that moment. The situation at hand felt too important for her small life.

"This will certainly complicate our lives. Though he is a Deviant, the biggest problem is that because of his core, he will stand out as he grows into a divine artist. To my knowledge, there have not been any Primals in centuries. There are old factions that would see him dead if they knew of his existence. Still, the Silent Father must have had a reason for bringing him here," Onki said. He put on a weary expression as he stared at the young human, but he came to a decision. He continued, "We will care for him until he decides to leave. That is all we can do."

Hearing his words eased Nin's nervousness a bit, but it also filled her with a deep sadness. The Silent Father had shown her what had happened to the child. His own kind had betrayed him. She knew there were scars on the boy's mind and soul that would need mending. She had no idea if she could help him, though she intended to try.

As they contemplated the challenges of raising a human among beasts, Nin watched a small wisp comprised of dream anima slip out of a pocket on the boy's robe. She stared at the spirit which drew Onki's attention. Nin hadn't sensed the wisp at all. Generally, they had very small spiritual presences, so it wasn't uncommon that they went unnoticed. To Nin's knowledge, they were also completely harmless. She wondered if Onki had noticed the wisp but deemed it not worth mentioning, however, she didn't have to wonder for long.

"Interesting," he said softly. Before she could really respond, a wave of power spread from Onki hitting the wisp. Like mist in a strong wind, the wisp dispersed.

Nin blinked at Onki, a bit surprised. Confused, she asked, "Was that really necessary? It was just a wisp."

"Just watch," he said, so she did. Not even a minute after the wisp was destroyed, tiny purple strands began emerging from the boy's navel. Another minute later and a newly formed wisp floated above his stomach. Nin looked to Onki, still confused, though for a different reason.

Thankfully, Onki elaborated, "The human child has bonded with the wisp. Normally, wisps reformed at their source, but if a bond is established with another creature, the wisp will reform within the bonded creature's core. They are also impossible to sense when near their bond partner because their spiritual presence is masked by the bond."

As she looked back and forth between the wisp and Onki understanding dawned on her. "So, you were just testing to see if it was bonded?"

Onki snorted, then said, "Yes, though I find wisps to be little more than pests. It's a shame this one will be sticking around."

Nin stepped next to the boy. The wisp landed on her shoulder as she pondered how well the boy would get along with her other children.

"Take the brat back to your burrow, little rabbit, but leave the human here. Though he may be less volatile, he's still a Deviant. I will monitor him for the night and ensure nothing is amiss," Onki said. Nin nodded her head, feeling truly relieved. While Onki assured her that the human wasn't dangerous, she could prepare her children for the new member of their family. She had no idea how they might react.

"Thank you, Onki. I'll come back for him tomorrow," she replied. Wasting no time, Nin gathered Brem then set off for her home. The day had been long and exhausting. She looked forward to getting some rest before anything else exciting happened.

***

Enkai woke in darkness. He tried to recall where he was or what had happened, but his thoughts were so muddled he could barely think let alone remember anything. Not to mention, his entire body ached especially his back. It felt like there were rocks digging into his spine and shoulders. Frustratingly, he could barely move any part of his body. With tremendous effort, he managed to lift his head and look around. Enkai saw nothing in the darkness; however, a faint glow caught his eye. From his robes, a ball of purple light emerged. He stared at the dream wisp as it settled on his chest. Its purple light allowed him to see a bit better. He was dismayed to see that he was, in fact, lying on a rock which would explain the aches in his back and shoulders. Enkai also noticed a hole in his robes near his heart. The skin there was mottled with a dull reddish color that made it look like an old scar, so he stared at the spot for several moments. Then like a river breaking through a dam, his memories came flooding back through the fog.

In just a few moments, he relived the last week of his life. He felt the heartbreak and frustration of finding out he was Forsaken. He recalled the relief of hearing the Matriarch's assurances. His heart soared as he remembered the anticipation leading up to their arrival at the Sacred Vas tree. The wonder of the sight assailed him once more. The memories built up as they flowed through his mind until it all came crashing down. He remembered his father's betrayal. A knife thrust into his heart by the man he'd trusted more than any other, his hero. All the emotion crushed Enkai. Tears formed in his eyes as his gut wrenched and his chest heaved. It was all too much. He had just wanted to be like his father. He'd just wanted a chance.

The dream wisp floated next to his face. Its gaseous body pressed against his cheek as if the creature was trying to comfort him. It didn't help.

Enkai recalled the sight of his father's death at the hands of a woman he'd come to trust. Muddled memories of whispers and fog trailed through his thoughts. He vaguely remembered a voice, but could not recall its words. He remembered his fear as the dagger bled the life from him.

In one go, he had lost everything. He couldn't understand why his father had sacrificed him and the Matriarch's motivations were another mystery. Why would she trick him and kill his father? If she'd planned to betray them, why had she been so kind to him? Weren't the Lin and the Du supposed to be allies? Had it all been a lie? Could the woman he'd felt such warmth from really have been so cruel? Enkai could barely begin to comprehend such things. His young mind was too preoccupied with the hurt.

The worst part was that as his heart quaked from the pain of betrayal, he missed his father. Even after watching her kill his father, he missed Lin Chun's warmth and the sweet smell of her robes. As the sobs wracked his small frame, his heart fostered the hope that this entire situation was just a bad dream he'd wake up from at any moment.

"Cease your mewling and calm yourself, little human," a voice rumbled from the darkness. It sounded like a mountain that had learned to speak. From the gloom beyond the wisp's light, a massive rocky snakehead emerged. Enkai screamed in horror, but only a hoarse croak emerged from his parched throat. Once again, he attempted to move, but his muscles refused to listen. His panic increased when the giant snake lowered its head toward him. It was going to eat him; he was certain of it. He closed his eyes and trembled yet nothing came. When he opened his eyes again, the creature stared directly at him with what he could swear was amusement. "Calm yourself or you will jeopardize your already weak spirit."

Confused by the creature's words, Enkai looked down at his body. Bands of faint red energy were forming around his arms, legs, and torso. As he focused, he sensed something roiling inside him. When he felt it, he recoiled but then a realization hit him like a red mare's kick. Tempering his excitement, he calmed his breathing and turned his focus inward as he'd been taught by his father in preparation for his Awakening.

In his mind's eye, Enkai saw his spirit. At the center of his abdomen, a dark sphere about the size of his fist floated. Stemming from the sphere, vibrant pathways filled with the faint glow of silver-white vital anima ran throughout his spirit. From his father's lessons, he recognized the pathways through his spirit as his anima channels and the dark sphere at the center as his core. Cords of scarlet energy writhed around his anima channels in a frenzy. He sensed predatory hunger and volatility from the energy even as his steady breathing calmed it. He focused on his breathing and fell into the old habit drilled into him by his father. In moments, the scarlet energy settled and the band's around his body dispersed.

The reality of what had just happened settled on Enkai. He could *feel* his spirit. He could *see* it. Only those whose spirits had been truly awakened could perceive the inner workings of the spirit.

The joy was bittersweet next to the harsh reality of the other events, but it gave him some relief amidst the hurt. Despite his inner turmoil, his apprehension of the scarlet energy ruining his spirit and the looming presence of the snake creature kept him focused enough to overcome his emotions. Enkai opened his eyes to see the snake beast still observing him.

"You are fortunate the Sin did not overtake you," the creature said.

"Sin? Do you mean this red stuff?" he asked, his voice nothing more than a raspy whisper.

"You do not know it?" it said, sounding surprised. Enkai shook his head. The beast grunted, then explained, "It is anima, but it mars the soul. Few survive the initial contact with it and those that do are usually warped into monstrosities with little of their sanity remaining. Man and beast fear it."

Enkai didn't like that answer. He glanced at the dormant anima. He knew it was dangerous just from the feeling it gave off, but he'd never imagined anima could be so terrifying. He had to take several more calming breaths to stop his heart from racing. After a moment, he asked, "But where did it come from?"

Perhaps Enkai had simply missed it because he couldn't sense his spirit until now, but none of the Du elders nor his father had ever mentioned it. If the anima was as dangerous as the giant beast said, surely someone would have said something. In fact, the only comment that had been made about his spirit was that it looked blackened or something.

The snake beast responded, "It depends. Sin can manifest in those who know great suffering. Other times, it is taken in willingly." The creature looked away gazing into the darkness above them before it continued, "Just be glad you are alive and whole."

A quick inspection of his body told him that nothing strange was amiss, so Enkai asked the creature, "If it turns people into monsters, then why do I feel fine?"

The creature chuckled which caught Enkai off guard. The stone beneath him trembled. "You are a Deviant, child. A stable host for Sin. So long as you keep your emotions in check, the Sin won't overtake your spirit and body."

Relief spread through Enkai's mind joining the dozens of other emotions occupying it at the same moment. At the very least, he wasn't in any immediate danger. Enkai understood the importance of controlling his emotions even without the threat of Sin, as Kai had constantly drilled lessons of self-control and discipline into him. Still, he was beginning to believe the heavens really had forsaken him. The entire affair made him feel exhausted mentally in addition to his physical fatigue. He let his head fall back as his neck began to ache but winced when it smacked against the rock. The snake beast watched him then shifted. He couldn't see the creature in the dark, but the earth shook when it moved. All of a sudden, something yanked Enkai into the air by the collar of his robes. The wisp followed. Its light allowed him to see that the creature had picked him up. Each step it took made the earth tremble. Oddly, he didn't panic. Somehow, he knew the creature had no intention of hurting him. He also noticed the snake's neck ended abruptly in a large shell made of moss-covered stone.

"Are you a turtle or a snake?" Enkai asked, purely out of curiosity. Already, he was getting used to his situation. He would probably cry again later, but for now, he'd managed to bury his pain and the strange creature provided a nice distraction especially since he was pretty sure it didn't want to eat him. It placed him on a flat stone covered in thick moss. After putting him down, the massive beast brought its head around in front of Enkai.

"I. Am. A. Tortoise," it rumbled, huffing a gust of hot air into his face through its nostrils. Enkai blinked a few times as the hot breath made his eyes water. It seemed he'd hit a nerve.

"Apologies, Elder Tortoise," he said. He had no intention of getting on the bad side of a creature capable of accidentally killing him by rolling over in its sleep. "I did not intend to offend in my ignorance."

"You may call me, Onki," the tortoise said lying down next to the stone upon which he'd been placed. Enkai looked up at the creature with many questions on his lips, but before he could say anything, Onki said, "I know not why the Silent Father brought you here, but you will stay until you can find your own way."

The Silent Father? Enkai thought to himself. Who was that? That and many other questions filled his mind, but he kept his mouth shut and turned his attention inward to observe his spirit instead. Despite everything, knowing he now had the ability to practice the divine arts gave him hope. The web of anima channels running through his spirit pulsed subtly every few seconds with a thin trickle of vital anima. Retracing the anima's path back to his core, Enkai inspected it. Its color bothered him. Even with his limited education on the divine arts, he knew that the core of a newly awakened divine artist was supposed to be golden, not black. Enkai wondered if the strange color of his core had been the reason Elder Win had called his spirit blackened. Since the core was the center of the spirit, any problems with it would affect everything.

"Excuse me, Elder Onki?" Enkai asked, his concern for his spirit outweighing his fear of annoying the massive beast. Besides, the tortoise appeared to know a lot, so perhaps he could give Enkai the answers he sought. The creature raised its stone brow at him which Enkai interpreted as permission to ask his question. "Why is my core black? Is there something wrong with it?"

"You are a Primal, little human," Elder Onki said as though it were obvious. When he saw the confusion on Enkai's face, he preempted the coming question by adding, "Your core is simply different from those of other humans, but there is nothing *wrong* with it."

Enkai made to ask a follow-up question, but Elder Onki was having none of it. With a grunt, he said, "Enough, I am tired, so save your questions for the morning. Rest. You will need it."

He watched as the tortoise withdrew his snake-like head and neck into his shell. For a few hours, he thought about his situation. Even knowing his father had attempted to sacrifice him, he couldn't help but default to the teachings Kai had instilled in him. Once, his father had given him advice to consider when he felt overwhelmed.

If you ever feel overwhelmed and helpless. Calm yourself with a breath and do three things. Assess the information at hand. Consider what you can do. Form a plan of action. He mentally reviewed his father's words repeating them to himself over and over. He almost wept a few times, but he managed to hold himself together despite the ache in his heart.

He was in an unknown location with an enormous tortoise who thankfully wasn't hostile. At some point after his father stabbed him, the Lin Matriarch had killed his father. A thought occurred to him that brought his churning mind to a halt. Had the Matriarch known of his father's plan to sacrifice him?

The faltering innocence in him hoped that she hadn't known. If she had been ignorant, she may have killed his father in anger. However, Enkai quickly realized the likelihood of her being ignorant of his father's intentions was nearly nonexistent. His father had stabbed him in front of the Sacred Vas tree. If the sacrifice had to be performed at the Sacred Vas tree, then Lin Chun must have known about it. The Lin clan knew the most about the Forbidden Forest out of all the clans. What's more, he had overheard his father talking about the Matriarch's knowledge about his fate and she had admitted to him that she could potentially see the future. Enkai was also certain that Elder Win had mentioned the Lin clan had similar records to the Du clan concerning the Forsaken. If that was the case, the Matriarch definitely knew about the sacrifice, but that left him baffled as to why she'd killed his father – or how for that matter. She'd dispatched his father with such ease that he doubted the entire scene. If it weren't for the deep certainty that his father was dead, Enkai would have thought it was a dream. He simply couldn't begin to parse through such a complicated web of information. He was only six summers. His only hope was to find the Matriarch and get some answers.

Thankfully, he could sense his spirit which meant he had been properly awakened and could practice the divine arts. The thought filled him with anticipation despite his less than ideal situation. Based on the strength displayed by the Matriarch, he would need to be much stronger – stronger than even his father. His goal in mind, he laid his head down and let sleep take him. Tomorrow, Enkai would face his new reality.

Chapter 7

One year later, Enkai climbed the stone ridges of Old Omen. With winter around the corner, cold wind was continuously battering the higher reaches of the mountain where the bare rock face provided little cover. Enkai was progressing nearly on all fours, hunched over against the howling winds to resist being blown off the mountain. This was his first time climbing the mountain alone, so his nerves were on edge. He knew the route for safely traversing Old Omen to its peak, yet without Nin, the strange humanoid-like great beast that had been caring for him over the last year, he questioned his ability to finish the journey. Because the winds grew more intense the higher he climbed, he typically needed to hold onto her in order to keep his bearings. Not to mention, the path became narrower and more treacherous the closer he drew to the mouth of the sleeping volcano. All in all, he feared the journey as much as the mountain's fury.

At the same time, Enkai needed to succeed. Elder Onki, the powerful great beast that ruled over Old Omen, had agreed to train him in the divine arts if he could successfully climb to Old Omen's peak from its base without assistance. At first, he'd had doubts about how effective training from a great beast would be, but Nin assured him that Elder Onki knew more about the divine arts than any human. Whether that was true or not, Enkai was sure the old beast knew more than him, so he was willing to learn.

After arriving at Old Omen, much of his time had been spent adjusting to his new life. While difficult at first, several factors played in his favor. The greatest boon was that many of the great beasts in the forest were able to speak, which while shocking at first, nevertheless, made the transition much smoother. Not all beasts spoke well though. For instance, Brem and Jak, the two great beasts also in Nin's care, had trouble expressing much beyond simple thoughts. Enkai surmised that their difficulty was connected to their age since they were both still young.

Additionally, Nin constantly displayed an unreal amount of patience in caring for him, so much so it made Enkai feel guilty. He'd been taught that he should always be conscious of disturbing others especially adults since their time was valuable. Enkai remembered several times when he'd suppressed his desire to ask for something or disturb his father for fear of being reprimanded. So, when he woke screaming from nightmares about his father bearing down on him, dagger in hand, he felt guilty because every single time without fail, Nin woke as well and held him while he cried. He adored her for it, but he hated himself for his own weakness. It was even worse when he woke up Brem or Jak and Nin was forced to console them.

Brem and Jak also made living on the isolated mountain easier despite their limited speech. As Nin's wards, the three of them were like kin, often playing together and exploring the forest while Nin gathered herbs or worked on her alchemy. Brem, a temperamental black fox, enjoyed competitions like races while Jak, an energetic yellow monkey, preferred cooperative activities like exploration. Enkai had discovered his own sense of competition which meant he butted heads with Brem every now and then. Even when their scuffles sometimes got physical, Enkai couldn't say he hated the fights, though he had to be wary of exciting the Sin inside him. Together, the three great beasts made him feel at home. Despite his past, he saw them as family, though he might not have been comfortable enough to admit it yet.

Sadly, not everything was good. Aside from his nightmares, Enkai also struggled with constantly questioning his self-worth. His father had been willing to sacrifice him. Did that mean he was an unworthy son? Now that he could practice the divine arts, did that mean he could go home? If the answer was yes, could he even get home from where he was? Back in the Maro Province, the only mountains had been the Sky Tooth range occupied by the Hu clan, yet even at the peak of Old Omen, he could see no other mountains, only miles of forest. In his nightmares, Enkai sometimes dreamt of never being able to return home. To make matters worse, he simply couldn't bring himself to talk to anyone about it. It felt like his burden to bear, so asking for help meant admitting to his perceived failings.

"A man should be master of his own mind, not the other way around," he told himself parroting his father's words.

As if that weren't bad enough, the strange scarlet anima nesting in his spirit made everything worse. Elder Onki called it Sin. He had no idea where it came from or how it had got within his spirit. Apparently, it was a volatile anima that amplified and fed off his negative emotions. Whenever he got upset, the threat of the Sin becoming active loomed over his head. Elder Onki assured him that Sin ruined the spirits of all who succumbed to it.

He was painfully aware of it as he climbed the mountain. Not only did he have to physically make the journey, but he also needed to keep calm until he got to the summit. It was a two-sided battle against fear and nature.

Gritting his teeth, Enkai pulled himself up to another ridge, his eyes watering as dirt dislodged by his fingers blew into his face. The heights of Old Omen stretched above him. Based on his memory, he was approximately three-quarters of the way to the peak and the hard part was to start now. His muscles were already sore from the climb thus far, yet he pressed onward. For not the first time, Enkai wished he had an Enhancement technique to make the climb easier — but he continued climbing for another hour before he ran into any issues at all.

He arrived at a wall of rough stone that towered nearly two dozen feet. It led to a small plateau that extended upward into a steep slope of bare stone and loose earth. Normally, Nin carried him up this wall, but he was on his own this time. Taking a deep breath, he rubbed his dirt-covered hands together and leapt up using a knot protruding from the rock face as a launch point. The first dozen feet went smoothly which instilled a sense of confidence in Enkai that fueled his waning strength. Then, the wind picked up.

Howling gales ripped across the mountain buffeting him while he clung desperately to the stone face. The cold wind chilled his bones after blowing right through the green robes Nin had made him. He knew he was in trouble when he began to lose feeling in his hands. Briefly, he considered waiting for the winds to die down but then dismissed that notion. The late autumn gales were erratic. They began at random and sometimes died down after a few minutes while other times they lasted entire days. At best, he had a few minutes before the frigid winds posed a real threat to him, given how exposed he was.

Carefully, Enkai reached for the next groove in the stone and pulled himself up after testing it. At the same time, a particularly vicious gust blasted the mountainside, nearly knocking him from his position. Not wanting to fall to his death, he pulled himself upward a few more feet. Enkai thought everything would be alright until the next foothold broke beneath his weight. He screamed as the sudden lack of support under one of his feet ruined his balance. An ill-timed wind hammered into him pulling his grip from one of his handholds while the slopes of Old Omen stretched out beneath him. If he fell, he would tumble down more than a dozen feet against the bare stone at best. At worst, the wind would ruin his ability to catch himself and ensure his death. In his spirit, the Sin stirred. His fear and panic grew worse as he realized he might actually die. The Sin slowly started to shift and coiled around his anima channels in anticipation. Then, a new thought occurred to him.

Can I use Sin? The thought slithered into his mind as enticing as a rope extending from the clifftop. Elder Onki had said he was something called a Deviant, an individual whose Sin was naturally calm. If his Sin was special, maybe he could tap into it for a quick boost. He needed to do something before he fell to his death. He nearly gave in to the temptation as he dangled from one arm, shoulder burning from the strain of supporting his entire body weight.

In the end, reason saved him from the decisiveness of fear. He had no idea how to tap into the Sin, not to mention, any way of knowing if it could even provide him with any kind of benefit. Enkai had literally been told that the Sin could destroy his spirit if it got out of control. Honestly, he questioned where such a foolish thought had even originated.

Perhaps sensing his distress, a small cloud of purple anima emerged from his chest. It was the dream wisp that he'd kept since his journey to the Sacred Vas tree with his father.

Taking a deep breath, Enkai swung himself toward the nearest handhold, arm outstretched. When he gripped it, he immediately used the support to find new footholds. Afterward, he wasted no time scrambling to the top.

By the time he'd pulled himself onto the plateau, his breath came in ragged gasps. The air was getting thin and each breath came harder than the previous one as he ascended. Once safely on the plateau, he laid flat on his back questioning his wisdom in accepting this test. Looking up from his position, he spied the peak high above him and suppressed a whimper. He got to his feet groaning as he trudged toward for the peak.

***

Nin watched Onki lounging next to her alchemy station, her brow furrowed in annoyance. Both of them were waiting within the mouth of Old Omen for Enkai to complete his trial. Nin paced back and forth, trying to ease her ever-increasing worry.

"Where is he?" she said wringing her hands furiously and increasing her pace. Onki peeked out of his shell to give her a look of bemusement that made her want to hit him. She turned on him balling up her fists. "What's so funny?!"

Onki recoiled into his shell slightly and said, "Oh my, how frightening. Motherhood has changed you, little rabbit."

"Onki, it's been twelve hours since he started!" she cried.

Onki huffed blowing a thick billow of breath from his nostrils that frosted in the near-winter air. He emerged fully from his shell and looked down at Nin with the same bemusement that had incited her irritation just before. "You worry too much. Life is full of uncertainties."

Nin froze, her heart skipping a beat at his words. Her ears drooped as a horrible realization dawned on her. She asked, "Wait! What do you mean *uncertainty*? Didn't you give En this test because you knew he'd pass?!"

Onki's amusement faded and he wore a confused expression arching the stony growth above his eye that reminded Nin of an eyebrow. He said, "What kind of test would it be if I was certain he would succeed? A test one can't fail is just a task to be completed, not a genuine evaluation of one's ability to succeed."

"What?!" Nin screamed. Moonlight-colored anima radiated from her jade fur in a sudden wave of power. She took a step toward Onki cracking the ground with the force alone, fists balled once again in anger. "I trusted your judgment and you're telling me he could die because of your test?!"

Onki showed no sign of alarm at her explosion which made sense since she posed no threat to him, angry or not. Instead, his expression softened and his tone became gentler. "Calm yourself, little rabbit. You forget that nothing happens on this mountain without my knowledge. The boy will never be in danger so long as he resides here." Though his words helped to calm her, Nin's worry showed plainly on her face. She understood that she probably looked as bad as she felt: nose twitching, eyes on the verge of tears, and ears drooping. Onki recognized this and added, "I'll check on him."

His eyes began to glow with rich yellow light. He was silent for several moments before his expression became troubled and he said, "Oh dear…"

Nin's heart sank.

***

Enkai was in trouble. The frigid wind chilled the marrow of his bones and made each step feel like hell as his joints groaned against the cold-borne stiffness. Snow and ice coated his surroundings making each step potentially disastrous. Trembling from overexertion and exposure to the cold, his muscles struggled to support him as he continued forcing himself to crawl when walking became too hard. His hands, bloody and cracked from hours of climbing in the cold, barely supported him as he dragged himself up the mountain.

I can do this. I'm a Du warrior. I can do this. He repeated this mantra over and over, his conviction being the only thing staving off panic.

Enkai saw the summit a few hundred feet above him. Another blast of wind disrupted his balance by knocking him onto his side. As he made to get up, his weary body resisted. He realized how tired he was as he lay there on the frozen earth. In his thoughts, the mantra grew hushed, barely audible over the wails of Old Omen.

Maybe I should rest. Just for a moment ... As the mantra faded, this thought emerged from his weariness and pushed its way to the forefront, overshadowing all other concerns. It held him within its clutches turning his exhaustion into a treacherous force that degraded his resolve. He closed his eyes preparing to succumb to it if only for a few moments.

He settled into blissful serenity which banished his panic and anxiety. Warmth spread through his body starting from his torso and working its way out steadily to the tips of his fingers. He curled up into a ball feeling as though he were cozy under a warm blanket. Enkai found his thoughts clear as the warmth spread through him making his skin tingle with a delightfully distracting sensation.

Yes, I'll rest for just a moment. It made perfect sense. The journey had been difficult. Climbing thousands of feet in the near-winter conditions was taxing. Once he'd rested a bit, he'd continue his journey and pass the test. A passing memory swept through his mind taking him to a safer place and a simpler time as he drifted into unconsciousness.

It was the Sin that saved him. Just as he began to slip into darkness, he felt it shift. Immediately, his spirit burned as if it was being branded with hot irons. Enkai growled a deep guttural sound that seemed more beastly than boyish, angry that this pain was pulling him from the comfort sleep offered. The Sin fed off that spark of anger growing stronger which in turn increased the pain. It reinvigorated his mind, jolting him awake. His adrenaline spiked in response to his distress sharpening his senses and breaking his serene calm. He bolted upright looking around frantically in search of an attacker, only to realize he was still alone. His renewed anxiety offered another source of sustenance to the Sin.

Enkai turned his gaze inward in the hopes of stopping the pain. The bands of Sin writhed around his anima channels like an agitated nest of vipers burning them wherever they made contact. His entire spirit was dim with the exception of the Sin. The silver-white flame of vital anima in the center of his core representing the vital essence that bound his spirit to his body flickered as though it might go out at any moment. He was dying. The realization hit him like a kick to the gut. Fear gripped his heart invigorating the Sin which increased the pain another step.

He rolled over onto all fours, his breath coming in short heaving gasps as the searing pain grew so great that it felt like his entire body was burning from the inside out. Strangely, Enkai still felt warm despite his surroundings. He frantically scrambled to his feet, heart full of anxiety. If he didn't make it to the summit quickly, he would die on this mountain.

For the next hour, Enkai wandered upward in a state of near-panic. At some point, the burning from the Sin reached a crescendo, so he nearly lost consciousness with every other step. He picked up his mantra once again while taking deep calming breaths. Soon after the pain stopped growing and ominous crimson steam began to rise from Enkai's skin. Instead of evaporating, it curled around him surrounding his body with a haze; however, Enkai paid little attention to it as he knew dwelling on it would only make him more anxious.

His sole concern was to reach the summit. The cold, the Sin, and his weariness were all mere distractions. In his mind, he visualized his family, the Du clan. Though the Du Patriarch probably knew of his father's plan to sacrifice him or had even ordered it himself, he couldn't assume the rest of the clan was guilty especially his grandfather. If his grandfather had known, Enkai was certain he would have stopped his father. Before attempting to kill him, his father had named him a Du warrior and Enkai had accepted. Despite his father's betrayal, Enkai still considered that oath binding. If he died on this lone mountain in the middle of the wilderness, he would never make his way back to his family. He would never make good on his oath or find out the truth of what had happened at the Sacred Vas tree.

"I can do this. Du warriors never falter. I can do this," he said, mumbling his new mantra aloud between ragged breaths.

The wind picked up again blowing flurries of snow all around him, yet he continued undaunted. His entire being was focused on pressing forward fueled by the burning in his body and spirit. The pain kept him awake and alert while the heat of his spirit warmed his body. Any snow that touched his skin immediately melted soaking him through in seconds. Regardless, he kept his gaze fixed on the peak only a few hundred feet above him.

***

Nin raced down the mountain alongside a stone puppet created by Onki. Her heart was pounding as she imagined En all alone freezing to death. She was furious with Onki, but her attention was bent entirely on reaching her child before it was too late. Onki's puppet led the way. Even though the puppet was only a temporary construct, the tortoise had complete control over it and could perceive things from its perspective.

They had barely trekked for a minute before the puppet stopped and pointed at a section where the gradual decline of their path tapered off into a steep decline that led onto a platform of sorts.

"There," Onki said through the puppet. Nin narrowed her eyes squinting at the indicated spot. A human hand crested the edge of the platform lingering there for a moment as though its owner was having some difficulty. Nin immediately made to rush forward to help, yet the puppet held out a hand barring her path. Onki's voice rang from the stone figure, "Wait, little rabbit."

Something in his voice gave her pause causing her to look again. The hand shifted as Enkai pulled himself over the edge, only to roll onto his back breathing raggedly. Wisps of crimson steam rose from his skin covering his body in a sinister haze. Nin opened her Spirit-sight and gasped.

"What is happening to him?" Nin asked. Enkai's spirit churned with Sin making her nauseous just from the sight of it. Additionally, she worried about his behavior. Enkai got to his feet and moved forward, but his movements were sluggish and clumsy. Worst of all, Nin couldn't see his core or anima channels through the coiling Sin.

The puppet stepped forward, its stone joints grinding against each other loudly. After a brief pause, Onki said, voice full of surprise, "He is channeling his Sin."

"No!" she cried, eyes widening in horror. Her ears drooped and tears gathered in the corners of her eyes. She thought of her apprehension in allowing Enkai to undertake the trail. She berated herself, her gut twisting into knots. She had failed as a mother and her child had paid the price. She looked at the puppet which had been silent for a long moment and asked, "Can we do anything to save him?"

"Of course," Onki said calmly. The puppet turned its dark eyes onto her and Onki continued, "You misunderstand, little rabbit. He isn't lost, but he is straying from the path."

Her heart soared with hope, yet the reality of what she saw in Enkai's spirit weighed on her. She hoped with all her soul that Onki's words were true but she needed to make sure. She asked, "I thought only demons could channel Sin?"

The puppet nodded slowly. The late autumn wind picked up around them whipping up snow and small ice shards into a flurry. Nin covered her eyes while the puppet stood unperturbed as though rooted to the mountain. On the platform below, Enkai trudged forward through the squall of frost seemingly unaware of the ice slicing into his flesh or the snow pelting him from all sides. When Onki spoke, it was like a deep rumble from the mountain itself that cut through the din of the howling winds.

"Normally, you'd be right," he said. The puppet set off down the slope toward Enkai's stumbling form with Nin in tow. "As creatures consumed by Sin, demons can and do channel it. However, Enkai is a Deviant, one whose spirit houses Sin without being consumed by it. It is possible for Deviants to channel Sin though they risk transforming into demons themselves by doing so. Still…"

Nin recognized the telltale sound of contemplation in Onki's voice. As he often did when in deep contemplation, he trailed off before finishing his statement, while mulling over some question he'd yet to voice. Filled with anxiety, she asked, "Still what? What is it?"

The puppet grimaced reflecting Onki's own consternation. He responded, "It's just that something is off about his Sin. Look closely at his spirit. His Sin is incontestably hurting him, but it hasn't managed to breach his anima channels or compromise his core. It's almost as if something is holding it back."

They finally reached Enkai and Nin barely choked back tears. Enkai's body was covered in bloody scrapes and bruised flesh. The leaf woven robes she had made for him were torn and soaked through. His hands dripped blood from the skin that had been cut and rubbed raw by the climb while the foot-wraps she'd made to protect his feet during the climb were in tatters. Beneath his mop of hair, his face was smeared with mud telling her he had collapsed at some point. The puppet placed a steadying hand on Enkai's shoulder, unconcerned with the ominous red haze. Despite the stone puppet's grasp, he continued trying to move forward, nearly colliding with it before it used both hands to restrain him.

Nin glanced into Enkai's spirit once more using her Spirit-sight. Pushing past the initial feeling of nausea caused by the Sin's disconcerting movements, she confirmed the truth in Onki's words. Sin thrashed within Enkai colliding with his anima channels and disrupting the balance of his spirit which Nin had no doubt was incredibly painful for him. However, his spirit endured despite the violent movement of the hostile anima. Strangely, the Sin continuously failed to breach Enkai's core or anima channels, though not for want of trying as far as she could tell.

"I'm so sorry, En. I should have never let you do this," she said stepping forward to take his battered hand in hers. As soon as she touched him, she felt the probing touch of Sin on her spirit. She erected her defenses and stepped forward embracing

Enkai. The puppet released him allowing Nin to have her moment. He stopped struggling as soon as she embraced him. Encouraged by the response, Nin pulled back holding his face in her hands and said, "It's okay En. I'm here I won't ever let you down again. I prom—"

She stopped mid-sentence as she caught sight of his eyes barely showing beneath his wet hair, half-lidded and unfocused. Nin stared at her child in shock. It was Onki that spoke first after a pregnant pause.

"He's unconscious," he said. The puppet placed a hand upon Enkai's brow. Nin watched Onki's power swell within the construct until it glowed like the noonday sun in her Spirit-sight. The haze curled away from the puppet's hand as though retreating from Onki's grasp. After another moment of silence, Onki said, "Impressive."

"What now?" she asked getting tired of being in the dark.

"It's him. Enkai is the one halting the advance of his Sin," he responded. Nin heard a rare hint of admiration in the ancient beast's voice and she understood why. From what she knew of Sin, it corroded the souls of those afflicted with it. Deviants like Enkai benefitted from Sin that was normally dormant, but if their Sin became active, they were as much at the mercy of its dangerous anima as anyone else. Keeping the Sin from compromising one's soul took an extraordinary amount of willpower, so much so that most individuals broke down in minutes. To be able to not only channel Sin but also keep it under control while unconscious should've been impossible.

Before Nin could dwell on her incredulity, Onki sent a pulse of spiritual power through the puppet into Enkai. Immediately, the crimson haze dispersed and Enkai collapsed into Nin's arms like a puppet cut from its strings. One quick look into his spirit showed that the Sin had been quelled into dormancy once more. Nin shifted Enkai in her grasp so she could carry him, but then she heard his voice, barely audible over the winds. She leaned forward placing her ears close so she could hear anything he might be trying to say.

"I ... can ... do ... this," he murmured weakly. Even with her exceptional hearing, Nin nearly missed his words. Enkai continued to repeat the words over and over as she held him. Wasting no time, she reached into the backpack she carried and pulled out a slender wooden case. The puppet watched silently as she opened the elixir case pulling out a clay vial marked with vibrant orange paint. Carefully, she administered the elixir to Enkai, steadily easing the liquid down his throat. Once she'd finished, she replaced the case in her bag.

She hefted Enkai up with both arms. His skin was beginning to warm up despite the chilling weather around them which told Nin the elixir was taking effect. When she got to her feet, she locked eyes with the puppet. She made sure her expression conveyed her opinion of Onki's test. Nin opened her mouth to speak, but Onki forestalled her tirade with a raised hand.

"Take Enkai home, little rabbit. We'll speak once you see to him," he said, his rumbling voice was gentle but brooked no room for argument. She scowled at the puppet but chose not to argue. She needed to see to Enkai's wounds and check for frostbite. Without another word, she turned to make her way down the mountain. Just as she initiated her Enhancement technique, Onki spoke again drawing her attention back to him. "When the boy wakes up, tell him he passed."

With that, the puppet crumbled into dust only to be spirited away by the howling wind. Despite herself, Nin felt a smile curl onto her lips as she made her way down the mountain to her burrow. She looked down at Enkai, unconscious in her arms and said, "Did you hear that, En? You did it.

Chapter 8

Sweat beaded his brow as Enkai pulled himself onto the rocky lip at the peak of Old Omen. Within the mouth of the dormant volcano, Elder Onki waited for him, lounging leisurely in the noonday sun which shone bright overhead. Enkai took a moment to catch his breath then slid down the bowl-like slope onto the hard-packed dirt and ash below.

One serpentine eye popped open as Enkai approached, flickering from Enkai to the sun in the sky and Elder Onki said, "Bah, you're done already? I've barely had any time to nap."

Enkai stretched his arms and shoulders which were sore from the climb. He also glanced at the sky before he responded to his master. "It's been at least six hours since I started. How is that not enough time for a nap?"

"Hmph, you youngsters are always in a rush. Six hours is hardly enough time to get comfortable," Onki grumbled.

Enkai shook his head. In the past several months, Elder Onki had started training him in the divine arts. At least, that was the idea. Enkai hadn't even caught a whiff of anima in his training so far. Most of his time was spent climbing up and down the mountain, running through the forest, lifting heavy stones, or performing a harsh routine of calisthenics at Onki's behest. He was beginning to wonder if the ancient tortoise did know anything worth teaching.

His skepticism must've been plain on his face because Onki said, "What're you scowling about over there? Got a rock stuck between your toes?"

"It's nothing, Elder Onki," Enkai said reflexively. Mentally, he pushed the matter aside and prepared to ask Onki what he should do next. His master wasn't having any of that though. The ancient tortoise slammed his tail down which shook the ground so much Enkai stumbled a bit. When he looked into Onki's eyes, Enkai froze under their stern gaze.

"I don't like that, little human," he said. He lowered his head so that they were eye level and blew a gust of hot air in Enkai's face causing the boy to recoil and fall over onto his backside. "If you've got something to say, then spit it out."

Enkai's eyes widened then he started to laugh, but only for a moment before Onki's brow furrowed and he quickly explained himself. "Apologies, I didn't mean to laugh. You just reminded me of my grandfather. He used to always scold me for doing the same thing." His expression grew sad as he remembered his family that still lived in the Maro Province. How was his grandfather doing? Losing his son and grandson would've hit him hard. Enkai hoped his grandfather wouldn't seek vengeance against the Patriarch or the Lin clan. He shook these thoughts away as they grew dark. He didn't want to dwell on such things, not now.

Onki snorted. "Well, I'm not your grandfather, but I do expect you to speak plainly."

It was hard for him to speak his mind. In truth, he wasn't even naturally meek mannered. It was because most of the adults he'd interacted with in the Du clan, including his own father, had expected him to be silent and obedient, and had often become annoyed if he'd asked too many questions. Only his grandfather had ever encouraged his curiosity, but as a clan elder, he'd had limited time to indulge Enkai.

Standing up, he pushed past the urge to reassure Elder Onki that it was nothing and said instead, "Alright. I was just wondering about how effective my training is. I mean, I'm getting stronger sure, but what does that have to do with the divine arts?" Onki frowned and his brow furrowed once more. Enkai waved his hands in an attempt to cool the rising ire he sensed from his master. "Please don't take offense. I merely wondered if your training was well suited for me since I'm human and... well... you're a great beast."

"So, you're questioning my knowledge of the divine arts then, little human? Think I've got nothing to teach you?" Onki asked, his voice low and dangerous. Enkai floundered for several seconds his mouth flapping like a fish out of water. The ground shook. Onki's eyes flashed golden and an explosion of force blasted Enkai off his feet. A wave of ash and dirt washed over him sending him into a coughing fit. When the air cleared, he looked up at Elder Onki and trembled in fear.

His serpentine eyes radiated a golden glow rivaling that of the sun. More golden light spilled out from beneath the black scales running down his long neck making him appear as though he was brimming with barely restrained power.

Enkai scurried backward several paces using his hands to pull himself. Then, he noticed his surroundings. The mouth of the dormant volcano had been blown apart. The ground was flat as though something had sheared the majority of stone from the mountaintop. Around them, countless pieces of earth and ash were frozen in mid-air. The sizes and shapes of each piece of debris varied from specks of ash to massive sections of stone.

Another surge of power rippled through the air. Unlike before, the force was like a whirlwind, not an explosion. Enkai ducked as several dozen pieces of earth whizzed overhead. He covered his head with his hands as the *mountain* shook. Moments later, all the noise stopped and his surroundings grew still. His breath came in quick nearly panicked gasps. Only when things quieted down did his Sin begin to stir, as if it had been afraid to do so beforehand. His hands and legs shaking, he got to his feet. Elder Onki still lay in the same spot watching Enkai, the golden glow gone from his eyes. Enkai glanced around and couldn't contain his shock. The mouth of the volcano was untouched. All the devastation and broken earth were gone. As if it had never happened. If not for the ash covering his body, he might've thought he had imagined the entire thing.

Onki favored Enkai with a decidedly amused expression. "Still doubting, little human?"

Enkai winced. He immediately launched into a series of apologies to ensure his master that he'd learned his lesson. His motions were so frantic that he disrupted the ash coating his robes and choked on it mid-sentence, which sent him into an undignified fit of coughs and broken apologies.

Onki laughed uproariously shaking the ground with each breath. Enkai feared he might accidentally blow everything up again, but when his laughter settled the earth was still whole. "I'm glad we settled that. Now, hike up and down the mountain once more." Enkai balked and started to protest before his instincts kicked in. Onki raised an eyebrow as Enkai shut himself up. "Something else you want to say?"

He started to shake his head, but Onki's eyes began to shine gold once more. Quickly, he said, "If I do the trip both ways, it'll take me the rest of the day and I'll miss dinner. Nin will be upset." Enkai hoped Nin's ire was enough to sway the tortoise to mercy. Sadly, he was disappointed.

"I supposed you'd best get moving then," his master said.

Chapter 9

Enkai ran through the underbrush leaping over patches of shrubbery and fallen trees in his flight. Behind him, the calls of his pursuers grew ever closer. Normally, their skill made it near impossible for him to hear them, but they were enjoying the chase too much which meant they were sloppy. After a few more minutes dashing through the forest, Enkai realized he couldn't outrun them for much longer. Not only were his pursuers faster, but he also lacked the stamina to keep up his current pace. Fortunately, he'd had a head start which gave him a bit of room to maneuver.

The uneven terrain of the forest at the base of Old Omen offered a lot of possible avenues to escape, but a good number of them were either too dangerous or too roundabout for Enkai's liking. Thinking quickly, he devised a plan. As the terrain unexpectedly dipped in elevation, he leapt down a slope turning the landing into a roll to mitigate the impact when he hit its base. Following through with the tumble, he popped back to his feet and veered off to the right alongside the slope. He heard the sound of rushing water which meant he was going in the right direction. As he reached a wide flowing river, he heard one of his pursuers call out.

"I see him! I see him! He's going for the river!"

Enkai stifled a smirk. Everything was going according to plan. Preparing himself mentally, he dove into the mountainside river. Frigid water washed over him making his mind freeze as his nerves screamed. He pushed through the shock and then submerged himself in the rushing water. Normally, the river would carry him farther away from the mountain, but he had another plan.

Cycling vital anima from his core in the way he'd been taught, he felt the anima empowering his body and reinvigorating his muscles. Enkai lacked a true Enhancement technique, but his training had revealed he had an affinity for vital anima and essence. While any divine artist could cultivate vital anima they received from natural treasures, medicinal pills and elixirs, and other such methods, very few, if any, could cultivate vital essence to create vital anima within their own spirits. It was an extremely rare talent according to Elder Onki, though Enkai couldn't help but feel disappointed when he discovered that he lacked affinity in either earth or water.

While vital anima offered very little in terms of flashy offensive capabilities, it worked very well for strengthening his muscles and improving his stamina.

Using his heightened strength, he plowed through the river toward the mountain. He struggled furiously against the current hoping the white foam created by the rushing water would hide his progress from his pursuers. His muscles cried out as he forced his way upriver. Even when cycling anima, the river's current was too strong for him to travel against it for an extended period of time.

Just a little bit more. For a full minute, he'd held his breath. His lungs burned from the effort especially while exerting himself against the river's currents, but after tons of practice the vital anima powered him through. Enkai strained until he finally felt his hands wrap around something smooth and hard. He'd reached his goal: one of several large rocks that dotted the river and broke the water's flow. At last, he emerged from beneath the water's surface to take a deep breath of fresh air and, using the rock as an anchor to keep himself from being washed away, rested his overworked muscles.

Still holding onto the rock, Enkai scanned the area around the river for his pursuers. There was no sign of anyone. He sighed in relief pushing himself off the rock against the current and cycling more anima to propel himself to the riverbank opposite to where he'd first dived into the rushing waters. Still cautious, he kept low. One of his pursuers was skilled in stealth, so it was possible they were lying in wait for him. Thankfully, it looked like his ploy had worked. They were presumably traveling downriver waiting for him to resurface.

Just to be safe, he decided to continue cycling anima despite the risk of spiritual exhaustion. Moving quickly, he stalked through the forest back toward Old Omen. It took half an hour to find his usual path up the mountain and another hour to hike up the mountainside back home.

As soon as he entered the burrow, Nin looked up in surprise from a pile of herbs she'd been sorting through. He waved at her with a smirk flashing across his face before plopping down in his usual spot.

"You're back early," she said tilting her head to the side. She looked at the entrance then back at Enkai. "Where are Brem and Jak?"

"No idea," he said, shrugging, as his smirk spread into a mischievous grin. Seeing this, Nin put her hands on her hips and gave him a look only a mother could muster. He gave her an innocent look then said, "Well, I might have tricked them into following the river downstream while we were playing Hunt."

Nin's nose twitched. She obviously didn't appreciate his trick as much as he did. Her brow furrowed as she scowled at him. Honestly, she just wasn't very imposing, due to her appearance and stature. In her current form, Nin appeared as a rabbit-like humanoid except that her features were more rabbit-like than not. Additionally, she stood no taller than a child. Six years ago, when Enkai had first been adopted by her, he had been the same size as her. Now though, he was over twice her size. Still, he knew she could overpower him with ease if she wanted to. He'd seen her small frame lift boulders ten times his size.

"So, you tricked Brem and Jak, so you could come back here and take a nap while they search for you?"

"Yeah," he responded, unsure why she was so upset. She placed the bundle of herbs she was holding down next to the pile she'd been sorting before walking over to him. She leaned down to stare at him accusingly.

"In Hunt, the Prey is supposed to evade the hunters until the time is up. You all agreed to play in the forest. If you're on the mountain, they'll never have a chance of finding you in the forest."

Enkai looked up at her, tilting his head to the side as she had done when he'd entered. Scratching his head in confusion, he nodded saying. "Uh-huh, that's the idea. Besides, we never said the mountain was off-limits and I have training later, so I wanted to take a nap before I go."

"But that isn't fair to them. You have to at least be out there with them, or you aren't even playing the game," she said, still scowling.

"Only the strong have the luxury of playing fair, the weak must do what they can to survive," Enkai replied, his smirk returning. Nin gave him another sharp look.

"Don't you quote that old layabout to me, little one," she said smacking the side of his head. She didn't hit him very hard, but he met her gaze with mock hurt in his eyes.

"But I can't keep up with them. It isn't fair for me to be the prey," he cried adopting a distressed expression. "They're picking on me; I'm the victim here!"

"Stop," she groaned swatting at him again. He dodged this time. "Onki is having a bad influence on you. I knew I shouldn't have let you train with him."

"No idea what you mean," he said while pulling out a twig that had gotten snagged in his hair. "Elder Onki is a sage and diligent teacher."

"Diligent? What about last month when he let you fall from a ledge during training and you broke your leg? Or how about when he made you wrestle that jaguar puppet of his and it turned you into a bloody mess? Who had to tend to you while you recovered?" she asked, stepping up so they were nose to nose. He averted his gaze, as he'd found the adjacent cave wall very interesting all at once. She scoffed, "I bet he feeds you lines to tell me when I bring up your training."

"You can prove nothing," he said, suppressing a smirk.

Nin snorted then walked back over to her bundles of herbs. Enkai began to make himself comfortable for his nap when he heard her speak again, "Nope, get up. If you don't want to play with your brother and sister, then you'll help me sort through these herbs for Elder Jagan."

Enkai groaned. He gave Nin a pleading look, but her gaze held no mercy. Silently grumbling to himself, he got to his feet and made his way over to her. Without a word, he started sorting the herbs based on memory. During the first year of his stay, Nin had refused to let him out of her sight because she was afraid, he would injure himself while wandering the mountain or get into trouble. While with her, he'd spent much of his time learning the layout of the mountain and gathering herbs. However, after he started training with Elder Onki, he'd continued his walks gathering herbs with Nin as he'd found that he liked helping her gather ingredients then combine them into elixirs and medicines. About a year ago, she had started teaching him alchemy though most of his alchemy training consisted of memorizing ingredients and recipes that she showed him.

An hour passed as the two of them sorted through multiple bundles of herbs. When they were almost done, they heard voices coming from the trail leading up to the burrow.

"Brem, I'm starting to think you have no sense of smell."

"Shut up! I'm telling you I couldn't find his scent until we got back to the mountain."

"Well, how in Kong's name did he get past us, unless you just missed him!"

"You were in the trees, Jak! How did you not see him, huh? Are you blind?"

"Don't turn this around on me, Brem. You're older, so I should be able to rely on you."

Their bickering continued as his siblings grew closer and closer. Nin sighed, plainly lamenting the departure of her peace and quiet for the day. In a rush of dirt and fur, a black fox darted into the burrow followed quickly by a yellow monkey holding a big stick.

"Mama, did En come here? We—" the fox skidded to a stop and was silent as soon as she saw Enkai who waved at the two great beasts with a full-blown smile on his face. Both of them gawked at him before the fox whirled on the monkey. "I told you!"

"How did you get past us?" the monkey demanded, pointing his stick at Enkai accusingly. He walked over to stand next to the fox, then added, "I had a clear view of the river all the way till the rapids and Brem ran up and down the riverbank looking for your scent. There's no way."

Enkai scratched the back of his head as he thought about how to respond. He looked at Nin, but she'd already gone back to finishing up with the herbs while pointedly ignoring the conversation. He shrugged deciding to just go with the truth. "Didn't swim downriver."

His statement hung in the air for a few seconds. Enkai saw the suspicion grow on his siblings' faces, and even Nin gave him a look of disbelief.

"So, what are you saying? You swam up the river like some kind of fish?" the fox asked, his tone heavy with skepticism.

"Yep," Enkai said, nodding.

"You swam upriver against the current?" the monkey asked, repeating the question.

"You got it, Jak."

Jak's face was deadpan as both he and Brem looked at Nin, who held Enkai in her gaze for almost half a minute before saying, "He isn't lying though he's trying to show off, so there's probably more to it."

Enkai's smile faded a bit while his brow twitched in annoyance. Nin could always tell when one of them was lying or leaving information out. Really, she was just unnaturally good at reading Enkai and his siblings. Jak and Brem still seemed doubtful.

"What's your secret? You really a fish or something?" the monkey asked waving his stick at Enkai with squinted eyes.

"I can't reveal all of my secrets. Where's the fun in that?" he said, chuckling and getting up from his sitting position. Making his way over to them, he knelt down and patted them both on the head. "Maybe when you guys are half as skilled as me, I'll tell you."

"What?! I'm stronger than you are!" Jak said, swatting his hand away.

"Yeah and I'm faster. Besides, you can't even do much other than cycling your anima," Brem shot back, and followed up with another stinging retort, "Plus, it's been almost five winters since you started training with that old geezer and you haven't even advanced to Bronze. Where's the skill there, huh?"

Enkai resisted the urge to grit his teeth and kept his smile. He saw Jak wince at Brem's comments though Nin just sighed. Frustratingly, Brem wasn't completely wrong in her assessment. For almost five years, he'd been training with Elder Onki, yet he'd barely made any progress in the divine arts. He still didn't even know a single technique despite finding his affinity for vital anima. His agonizingly slow progress wasn't from lack of trying. Much to his chagrin, Elder Onki insisted he perform only basic cycling forms and physical exercise. No matter how much Enkai asked about advancing his training, the elder refused. When Enkai pressed him on the matter, he just got nonsense about "setting a rock-solid foundation." Despite his frustration, he chose to trust the old tortoise though it was still a sore spot for his ego. His father had been almost Bronze by his age. He also felt like he was falling behind his siblings who were both a half-step from Bronze, despite the fact that neither of them trained as he did. It was especially humiliating since he was older than both of them combined. Of course, his siblings knew all this, yet Brem had chosen to be mean anyway. Regardless, Enkai didn't let the comments bother him too much. He could tell Brem was angry, that she had been outsmarted and was lashing out at him. The fox had a mean competitive streak.

"Well, go ahead and talk big now. Once I really get serious, I'll leave you in the dust," Enkai taunted, and standing up so he was looking down his nose at Brem. It was a little petty of him, but it felt good, so he didn't care. He'd decided he would ask Elder Onki about advancing his training again during his upcoming session. It'd been several months since the last time he'd asked.

"Oh yeah, wanna bet?" Brem snapped. She lowered her posture and growled. Enkai stood his ground crossing his arms. Jak stepped between them smacking the ground with his stick.

"Guys, stop it, did you forget Mama is here?"

"Yes, thank you, Jak. I think that's quite enough from you two. Apologize to each other," Nin said leveling a stern look on Brem and Enkai which caused both of them to sheepishly mutter apologies. Though small in size, Nin's piercing jade green eyes and powerful spirit made her gaze rather imposing when she got serious. Nodding in satisfaction, she walked over to a hole in the wall of the burrow. She pulled out a basket woven of braided silk leaves treated with an alchemical mixture. The basket was full of nuts and fruit of various shapes, sizes, and colors. After setting it down, she sat down next to it and waved them over. "Come eat. En has training soon."

All four of them situated themselves around the basket before they ate. They always ate together when possible since Nin thought it was important for families to dine with each other. Even after the spat between Enkai and Brem, they were all soon chatting happily amongst themselves. Nin complained about how the Elders of the forest were so demanding of her time for alchemical work. Enkai laughed and told her that it was because she was the only alchemist in the forest, while Jak told Brem about a cave he'd found a few miles from the mountain while exploring. As he sat there with his family, a deep sense of contentment washed over Enkai. During his first few months on Old Omen, he'd found the concept of eating together to be strange especially when there were other things to be done. In his early childhood, he had eaten alone for the most part. Occasionally, his grandfather would join him for dinner, but he actually couldn't remember a meal he'd eaten with his father before they'd begun their journey to the Sacred Vas tree. It was a uniquely human sentiment Enkai hadn't expected from great beasts when he first came to Old Omen.

As they often did when he thought of his father, memories of the trip and the events in the Sacred Vas glade began to resurface, but he quickly pushed them back down. The last thing he needed was to have another episode where his emotions got the better of him. His smile never wavered, but Nin gave him a concerned look.

She's too perceptive, he sighed mentally. Looking her in the eye, he gave her his best reassuring smile then jumped into the conversation with Brem and Jak.

"So, what's the plan with this cave?" Enkai asked Jak.

"Well, I was going to explore it tomorrow if Mama is okay with it," the monkey replied looking at Nin expectantly. Nin took her eyes off Enkai and adopted a thoughtful expression.

"Alright, but you aren't to go alone. Take at least one of your siblings with you. I haven't been to that area in a few years so I can't be sure if it's safe. Make sure you tell Elder Onki where you are going, so he can watch the area," she said. Jak immediately looked at Enkai with an eager gleam in his eye.

"You'll explore the cave with me, right En?"

Enkai chuckled. He threw his arm around Jak's shoulders then said. "Of course, who's going to keep you out of trouble if I don't?"

"Great, I can't wait to see what's inside!" he exclaimed between shoving pieces of fruit into his mouth.

"Hey! What gives?" Brem asked scrunching up her face at Jak.

Jak laughed, mouth full of half-chewed fruit. He scratched the back of his head sheepishly and said, "You can come with us too, Brem. I just figured there might be a lot of climbing in the cave and well... you know..."

Jak held up his hands then grabbed Enkai's wrist and waved his hand around. Enkai burst into laughter when he understood what Jak meant. Brem's fur bristled and a look of pure offense adorned her face.

She growled at them both. "I can manage without hands! You watch."

"I'll ask Elder Onki about the cave when I go for training," Enkai said to Nin while Jak awkwardly attempted to apologize to Brem.

After they'd finished eating, Nin turned to Enkai. She tilted her head pensively looking at him as if she were considering something serious. A few moments later, she asked, "En, do you want to come with me to see Elder Jagan tonight? Assuming you feel up to it after your training, of course."

Both Jak and Brem shivered. Jak went pale while the fur of Brem's tail lowered.

"That old owl is so creepy. Don't go En, you'll regret it," Brem said matter-of-factly. Jak nodded fervently in agreement though he stayed silent. Nin glared at the two of them though they seemed resolute in their opinion.

"Don't be so rude, you two!" Nin sighed. "She is a very kind and wise Elder. She's just a bit... intense."

Enkai had heard of Elder Jagan from Elder Onki a few years ago. According to Elder Onki, Jagan made frequent use of Nin's alchemical knowledge. His siblings had both met Jagan and the experience had resulted in both having nightmares for a week straight. Despite the drama that had caused, Enkai was interested in meeting the great she-owl when he learned she was a great beast that utilized dream anima.

His familiar, a dream wisp that had formerly been a wisp lantern for the Lin clan, didn't seem all that useful, so he'd been wanting to ask someone knowledgeable about it. Additionally, Lin Chun, the woman who'd killed his father and tricked him, was a dream artist, so he might be able to get some information from Elder Jagan about her. Admittedly, it was a long-shot which was why Enkai hadn't really been worried about it and had instead chosen to focus on his training to get stronger — slow-moving as it was. He nodded, "Sure, I'll go."

About a quarter of an hour later, Enkai got up from his seat. After stretching his cramped legs out, he prepared to leave, "Alright, I'm heading to training."

"Don't forget to bring up the cave, En," Jak called as Enkai walked into the tunnel near the entrance to the burrow that led down to Onki's lair.

"I'll meet you down there when the time comes to visit Elder Jagan," Nin called after him. Enkai raised a hand and gave a single wave to his family as he trekked through the mountain tunnel to continue his training.

Chapter 10

As Enkai drew deeper into the tunnel, a ball of purple light emerged from his torso. It floated slightly above his head providing him with a convenient lantern to light the way while he traversed the tunnels leading to Elder Onki's lair. Over the years, he'd grown accustomed to the wisp's company During the first few weeks, he had hated the dream spirit since it only reminded him of the pain he'd undergone, but now he treasured it as a token of his former life. Even if his father had tried to kill him, he still had family in the Du clan. Given his certainty that the Du Patriarch knew of Kai's intentions, he still wasn't sure he wanted to return to the Maro Province although it would almost certainly be necessary if he wanted to confront the Lin Matriarch.

The trek through the tunnels took a little over an hour before he emerged into the cavernous chamber full of boulders Elder Onki called his lair. The walls were covered with entrances to other tunnels, large and small, which snaked throughout Old Omen. Elder Onki forbade access to the tunnels that led below his lair, so Enkai knew little about where they led. The tunnel that led to Nin's burrow was a dozen feet above the floor.

Backing up a bit to get a running start, he leapt down to the nearest boulder where he landed in a roll that nearly sent him tumbling to the ground. Thankfully, he stopped his momentum at the last second then surveyed the room for his master. Toward the middle of the chamber, he was resting on a sizable circle of soft earth which was in contrast with the hard-packed ground in the rest of the chamber. It was Enkai's training area. Elder Onki had created it when he first began training. Jumping from boulder to boulder, he decided to put on a show, so he executed a series of flips and rolls as he wove his way toward the training area. Upon reaching his destination, he executed a forward front flip onto the ground then bowed sweeping his arm out with a flourish.

From within his massive moss-covered shell, Onki sighed. Enkai crossed his arms, a grin plastered on his face, waiting for the ancient tortoise to emerge from his shell.

"Well?" he asked as Onki's snake-like head turned to him. In the wisp light, the black scales that covered the elder shimmered in sharp contrast to the dull earthy tones of his shell. He situated himself in front of Enkai.

"Yes, you did a fine job impersonating a monkey with your aerial flailing," Onki said, yawning.

"Flailing? Please! It was impressive and you know it. Also, are you implying there's something wrong with monkeys?" Enkai replied placing his hands on his hips.

"Yes, they are loud, rude, and smelly."

"I don't smell!" Enkai exclaimed though he did give himself a sniff to make sure. He smelled like leaves and dirt. He'd be surprised if a tortoise that lived in a mountain cave in the middle of sprawling forestland found those scents objectionable.

"By the way, speaking of senses, when will I learn to sense anima and essence without my spirit-sight?"

Instead of answering, Onki grunted and stomped a foot into the ground while his eyes flashed. Abruptly, five mounds swelled from the soft earth. They continued to grow in size while their shape became vaguely humanoid. When the earth grew still more, five human-shaped figures composed of soil and rocks stood before Enkai. Several glowing yellow lights also appeared around the training area which provided further illumination for Enkai who couldn't see in the dark.

He opened his spirit-sight which he'd earned upon reaching Lead a few years prior. His perspective changed from a dim cave filled with boulders to a vivid landscape of yellows and greens with tiny strands of silver-white threaded throughout. The five figures were completely shrouded in rich yellow. Soon after they'd finished forming, each figure adopted a fighting stance. As extraordinary as the display was, Enkai had experienced it many times prior.

Puppets as Elder Onki called them were temporary constructs created by moving one's anima into a compatible vessel. If done correctly, the process allowed a divine artist to control that vessel with their will. Enkai had never heard of such a technique before Elder Onki explained it to him. The closest equivalent he could think of was Creation techniques which allowed a divine artist to create temporary objects like armor and weapons from their anima. However, Creation techniques were the most difficult of techniques. Of all the clansmen in the Maro Province, very few divine artists had ever been capable of using them.

"You will gain the ability in time," Elder Onki said dismissively. He yawned once more before adding, "Now, since you are so energetic, we'll start with your martial training. Attempt to defeat these puppets."

Enkai raised no argument despite his question being brushed aside. He preferred the more practical aspects of his training anyway and the puppets were nothing new though he had never faced more than three. As soon as Onki's words echoed out, the puppets moved.

Instead of creating distance or attacking, Enkai cycled anima and watched. None of the puppets charged him directly but spread out surrounding him on all sides. Two took up a flanking position behind him while three were positioned in front of him. There was no escape. However, despite being surrounded on all sides, Enkai waited. These puppets weren't of the same caliber he typically faced while training with Elder Onki. He could tell by the amount of residual earth anima around them which he'd learned denoted their overall combat strength. He guessed these puppets were roughly half and again as strong as the usual batch Onki created based on the density of their anima.

The first strike came in the form of a pincer attack from his front left and back right. The two puppets charged him, one going for his legs while the other aimed for his head. They were fast; one mistake and he'd be overwhelmed. When they neared him, he noticed out of the corner of his eye that the puppet on the front right was also moving in to attack. If he dodged the first two attacks, he'd be wide open to the third.

This seems like a bit much, he thought as attack closed in on him like a vice. Instead of blocking or dodging either attack which would leave him open to an attack from another puppet, he stepped toward the puppet from the front left, ducked the powerful punch aimed at his head, and grabbed the inside of its arm. The arm was made of gritty stone which wasn't comfortable though it ensured his grip wouldn't slip. Following the momentum from the punch, Enka pivoted his hip then twisted to throw his attacker directly into the puppet diving for his legs from behind. The puppets were incredibly heavy, possibly twice as heavy as a full-grown man, but while cycling anima Enkai was able to execute the maneuver, albeit with some strain. The puppets collided with each other while the latter one was mid-dive. The ensuing cacophony of crashing earth rang through Enkai's ears.

Wasting little time, he dashed toward the third puppet meeting it mid-charge. Barely dodging the monstrous swing it threw, he delivered an elbow to its throat. He put his entire weight behind the blow while he increased the amount of anima cycling through his body. His strike drove through the puppet's neck creating a cloud of dirt and debris; however, a sharp pain shot up Enkai's arm from his elbow to his shoulder.

Before he could recover, something smashed into his back sending him sprawling to the ground. As he landed face down in the dirt, his instincts called out danger, so he desperately rolled in a random direction. Not a moment later, he saw a puppet's foot slam down on the place where he'd just been. His back ached something fierce as he got to his feet. He spat out the dirt in his mouth and squared off against the two remaining puppets.

He tried to collect himself, but the puppets didn't let him. They launched a series of coordinated attacks that kept him on the defensive with barely any time to think. Bobbing and weaving through the onslaught, Enkai took note of his condition. His left arm was basically useless due to the pain in his elbow which felt like a fracture, and the constant motion sent shocks of pain through his arm especially when he bent its elbow. Additionally, his back had suffered some damage, but thankfully, that didn't impede his movement much with the anima cycling through him, though it was still causing enough pain to distract him. Unless he finished the fight quickly, he'd be finished. He also knew from personal experience that his master would only stop short of life-threatening injury or death. Enkai had spent more than one night in the care of Nin and her elixirs due to a nasty beating from Elder Onki's puppets.

Certain that Onki was testing him, Enkai was determined to win. Over the past few months, he had started to blaze through his physical and martial training.

Personally, he associated the improvements with his growth. According to Nin, his body was beginning to mature into adulthood which meant he was getting stronger, faster, and larger. It made sense to him that bodily maturation would directly translate into better results for training. In response, Elder Onki had increased the difficulty and frequency of his training although today felt different. Such a drastic increase in difficulty was assuredly intended to test his limits. Enkai decided to rise to the challenge.

Unfortunately, he had a major problem. With his current arsenal, he possessed no way to disable the puppets without harming himself. Unlike previous puppets, these ones were almost as solid as the boulders littering the cave around him. He'd already suffered damage from striking one of them and he didn't want to think what would have happened had he not been cycling anima. Elder Onki had only taught him how to cycle the vital anima of his spirit through his body, so he had no real techniques he could employ. There was only one thing he could try, but it was a long shot.

As he dodged another blow, Enkai retreated. He didn't leave the training area since Onki would consider that a forfeit. Instead, he simply ran away from the puppets. He knew he wouldn't get very far because there were two of them, which meant they could cut him off fairly easily once he committed to a direction, but he didn't care. He just needed some time.

Turning much of his focus inward, Enkai tracked the motion of his cycling anima. He narrowed his focus to the anima channels that carried his vital anima from his core through his body, specifically, those that ran through his right arm. Carefully, he stopped the flow of anima out of his arm to create a stockpile as more flowed into it. More and more anima coalesced in his arm until there was a noticeable difference between the density of the anima in his arm compared with what was in the rest of his body. He increased the amount of anima being cycled from his core to the maximum in order to maintain his speed. By the time he reached the other side of the training area, the anima in his right arm had gotten as dense as he could make it without losing control. A trickle of vital anima spilled out of his skin of his arm in a pale silver-white glow.

Praying to the ancestors, he abruptly reversed his direction and dashed toward the charging puppets with as much force as he could muster. The puppets matched his charge. As they met, he launched his right arm into a massive cleaving haymaker aiming to take both puppets out with one swing.

Like a comet in the night sky, his fist sailed through the air crashing into the first puppet. There was a dull ringing of pain, but he kept his body turning with the punch and following through with his weight. The resounding boom that followed the impact made his heart jump. The first puppet exploded from the neck up creating another cloud of dirt and dust, but he continued the swing to take out the second puppet. However, his strike whizzed through the air hitting nothing. With nothing to catch the momentum, his shoulder wrenched as the swing continued throwing him off balance. His gaze snapped downward, and he caught a glimpse of the puppet crouching slightly below the trails of vital anima left by his punch. The puppet sprung upward with its fist poised to deliver a merciless counterattack.

Before he could even attempt to dodge, the blow caught him in the gut and brought him to his knees. The force of the blow was so great, he nearly lost his dinner. As he clutched his gut, his vision swam with black spots. Pain trampled through his mind crumbling his focus like dry leaves underfoot. Without his will to manage it, his anima stopped cycling and dissipated leaving him completely drained. With titanic effort, Enkai lifted his gaze from the ground to look up at the remaining puppet which stood over him unmoving. Its earth-forged body reflected little light, thus giving it the appearance of a dark harbinger come to deliver his doom. Enkai had nothing left. Aside from the physical damage, his anima channels were dry, and his core was so strained he felt physically ill.

Despite knowing that he had no chance without anima, he still wanted to win. After it became clear he didn't plan on surrendering, the puppet threw a punch at his head. Enkai lifted his arms and leaned forward with the intent to intercept the punch in order to create an opening for an attack on its legs. However, the attack stopped short. Lacking the muscle strength to stop his forward momentum, Enkai simply tumbled forward face-first into the soft earth. The puppet stepped back to avoid his collapsing form.

As soon as he hit the ground, thunderous laughter filled the cavern. Enkai felt the bones in his body vibrate from the sheer power behind the sound. He groaned and rolled over so at the very least he wasn't eating more dirt. The ground rumbled as Elder Onki walked over to him, looking down with clear amusement.

"There's no need to laugh at me because I lost," he said staring up at Onki. He felt like one of the boulders in the cave had rolled over him. His master stopped laughing, but the amusement stayed on his features.

"Don't take it too badly," Elder Onki said. He settled down next to Enkai. His master's eyes flashed once again. The last puppet walked away so it wasn't standing over Enkai, then broke apart and returned to the earth. "You did well."

"But I still failed."

"Did you?"

The question hung in the air for almost a full minute before Enkai finally spoke. Hesitantly, he asked, "But I couldn't defeat all the puppets. If this was a real fight, I would have died. You said almost winning means nothing, because you still lose, and losing means death."

Onki nodded along as Enkai spoke. His demeanor changed becoming serious and pensive. He turned his head away from Enkai to look into the distance as if there was something only he could see. Even if there was something there, Enkai didn't have the strength to lift his head from the dirt, so he just assumed the Elder was contemplating. Several minutes passed which Enkai used for resting. He had many questions for Elder Onki, but a major thing he'd learned over the years was that there was no rushing the ancient tortoise.

"Do you know why I made tonight's combat trial so difficult?" Onki asked. Enkai opened his weary eyes. He thought about it for a moment. A number of snarky and clever responses passed through his mind, though he held them back and decided to just give the answer Elder Onki always gave him.

"No," he answered. The difficulty frustrated Enkai. Despite his years of training, he had barely made any progress in the divine arts. Sure, he had made significant progress physically, but any divine artist with an actual Enhancement technique could wipe the floor with him. He needed to cultivate essence into anima and learn its techniques in order to advance, yet at twelve summers he still hadn't done either despite his spirit having awakened years ago. How was he supposed to overcome increasingly difficult tests when he wasn't allowed to get any stronger?

"I see. Over the past few months, I have sensed much unrest in your spirit. I had thought that it may be the influence of the Sin nested in your spirit, but if you had been compromised by Sin, you wouldn't have been able to hide it while straining your spirit as you just have. Thankfully, it appears I was wrong," Onki said.

Enkai was surprised. He knew his frustration was apparent to his family, but he thought he had done a good job hiding it from his master. It wasn't as if he didn't want Elder Onki to know. Enkai had just been raised not to let his emotions affect his training. Although, Elder Onki made suppressing his frustration hard at times since he did nothing but sleep and torment Enkai with hours of repetitive, grueling training.

Even so, he disliked the notion that Onki's test was just aimed at ascertaining the state of his Sin rather than his potential. In the face of all the concern Onki and Nin paid to it, his Sin rested peacefully in his spirit. Over the past six years, he had only had one incident with it. According to Nin, he'd nearly frozen to death climbing Old Omen during his test to prove himself to Elder Onki and his Sin had woken up. That said, nothing bad had happened as a result and he'd passed the test, so Enkai wasn't sure what the big deal was. Looking inside his spirit, he observed the cords of red anima. They rested calmly waiting for him to tap into their power. He never did though. Whenever he touched his Sin, it sent impressions of hunger and volatility through him.

Seeing his furrowed brow, Elder Onki caught his gaze and asked, "What troubles you?"

The question caught him off guard. Of course, he was glad his master had given him an opening though now he was confronted with an opportunity, he struggled for the right words to explain the root of his frustration. Despite his issue with the pace of his training, he respected Elder Onki. Simply based on what his master showed him during training, he was certain the ancient tortoise was stronger than anyone he'd ever met except, perhaps, the Lin Matriarch.

"I..." he began but paused as he attempted to formulate his thoughts. Taking a deep breath, he chose to take the direct route. Elder Onki hated it when he danced around a subject. "I feel like I am moving too slowly in my training. Even though you keep pushing me forward in my martial and body training, I haven't progressed in the divine arts in years. I have no idea how to use techniques and I don't even know where to start. Meanwhile, Brem and Jak are ahead of me even though I'm the oldest. Brem and I had an argument today and she said I have no talent because after five years of training with you I've barely passed Lead rank. I know she didn't mean it, but I can't help but wonder if it's true. My father was nearly Bronze by my age."

Once he started talking, the words just poured out like a river through a broken dam. He continued, "All I do is physical training and anima cycling. Five years of just the basics. What is the point of holding me back? In my clan, I would have at least moved on to learning a technique by now, but I don't even have a proper breathing exercise for cultivating essence into anima. When we first met, you told me that I could stay until I found my own way. I want to find the woman that killed my father, but I can't because I'm too weak. How am I to do anything without the divine arts? I might not know everything but I know that I need to learn powerful techniques as I advance or I'll never be strong enough. Is it my fault? Do I have no talent?"

By the time he finished, his voice rang with desperation and frustration. Enkai hated it. He sounded like a petulant child, but he couldn't help it. His dream wisp floated in front of his face bobbing up and down like it was agreeing with him. During the whole tirade, his master listened patiently. When Enkai finished, he shook his head then sighed.

"Forgive me, young Enkai. It seems I have failed you," he rumbled. The statement made Enkai feel even more like an ungrateful child. As far as he knew, a mysterious great beast had saved him from death's door all those years ago then left him with Nin who lived in Elder Onki's domain. Elder Onki had not only allowed him to stay within his domain as Nin's ward, but he also agreed to train Enkai in the divine arts despite being under no obligation to do so. And how did Enkai repay his kindness? He got frustrated and convinced himself Onki was stunting his growth. Before Enkai could truly immerse himself in his guilt, his master snapped him out of it by continuing, "I made the assumption that you had been educated in the divine arts, but it seems you were raised by imbeciles."

If he weren't completely exhausted, Enkai might have physically reeled at this. The ancient tortoise might as well have slapped him in the face. Onki's tone dripped with disdain which left Enkai confused.

"You mentioned your father was nearly Bronze by your age. What rank was your clan's most powerful divine artist?" Onki had evidently reached some sort of conclusion that Enkai didn't understand

"My father was the strongest. He was Silver," he answered hesitantly.

Upon hearing this, his master burst into a fit of laughter for an entire minute. Meanwhile, Enkai started to feel angry. Even though he hadn't seen them in half a decade, he chafed as Onki seemingly found humor in the devotion his clansmen had for the divine arts. As his master's laughter died down, he angrily asked, "What are you laughing at?"

"Ah, I just realized the reason you must feel so frustrated. Forgive me for my foolishness, En," the black tortoise said. He shook his head chuckling once more. "When you said your home bordered the forest, I assumed you came from one of the northern human kingdoms south of my domain, but that patently isn't the case. Where is your home?"

Enkai paused a moment before answering. The notion of *other* human settlements, kingdoms at that, caught his attention but he resolved to ask about them later in order to stay on topic. The Maro Province was technically a secret refuge for the five clans. They had fled there during the Fall of Heaven after all. However, he trusted Onki, so he told him.

"The Maro Province."

"Never heard of it," Onki grunted. His master's ignorance made sense; however, the dismissiveness in his tone irritated Enkai — despite his long years away from his old home. He wanted to defend the Maro Province, however, Onki interrupted him, "Your ignorance makes sense now. I should have realized sooner."

"What do you mean?" Enkai asked.

"Do you know what lies at the pinnacle of the divine arts?" Onki asked instead of answering his question. Despite his annoyance, Enkai went along with Onki.

"Gold. The founders of the five clans were Gold," he said smiling smugly. Of course, he knew about the Gold rank. Back in the Maro Province, few had reached that rank other than the clan founders and none within recent history. The rank of Gold was mythical amongst the clans and any divine artist who reached such heights would be like a god among men. Onki appeared to be considering something before he responded.

"While it might amuse me to burst this bubble myself, I think it would be best if you saw the truth for yourself. When you visit Elder Jagan, ask her to show you the Apostles of the Green Mother. After you have seen what she has to show you, my amusement will make more sense and we shall correct the error in your education."

"Okay …" Enkai responded though he was still unsure what exactly Onki meant. Honestly, the entire conversation was just confusing. "How did you know I was going to see Elder Jagan?"

"I may appear easygoing but make no mistake: there is little that happens in my domain that I do not know," Onki said. The old tortoise withdrew his legs into his shell and yawned. Enkai knew from experience that this meant the conversation would be over soon since the ancient tortoise planned on sleeping. Before he withdrew completely into his shell, he said, "Now that I know your knowledge of the divine arts is so fundamentally lacking, I will have to adjust my plans for your training. However, there is one misunderstanding I will not allow to continue."

"What?" Enkai was curious about what knowledge he lacked. After all, the entire basis of his frustration was feeling like he didn't have the knowledge necessary to advance in his study of the divine arts. He gave Onki his full attention.

"Your understanding of techniques is deeply flawed. Techniques are not simply a means to power. They are integral to the divine arts, yes, but not because they are the most important part of a divine artist's strength. Having them alone will not grant you strength. The anima cycling that I taught you which you referred to as 'just the basics'," the black tortoise snorted as he quoted Enkai before continuing, "is, in fact, a rudimentary form of Enhancement technique. I designed it specifically for you to strengthen your spirit and grant you better control over your anima. It is for training yet it is undeniably a technique; a quite effective one, I might add."

Enkai blinked a few times as he processed Elder Onki's words. He felt his heart flutter a bit; however, it seemed Onki was not done talking, "Given your frustrations, I will be honest with you. Though you didn't win, you performed beyond my expectations today. Each of the puppets you fought possessed roughly the same physical capabilities of an average Silver ranked human. Not only did you defeat four of them, but you have also unmistakably mastered the cycling technique I taught you. On top of that, you applied the technique in a way I did not teach you by pooling anima into your arm to increase your attack power. What you did is called a Strike. It is a basic application of the core principles of Enhancement which you discovered on your own. If you have doubts about your talent, think on that."

With his piece spoken, Onki withdrew his head into his shell leaving Enkai in shocked silence. He couldn't believe what he'd heard. Each puppet was equivalent to a *Silver* human? It was ridiculous. There was no way Onki was telling the truth. Not only could Enkai not believe he'd disabled four Silver opponents, but he also couldn't believe that Onki was powerful enough to create five such opponents so easily. He knew Onki was powerful, but still.

Who is this crazy old beast? Enkai couldn't help but wonder. Not for the first time since he'd woken in a cave with talking great beasts, Enkai wondered if he had truly died the day his father had stabbed him and was trapped in some whimsical afterlife. He gave an accusing look at his dream wisp familiar and reached into the connection between him and the wisp to send a thought.

You would tell me if I was dreaming, right? As expected, the dream wisp didn't respond. It never did. He lay there in the dark for a quarter-hour pondering Onki's words. The tortoise had said that the puppets were physically equivalent to Silver ranked humans. Enkai realized that meant they only had the physical strength and speed of the Silver rank. Obviously then, at least as far as he knew, the puppets couldn't use techniques while Enkai had been Enhancing himself by cycling vital anima, and, even then, he'd come out bruised and battered. If his opponents had been true Silver divine artists, Enkai knew he'd have been torn apart. On top of all that, Onki had called them "average". He shivered at the thought of facing even one opponent of his father's skill level.

He'd also discovered an entirely new technique on his own. Enkai contemplated whether *intermediate* meant it was more powerful or more difficult to learn than basic techniques. He hoped it was both.

"A Strike technique, huh?" he said punching the air with his right arm and wincing slightly from the motion. He laughed as anticipation washed over him. Pain lanced through his back and left arm while he laughed yet he didn't care. He had a technique! Despite Onki's words, it was an accomplishment that he could be proud of. Each ache felt like proof of his accomplishment. In less than an hour, he'd gone from frustrated by his lack of progress to giddy about the possibilities to come. Already, he was considering new applications he might discover by experimenting with the distribution of his anima.

As his laughter faded, the cave grew quiet. His aching body saw fit to remind him that he needed to rest, so he futilely attempted to get more comfortable. As he dozed off, he prayed Nin would bring some healing salves to ease his pain, so he could meet Elder Jagan, who now potentially held even more answers for Enkai than before. Looking forward to the meeting, he slipped into sweet slumber.

Chapter 11

Hours later, Enkai was prodded to consciousness by a worried-looking Nin. He felt the warmth of her spirit sweep across his own as she scanned him. He knew she was just attempting to gauge his condition. One of her abilities allowed her to ascertain not only a creature's spiritual condition from scanning their spirit but their physical condition as well. Based on what Enkai had seen of the ability, she could discern the specific ailments a person suffered, so when she spoke, he wasn't surprised by her detailed diagnosis.

"Onki!" Nin shouted. She didn't look happy at all. Elder Onki yawned loudly as he emerged from his great mossy shell. Nin pointed a finger at Enkai then back at Onki in accusation. "Please tell me why my son whom I entrusted to your care has two hairline-fractured ribs, a fractured elbow, and spinal bruising?"

Onki blinked at her sleepily then blinked once more at Enkai before replying, "Is that all? You did better than I thought En. I was sure something was at least broken."

"Thanks," Enkai said and laughed awkwardly before one look from Nin silenced him. She glared daggers at Elder Onki. From Enkai's perspective, it was all quite humorous though he would never say such a thing to Nin. Even in her humanoid form which was the only form Enkai ever saw her in, she was diminutive by human standards. So, Enkai couldn't help but find humor in the image of a child-sized rabbit-woman staring down a massive tortoise. The scene was especially funny because Onki didn't seem to find any tension in the situation.

"What?" Onki asked innocently. She just continued to glare and crossed her arms. Despite the throbbing pain from his torso and arm, Enkai raised his arm to get Nin's attention but immediately regretted the motion.

"Nin, guess what?" he said excitedly. Uncrossing her arms, she looked over to him. Seeing the look in his eyes, she sighed as if she was about to hear something bad. He was happy he only had good news. "Elder Onki had me fight *five* Silver level puppets and I almost won! And I discovered a technique all on my own!"

"You what?!" Nin shouted at Onki again. This time Enkai winced. He'd really expected a more positive response. Even though it was directed at Onki, Enkai couldn't help feeling as though he were in trouble. She gestured at him emphatically. "He is still a *child*, Onki. What if one of those puppets had caused damage I couldn't heal? He's barely a step into the Lead rank!"

"You worry too much, little rabbit," Onki said smiling amiably which only seemed to make Nin more exasperated. "Children need to get banged up and broken a little for them to grow. Besides, I wouldn't have let things get out of hand. You pretend that I do not know my own disciple's strength."

Nin appeared less than satisfied with his answer but dropped the matter in order to tend to Enkai who admittedly was beginning to wish for a reprieve from his pain. He'd decided not to mention the fact that Onki had just withheld the truth from Nin. He wondered how she would feel if she knew Onki had purposefully made the fight unfair in order to ascertain whether he had been corrupted by the dormant Sin in his spirit.

Nin treated Enkai carefully over the course of the next hour. Nin's healing elixirs and restorative techniques amazed him every time he observed them in action. He felt the fractures in his bones knitting themselves together as her hands passed over the injured areas cloaked in waves of moonlight-blue anima. By the time she finished, he was feeling much improved, though he still ached. Once on his feet, he inspected her handiwork. His elbow sent dull jolts of pain up and down his arm when he moved his left arm too much and he suffered occasional throbbing from his chest and back, but Enkai was grateful. He surmised Nin had saved him weeks of recovery time in only an hour.

Before they left, Enkai asked Onki about the cave Jak wanted to explore. The answer was a simple grunt of approval from his master as he attempted to go back to sleep. When they exited Onki's lair, the sun had long departed leaving the moon and stars to reign in the sky. Enkai instructed his dream wisp to hover in the air above them to help them see when the ambient moonlight wasn't enough.

The dream wisp had grown brighter thanks to his advancement to Lead a few years beforehand. According to Nin, the wisp gained many benefits from their link including an ongoing supply of anima to keep it from fading. His wisp would gain more strength as he progressed in the divine arts, though what benefit increased strength would grant a wisp was beyond Enkai. Wisps were minor spirits born from various types of essence in the world.

As Enkai lost himself pondering the mysteries of his insubstantial companion, Nin guided them through the forest at a brisk pace. They passed over the river where Enkai had tricked his siblings. A mile past the river the vegetation took on a lavender tint. Continuing another few miles to the southeast, they began to see dream wisps of various sizes floating through the air. Enkai had to force his wisp to stay near him multiple times as it attempted to drift away toward other wisps. The number of wisps increased the closer they ventured toward their destination.

"Hey, how come there are so many wisps all a sudden?" Enkai asked. Nin looked mildly surprised at his question, but the surprise faded after a moment.

"Sometimes I take for granted the things I know because I was born here," she said, her expression reminiscent. "Our forest is dense with essence of all kinds. Several places here overflow with it. These essence-rich sites attract wisps. Some of them even create new wisps. They are called Essence Fountains. Elder Jagan's home sits on top of a Dream Essence Fountain that she guards."

The new information made Enkai recall the Sacred Vas tree. He wondered if it had been a Vital Essence Fountain. He could understand why someone would guard such a place, though one thing did bother him.

"What does she guard it against?" he asked. As far as he knew, great beasts within the forest didn't fight with each other very often. When they did, it was usually the result of a hunter-prey relationship or a territorial dispute more than any malicious intent.

"Ah. Well nothing nowadays, I suppose. But Onki used to tell me stories about humans who would try to steal the power of her fountain a long time ago," she said shrugging.

"How long ago?"

"I can't be sure. Elder Onki and Elder Jagan are the oldest beasts in our forest. All I know is it was long before I was born," she replied. Truthfully, her answer didn't tell Enkai what he wanted to know, which was whether she was referring to before the Fall of Heaven. Then again, he had no idea exactly how old Elder Onki was. The massive tortoise was discernibly ancient yet for Enkai the idea of a thousand-year-old creature seemed more at home in his imagination than in reality.

About half an hour later, Nin stopped between two massive trees with purple leaves and waited. Before Enkai could ask why they had stopped, an enormous spider descended to block their way. Its black beady eyes and hairy body startled Enkai so much he cycled anima and leapt backward to create distance. Thankfully, the scare wasn't enough to cause any disturbances with his Sin. Nin, on the other hand, stood there unperturbed. Instead of creating distance, she greeted the creature like an old friend.

"It's been a while, Anansi," she said with a smile. Then to Enkai's utter shock, she reached out and hugged the spider which was several times her size. He watched on in horror as the spider returned the embrace. When the creature's front legs wrapped around Nin, he was certain it was going to eat her, then a warbling voice filled with cheer reverberated through his mind seemingly from all directions.

It truly has, Nin! You haven't been by in months! Enkai's understanding of the world broke down just a little bit more as he watched the spider nuzzle Nin affectionately. For the second time that night, Enkai wondered if he had been living in some strange dreamland all these years. All of a sudden, shivers ran up his spine as something scanned his spirit. He looked over to see the spider creature staring directly at him. Once again, the strange voice echoed through his mind. *This must be the little human boy you adopted. Enkai, isn't it? Why look at that, he's already bigger than you! Oh, but he's a bit pale though. Are humans normally like that?*

Anansi looked between Enkai and Nin inquisitively — or at least that is what Enkai hoped. Honestly, any *expression*, if it could be called that, that the spider adopted made it look like it wanted to eat them. Thankfully, Nin walked back over to him grabbing hold of his hand as she answered Anansi's question.

"No, he's just a bit startled is all. I don't let my children stray too far from the nest, so they get startled by the silliest things," Nin explained patting Enkai on the hand. He just stared at her, dumbfounded. How was getting startled by a giant talking spider silly? She was being unreasonable. Then to top things off, the spider began nodding its head in understanding.

Well, that makes sense. You always do worry too much. You should let them explore a bit or they won't grow. I can remember a time not too long ago when a little rabbit got into all sorts of trouble in Elder Karn's territory looking for mandrake root. Anansi's mouthparts twitched as the voice rang through their minds and gave Enkai the impression that it might pounce on them at any moment. While he fretted, Nin laughed and laughed. The spider laughed too. Its laugh echoed from all sides with a sound akin to a hissing banshee. Enkai tried not to panic, but despite his best efforts, his heart rate spiked dramatically. Nin's ears twitched, as she could probably hear his increased heartbeat.

"Well, as always it is wonderful seeing you, Anansi. We need to catch up next time, but I must be going. Elder Jagan doesn't like to be kept waiting," Nin said. She squeezed Enkai's hand which helped ease his anxiety a bit.

Don't make me wait too long or I'll come and find you next time. It gets awfully boring around here, Anansi said before levitating through the air into the trees. Enkai gaped at the display.

"A flying spider?" Enkai gasped, half-incredulous, half-horrified. Nin chuckled at his reaction.

"No, silly. He was using his webs. Look," she said pointing upward. Enkai looked up yet he saw nothing except for dozens of dream wisps floating high in the air. He looked at Nin, confused. She smiled then pointed at her eyes. "Use your Spirit-sight."

Doing as she said, he activated his Spirit-sight. His eyes widened from what he saw. Above him, a massive web hung high in the air. Its strands of webbing were all made of dream essence. The dream wisps he thought were just floating high above were actually caught in the web. Based on what he knew about wisps, they were probably drawn to dream essence. He wondered why a huge spider would trap dream wisps; however, Nin answered his question before he had a chance to ask.

"He eats them. The dream wisps. Unlike most spiders, Anansi doesn't feed on other great beasts. He subsists on the dream anima in the wisps," she said. On hearing her explanation, he realized that was beyond question the reason Nin felt so at ease around the spider, and he relaxed a bit after hearing it. Knowing the massive spider floating overhead didn't want to eat them helped his anxiety a bit; but, he did check to make sure his dream wisp was staying close to him since he would hate for it to get eaten. Marveling at the sheer size of the web, another question occurred to him, but Nin predicted that as well. "Since he spins the web from dream essence, it's invisible to the naked eye. Anansi uses the dream essence to attract wisps. He can also make himself and his web completely invisible so other great beasts do not bother him."

"I don't think I like spiders very much," Enkai said frowning. It was the only thing he could think of at that moment. This newest piece of information caused a bit of his anxiety to return, as his imagination conjured up all types of invisible creatures stalking the area around him. Nin found humor in his apprehension. He decided he would keep his Spirit-sight going regardless of the drain on his spirit, even though it hadn't fully recovered from his fight with the earth puppets. Unfortunately, it would take a few days of rest for it to recover completely.

The pair arrived at their destination when the moon was highest in the sky. Enkai recognized they were very close because dream essence was thick in the air. While using his Spirit-sight, the area appeared to be covered by a thin mist that became denser the closer they came to Elder Jagan's home. The dream mist struck a chord of familiarity with him though he couldn't place his finger on why.

He didn't waste much time thinking about that since something else caught his attention. The landscape changed as they crossed into the heart of Elder Jagan's territory. Thick lavender trees gave way to large stone ruins that jutted from the earth at all angles. Enkai recognized a number of features that marked the architecture as human including among other things, ruined doorways, overgrown windows, and walls marked with runes long drained of their power.

"What is this place?" Enkai asked with wonder plain in his voice.

"Onki calls it the 'Lost City of Dreams' though I'm not sure that's its actual name," Nin said. She adjusted the pack on her back before looking up at him. "It used to be a human city where great dream artists gathered to create wondrous works of art and cultivate their spirits before it was destroyed in a great war over a thousand years ago."

Enkai didn't think it was a coincidence that Nin's 'great war' matched the timeline of the Fall of Heaven. Even in its ruined state, the city was amazing. He was overwhelmed by the sheer scale of the place as they continued through its ruins.

The decrepit buildings they passed by shamed anything Enkai had ever seen. Some were small and made from basic materials like stone while others were grand affairs with decorated walls, spires, wrought metal fences, and stained glass. Enkai wished he could have seen these places in their full glory. However, the buildings were only one of the many wonders of the lost city.

Obelisks and statues dedicated to long-dead ideas and figures looming in the wisp-lit night dotted their trail. One featured a man with three sets of wings who raised a shimmering blade of prismatic glass in triumph. Another depicted two serpentine dragons coiled together in a ring each eating the other's tail. One dragon had eyes set with golden gems while the other had eyes of onyx. Near the place where they first entered the city, two obelisks sat side by side each made of some unknown material riddled with holes. Every time the wind blew, a soft flute-like note drifted from the structures. No two notes were the same, as each wind changed the pitch and tone of the sound. The notes wove together in a haunting tune that followed them as they walked.

The number of dream wisps grew significantly with every step they took until he could spot more than a dozen no matter where he looked. In his Spirit-sight, the world became a hazy landscape of foggy dream essence dotted by the lights of dream wisps. Another pang of familiarity echoed through his memory though he couldn't put his finger on its source either. The ever-thickening dream essence, the light of the wisps, and the strange music filled the air with a surreal atmosphere as though they were walking through a dream.

Nin led him to one of the grander buildings in the city. In its prime, he believed the building had to have been several times larger than even the largest structures built by any of the five clans of the Maro Province. Even in its dilapidated state, it was still impressive. Hundreds of runes covered its walls. The windows were made of stained glass which depicted scenes of divine artists in various meditative positions. High above their heads, the remnants of four towers occupied the corners of the structure giving Enkai the impression that this place had been of great importance even before its destruction.

They tracked around the building to where a large portion of the back wall had collapsed. Nin hopped over the rubble with relative ease compared to Enkai who had to carefully navigate through it. When he finally made his way through, Nin was waiting for him at the bottom of a large staircase leading up to the second floor. As he reached her, he bent down placing his hands on his knees and took a moment to catch his breath. Although Nin had healed him, his body was still exhausted from his earlier exertion as well as the several mile journey through the forest which had hardly been easy with the heavy undergrowth, fallen trees, and uneven terrain. Nin allowed him to rest for a moment while she checked the contents of her pack.

"When you meet Elder Jagan, make sure to be on your best behavior. She isn't like Elder Onki," she said looking him directly in the eye to make sure he was paying attention. "We are here as members of Onki's family, so if you disrespect her, you'll only cause trouble for him."

This was news to Enkai. He thought of Jak, Brem, and Nin as his family, but Elder Onki had always been his teacher. Then again, he did spend a large amount of his time with the ancient tortoise. Onki had also raised Nin and they all lived on his mountain. Now that Enkai thought about it, the idea that they were a part of Onki's family did make sense. If he thought about it as a human family, Onki would be the grandfather while Nin was the mother. Enkai nodded to show he understood and the two of them ascended the stairs.

The stairs led into a hallway lined with the forgotten tatters of a lost age. Paintings, vases, suits of armors, mounted weapons and much more filled the hall setting Enkai's head on a swivel as he tried to take in everything. The objects had been broken down by the fetters of time which had left many in a barely recognizable condition. That was the case for their physical forms at least. Astoundingly, each of the objects was covered in dream essence which completed its broken form. A mostly rusted suit of armor looked brand new in his Spirit-sight as the dream essence recreated the bronze and iron plates which had long fallen to time. Age-torn paintings became life-like recreations of divine artists and great beasts. He lost himself in the sights while following Nin. The dream essence seemed so real he passed his hand through several of the objects just to check. Unsurprisingly, his hand either passed through the insubstantial essence or found only their broken remnants. Still, even if they were all illusions, he was impressed by Elder Jagan's home.

The hall opened up into a grand chamber with rune-inscribed stone pillars lining the sides of an illusory carpet leading up to a large dais. Above the dais, a crystal chandelier hanging from ephemeral chains swung back and forth. Upon the crystal framework of the chandelier, a large owl rested. It had deep indigo feathers tinged with red at their ends. At the top of its head, its feathers swept up in tufts that resembled great horns giving it a fearsome appearance. When they entered, the creature lifted its head and all around them dream essence shuddered.

Nin stepped forward bowing her head. She spoke in greeting, "Hello, Elder Jagan. I have brought the elixirs and herbs you requested."

Instead of responding, Elder Jagan spread her massive wings and leapt from the chandelier. She glided silently to the chamber's floor in front of Nin, and Enkai got a full view of her. She was more than twice his height easily breaking ten feet. Her beak and talons glinted in the wisp light which illuminated their disconcerting size and sharpness. When Enkai met her gaze, her eyes seemed to pierce through him and stare directly into his soul. The dream essence around the room pulsed like a heartbeat and his eyes were drawn to the space above her eyes where a third eye opened. The eye radiated dream anima and looked completely alien with an indigo iris and sclera as black as the void. Completely ignoring Nin, the third eye looked directly at Enkai. A voice flooded his mind.

Young Enkai of the Du clan. At long last, we meet.

Chapter 12

Jagan craned a long, feathered neck over Enkai. Her three eyes bored into him as if she were searching for something. The familiar shiver of spiritual contact ran through his body confirming his suspicions that she was looking directly into his spirit. Whatever she was looking for, she would find. Enkai very much doubted he could hide anything from her.

How astute, young Enkai. There is little I cannot see. Enkai froze, eyes wide open. Had she just read his thoughts? Was such a thing possible? It had to be related to her abilities as a great beast that utilized dream anima. In the Maro Province, stories of the Lin clan spoke of their dream artists being able to attack the minds of their enemies in addition to casting illusions. While Enkai knew very little about the specific properties and abilities of each type of anima, he knew dream essence was intimately connected to the mind. So, as shocking as mind-reading was, he could only accept his own ignorance in the matter and keep it in mind in the future. A laugh like tingling bells drifted into his mind, clear and full of amusement. *Very good. Those who acknowledge their own ignorance have already taken the first step to finding truth.*

"Uh… excuse me, Elder," Nin said awkwardly. She looked uncertainly between Enkai and Elder Jagan. Based on the slight look of confusion on her face, Enkai guessed she hadn't heard any of what Elder Jagan had said. Elder Jagan turned her head to gaze down on Nin's petite form. Nin continued, her voice growing more resolute, "I'm glad you are getting acquainted with En, but I'd prefer that you did not menace over him like that. My other two children are still afraid of you after you threatened to drop Brem off one of the towers."

It was a simple jest, Ninsa. Besides, your little fox has quite the mouth on her, Jagan said. Enkai took note that she used Nin's full name. Elder Jagan tilted her head back and forth in a curious motion. The feathers of her face bunched up in what Enkai thought must be a smile. He chuckled. He had no trouble believing that Brem had said something that prompted the Elder to put her in her place. His little sister had a habit of sprouting whatever came to her mind which was usually something disrespectful and abrasive. It was because of several similar incidents that Elder Onki referred to Brem exclusively as *the brat*. Elder Jagan extended a wing toward Enkai. *See? Even young Enkai knows the truth in my words.*

Nin favored Enkai with a frown, then shook her head. Somehow, Enkai felt like he had done something wrong.

"I know she can be difficult, but she's a sweet child at heart," Nin said. Enkai understood why Nin thought that way: he doubted that Nin believed anything bad about any of her children. She saw the best in everyone.

Elder Jagan let loose another tingling laugh, overtly amused. Nin frowned a bit more, but let it pass. She thrust the bundle of herbs and elixirs at Jagan and said, "Here are the items you requested. Also, En has something he—"

I am aware of young Enkai's desires, Elder Jagan announced interrupting Nin mid-sentence. She scooped the bundle out of Nin's hands with her beak and tucked it under one wing where it mysteriously disappeared. While her two golden eyes watched Nin, the mesmerizing third eye remained trained on Enkai. He couldn't help but feel unnerved by its unwavering gaze. *Before we get too ahead of ourselves, what do you desire as payment for your service this time, young Nin?*

Nin appeared to think about the question for a few moments before shrugging as she responded, "Since you know what Enkai wants, could you do your best to help him?"

That is fine with me, however ... the elder responded before pausing. Her golden eyes twitched to the side locking on Enkai. Under the gaze of all three eyes, he felt cornered as if she had caught him in a trap he couldn't escape. *I have a proposal.*

"Oh, what kind of proposal?" Nin asked looking up at Jagan who turned her eyes to the small rabbit-woman.

I see that young Enkai is a Deviant.

Nin's brow furrowed. Enkai knew, based on her conversations with him and Elder Onki, that Nin was wary of the Sin lying dormant within him. Her frown which had begun to wane returned deeper than ever. "Yes, he is. What about it? He has never had a single outburst, so it isn't an issue. Since you've looked at his spirit, you know the Sin is dormant. I—"

Come now, young Nin. We both know all creatures marked by Sin only have a matter of time before they lose control, Deviant or not. Once again, she turned her gaze to Nin and Enkai got the feeling of a predator watching its prey. Jagan's words rang through their minds like a tolling death bell and evoked a sense of foreboding and dread. Seeing the clear distress in Nin's eyes, Enkai who had been too overwhelmed by everything happening to do more than stand and contemplate, chose to intervene. He stepped between Elder Jagan and Nin.

"I won't lose control. As long as I train hard enough, Elder Onki says I'll be fine," he said. Jagan blinked at him a few times before belting out a tinkling laugh that filled the chamber around them. Her laughter annoyed him. Did she think he was wrong? He would show her.

Oh, you'll show me will you, young Enkai? Enkai frowned. It was hard to account for her ability to read his thoughts. Nin who had gone quiet grasped his hand. When he looked down at her, she smiled brightly up at him. Then, she turned a scowl toward Elder Jagan.

"I assume your proposal has more to it than provoking me and my son," she said. Elder Jagan tilted her head observing Nin as if for the first time.

Forgive my impropriety, Ninsa. I sometimes forget you have grown since Onki first introduced you to me. Nin's displeasure broke down a little and her glance went askance for a moment. Enkai wondered what Nin had been like as a child. He resolved to ask Onki. Elder Jagan turned away from them and walked a few steps toward the raised dais beneath the chandelier. Her talons clacked against the stone floor sending echoes through the halls. *However, my prodding did have a purpose. You may wish to protect him, but eventually, that won't be enough. Onki knows this and so do you. My proposal is this: as payment for your services, I volunteer to train young Enkai's will. With Onki training his body and spirit while I train his mind, he will have the best opportunity to overcome his Sin.*

Enkai looked between Nin and Elder Jagan, eyes wide. He still wasn't sure what to think of Elder Jagan or rather if he should think anything at all given that she could read his thoughts. He didn't trust her. There was something ominous about the sinister-looking owl. Nevertheless, he didn't think he needed mental training that would take time away from his actual training in the divine arts. "Elder Jagan, apologies, but I don't need your training. I trust Elder Onki."

Oh? Jagan twisted her neck so that she faced him without moving her body. The mysterious third eye bored into him once more and sent chills down his spine. Nonetheless, he didn't back down. He would not be thrown off by her strange mannerisms. She appeared to take note of the determination in his gaze. *You have a strong will, young Enkai, even for a Deviant, however, right now it is no better than a hunk of raw precious metal. If not cultivated properly, even the greatest talent means nothing. You could gain much from my tutelage. I could even teach you how to utilize your little wisp.*

Her last words caught his attention. The dream wisp which had wandered away from him during the conversation with Elder Jagan floated back to him after a bit of mental prompting. Elder Jagan's third eye locked onto the spirit and her feathers bunched up in another smile. Enkai noticed her two normal eyes went all squinty when she smiled. Oddly, that small realization made her seem less threatening: it reminded him of the old women in the Du clan who would oversee unattended children while their parents were away.

"I will consider your proposal, Elder Jagan," Nin interjected politely if a bit tersely. Elder Jagan nodded. She twisted her head back around and continued walking toward a large set of double doors near the dais on the left wall of the room. Both Nin and Enkai looked at each other, uncertain if they should follow. They only wondered for a moment before the she-owl called out.

Come along. Now that we have sorted our business, we must see to young Enkai's request and the assignment given to him by Onki. They both followed her though Nin gave Enkai a questioning look. After a bit of confusion on his part, Enkai realized Nin didn't know about Onki's order to ask Jagan about the Apostles of the Green Mother. As they followed Elder Jagan across the large chamber, he told her about it. Strangely, his explanation seemed to only add to her confusion.

"Onki has told me stories of Apostles, but I've never heard of the Green Mother," Nin said. Elder Jagan looked back at them. Enkai found her ability to twist her neck so far disconcerting especially when her body continued forward without missing a step.

Oh, Ninsa does not know of the Green Mother? I am not surprised. She has always been fonder of Onki's human-centric stories. A hint of embarrassment flashed across Nin's face and her ears twitched slightly. She looked as though she would protest but seemed to think better of it.

The trek through the dream-filled structure took a few minutes. During the silence of their walk, Enkai had time to become truly enraptured by the wondrous sights around him. He was glad they had made their trek during the night. The starlight and night air coming through the windows provided the perfect complement to the dream essence fueled illusions and wisps. Elder Jagan led them through a series of halls ending in a tight stairwell that led downward. As Enkai wondered if Jagan would be able to fit down the stairs, her body shrank to nearly half its original size. Enkai missed a step and nearly fell flat on his face before he caught himself on one of the rusted suits of armor. He stared dumbfounded at Elder Jagan who was now eye-level with him. Elder Jagan answered his unspoken question as they descended.

The divine arts give many boons to those who dedicate their lives to them. For us beasts, one such boon is a varying degree of control over the form and shape of our bodies. Enkai glanced at Nin. He'd always wondered about Nin's ability to assume the humanoid form she favored.

"Does that mean any great beast can do what Nin does?" he said. If so, he didn't see any reason why great beasts wouldn't assume more humanoid forms especially when he accounted for all the things Nin was able to accomplish. Elder Jagan shook her head.

No, young Enkai. A transformation like hers, she said gesturing at Nin with her wing, *requires a deeper spiritual commitment than many of us are willing to give. In the lands beyond the forest, there are some great beasts who live among your kind and imitate the human form, but they are uncommon. Besides, it is not in the nature of most living creatures to abandon the form they were born with. Would you choose to abandon your human form for that of an owl or rabbit?*

Her explanation made some sense to Enkai, but something still bothered him. Why exactly did great beasts have such an ability? According to the lessons he'd received from his father and grandfather, the only difference between people and great beasts in the cultivation of the divine arts was that beasts had stronger bodies while people had stronger spirits. Perhaps their more powerful bodies granted them more control over their forms? His slight mistrust of Jagan drove him to believe she was hiding something from him. Abruptly, Elder Jagan erupted in a ringing cackle, unlike her previous more melodic laughter. The dream essence around them visibly shifted once more in his Spirit-sight as a mirror image of Jagan's third eye appeared on the back of her head staring directly at Enkai. *I see why Onki wishes to educate you. With your current understanding of the divine arts, you might doom yourself to unwitting incompetence and waste all the time he's spent on you.*

Enkai blushed fiercely as he bit back the sting of embarrassment and his mounting annoyance. Jagan's ability to read his mind was quickly becoming frustrating to deal with. Being unable to hide his thoughts from her, made him feel even less desire to receive her tutelage. His father had always said that pursuing the divine arts meant constantly putting oneself at risk in order to reach new heights, but why would he put himself in a situation where even his thoughts weren't secure?

Nin scowled once again at Elder Jagan as she saw Enkai's reaction. She couldn't know what had prompted the Elder's last statement, but she could guess. "Elder could you please refrain from reading En's mind. It's making him uncomfortable."

I'm afraid I can't help it. His untrained mind and strong will work against him here where dream essence runs thick and thoughts flow as freely as words. Honestly, it's as if he's shouting his thoughts at me. Nin's ears drooped and she gave Enkai an apologetic look. He smiled and lightly squeezed her hand to let her know he appreciated the attempt.

As they descended the stairwell which spiraled downward, Enkai realized they were descending within one of the four broken towers he had seen when they'd entered Jagan's lair. The stairwell led into another hallway which ended in two divergent paths, one to the left and another to the right. To the left, the ground sloped downward leading to a stone door lined with purple runic symbols that Enkai couldn't even begin to understand. To the right, another hallway led to yet another stairwell leading farther down. His dream wisp broke away from them and bolted down the hallway toward the stairwell before Enkai even realized what had happened. He reached out with his will and attempted to call it back but got no response.

"What was that about?" he asked, worry thick in his tone. He stared at the rapidly fading purple trail of light left by his bonded spirit.

Worry not, young Enkai. Your wisp will be fine. It has merely heard the call of the Dream Essence Fountain beneath us.

Together, the trio turned to the left and approached the stone door. Enkai swallowed his disappointment at not getting to see the Essence Fountain. Elder Jagan waved her wing in front of the door causing the runes to flare to life. The sound of a ringing bell chimed through the hallway followed by several pulses of dream essence that made Enkai dizzy. After the last pulse, the door shimmered like a fading illusion and disappeared. Enkai thought an illusory door made for very poor security but second-guessed himself when Jagan laughed. Somehow, he knew she was laughing at him which brought a blush to his cheeks.

Beyond the door was a medium-sized room. Interestingly, the floor sloped down from the walls toward the center of the room giving it a bowl shape. The design served a purpose because a large pool of clear water filled nearly half the room. His eyes swept through the strange chamber as he tried to puzzle out its function. They stopped just short of entering the room which was good as far as Enkai was concerned. Not only did the floor's downward slope leave them no place to stand, but the stone tiles were so smooth he was sure anyone who tried to walk on them would slip into the pool. Elder Jagan gestured toward the pool in the center of the room and smiled at them.

Here lies the Well of the Dreamer. One of the many wonders within this once great city. In times long lost, divine artists went through great lengths for a chance to use it. Consider yourselves lucky. Elder Jagan gazed at the pool for a moment. Her eyes were full of a strange sadness he couldn't understand.

"What did they come to use the Well for?" Enkai asked, genuinely curious. Elder Jagan brightened as she answered.

The Well has many functions, but its primary use is divination and preservation of knowledge. It allowed skilled dream artists to scry others with no chance of detection, to peer into the past, and to experience the memories others had placed into the Well.

His eyes widened in surprise. The Well sounded truly amazing and according to Elder Jagan, it was just one of the wonders in this place. Enkai's latent wanderlust kicked in as he imagined the kinds of treasures he could find in exploring the ruined city. He did have a question for her though regarding the Well. "What do you mean by 'memories placed within the Well'?"

Why, I mean just that, of course. Great divine artists left their memories here to be passed down. Though, this usually only happened when they lacked a clan or sect to whom they could pass on their knowledge. For the most part, divine artists would store memories here as payment for using the Well or one of the city's other treasures.

"People in reality paid to use these treasures with their own memories?" Nin asked. Her voice reminded Enkai of a child's, full of wonder and curiosity. Then again, he would sound about the same if he asked, so he couldn't fault her. This place was proving very interesting, mind-reading ancient owls aside.

Yes, the woman who ruled over this place was a true visionary. She understood that while she could obtain great riches from those seeking to use the city's treasures, the true value rested in the secrets of the mind which few could claim to possess. Over the city's lifetime, the Well which started as a simple, if powerful, tool for divination became a one-of-a-kind treasured repository of knowledge from countless divine artists.

After hearing her answer to Nin's question, Enkai became even more excited. If the Elder spoke the truth, this mundane looking pool of water held age-old secrets from before the Fall of Heaven. Such a treasure was beyond priceless. The Well could solve one of his biggest concerns. Although Onki had convinced him he was making progress, his master had also made Enkai wonder how complex the divine arts were. If he could use the Well, he would have access to the knowledge of ancient divine artists, some of whom may have been even greater than the five clan founders.

Furthermore, he would finally be able to see his clan again. He could spy on the Lin clan, as he planned to confront Lin Chun for killing his father and being complicit in his sacrifice six years ago. He would finally be able to gain some perspective. How was the Du clan faring since he and his father had departed? Had they learned of Lin Chun's betrayal? If they had, was there retaliation? That last question had worried Enkai for many years. The five clans of the Maro Province had been at peace since their founding. There'd been minor skirmishes or power struggles born of clan rivalries, but it had never escalated to full-on conflict. The worst it ever got was the feud between the Du and the Hu clans which, according to his grandfather, amounted to a few hundred years of posturing and brief skirmishes over territorial borders. If the Du clan sought vengeance against the Lin clan, the Maro Province might erupt into a conflict never seen before on its fertile soil.

I see you have much you wish to see. Elder Jagan gave him a knowing look as her words echoed through his mind. The voice broke him out of his contemplation bringing him back into the moment. His concern must have been plain to see because Nin was giving him a worried look.

"Yes. Elder Jagan, please permit me a few selfish uses of this great treasure," Enkai said bowing, one fist pressed to his heart. "I am willing to pay the cost, whatever it is."

Elder Jagan stared at him with her big golden eyes before chuckling. Her head tilted to the side as she considered him. *And what would you in your barely more than a decade of experience have to offer? Knowledge of techniques? Of a unique understanding of anima or essence? I think not. But do not worry yourself, young Enkai. The time when men had to pay to use the Well is long gone. Only I remain as its keeper and I say you may use it.*

"You have my deepest gratitude, Elder," he said. Despite her playful taunts, Enkai truly appreciated her gesture. It genuinely made him seriously consider her offer of tutelage since it would mean he would have more opportunities to use the Well.

Let us begin. Elder Jagan turned to the pool and her third eye flashed. The room slowly came to life. Small dancing lights popped into existence above the pool lighting the dark room up. Along the walls, runes similar to those on the door shone with soft light. Just above the pool, something shimmered. It started at the very center of the pool and slowly bloomed outward until it reached the walls and the entrance to the room. When the shimmer ceased, nothing visibly changed, but Elder Jagan casually stepped out into the room. Instead of her talons hitting the smooth sloping tiles, they met with something unseen. As if nothing was amiss, she walked to the center of the room seemingly on thin air.

Both Nin and Enkai gaped at her for a moment before Enkai's curiosity moved him to take a tentative step forward. To his shock and delight, his foot touched something invisible yet firm. Another step brought his full weight onto the surface which reassured him it wouldn't vanish. Together, he and Nin made their way to the center of the room where they joined Elder Jagan. Under their feet, the surface of the pool had gone from crystal clear to cloudy as it had been filled with dream essence.

Elder Jagan waved her wing once more and the stone door appeared sealing the exit. She turned to Enkai fixing all three eyes upon him. *Now, unfortunately, you are not powerful enough to use the Well of the Dreamer on your own. Yet worry not, picture what you wish to see and I shall guide your will so that the Well responds.*

Following her instructions, Enkai pictured the Du settlement within the Maro Province. As the image solidified in his mind, the world was swallowed by a surge of purple mist.

Chapter 13

When reality took shape once more, a vast plain stretched far off to the north, west and, south. To the east, he could barely make out the outline of many jagged mountain peaks attempting to devour the sky. Under the brilliant light of the moon and stars, the Maro Province slept. Directly below him, Enkai spotted a small collection of lights around a massive oak. He took a deep breath to calm his heart which was racing from a cocktail of excitement and nervousness. Someone squeezing his left hand startled him. He looked over to see Nin giving him a reassuring smile. For some reason, her eyes shone with excitement. Checking to his left, he saw Elder Jagan floating beside him as well. She gave him a single nod.

"Simply think where you want to go and the Well will do the rest," Elder Jagan said, shocking Enkai. She had in fact spoken aloud and he'd heard her words with his ears instead of his mind. He glared at her thinking she had continued speaking into his mind for her own amusement or convenience. She found his glare amusing.

"Believe it or not, young Enkai, I do not speak with my mind simply because it annoys you or because it is convenient. There are reasons I must do so, though none of those reasons restrict me in visions of the mind such as this," she said, though her eyes held a hint of laughter.

Dismissing the old she-owl's shenanigans, Enkai willed himself to move toward the largest source of light beneath the tree. The largest building in the settlement. This was the Du Patriarch's home. The same place where he'd discovered he was Forsaken so many years ago. As he reached the door he paused, all around him the Du encampment was quiet except for inside the house. He heard voices through the thin wood. Steeling himself, he pushed forward and passed through the door like a specter.

The interior was well lit. Four men sat around a small table drinking liquor from saucer-like cups as they spoke. Enkai recognized three of the four men. Sitting directly across from the door, the Du Patriarch looked to have aged several decades since last Enkai saw him. To his left, Ba Ren sat having a conversation with the man sitting across from him whom Enkai did not recognize. He was bulkier than any of the other men present, so much so that he could have given Enkai's father a run for his money. Light-colored furs matching his tan-colored hair were draped over his shoulders despite the summer heat. The last man sat across from the Du Patriarch with his back to Enkai which meant Enkai couldn't see his face. As fate would have it, he didn't need to see the man's face to recognize him.

His grandfather, much like the Patriarch, had not aged well since the last time Enkai had seen him. His hair once a knot of smooth gray hair tied up neatly behind his head hung loosely about his shoulders, thin and wispy. He wore the decorated robes of a clan elder, but the color was faded as if he hadn't been caring for them properly. Shockingly, his back and shoulders were also hunched as if bent by old age. For other elders, such a posture would simply mean they had reached the age where their bodies began to wane, but for Du Makai, it meant something different. His grandfather believed in putting the best image of oneself forward at any given time. He would say "putting forward the perception of strength is just as important as being strong." Seeing him sitting there slouching, Enkai's heart ached. The Patriarch spoke breaking him from his reverie.

"So, Makai, what say you?"

His grandfather swayed slightly and grabbed the yellow wooden jug holding the liquor. He poured a generous helping into his cup and drained the liquid in one go as the other three watched. Enkai noticed the Patriarch and Ba Ren exchanged a meaningful look that went unnoticed by the stranger.

"Why does it matter what I think, hm, *Patriarch*?" Makai said glaring at the assembled men. He infused "patriarch" with such venom that Enkai winced. It sounded nothing like the grandfather he knew who would've tanned his hide for showing any form of disrespect. "If you wanted my say, you would've asked when it truly mattered. Besides, it was your patriarchal wisdom that led us here, so that should be enough to sway the clan warriors without my input. No need to call me here in the middle of the night. It's your business if you want to marry your granddaughter off to the Hu brat. We both know our feud with the Hu clan is nothing but a farce to keep the hot-bloods satisfied."

The Du Patriarch smiled, though Enkai could tell from the strained set of his face that he didn't appreciate his grandfather's words. However, what Enkai found interesting was the content of his grandfather's response to the Patriarch. Shana was getting married to someone in the Hu clan? Beyond doubt, such a union would cause unrest among both clans. How much had changed since he left?

He took another look at the unfamiliar man. During his life in the Maro Province, he had never seen a member of the Hu clan since they'd never come to Du settlements for trade. The man's demeanor marked him as someone of importance. He had a sleeve of tattoos on his left arm along with two silver bracelets on each wrist. His face was average looking while his robes beneath the furs were gray with brown accents. Enkai recognized the colors. The stranger was from the Hu clan. Enkai suddenly understood why this meeting was being held in the middle of the night. Most of the clan would be none the wiser.

The stranger turned to Makai and flashed a smile. He said, "Honored Elder Makai, I am told you have been in mourning since you lost your family some years ago. A great shame what happened. You have my condolences. However, I think what happened to the late Du Kai should serve as a lesson to us all. We are stronger together and we must not let our hubris lead us down an unwise path."

"Watch your tongue, Hu pup. Do not speak as if you knew my son. You are not half the divine artist he was," Makai snapped. Enkai flinched, while the Du Patriarch and Ba Ren looked uncomfortable. Conversely, the Hu clansman maintained his smile though something sinister flashed through his eyes.

"With all due respect, your son is dead, most assuredly torn to pieces by the great beasts of the Forbidden Forest during a fool's errand that claimed not only his life but those of the late Lin Chun and your own grandson. Why the man would take a child into the Forbidden Forest is beyond me, but I'm sure he had his reasons." The man shrugged, his expression filled with mock sadness. "While I am sure he was a great warrior, your clan must go on in his absence. As an elder, I believe it is your duty to help shepherd a brighter future for those that will live on after you."

Ba Ren physically cringed as the man spoke and the Patriarch looked displeased but neither said a word. His grandfather was still and Enkai feared he would strike the stranger. After a moment, Makai took a deep breath in much the same way he had taught Kai who in turn had taught Enkai. Without realizing it, Enkai mirrored the motion. He was furious with the Hu clansmen. Even though he had more reason than anyone to disparage his father, he couldn't bring himself to do so. The man's disrespectful tone needed correction.

After exhaling, Makai turned to the Du Patriarch. When he spoke, his voice was full of weariness and disinterest, "I give my approval. I will talk to the warriors after you make your announcement."

The Patriarch nodded while Ba Ren showed visible relief. Enkai watched his grandfather get to his feet and excuse himself before pushing his way into the night. All the while, the Hu clansman continued to smile. Enkai wanted to punch him in the face.

He contemplated following his grandfather but decided against it. The look on his grandfather's face as he left broke Enkai's heart. He didn't like seeing his grandfather in such a sad state and he had no desire to see more. With a heavy heart, he turned to Elder Jagan. "I'm ready to go, but I have one more place I want to see before we move on."

Elder Jagan tilted her head to the side then responded, "Very well, simply picture it in your mind."

Enkai nodded. The Hu clansman had said that Lin Chun was dead. He didn't believe that for a second. It made no sense. Not only was she powerful enough to kill his father, but she was also an expert guide and could mask herself from any great beast that might pose a threat to her. It simply wasn't possible that she had died in the Forbidden Forest. He needed to check the Lin clan settlement.

He noticed Nin was giving him a curious look as if she had a question she wanted to ask. He could guess what it was. After all, Enkai hadn't told anyone about what had happened to him in the Forbidden Forest and no one had pressed him on the matter. Though he knew he should tell them, he'd never quite worked up the will to relive the experience. He had enough of it in his nightmares. Avoiding her gaze, he focused his mind on their next destination. The Du camp faded away as the Well transitioned.

***

The space around them filled with thick fog blurring out any definition or clarity in their surroundings. Within his mind, Enkai pictured the audience chamber in the Lin clan settlement where he'd first met Lin Chun. Gradually, the audience chamber began to take form. Enkai recognized the silver leaf decorations on the walls and the pattern of the wooden floor.

However, the rest of the chamber was not as he remembered it. In it, there were tables placed in sets of two every ten feet which were covered in various herbs and alchemical tools. Each table was manned by two Lin clansmen at different stages of the alchemical process. At the center of the room where Lin Chun's pallet of furs had been, a large oak desk sat emblazoned with the green and silver colors of the Lin clan. As the chamber materialized, Enkai swept his gaze over the room looking for the woman who had killed his father. While he scanned the faces of every red-haired woman in the room, a voice cut through the general din of people conversing within the room.

"Matriarch, you've returned!" said a young man with ruddy brown hair as he stepped from behind one of the tables nearest to Enkai. His gaze was fixed on a point behind Enkai which sent his heart racing. Steeling himself, he turned around ready to confront his past. Unfortunately, he was met with confusion and disappointment.

When he turned, it wasn't the strange golden eyes of Lin Chun that met him, but the gray eyes of Lin Fa. The man who had called out ran through Enkai and bowed to Lin Fa. She wore the robes of the Lin Matriarch, the very same robes Lin Chun had worn the last time Enkai had seen her. The young man presented a vial of cloudy silver liquid to her with a bright smile. She took the vial from him and asked, "Is this what I think it is?"

"Yes, Matriarch. I've finally succeeded in creating my first Silver Leaf elixir," he answered with a voice full of pride. Lin Fa favored him with a slight smile as she handed the vial back to him. He accepted it with a bowed head.

"Fine work. The elixir has a few flaws, but it is an admirable first effort," she said patting the man on the shoulder. The young man beamed at her and walked back to his table to resume his work. Lin Fa took in the room for a moment before striding confidently to the large desk in the center of the room.

A sinking feeling gripped Enkai as he watched the exchange. Where was Lin Chun? Another careful scan of the room revealed she was not within the audience chamber. His mind raced. Focusing his will, he moved their perspective to the lower floor. One by one he checked each of the rooms on the first floor. Once he had finished, Elder Jagan spoke.

"What are you looking for, young Enkai?"

"The woman who killed my father," he responded without thinking. His words trailed off as he tried to process his next plan of action. Elder Jagan abruptly appeared in front of him.

"Don't fret," she said. "Picture her in your mind. You needn't have an exact image. Simply focus on a few of her defining features and the Well will bring the memory forth to guide the divination."

Enkai did as Elder Jagan instructed. He fell into a pattern of deep breaths in order to center his mind. He pulled forth the image of Lin Chun's strange golden eyes. He remembered the smell of dried flowers and rich earth that had filled his nostrils when he fell asleep in her lap. He recalled her voice telling him stories to help him sleep as they traversed the Forbidden Forest. Gradually, the scenery shifted once more blurring then reforming.

For a moment, *something* began to move at the edges of Enkai's sight like encroaching darkness. Abruptly, a piercing pain spiked through Enkai's mind. He cried out as the pain unraveled his focus. The world projected by the Well of the Dreamer began to spin. He gasped falling to his knees as the pain grew greater threatening to overwhelm him. Taking deep breaths, he struggled to keep himself calm. Within him, he felt his Sin stir as it sensed weakness in his will. As soon as the scarlet anima shifted, the world of the Well collapsed and they were back in Elder Jagan's lair.

All at once, the pain disappeared. Without it, he quickly collected himself forcing his Sin back into a dormant state. Beneath him, the Well of the Dreamer rippled.

Nin placed a hand on his shoulder. Her face bore a mask of barely concealed fear and outright concern. He gave her a half-hearted smile which prompted her to hug him. For the first time since coming under her care, Enkai noticed how similar her smell was to Lin Chun's. He wouldn't have noticed if he had not just intentionally recalled the former Lin Matriarch's scent. Strangely, it didn't bother him.

"Are you alright, En?" Nin asked. Her jade green eyes sparkled in the light as she looked him up and down.

"I'm fine. I don't know what happened."

A few feet away from them, Elder Jagan stood with a fearsome scowl aimed down at the Well. At least, Enkai thought she was scowling. It was hard to tell given he wasn't sure what a scowling owl would look like, but the general disposition of her face didn't seem pleased. He exchanged a look with Nin then shakily got to his feet.

"Elder Jagan, what happened?" he asked. Based on the pain he'd experienced, he figured he must have done something wrong. The she-owl was silent for several moments.

Young Enkai... she said speaking as if she were still formulating her thoughts. He once again heard her words only in his mind. *Is the one you wished to see still among the living?*

"She was when I last saw her," Enkai said with a hint of uncertainty. "It was roughly before I came to Old Omen. Around six summers ago."

Ah, she replied vaguely. Enkai met her gaze, confused. She continued: *I have seen the Well react this way before. Long ago, when the city was still in its prime. Once or twice every decade, a divine artist would come seeking to use the Well of the Dreamer as others did, yet when they activated it, those they were attempting to divine were either dead or too powerful for even the Well to glimpse. The divination failed in every such case causing the Well to backfire on the user. If the user's will was not strong enough, his or her mind collapsed as a result. Thankfully, I was able to deactivate the Well before anything serious happened.*

Enkai shook his head in denial. Lin Chun couldn't be dead. After all, she had killed his father. Du Kai had been the strongest divine artist in the Maro Province as far as Enkai was concerned. While the clan leaders had greater authority, his father's devotion and talent to the divine arts made him their equal and more. If Kai had lived, Enkai had no doubt he would have eventually reached the mythical heights of Gold. His father represented everything a divine artist should strive to be. Yet, Lin Chun had struck the man down with a wave of her hand like one might shoo away a fly. Over the years, Enkai had concluded that Lin Chun must have somehow broken through to Gold. While such a thing was hard to fathom, it had made sense once he'd learned more about alchemy from Nin.

The natural treasures harvested for use in alchemy were potent tools for divine artists and great beasts who sought power. The primary benefit of harvesting and processing natural treasures was their high concentrations of anima. According to Nin, individuals sought these objects in order to strengthen themselves. If the natural treasure had a high concentration of anima compatible with the individual's spirit, they could incorporate its anima into their own to potentially gain years' worth of cultivation in one go. Alchemy allowed those skilled enough to refine some natural treasures and other anima-rich ingredients into elixirs, pills, and other mixtures which increased the potency of the base ingredients manifold.

Since the Lin clan was comprised of alchemists who guarded a trove of natural treasures, it stood to reason that the Lin Matriarch could reach Gold if it was even possible. She could have all the resources funneled to her. Enkai didn't enjoy reaching this conclusion since it meant he would have to reach a level of cultivation equivalent or even beyond that of the clan founders. The thought both scared and excited him.

"She isn't dead," he said to Elder Jagan with all the confidence he could muster. He thought about the former Lin Matriarch. He considered the ease with which she'd killed his father then recalled the purpose of their journey so many years ago, the Sacred Vas tree. Based on what he remembered of the conversations between his father and Lin Chun, the Sacred Vas tree produced an extremely powerful natural treasure. If Lin Chun had consumed the Sacred Vas fruit after killing his father, she would be far more powerful than he could imagine. "She has to be too strong for the Well. I'm pretty sure she's ascended to Gold."

The tingling melody of Elder Jagan's laughter filled his mind. He noticed Nin give him the same curious look she'd had after they saw his grandfather.

"What?" he asked looking from Nin to Elder Jagan. Nin glanced uncertainly between Enkai and the she-owl which prompted Enkai to ask once more, "What is it?"

Young Enkai, do you believe that Gold is the pinnacle of the divine arts? Elder Jagan asked. Her third eye flickered left and right as if it was following something unseen. For some reason, he felt nervous. Elder Onki had asked something similar before he had instructed Enkai to have Elder Jagan show him the Apostles of the Green Mother. His chest tightened as his nerves went on edge.

"I'm not sure but our great ancestors, the clan founders, were Gold. They fought in the Fall of Heaven which ravaged the entire world more than a thousand years ago," he said frowning. Filled with uncertainty, he added, "Why do you ask, Elder?"

Perhaps it is best that I show you, Young Enkai. Prepare yourself. Before Enkai could ask what he should prepare himself for, the chamber filled with fog once more as the Well of the Dreamer activated.S

Chapter 14

Enkai heard the wildlife first. Next, the landscape took form materializing as a vast jungle surrounding them on all sides. All around them, life thrived. Unlike the quiet forest he called home, the jungle teemed with activity and noise. Everywhere he looked, densely packed wildlife and plant life created a painting of the unrestrained diversity that illustrated the majesty of mother nature.

Several feet from where Enkai floated, a hive of insects flitted about an enormous tree. They had shining carapaces with great iridescent wings which were just a blur as they moved through the air. Taking a closer look, he realized the entire tree was its own ecosystem. Insects of all types crawled or flew around the tree landing either on the tree's large fleshy leaves or the plants sprouting from its trunk and roots. Plants of many different shapes and sizes grew from the trunk of the tree. They ranged from small flowers at the base of the tree to huge fleshy bulbs that looked like fruit higher on the tree, which snapped up any insects that made contact with them. High above in the tree branches, Enkai heard the call of birds, monkeys, and even a snake-like hiss, though he couldn't see most of the creatures making the noises. The beasts and plants he saw were far more colorful than any he had seen within the Forbidden Forest. The flowers and fleshy bulbs were brightly colored while the birds and even a monkey he glimpsed had vivid red, blue, and orange patterns.

"Beautiful isn't it?" Elder Jagan said wistfully. Both Nin and Enkai exchanged wide-eyed looks. Nin looked as amazed as Enkai did, perhaps, even more so.

"This is like an alchemist's paradise…," she whispered.

"You will find no greater diversity of life, plant, beast, or otherwise that is for certain. This entire jungle exists because of the Green Mother who sleeps at its center. This is her domain," Elder Jagan explained. They began to move upward as she continued, "However, we have not come here to admire the majesty of the Kazoan Jungle. Young Enkai, pay close attention."

As they crested the treetops, Enkai balked at the vastness of the jungle around him. It easily rivaled the scope of Forbidden Forest which he had glimpsed several times while standing high on Old Omen. In the distance, something truly gargantuan moved. The size of the creature beggared belief. It towered over even the tallest of the trees which stood at hundreds of feet. Enkai was horrified when he realized they were moving closer to the behemoth. Nin gave his hand a squeeze of solidarity. Her ears were flattened against her head showing she too had no wish to get any closer. The creature released a bone-rattling roar which only increased their anxiety.

When they were close enough to be dwarfed by the behemoth's shadow, a man's voice cut through the thunderous din created as the creature moved.

"Be at peace, Favored of the Mother. I have come to shepherd you back on your way."

The words echoed through Enkai's very soul. He quaked at the voice's power, confused and afraid. It was like he was hearing a god of old speak the tongue of man. A moment later, dream anima radiated from Elder Jagan and surrounded them like a protective blanket of cool mist. The pressure on his spirit dulled significantly. Once he'd collected himself, he looked for the source of the voice. Who could speak with such power? His eyes roamed the surroundings.

Because they were close, Enkai could see the creature's face which was like a mountainside of thick brown hide. Two massive eyes with horizontal pupils rested beneath a thick ridge of bone. A long thick trunk extended from the place Enkai expected to see a nose. The trunk swayed back and forth as the creature moved knocking over enormous trees as if they weren't there. On either side of its trunk, fearsome tusks of ivory protruded from the corners of the creature's jaw curling into wicked points. Atop one of these tusks, there was a man.

In many ways, he was unremarkable. He had a somewhat impressive physique that spoke to a life lived outdoors. He wore almost nothing except a torn pair of hide leggings that stopped just above his knees. His entire body was covered in dirt while twigs and leaves littered his unkempt hair. He was of average height and probably would be considered unattractive by most. In his right hand, he held a spear made of moss-covered gray wood with a bone-like spearhead. Despite his looks, the man radiated an essence of absolute confidence.

"Let us walk, Favored. You have fallen many days behind the herd, but I will see you to them," the man said. The behemoth's movements became calmer as it continued to move forward. It roared shaking the earth yet somehow Enkai could tell the creature was happy. The man jumped from the tusk to the top of the creature's head in a single bound. Once atop the creature's head, he laughed and pointed his spear to the east.

"Kartuk, Apostle in service to the Green Mother and master of the Kazoan Spear," Elder Jagan said plainly. "He shepherds the Kazoan Behemoths, titanic great beasts. If every member of your five clans reached Gold, they wouldn't even be able to scratch its hide. Kartuk himself could decimate them with barely a thought."

Enkai could only stare dumbly at the retreating form of the hulking great beast as he tried to process her words. Before he could even begin comprehending the truth of what he just witnessed, their surroundings blurred and shifted once more.

***

Dark smoke filled the air. Below them, the maw of a massive volcano yawned open threatening to consume the sky. Unlike Old Omen, this volcano brimmed with life. Waves of heat rolled from its mouth distorting Enkai's vision. He thanked the ancestors that he was not really being subjected to the heat of this leviathan volcano. He knew with absolute certainty that he would not survive such conditions. Looking out below the mouth, Enkai saw a distorted image of a vast jungle and he assumed that they were still within the Kazoan Jungle.

They moved down into the volcano's roiling maw which prompted Nin to squeeze Enkai's hand once again. However, Enkai felt no anxiety this time. Though overwhelmed, his curiosity had taken control. The smoke, ash, and heatwaves became so thick that seeing anything proved difficult, yet Elder Jagan continued to guide them downward.

They stopped a few feet above the waiting pool of liquid fire. As they hit the pool, they continued moving across the flow toward the center. Although he knew the lava could do no harm to him, he still had to suppress a shiver when a piece of rock tumbled into the lava only to be quickly consumed like ice in boiling water. In the time they'd glided across the lava, Enkai noticed dozens of small orange lights floating lazily through the air.

Those must be fire wisps, he thought. When they stopped, he looked to Elder Jagan for direction. She peered into the fumes directly in front of them. Following her gaze, Enkai struggled to perceive anything through the veil of ash and smoke, but after allowing his eyes to focus, he finally saw her.

A woman sat cross-legged on the bubbling pool of lava as one would sit on a stone floor. She was covered in ash though Enkai did glimpse simple red tattoos all over her body. He was able to see them because unlike Kartuk she was completely nude which might have made Enkai turn away if he weren't still trying to process the fact that she was meditating on a pool of liquid fire. To his left, Elder Jagan spoke.

"Watch and listen, Young Enkai."

With a single uncertain glance at Elder Jagan, Enkai focused his senses. He steadied his breathing into a slow rhythm tuning out as much as he could while honing in on the meditating woman. Gradually, he began to hear it.

She had an agonizingly slow pattern to her breathing. He watched her chest rise and fall slightly with each breath. She was as still as a statue, but something strange stood out to Enkai. He listened to her breath and to the ambient turmoil of the volcano. For several minutes, he concentrated on the flow of sound around him taking care to watch her as he did. Eventually, he realized what Elder Jagan wanted to show him.

Each time the woman inhaled, the heat and smoke within the volcano settled. When she exhaled, the heat and smoke surged, billowing from the mouth of the volcano. She and the volcano were perfectly matched. Enkai wondered whether it was the volcano that set the pace or the woman.

"Who is she?" he asked, incredulous.

"She has no name, though the great beasts of the Kazoan Jungle call her the Daughter of Fire," Elder Jagan explained. Her third eye fixed on the woman as she resumed her explanation. "She was abandoned as a babe deep in the Kazoan Jungle by one of the many tribes that live on its fringes. She was one of many sacrifices made each year to appease the powerful great beasts who ravage the tribes. No one is sure how she survived, but many believe it was under the watchful eye of the Green Mother. By the age of five, she had already reached the peak of the Gold Realm."

Enkai balked. Elder Jagan had to be lying. This woman had been Gold at the age of five? How could such a thing be possible? Also, what did she mean by "Gold Realm"? He wrestled with these questions while Elder Jagan continued speaking.

"Many divine artists and great beasts come to this volcano because it is a fountain for fire essence. However, the Daughter of Fire was entrusted with this place by the Green Mother and only allows those she deems worthy to use its power for cultivation. Because of this, she has spent her life guarding this volcano against those who seek to take the volcano's power by force. Nations have sent full raiding parties against her, but she has never once yielded. As you can see, her body bears marks of a divine artist forged in the fires of war."

As Elder Jagan finished, Enkai paled as their full weight settled on him. The red markings covering her entire body weren't tattoos – they were scars. The volcano started to blur as Elder Jagan's will shifted them to another location, yet Enkai caught one final glimpse of the woman. She opened her eyes and stared directly at him. In his rational mind, he knew she was not looking at him in truth, but he trembled under her gaze. Like an erupting volcano, her eyes were simultaneously beautiful and terrifying.

***

When the world took form once more, they viewed a landscape at the edge of the Kazoan Jungle. Enkai surveyed the terrain which changed into a desert with red sand as the jungle came to an end. Nonetheless, the environment was not what drew his eye.

Stretched out across the desert, a warzone raged in full force. Men fought against beasts in a savage battle with no foreseeable end. On one side, men called forth massive roots and vines from the sand to bind their enemies as others impaled the trapped beasts with massive spears. On the other side, monstrous beasts drawn from some kind of nightmarish hellscape threw themselves at the men. They drifted down to the edge of the forest. Enkai was thankful they didn't move closer to the monsters, as he had no wish to get a closer look at those creatures.

"Do they frighten you, young Enkai?" asked Elder Jagan startling him. He wondered if she could read his mind even in the dreamscape of the Well, but then he realized she didn't need to. He was trembling uncontrollably. Too terrified to put up a front, Enkai nodded. After being unnerved by the Daughter of Fire, he hadn't been mentally prepared to see the monstrosities pouring over the red sand dunes. The worst part was the noise. The creatures screeched, screamed, yowled, roared, and howled with a mad ferocity he couldn't comprehend. They battled with no regard for their own lives as if driven by some outside source to violent madness. "Look closely, young Enkai. Before you lies the border where the Kazoan Jungle meets the Sin Wastes. Those creatures are demons, divine artists and great beasts corrupted and twisted by Sin. Day in and day out they throw themselves at the border of the Kazoan Jungle seeking to spread their corruption into its fertile soil."

"Is ... is that what's going to happen to me?" Enkai asked. All of a sudden, his Sin which he had viewed as more of an inconvenience felt like a fresh brand upon his spirit. The familiar cords of mysterious red anima he was constantly warned about were waiting for his will to falter so it could warp him beyond all recognition.

"As a Deviant, you would not become a demon if you succumbed to your Sin," she answered causing a wave of relief to wash over Enkai. Unfortunately for him, it was not long-lasting. "Your fate would be much worse."

His heart nearly stopped. Next to him, Nin grabbed hold of his arm. Startled by the sudden touch, he flinched away from her. She held firm and used one hand to bring his face to hers. Looking into her jade eyes, Enkai saw no worry in them only resolve.

"That will never happen to you, En," she declared.

"But I ..."

"It won't happen, En. I promise. I won't let it," Nin said firmly pulling him into a hug. Gradually, his body stopped trembling and his breathing which had become ragged as his fear had risen calmed. Elder Jagan who watched this entire display quietly nodded approvingly.

"It is good that you see the true face of the cursed anima within you. Some of the greatest divine artists in history have fallen prey to their own hubris when dealing with Sin," the ancient owl said. "However, take heart in knowing you are not doomed, young Enkai. Deviants are unique among those corrupted by Sin. You can learn to control the Sin within your spirit through the strengthening of your will."

She looked out at the battle raging below. With one wing, she pointed to a nearby treetop and said, "Look there."

On the highest of branches, a man stood, surveying the battlefield. In his hands, he held a bow as tall as he was. He had no arrows with him, but as Enkai watched an arrow of crackling green energy formed in his hand. He nocked the arrow with practiced ease. As he pulled the bowstring taut, bands of scarlet anima coiled around the arm holding the bowstring. Enkai's eye widened. He recognized that anima. It was Sin. The moment the Sin made contact with the arrow, there was a flash as the man fired.

Enkai tried to follow the arrow's flight but it was too fast. He only knew it hit its target when a thunderous eruption of power exploded in a distant part of the battlefield. Straining his eyes, he saw a crater blasted into the sand. Around the crater, the bodies of dozens of demons lay still in death. For one long moment, Enkai looked from the crater to the man in shock. Meanwhile, the man had already gone back to surveying the battlefield.

While Enkai was gawking, the man repeated the process destroying a hulking demon comprised of fire and darkness. Incredulous, Enkai looked to Elder Jagan for an explanation. She smiled and said, "To those who know of his post, he is called Purifier. Alone he guards the border of the Kazoan Forest protecting it from the grips of Sin. For nearly three decades, he has manned this post knowing rest only when he kills enough of the demons to drive them back. In exchange for his service, the Green Mother gifted him the bow he wields crafted from the heartwood of a Kazoan Ancestor Tree."

"Is he ..." Enkai began glancing furtively at the man's arm as the Sin faded.

"A Deviant? Yes," Elder Jagan said answering his unfinished question. His heart sped up a little as he viewed the man in a new light. Could he be that powerful one day? He pondered the possibilities as she continued, "Some Deviants like Purifier wield their Sin to enhance their divine arts yet doing so harbors great risk. Keep that in mind before you start fantasizing, young Enkai."

A thought occurred to him as he contemplated her words. "What do you mean? He guards this place alone? There are hundreds of warriors down there."

Elder Jagan continued to smile as she answered, "I mean what I said, young Enkai. Purifier fights alone. Those you see below are simply an extension of his power and will."

Skeptical, Enkai focused on the warriors fighting the horde of demons. After only a few moments of observation, he had two startling epiphanies. The men below were not men at all. They were extremely detailed wooden puppets and they were all identical in appearance. At first, he'd thought they were all earth divine artists using the same Enhancement technique, but he'd been mistaken. Enkai recalled Elder Onki's puppets and how he had directed them to fight Enkai with only his will. This implication defied reason. He took in Purifier once more. The man appeared weary, though Enkai couldn't tell if it was actual fatigue or simply the set of Purifier's face. Could Purifier truly be controlling hundreds of puppets? Not only was the number ridiculous, the strength of each one boggled Enkai as well. They all displayed superhuman strength, speed, and durability. As if that weren't enough, they were using techniques— something Enkai didn't think was possible. If Purifier wished it, he could conquer the entirety of the Maro Province in a single night and the clans would be powerless to stop him. Enkai immediately felt extremely small like a baby rodent leaving its burrow for the first time only to realize the world is large and full of predators.

"The three individuals I have shown you today are known as the Apostles of the Green Mother. In their own ways, they each serve the Green Mother and protect her domain. Each of them has attained incredible power by dedicating themselves to the divine arts. Think on this, young Enkai. Only by understanding your own ignorance can you truly begin to learn," Elder Jagan said. He got one final look at Purifier before her third eye flashed. Around him, the scenery faded away leaving Purifier to his solitary struggle.

***

The comparatively dull sight of the Well's holding room greeted them as Elder Jagan dismissed its power. The next few hours passed by in a blur. After leaving the Well, his familiar returned to him. The little wisp had gotten slightly larger, but Enkai barely noticed since it retreated directly into his spirit where it went dormant. Although its behavior had been strange since coming to Elder Jagan's domain, Enkai had dismissed it as having to do with the superfluous amount of dream essence in the area.

Back in the main chamber, Elder Jagan spoke to Nin about Enkai becoming her disciple at some point in the future. Before Nin and Enkai left, Elder Jagan said one final thing to him which left him even more at a loss.

Young Enkai, you claimed that perhaps the woman you seek might be too powerful for the Well of the Dreamer. Know this, if she is indeed alive, her power would dwarf even the combined power of the Apostles of the Green Mother.

"Thank you for your wisdom and for allowing me to use the Well, Elder. I will think on what you have shown me," Enkai humbly replied.

Her parting words left him completely dejected. What was he supposed to do? He questioned his earlier assertion that Lin Chun was alive. If she was, it meant she was more powerful than the people he had seen within the Well. Was that even possible? Kartuk, the Daughter of Fire, and Purifier were like the gods who battled each other in the old clan stories of the Fall of Heaven. And to add salt to the wound, if Lin Chun did live still, it was unlikely he would find her in the Maro Province, which meant if he decided to seek her out using his own power, he would have to choose between finding her and returning home.

As Nin led him back home to Old Omen, he fell deeper and deeper into a mire of doubt and frustration. By the time they got back home, night had died giving birth to early morning. Nin said a few words of encouragement along the way as she sensed his turmoil, but they didn't do much to help.

Enkai lay down in his usual spot. For a little while afterward, he thought about his day. A lot of things had happened. Enkai admitted to himself that he didn't understand much of what he'd seen. Before his experience with the Well of the Dreamer, he wasn't sure he could have imagined such power and scale. In the stories of the Fall of Heaven, only the gods wielded the type of power exhibited by the Apostles of the Green Mother. The story of the Fall of Heaven painted the catastrophe of a conflict between the gods. In the face of such divine conflict, the clan founders had been forced to flee the battle to ensure mankind's survival which had led to the formation of the five clans of the Maro Province. However, the Apostles made him doubt the story. Despite their immense power, they seemed human. They were divine artists, if Elder Jagan was to be believed. The implication troubled Enkai just as much as their incredible strength. Had divine artists caused the Fall of Heaven?

He also thought about the world beyond the Forbidden Forest. The people of the Maro Province believed the world was nearly destroyed during the Fall of Heaven. Consequently, though it was never explicitly stated in the stories, most people in the Maro Province believed that the five clans were all that remained of humanity. In fact, some believed the five clans were the chosen people of the gods destined to one day leave the Maro Province and usher in a new age of humanity. That said, his time outside the Maro Province had led him to believe the world was much larger than he could imagine. At the very least, he understood that some of humanity had survived the Fall of Heaven and, by the looks of it, they had advanced further in the divine arts than anyone in the five clans.

Eventually, he closed his eyes and got comfortable in an attempt to sleep; however, he failed for the better part of two hours. His mind refused to let him rest while spinning with all the new information he'd gained as well as the implications such knowledge brought. Ultimately as the sun began to dawn in the sky, he succumbed to the combination of bodily exhaustion and mental fatigue and slipped into a deep sleep.

***

In the fallen city of Somn, Elder Jagan strode down the halls of the Citadel. As she often did when walking the halls, she reflected on the city's former glory. In the time before the Usurper had waged war on the heavens, Somn had been one of the three great cities of the world. Its ruler had opposed the Usurper, so the city was one of the many places to suffer his wrath once he ascended to power. In the current era, no one aside from Jagan even knew its original name.

Unfortunately, the ruler, Jagan's mistress, fell in battle and Jagan survived but was severely injured. The wound in her throat stopped her from speaking as she once had. Thanks to much time spent healing and eventually using Nin's medicines, Jagan had regained some minor vocal capacity. Sadly, the wound went deeper than the flesh. It marred both her body and spirit. Such wounds rarely ever recover completely. Had her mistress been alive, she would have been able to restore Jagan. The old owl often dreamt of her old mistress returning from the dead in order to rebuild what was lost. Sometimes, she almost managed to convince herself that she was dreaming of events to come, but she knew such a thing wasn't possible. She'd witnessed her master's demise with her own eyes. Her body and spirit had been utterly eradicated.

With a heavy heart, she stopped in the chamber that had served as her mistress's private study. The walls were lined with bookshelves containing hundreds of ancient texts both real and illusionary. The tattered remains of an ancient carpet covered the floor of the stone chamber while two crystal chandeliers hung from the ceiling. There had once been three but the third had not withstood the test of time. On the far side of the room opposite the door where Jagan entered, a grand portrait dominated the wall. The portrait depicted a tall woman of regal beauty. As she often did, Jagan gazed sorrowfully at the image of her former mistress. Her beauty and intelligence had been only matched by her mastery over dreams.

Taking one final look, she turned away. Her mistress would have wanted her to keep her sights fixed on the future, not the past. Though her dreams of her mistress were only fanciful wishes, her other dreams had shown her portents of the events to come. For not the first time, she wondered if she should have warned Enkai; however, she had resolved herself years ago to face the consequences of her inaction. *Enjoy the limited time you have left, Young Enkai. You will know little peace in the times to come.*

Chapter 15

Enkai slept through almost all of the next day. He vaguely recalled Jak attempting to wake him up then being chastised by Nin. By the time he finally awoke, the day was already well into the evening. He groggily rose to his feet and glanced around the burrow. He was alone. He went through his morning stretches noting the aches from his left elbow had dulled dramatically. The rest of his body felt good as new. Hopping up and down, he marveled at the effectiveness of Nin's healing medicines. His injuries would have taken at least several weeks to heal naturally, but an hour of treatment from Nin and a good night's rest rendered him almost completely healed.

After completing his wake-up routine, Enkai wandered outside looking for his family. Jak sat nearby the entrance. He was playing with some rocks he'd collected. There was no sign of Brem or Nin, so Enkai walked over to the monkey and took a seat across from him.

"Hey, Jak," Enkai said smiling. Jak looked up from his rocks and favored Enkai with a smile of his own. Enkai pointed at the rocks. "What're you up to?"

"I was just drawing pictures," Jak answered nonchalantly. He glanced down at the dirt where he'd created a triangular arrangement composed of three spirals each with a stone at its center. It looked like a rune to Enkai

"What is it?" He asked.

Jak shrugged scratching his head. "I don't know. I saw it in the cave I told you about."

Oops ... Enkai thought as he remembered the cave he was supposed to have explored with his siblings. Instead, he'd slept the entire day. Thinking back, that was probably the reason Jak had tried to wake him. *I should apologize.*

"Um, sorry for sleeping all day by the way. I know we were supposed to explore the cave together," Enkai said.

"It's OK," Jak replied. "We saw a lot of neat stuff in the cave, like glowing mushrooms and big shiny rocks with pictures on them. The cave wasn't that big, but it did lead somewhere interesting. I actually got a present for you."

Jak's tail flicked to the side grabbing onto a small sack made from the same woven leaf material Nin used to make all her bags. He handed the sack to Enkai. The soft material felt cool against his skin. Enkai had no idea how Nin produced it though he was thankful for it. When he'd first arrived at Old Omen, he had been forced to abandon his Du clan robes which were mostly ruined. In order to make Enkai more comfortable, she had woven a set of robes for him. Inside the sack,

Enkai found a plump oblong fruit with rough orange skin. He recognized it immediately.

"Where did you find an Orlang fruit?" Enkai asked in shock. Orlang fruits were very difficult to find because Orlang Trees only produced a single fruit each year and the trees themselves were very rare. Orlang fruits contained a substantial amount of vital anima which made them prizes for any great beast in the forest that stumbled across one. Oftentimes, powerful great beasts sought Orlang Trees about to bear fruit, claimed the fruit prematurely, and chased away other great beasts. Enkai had only seen one Orlang fruit which had only been obtained because Nin had found the tree early. Due to her connection with Elder Onki, no great beasts were willing to contest her claim even if they could have overpowered her.

"It was outside the cave's exit. We almost didn't see it but since I climbed into one of the trees, I spotted it," Jak answered. He puffed out his chest with pride which earned a laugh from Enkai.

"Wow! That's pretty amazing, Jak," he said patting the yellow furred monkey on the head, and he honestly meant it. The likelihood of a great beast as weak as Jak getting ahold of an Orlang fruit was basically nonexistent. Not only had Jak found one of these rare fruits, but he was also giving it to Enkai. He didn't know what to say, so he just said, "Thanks, Jak. I really mean it."

"No need to thank me," Jak said with a toothy grin. His round blue eyes glimmered with amusement as he added, "It was really Brem's idea to give it to you, but she wanted me to tell you it came from me."

Enkai couldn't suppress his lopsided grin. A warm feeling bubbled up inside him. Despite his constant headbutting with Brem, it made him happy to know the little fox still cared enough to make such a gesture.

"I'll be sure to tell her," he said. Jak went back to drawing in the dirt with rocks while Enkai turned the Orlang fruit over in his hands. In his Spirit-sight, he saw thin wisps of vital essence leaking from it, which represented the fruit's fading lifeforce. Though it was a natural treasure, the fruit would still spoil and the anima contained within would disperse into essence if it wasn't properly preserved. He would have to make sure he gave Nin the fruit next time he saw her. He put the fruit back in the woven leaf sack and asked, "Where is she, by the way? Did she go with Nin to gather herbs?"

"Yeah, Mama asked if I wanted to go, but I stayed so I could give you your gift," Jak said. His arm moved in surprisingly complex motions as he drew five interlocking symbols in the soil. Enkai observed Jak for a little bit. The little monkey concentrated on his drawing for a full minute. He pursed his lips with his tongue sticking out the corner of his mouth. After he'd finished, he leaned back to survey his handiwork. Enkai was very impressed by the detail in the drawing. In a different life, Jak might've made a good runesmith. Apparently satisfied, he glanced at Enkai and said, "By the way, did you have fun last night?"

"Fun isn't the word I'd use, but I'm glad I went anyway," Enkai said as he pushed back a maelstrom of unresolved emotions threatening to resurface. His expression must have betrayed his internal turmoil because Jak spoke up. Or he was just a curious monkey.

"Did something happen?" asked Jak, while his tail flicked back and forth.

"Um," Enkai stuttered, unsure of whether he wanted to talk about it. Jak's big blue eyes peered up at him innocently waiting for his response. Unfortunately, neither Enkai's previous life in the Maro Province nor his training in the divine arts had prepared him with the skills necessary to say no to an adorable younger sibling. It only took a few more moments for him to crack. Sighing, he leaned back on his hands and looked up at the sky.

"You remember how I told you and Brem that my father died in the forest before I came here?" he asked. Jak nodded attentively so he continued, "Well, he didn't die from an accident or anything. He was killed"

"Was it another human?" Jak asked, eyes wide. When he'd told his siblings about his father, he'd been purposely vague about how Kai had died. He knew they'd assumed some sort of beast was responsible, as great beasts killed each other all the time in the Forbidden Forest. It was the natural cycle of life. His family was largely spared such danger because of Elder Onki's protection.

"Yeah …" he replied allowing himself to fall onto his back. Like a torrent, the memories came flooding back. Unlike what had happened previously, he didn't break down immediately because of the memories, but he did feel an overwhelming sadness mixed in with a bit of self-loathing. He hadn't started out hating himself, but it had developed over time as he slowly became convinced his inadequacy was the reason for everything that had happened. If he hadn't been Forsaken, none of it would have happened. His father would still be alive, he would still be in the Maro Province, and his clan would be prospering. He felt even worse after seeing his grandfather who was drowning his grief in alcohol. Before Enkai knew it, his emotions were tumbling through him barely being kept in check even though he was trying to control them. At some point, a hand touched his shoulder.

"It's okay, you don't have to talk about it if you don't want to," Jak said. His concern was plain to see. Inadvertently, Enkai reached up to wipe away the tears that had started to fall. They always did when he got caught up in his memories. While he liked to think he had come to terms with his past, he had really only succeeded in suppressing the memories and ignoring the emotions. Something his father once said to him echoed through his thoughts.

"Stop crying, boy. You must control your emotions, not be driven by them. You must discipline your mind or you will never truly master your spirit. Remember that the next time you choose to weep instead of act."

"I'm fine," he said choking back a bit of shame. He managed a half-smile, but Jak looked unconvinced. Then, Jak's face lit up as if hit with sudden inspiration.

He sighed heavily then flopped down on his back like a ragdoll with a dejected look. He turned to Enkai and said, "I'm fine ..."

His words trailed off and his face scrunched up as if he was going to cry. Despite his melancholy, Enkai laughed hard and Jak joined in.

"Okay, I get it. I was a little dramatic," Enkai chuckled as their laughter died down.

"A little?" Jak asked with mock outrage. Next, his face adopted a look of pure innocence mixed with clear distress. "I'm like four, En. How am I supposed to react to that?"

"Jak, this is your sixth summer," Enkai said raising his eyebrow. Jak's age was easy to remember since he had been a fresh newborn when Enkai had first arrived at Old Omen.

No, I'm—" Jak said, but stopped mid-retort. With a befuddled and slightly embarrassed expression, he started counting with his fingers which prompted Enkai to burst into laughter once again. He didn't even bother mentioning that his siblings aged differently because they were great beasts. According to Nin both Jak and Brem were well into adolescence in terms of physical maturity.

"You know I've never really talked about what happened," he said after he stopped laughing. Jak gave him a nod of encouragement. He sighed then added, "I haven't even told Nin or Elder Onki. I'm not even sure why I haven't told them or why I keep avoiding it."

"You can always start with me since I'm too young and naive to ask uncomfortable questions," Jak said. Enkai snorted despite himself, and without thinking, he affectionately tousled Jak's furry head. The monkey favored him with an earnest look saying, "I promise I'll keep it secret."

Enkai knew he had to tell someone eventually. After all, his current strategy of keeping it all bottled up was becoming more difficult day by day. On an impulse, he decided to tell Jak the entire story. Maybe it was because Jak was so unassuming and obviously innocent, but he found it fairly easy to open up to his little brother. Once he started talking, the words just came out one after another painting his story from the horrible moment when the Awakening Orb didn't respond during the Ritual to waking up in Elder Onki's lair. Part of him felt like there was something missing while he told the story. The vision of his father dying was strange, almost as if it wasn't from his perspective, but he'd never doubted its validity. Besides, his viewing of the Du clan confirmed his belief in the vision. By the end of his tale, he felt a little bit lighter.

They both were quiet for a long time afterward which was fine with Enkai. Jak looked perplexed though Enkai couldn't tell if his brother was confused or just thinking. While enjoying the quiet, Enkai relaxed. He thanked the ancestors that his Sin hadn't felt the need to rear its ugly head during his retelling. It was odd, but Enkai didn't want to question a good thing. Soon, he felt the tension that was bound up throughout his body bleed away. The relief was so great that his body felt lighter. Eventually, Jak collected his thoughts enough to ask a question.

"If he really did that to you, how come you always talk about how great he was?" Jak asked which confirmed that his earlier look had been one of confusion. "All the stories you've told us about him made him sound like some kind of hero."

Enkai nodded. He understood Jak's confusion intimately because he felt it every time he thought about his father. He simultaneously hated, loved, and idolized Kai. Despite everything that had happened, he couldn't just throw away all the feelings he'd developed as a small child. He also had no idea why his father had chosen to sacrifice him, however, he had become convinced his father had felt it was for the good of the Du clan. No matter how despicable Kai's actions were, Enkai could not bring himself to disparage his father's honor. Kai had lived his life dedicated to his principles and the divine arts. Of course, he knew the possibility existed that his father compromised his principles just for the power of the Sacred Vas fruit, yet, perhaps for his own sake, Enkai didn't believe that was the case.

Meeting Jak's gaze, he said, "He was my hero. In a lot of ways, I think he still is. I just wish I knew why they did it."

"Is that why you want to find the dream lady?"

Enkai honestly wasn't sure how he felt about Lin Chun. Already comfortable speaking to Jak, he simply vocalized his thoughts as they came. "At first, I just wanted to find her and get revenge because she'd killed my father. Even after what he did, I felt it was my job as his son. Eventually though, I was glad that she'd killed him because he'd betrayed me." He paused to look up at the clouds that trailed lazily through the darkening evening sky. "Now though ... I just want to know *why*, because I feel like there is something I'm missing. I don't believe either of them did what they did for power or specifically to hurt me."

Jak hopped up onto his chest while he was lying on the ground and looked down at him. "So, are you gonna go find her?"

"No idea. I have no idea where she is. Elder Jagan says she is either dead or really powerful — way more powerful than anyone I've ever seen."

"Stronger than Elder Onki?" Jak asked, eyes wide.

"Maybe …?"

They sat in silence for a few minutes. Enkai noted that he barely noticed Jak's weight on his chest though he attributed it to the monkey being less than half his size. Finally, Jak seemed to have an idea as he leapt off Enkai's chest.

"If you go find her, I'll back you up. Even if she is strong, we can take her together," Jak said with an infectious smile.

"It might be a little harder than that. We aren't exactly super powerful," Enkai pointed out which elicited a thoughtful expression from Jak. Then, he shrugged.

"Brem'll come too! No way the three of us can lose! We'll be unstoppable!" he gibbered practically bouncing up and down in excitement. Enkai couldn't stop himself from laughing.

"Alright, Jak. Sounds like a plan but let's train a little before we go," he said.

Chapter 16

Lin Chun flinched as a massive tendril swept through the air only a few feet away from her. It wasn't the tendril itself that prompted her reaction, as she had long since grown accustomed to those horrible black masses. No, it was the cacophony of sonic booms created by the larger tendrils as they lashed through the air that sent her heart racing. From behind her, a slender hand covered by a translucent purple glove grasped her shoulder and held her steady. Chun composed herself for the task to come.

"I am fine, mother," she said. The hand left her shoulder and Evaniel strode forward. As she passed, Evaniel favored her with a warm smile which filled Chun with confidence. Several years ago, she had learned the true nature of the guardian spirit called the Great Mother that had watched over every woman in her direct family line since the founding of the five clans. Not even in her wildest dreams could she have predicted the true power wielded by Evaniel. Focusing her attention on the anomaly, Chun asked, "Shall I begin the sequence?"

Evaniel paused a moment and considered her question. Below them, a world of metal and might burned in the ruination of war. In the center of chaos, an anomaly wreaked havoc. Men in metal suits fired light and heat at each other while skyships rained death from above. These extraordinary sights were among many Evaniel had shown Chun, yet they hadn't come to this world for her to marvel at its strangeness. Looking down at the doomed world with a hauntingly forlorn gaze, Evaniel spoke, "You may begin."

Chun initialized the sequence imprinted on her spirit. Power radiated from her and enveloped the apocalyptic landscape in a web of silver light. When Chun sensed her influence over the entirety of the small world, she initiated the next phase. Little by little, time began to release its hold on reality. Blasts of fire and light slowed to a halt as they shot through the air. Men and women froze in the midst of heated combat. The two women floated in silence over a landscape frozen on the brink of ruin.

"These moments never cease to inspire me," Evaniel said. Her voice was soft like a whisper even in the silence of a world frozen in time. Chun felt the tiniest pulse of Evaniel's vast spirit and, all of a sudden, the pair stood along the battlements of a bastion whose occupants were locked in the moment of their final stand. Metal warriors stood on the battlements facing a seemingly endless wave of fighters wielding far less advanced armaments. Despite being better armed, Chun could tell from a glance that the warriors holding the bastion were on their last legs. Their enemy outnumbered them, one hundred to one, and many bore signs of injury. At the edge of the fortification, a commander in a dented metal suit was frozen in place, an ax with a blade of fire raised above his head. Like a beacon of hope, he stood atop the wall, a shout half-formed on his lips as every eye in the bastion looked to him. Evaniel stepped over to the man and surveyed the warzone that stretched as far as the naked eye could see.

"These are the moments in which dreams flourish or fade. When hope and despair struggle for dominance amidst the winds of change, which will prevail?" Stepping lightly onto the air, Evaniel reached out her hand to touch the side of the commander's face. Chun sensed a distant ache from the spiritual connection with her mother. "At times, the victor can be determined through the actions of just one soul."

Though she wanted to respond as she sensed the dull echoes of pain in her mother's spirit, she could not. All her power along with the majority of her will was focused on maintaining the stasis. While she liked to think of herself as the same person who'd led the Lin clan, she couldn't deny that much had changed in the time since.

After agreeing to aid Evaniel, they had stepped into a realm of vast emptiness where worlds and stars were born. According to Evaniel, they walked within the Transcendent Realm, the domain of those who governed all worlds. While she still didn't know the entire story, Chun had learned that the Fall of Heaven had originated in the Transcendent Realm when two factions had waged war against each other. Much of her knowledge was inferred from her interactions with the Great Mother. The why of the matter was still a mystery to Chun since Evaniel shared very little information about those events. That said, she was certain of one thing: Evaniel had been on the losing side.

Moreover, Chun had grown much more powerful since their departure from Genesis. Though she couldn't hold a candle to her mother, the depths of power she wielded stretched far beyond anything she could've imagined before leaving the Maro Province. The only reason she could achieve such breakneck advancement was Evaniel's vast knowledge and power. Her mother's spirit was like an unending well of power for her to cultivate and she knew exactly what Chun needed to do in order to advance spirit and refine her Silver Leaf anima. Nevertheless, Evaniel's tutelage had not been spurred by generosity or motherly love. Without Chun to place the area in stasis, her mother would have been unable to do her part. Speaking of which, Chun grunted as a polite way of telling her mother to hurry up. With her level of ability, she couldn't maintain the stasis for long.

Looking back, Evaniel gave Chun an apologetic look. Space moved around them once more and they stood at the edge of the anomaly. Spirals of flame and explosions dotted the area around them. Several dozen cylindrical metal objects with tails of flame sat locked in the air. Evaniel approached the anomaly.

For the second time since leaving Genesis, Chun felt dread creeping into her heart. Anomalies sucked all the life out of the environment around them. Unnatural stillness pervaded the air around each one, no matter how large or small. Even in the Transcendent Realm in which she'd glimpsed foreign worlds and strange beings, nothing had evoked the same soul-deep terror in her as anomalies did. This was the second one she had seen. The first, nearly a year prior, had been much smaller and was meant to test Chun's ability. Currently, they were testing her capabilities on a larger target.

Spreading her arms wide, Evaniel brought forth her Semblance. Chun felt the tsunami of power rise within the ocean of Evaniel's spirit. A flowing mantle enveloped Evaniel trailing behind her as if caught in an ethereal wind. On her head, a bridal veil hung down to her shoulders framing her alien beauty and crimson hair. Solemnly, Evaniel extended her hands outward like a lover reaching out to a dying partner. The ethereal indigo fabric of her Semblance wrapped around her hands like a second pair of fine gloves. As she touched the sheer black stain of the anomaly's surface, golden sparks erupted from the point of contact. Chun felt her mother's power envelop her spirit to protect it from the coming conflict.

Something lashed out from within the frozen anomaly aiming at Chun; however, it crashed futilely against the protective cocoon around her. Several more attacks followed and each broke against Evaniel's power. Each attack was more powerful and desperate than the last, but all of them were purely spiritual since the stasis prevented the anomaly from attacking physically. None of the attacks broke through.

Chun gritted her teeth and narrowed her focus in order to maintain the stasis. Chun could feel her spirit straining to keep the stasis active. If the anomaly broke free, even her mother might be in danger.

At the same time, Evaniel's power flared up around her as countless fragments broke away from her Semblance and shot toward the anomaly and colliding with it in a spray of golden sparks. For hours the struggle continued as attacks sought to disrupt Chun's focus and Evaniel's Semblance collided with the surface of the anomaly. Each golden spark that touched the Anomaly's surface ignited a brilliant conflagration of purifying energy. The anomaly began to burn away under the pressure of Evaniel's assault.

Ultimately, the anomaly collapsed into itself. A bonfire's worth of golden sparks consumed its remains. When it was done, only the gaping chasm torn into the world's crust by the anomaly remained.

Evaniel stepped back and space folded to bring them amongst the stars once more. As if throwing off a physical burden, Chun released the stasis and sagged as exhaustion tore through her. She started the breathing exercise Evaniel had taught her for cultivation in order to steady herself. She balled her hands into fists to stop them from trembling, and Evaniel gave her a knowing smile.

"Very well done, dear daughter. How do you feel?" Evaniel asked placing a steadying hand on Chun's shoulder.

Swallowing her pride, she answered, "Exhausted. I'm not sure how much longer I could have held it." Though she wanted to put up a front and claim she was fine, she knew anything other than the truth would only lead to trouble. Evaniel cupped her face with one hand and brought it to mere inches from her own. Chun tried her hardest not to be transfixed by her mother's strange beauty — her features while still human were almost unnatural. It was as if someone had taken an already stunning woman and corrected every imperfection. The result was surreal.

"I'm not surprised. Handling a sequence of that size will take time to master," she said as her eyes peered into Chun's own in search of any potential irregularities. She released Chun seemingly satisfied there was nothing amiss, then added, "If ever you feel too taxed, tell me immediately. I already ask far too much of you."

"I agreed to perform this knowing the risks, mother," Chun replied. Before attempting to purify their first anomaly almost a year ago, Evaniel had given Chun the option of waiting until she was more powerful. She had shown Chun the anomaly which at the time had paralyzed her with fear. However, Chun had grown much in the years leading up to that point. After a few days, she overcame her terror. Evaniel's strength played a large part in bolstering her confidence. Although she looked human, Chun had grown increasingly convinced that Evaniel was some sort of goddess. Therefore, so long as Evaniel was with her, she could find the courage to do anything. With a weary grin, she admitted, "Honestly, I wish I could do more. I know I'm balancing on a knife's edge, but I want to help you in any way I can."

"You have always been such a sweet girl," Evaniel said brushing a stray hair from Chun's face as a comet streaked across the star-strewn darkness. Her eyes shone as she turned to gaze out into the sea of stars. When she next spoke, it was barely a whisper. Chun almost didn't hear her, but she felt the deep gratitude through their entwined souls. "Thank you."

***

Sometime later, they rested on the surface of a small moon orbiting the planet they had just saved. The dusty terrain of the lunar body shone with a strange silver luminescence that radiated from strange metal obelisks. One such obelisk towered over the pair while Chun waited patiently for her mother to scan nearby space for more anomalies. Though they had successfully purified two world-ending phenomena, their work was only just beginning.

Chun watched the star-filled void before her with pensive eyes. The day they'd left, Chun had put her priorities in order, so the clan wouldn't be left in chaos when she inevitably didn't return. Despite that, sometimes her thoughts drifted to the family she had left behind. Her hands played with the elaborate fabric of the matriarchal robes she'd retrieved from Evaniel after leaving Genesis. They were the only reminder she had of her old life. For that very reason, Evaniel had suggested abandoning them multiple times. They represented a position she had long since abandoned and they did little other than distract her with memories of her old life and trivial questions. How was her daughter, Fa, faring as Matriarch? Without the oversight of the Great Mother to advise her, would the Lin clan suffer? Would the five clans begin to quarrel without Evaniel's shadow influence keeping the peace? Could the Maro Province handle such conflict? Ultimately, these questions mattered little in the grand scheme of things. She knew that now. Her current role in aiding

Evaniel was much more important than anything else from her past life. Yet, she still couldn't bring herself to abandon her robes.

Sucking in a sharp breath, she shook the thoughts from her mind. Even if she found it difficult to let go of her past, she needed to devote herself to her current mission. If she and Evaniel failed, all, including her family, would share in the consequences.

With her resolve reaffirmed, she focused her mind. Flexing her will, she felt the essence of dreams and vitality around her. Vital essence was razor-thin in her current location but dream essence practically spilled from Evaniel. These two were the building blocks of Silver Leaf anima. She needed to be much more powerful if she truly wished to combat anomalies. While she'd successfully held two in stasis, they'd evolved as they devoured their host world and both the anomalies she'd faced were still in the early stages of development. At her current level of skill, she knew a more developed anomaly would overwhelm her stasis in seconds.

As she cultivated, essence swirled about her creating a whirlwind of power. Her breath slowed until it was nearly still. Within her spirit, she mirrored that stillness. As if it was being funneled, the essence began to trickle into her spirit. With each nearly imperceptible breath, she pulled more and more essence into her anima channels and guided it to her core to create Silver Leaf anima.

Sometime later, her focus shattered as something foreign and intangible pressed itself against her will. She recognized the distinct feel of dream anima, but couldn't quite grasp what was happening. Regardless, she understood the presence as alien.

Mustering her will, she pushed against the invading presence to drive it away. However, no matter what method of attack she used, the presence passed through the grasp of her will. It was like wrestling with a phantom. Moreover, she felt no sense of self from this foreign entity. There was no hostility or even desire, only unrelenting purpose. Sensing the futility of her struggle, she cried out knowing she couldn't keep the presence at bay.

Instantly, a wave of anima flooded her spirit and the presence simply vanished. Rising to her feet, she gazed at the spot where her mother had been standing. Evaniel stood still as stone peering at her with shining eyes welling with power. With practiced efficiency and speed, Evaniel combed through her spirit leaving no aspect unexamined.

Chun silently endured the search as shivers ran through her body and spirit. Such a thorough search of a divine artist's spirit by another was normally unheard of. Though divine artists could sense and examine the spirits of others once they reached Silver, most of those interactions were only at a surface level to ascertain an individual's spiritual strength. In order to go further, one needed to either forcefully probe deeper or be permitted entry and very few divine artists would willingly allow another person such an intimate view of their very soul. That said, Chun trusted Evaniel entirely. She offered no resistance and allowed her mother to sense everything including her fear.

While she had nothing to fear from Evaniel, the foreign presence was another story. During the invasion, she'd sensed the use of dream anima which explained the nature of the attack. For the most part, dream artists had few methods of directly attacking other divine artists. After all, dream essence and anima were naturally insubstantial. However, if a dream artist did launch an attack, it was often a multifaceted endeavor that was as devious as it was dangerous. The fact that she had only sensed one incursion during her struggle terrified her. Who was trying to invade her spirit? How many other aspects of the attack had she failed to sense? If her mother had acted a moment later, what would have happened to her? Evaniel had many enemies and most of them could crush Chun like an insect underfoot.

Evaniel withdrew from Chun's spirit. Anxiously, she waited for her mother to speak, yet Evaniel remained silent. The Great Mother shifted her fearsome gaze into the great expanse of the Transcendent Realm. For several agonizing minutes, she said nothing. Chun scanned her spirit several times during the interim doing her own search for potential abnormalities. She knew it was improbable she would find anything her mother hadn't, but it made her feel better to do something while she waited. Eventually, her mother stirred. A gentle touch alighted on the edges of Chun's mind as Evaniel spoke directly into her thoughts.

Forgive me, dear daughter, for keeping you in the dark. There is nothing amiss with your spirit; however, I wished to know who or what targeted it. Chun suppressed a shiver as her mother spoke. Her voice was like a dark wind full of anger and ill omen despite her calm demeanor.

Did you find the culprit? Chun asked mentally. Given their distance from one another, they could have conversed out loud, but since they were potentially under attack, mental communication was more secure. If they were being watched, there was a much smaller chance they'd be overheard.

Evaniel's lips curled into a haunting smile as she answered. *I did, in fact. They were clever hiding their trail, but I managed to trace them. However, there is a slight problem.*

What? Chun asked not bothering to mask the worry in her voice.

The source is on Genesis.

Chun froze. Genesis? How was that possible? She puzzled over the matter for several moments in stunned silence. Then, a revelation hit here. The Lin clan. Her family must be trying to locate her. Looking to her mother, she asked, *Would it be possible for the Lin clan to find me here?*

Evaniel assumed a pensive look. Knowing her mother, Chun doubted she was even thinking about her question. Evaniel almost certainly knew the answer already and was currently contemplating a completely different possibility.

Stepping across the dusty rock surface of the moon, Evaniel approached Chun. Motes of shining silver dust swirled around her as she walked, though they never sullied her flowing robes. Once again, Chun marveled at the otherworldly presence her mother emitted with so little effort. Evaniel stopped in front of her and extended a hand.

It is possible, though unlikely given how little time has passed on Genesis since we departed. Nonetheless, I believe this warrants investigation. Come, I shall

Shroud us. Do not leave my side while we are there, no matter what. We cannot afford to be detected.

Nodding, Chun reached out and took hold of her mother's hand. Once again, the ethereal veil of her mother's Semblance materialized and expanded until its insubstantial material surrounded them. Goosebumps ran down her arms and back as Evaniel activated her Shroud. As soon as it settled around them, the Semblance disappeared. Even though nothing appeared to have changed, Chun knew better. The effectiveness of a technique directly related to the skill of its user. Inside a Shroud created by the Great Mother, they were undetectable.

Pulling her forward, Evaniel stepped through space crossing unfathomable distances in a single step. They repeated this process multiple times until the pair reached their destination. For the first time in years, Chun was astonished by the size of Genesis. The Maro Province couldn't even be seen from their current perspective. A feeling of insignificance threatened to overwhelm her, but she pushed it aside reminding herself that the fate of thousands of worlds depended on the success of her new mission.

She steeled her resolve and gave Evaniel a quick nod. She was ready. Behind them. the flare of Genesis's sun reflected brilliantly off their crimson hair as they descended to the world they had once called home.

Chapter 17

Later that night, Enkai enjoyed a relaxing meal with his family. After leaving the Orlang fruit with Nin, he departed to Elder Onki's lair through the tunnels of Old Omen, choosing a different route from the previous night. It didn't really matter since there were dozens of ways to get to Elder Onki's lair. Dozens of tunnels ran throughout the whole of Old Omen. When he was younger, Enkai often got lost in them especially after he'd started training with Elder Onki. As a small child, he'd failed miserably at navigating the tunnels by himself; there had been many innocent mishaps then. Aside from getting lost a lot in his first year, he'd accidentally eaten a poisonous fruit, almost frozen to death at least twice, broken most of the bones in his arms and legs during his hikes up the mountain, and nearly drowned in the river near Old Omen.

Enkai chuckled as he jumped from the opening of a tunnel into Elder Onki's lair. Thinking back, he counted himself lucky he hadn't died while acclimatizing to life in the Forbidden Forest. There had certainly been plenty of opportunities. Not to mention, all of the times he'd been driven to his physical limits by Elder Onki. When he thought about those mishaps, he realized how much he'd grown. He had gone from nearly drowning in the river to swimming against the river's current. He knew the layout of Old Omen, inside and out and he hadn't broken a bone in years, not counting Onki's last test. He could even shatter Onki's stone puppets with his bare hands while cycling anima. Though the effort had fractured his bones, how many Lead rank divine artists could match that? He took a bit of pride in his accomplishments.

"Well don't you look pleased with yourself," Elder Onki remarked dryly as his head emerged from his shell. Enkai hopped up onto a small boulder adjacent to the Elder in the middle of the training area and sat down.

"I was just thinking about how I'm not the same as when I first came here," Enkai replied. He tilted his head upward to look Elder Onki in the eye since his master's long snake-like neck towered above him even while he lay on his stomach. The mirth faded from his face as he recalled what he said to his master in their last training session in the light of what he now knew about himself and the power he had seen wielded by the Apostles of the Green Mother. He bowed his head low and pressed his fists together. "I sincerely apologize for my words last night, Elder. I questioned your training yet again and let my frustrations—"

"That isn't necessary, En. I've always told you to speak your mind and I won't begrudge you for doing that. As your master, I should have realized there was a hole in your education," he said cutting Enkai off.

When Enkai kept his head bowed, Onki added, "Stop with your human etiquette. Or better yet, save it for your sister. Maybe you can teach the brat some manners." Enkai smirked. They both knew Nin had attempted to teach Brem basic manners more times than either cared to count. At first, Enkai saw little point in her attempts. What use were manners to a great beast in the wild? However, the hierarchy and sophistication of the Elders of the Forbidden Forest made it clear that great beasts had their own primitive form of etiquette that even the most savage of beasts observed. Perhaps it was because Brem was young, but she seemed to care very little for respect or manners which made most of her interactions with the Elders negative.

"I think we both know that's a lost cause, Elder," Enkai remarked. They both chuckled, but a pregnant pause followed. Onki seemed content to wait for Enkai to speak first. He took a moment more to collect his thoughts then said, "Elder Jagan showed me the Apostles of the Green Mother."

Elder Onki nodded. "And how do you think the warriors of your clan would fare against the Apostles?"

"I don't think they would stand a chance," Enkai said, remembering the unreal power of the Apostles. He suppressed the urge to grit his teeth as he thought about his father. When he continued, his voice was more bitter than he expected, "Even my father doesn't come close to their power."

"Good," Elder Onki said, "before we advance your training, you must fully understand the true depth of your ignorance. Speaking of ignorance, I wish to apologize."

"Huh?" Enkai said, donning a confused look.

"Last night, I condemned your Du clansmen for their ignorance and incompetence in teaching you, yet I made no mention of my own ineptitude. I will be honest with you, En — I am old. I've lived through entire ages, watched empires rise and fall, and said goodbye to old friends again and again. It's left me weary of the world." Onki sighed and readjusted his position. "When you arrived, I lamented that it would mean an end to my peace. I cut myself off from the humans to escape the complications that often follow them. I didn't even want to teach you in the divine arts. It was only as a favor for Nin that I agreed to give you a chance, and even then, I made your test much harder than it should've been for a small human child who'd yet to even hit Lead. I hoped you would fail so I could be done with it."

Enkai listened quietly but his stomach tightened. He kept his eyes trained forward, neither looking directly at Onki nor away from him. His face was a mask.

Onki continued, "When I discovered how much discipline and talent you possessed, I rejoiced. I've had talented disciples in the past and each one needed minimal guidance from me to flourish. Instead of starting from scratch and educating you as I should have for a disciple of your rank, I assumed you knew what you needed to know because it meant less trouble for me. I assumed you understood the basic importance of your cycling, physical training, and setting the foundation of your spirit. However, because of my own negligence, I didn't realize my error, so you have been operating at a disadvantage that could have been crippling had you not brought it to my attention. For someone of my rank and age, such a blunder is inexcusable. I hope you can forgive me, and should you no longer wish to be my disciple, I will understand."

It hurt to hear Onki's words, just like it hurt to admit that even his father, the man he idolized despite his horrible actions, was weak. Briefly, Enkai wanted to scream at Onki, but that gave way to shame at his own inadequacies, then acceptance. Du Kai had been killed by Lin Chun because of his own weakness. If his father were here now, Enkai knew he would chastise him for his feelings. There was no point in wallowing in self-pity or resentment when a light was shone on your shortcomings. One should strive to better oneself in all respects. Only fools choose pride at the cost of personal growth. Enkai wanted to be neither weak nor a fool.

Besides, if Onki was willing to admit he was wrong, Enkai could forgive him. Negligent or not, he owed much to the ancient tortoise.

Enkai rose to his feet. Crossing his arms then sweeping them out to his side, he bowed deeply to the ancient Elder. "Elder Onki, I could ask for no better teacher in the divine arts. My own ignorance far outweighs your mistakes. There is nothing to forgive. Please continue to grant this foolish disciple your wisdom."

"A simple 'yes, I forgive you' would have sufficed, En," Elder Onki said, and after a slightly awkward silence, he cleared his throat and walked over to the center of the training area. "Now that we've gotten that out the way, let us begin."

Enkai lowered himself into a kneeling position with his back straight. He gave Elder Onki his full attention as he began to speak. "Since I'm not sure how flawed your understanding of the divine arts is. I will start with the most fundamental aspects of the divine arts: anima and essence. So, I know where we stand, tell me what you know of them."

Nodding, Enkai answered immediately. It was the first thing young children were taught in the Maro Plain. Even after all these years, the information was still ingrained in him. "Anima and essence are the two energies divine artists and great beasts use to cultivate and perform techniques. Anima is the internal energy that exists within all things. World essence is external energy which has yet to be drawn into a vessel. They have a cyclical relationship. In order to grow stronger and use techniques, you need anima, but the amount of anima any one creature's core can hold is limited. In order to gain more anima, one has to gather essence into one's core where it is converted into anima. However, anima that is released through techniques or other methods such as when an Eidolon fades away becomes essence."

"A rudimentary answer but serviceable nonetheless," the Elder grumbled in response. Enkai bit down the desire to ask what was lacking from his explanation. Instead, he kept his mouth shut and waited for Elder Onki to finish speaking. "Now what do you know of the Realms of Cultivation?"

Enkai pursed his lips as he tried to recall any knowledge pertaining to Onki's question. He recalled Elder Jagan mentioning the Gold Realm while showing him the Daughter of Fire, but he had assumed she was talking about the rank of Gold. Was there more to it? He now knew that there were stages beyond Gold, but he was clueless as to what they might be. After about a minute of fruitless contemplation, Enkai was forced to face facts. Whatever the Realms of Cultivation were, he had no idea. They certainly sounded important which meant that he should know about them. Pointedly ignoring his own feelings of embarrassment, he admitted. "Apologies, but I don't know anything about the Realms of Cultivations. Are they related to cultivation ranks like Lead and Bronze?"

Elder Onki nodded. "Yes, they are. Each of the Realms of Cultivation refers to a different stage of spiritual maturation. The type of training a divine artist should undertake is usually determined by which Realm of Cultivation they are within. The ranks used to measure the strength of one's spirit each fall within one Realm or another."

Curious, Enkai asked, "Which Realm is Lead in?"

Eyes flashing yellow, the black tortoise summoned three humanoid stone puppets in a line. Two of the puppets were basically the same size while the third was larger and more imposing. Out of habit, Enkai activated his Spirit-sight. The puppets had earth essence gathered around them in increasing amounts with the largest puppet having the most.

"Lead, Bronze, and Silver are all within the first Realm otherwise called the Foundation Realm," his mentor explained. As he said each rank, a puppet stepped forward bowing. Unsurprisingly, the largest puppet presented itself as Onki called out Silver which made Enkai realize the puppet was identical to the ones he had fought the previous night. Onki asked, "Can you guess what type of training is most important within the Foundation Realm?"

Ignoring the feeling that he was walking into a trap, Enkai responded, "Since it's called the Foundation Realm, it must be most important to begin by choosing the type of anima you will use for your divine art based on your affinities and learn the techniques using that anima."

Shaking his head in apparent disappointment, Elder Onki looked Enkai in the eye and said, "Therein lies the root of your ignorance, En. In any other Realm, you would be partially correct. However, the spirits of divine artists in the Foundation Realm are still immature. It is within this Realm that one sets the proper foundation for practicing the divine arts. In most human societies, an individual isn't even considered a divine artist or allowed to practice techniques until they break into the Gold Realm. There are many different methods for this process, but they all center around preparing the spirit and conditioning the body. The reason is that anima is affected by the quality of its vessel. Anima that resides in an unsuitable or subpar vessel will worsen in purity and potency — a critical truth for those practicing the divine arts. Thus, the purpose of the Foundation Realm is to create the most ideal vessel for one's anima."

Enkai's chest tightened. Did that mean no one in the Maro Province would be considered a divine artist by the civilizations beyond the Forbidden Forest? For some reason, that notion sat wrong with him. He shook his head clear. He needed to focus on his own growth for now.

"So, all the training you've been having me do was part of my training for the Foundation Realm?" he asked although he suspected he already knew the answer.

"Correct," Elder Onki said confirming Enkai's suspicions. "Since you have an affinity for vital anima, preparing your spirit and conditioning your body was straightforward. The cycling technique I taught was designed specifically to strengthen your anima channels and increase your control over anima within your body. And I created your conditioning workout to maximize the strength, speed, and stamina of the human body."

Enkai couldn't help but think of all the times he had almost died because of Elder Onki's *conditioning*. Thankfully, Nin had been there to put him back together when Onki went too far.

"So, if I've been doing the right thing, how come I'm only Lead?" he asked. Feeling slightly annoyed, Enkai pressed further, "It's been five summers. The Daughter of Fire wasn't even half my age when she reached Gold, so there must be a faster method."

"Oh, so you think you are comparable to the Daughter of Fire, hm?" his master asked raising a stone eyebrow. Despite himself, Enkai blushed. The Daughter of Fire unquestionably had talent far beyond his comprehension. It was a bit silly to compare his progress to hers. Seeing Enkai had no retort, Onki continued, "To answer your question, the reason you haven't advanced yet is that you don't have the anima to do so. Even if a divine artist or great beast practiced the best methods of spiritual preparation and bodily conditioning, they wouldn't advance until they filled their core with anima. Given your progress, we could have advanced your spirit earlier; however, it is best to develop the body and spirit as much as possible while at the Lead stage, since it lessens the strain of advancement. Besides, as far as I am aware there is no rush. Better to move slowly and carefully than to jeopardize your future with impatience."

As Elder Onki finished speaking, a realization dawned on Enkai. The divine artists of the Maro Province held none of these notions as far as he knew. Physical exercise outside of martial combat training was seen as unnecessary because they relied on Enhancement techniques. Even worse, most divine artists Enkai knew within the Du clan used Enhancement techniques during their martial training, so the benefits to their bodies were minimal. Along the same lines, cycling was only used to teach newly attuned children how to control their anima in order to learn techniques. After a child learned their first technique, the practice was all but abandoned. A sinking feeling settled in his stomach as he thought about his old home.

"If someone didn't develop their spirit or condition their body properly in the Foundation Realm, how bad would it be?" he inquired in an attempt to address his creeping suspicions.

Onki gave Enkai a knowing look making it clear he knew exactly why Enkai was asking. "It would entirely depend on how far the divine artist pushed themselves. The effects of failing to condition one's body wouldn't become apparent until the individual attempted to advance beyond the Gold Realm, so you needn't worry about that. However, if one doesn't prepare one's spirit within the

Foundation Realm when it is most malleable, it becomes exceedingly difficult to do so later and will undeniably lead to bottlenecks."

Enkai fidgeted a bit to gain Elder Onki's attention which caused his master to pause. Seizing the opportunity, Enkai asked, "What's a bottleneck?"

Elder Onki raised a rocky moss-covered ridge that looked to Enkai like an eyebrow. Then chuckled again, "Right. I shouldn't assume you know these things. If you have a question, feel free to speak up. I would prefer you to interrupt me now rather than make a fool of yourself due to ignorance later. A bottleneck is when a divine artist or beast hits a wall, figuratively, in their advancement through the divine arts. Most beasts and humans experience a bottleneck at some stage of their cultivation, however, not all are able to overcome it. Many are stuck for the rest of their lives unable to advance. Bottlenecks are usually the result of failing to establish a firm foundation or lack of insight into one's spirit though other factors may play a part."

"Ah, that does sound bad," Enkai said. He thought about how none of the divine artists in the Maro Province had reached Gold since the time of the founders and his stomach clenched.

Nodding, Elder Onki continued, "Bottlenecks are frustrating and potentially ruinous for the ambitious, but they aren't the worst thing that can happen due to an underdeveloped spirit. Listen well, En. Techniques are expressions of the spirit that allow divine artists and beasts to perform amazing feats. However, they are also dangerous especially for those in the Foundation Realm. If divine artists use a technique too strenuous or too powerful for them, they will damage their own spirit. If the damage is not too extensive, this can be fixed through the use of natural treasures, healing arts, and elixirs, but every time this happens, the damage becomes more difficult to heal. That damage will inevitably hamper the cultivation process, lower the potency of techniques, and even prevent one from being able to practice the divine arts entirely. Now consider that for a divine artist who fails to develop his or her spirit, almost all but the most basic techniques are too strenuous and too powerful."

Lowering his head to Enkai's eye level, Elder Onki met his gaze as he dropped all pretenses and added, "Wherever this Maro Province is, forget about it. In my long life, I have heard of places like it. Places isolated from the world where the weak flee to escape conflict and hardship. Places where cowards and fools lead spreading their flawed understanding of the divine arts. That very same flawed knowledge festers as it is passed down the generations until a population of impotent divine artists is all that's left. Be thankful that you ended up here. Even the most bountiful tree will bear no fruit in infertile soil."

He thought about Elder Onki's words. Howling winds echoed through the multitude of tunnels that dotted the walls of the chamber adding a chilling atmosphere to their lesson. Somewhere in the cavern, displaced earth shifted, and the sound of rubble rattled amidst the howling.

Enkai found the entire explanation hard to swallow. His chest tightened and a knot of pain twisted in his gut. Worst of all, he felt like crying. Not because he couldn't believe what Elder Onki was saying. Not even because his understanding of the divine arts had proved incorrect. He had come into this conversation ready to correct his ignorance, not validate it. The reason was the disgrace welling up inside him. If everything his master said was true, then every divine artist of the Maro Province lived a life of ignorance and self-sabotage. They were doomed to fail in the divine arts and they didn't even know it. He thought of the proud Du warriors he had watched train with his father as a child. He remembered how they cultivated and trained with their techniques for hours each day in the hopes that they might one day advance to Silver, unaware of the ironic futility of their dedication.

Then, there was his father, the man he idolized despite everything. Du Kai had sacrificed much for the divine arts. When growing up, Enkai had spent little time with his father outside of their lessons, yet Enkai had never resented him. On the contrary, he admired him for it. He'd been inspired by his father's constant dedication, his strict code of honor and duty, and the innate talent he demonstrated. The other members of the Du clan shared in his admiration. His father had been the pride of the clan. Yet, what was left to take pride in? Over the past six years, he had continuously rationalized his father's actions convincing himself that though his father chose to sacrifice his only son, it had been a decision borne of duty. An exceptional divine artist, but a flawed man — that was the memory Enkai had molded of his father. When that crumbled, Enkai lost a part of himself.

What was Du Kai to the world beyond the Maro Province? According to Onki, the human societies of the outside world wouldn't have even considered his father a divine artist. Was Du Kai just another fool trapped by the incorrect teachings of his ancestors? And what of the ancestors and clan founders? Had they simply been cowards and failed divine artists who'd fled the Fall of Heaven, not heroic survivors that shepherded the remains of humanity to safety? He gritted his teeth and his nails dug into his palms. How much of the life that he'd known was built on ignorance and lies?

Hot air gusted over Enkai. It was such a contrast with the natural dank air of the mountain cavern that it snapped him back to reality. He looked up and realized Elder Onki was still holding his head at eye level with him. When their eyes met, Elder Onki said, "Breathe. "

His mind, previously clouded in melancholy contemplation, cleared and he grasped the situation. His entire body was trembling and his breath came in shaky fits. Within his spirit, his Sin pulsed. Though still dormant, it sensed his distress and would wake if Enkai didn't calm down. Centering himself, he forced his thoughts to a standstill. Doubt, guilt, and anger fought against his efforts and sought to claw their way to the forefront of his mind. With practiced efficiency, he calmed himself, one deep breath after another. Onki observed the entire process with quiet patience. When their eyes met, Enkai was reminded that Onki was a great beast bearing wisdom beyond his ability to comprehend.

Once he was calm, he chuckled which earned a questioning look from Elder Onki. Obviously, humor wasn't the expected follow up to his near emotional breakdown. Enkai explained, "Forgive me, I was just thinking about how ridiculous it was for me to think I knew better than you."

There was bitterness in his voice as he spoke and he hated it. Letting out a deep sigh, he let himself fall onto his back so that he was looking up at the rough moss-covered ceiling of the cavern. Out of his periphery, he saw Elder Onki shift doubtless to get into a more comfortable position. They sat there together in a silent moment of contemplation.

The silence broke when Onki said, "There is nothing wrong with questioning what you are told. There is wisdom in knowing when to listen, but blind faith is for fools and zealots. The greatest divine artists and great beasts of ages past blazed their own trails and found the truth for themselves." His snake-like neck curled into view so he could gaze directly down at Enkai. His amber reptilian eyes narrowed as he continued, "So, what are you going to do?"

The question caught Enkai completely off guard. So much so that he asked, "What do you mean?"

Elder Onki snorted as though he thought the answer was obvious, then said, "I meant what I asked. You've told me you wish to find someone, is that still your wish? You seemed quite shaken just then and it's plain to see you're doubting yourself. As your master, I will guide you as best I can, but it is you who must decide your destination."

Taking his Onki's words to heart, Enkai considered his choices. Despite everything, he still wanted to find Lin Chun, if only to gain closure on what had happened to him as a child. However, he wasn't so sure that was his number one priority anymore. Briefly, he entertained the notion of just living out his life on Old Omen. Family was important to him and Nin, Brem, and Jak were his family. That was the problem though. Enkai couldn't shake the memories of his clan. He wrestled with the memories of the celebrations held when a divine artist broke through to Bronze or, if his father's case, Silver. He remembered the joy-filled laughter and the tears of the clan as they celebrated the success of their family members and the strengthening of the clan as a whole. Knowing what he knew now, Enkai's stomach twisted at those memories. His clansmen knew nothing of their own ignorance, yet they struggled, laughed, and cried in pursuit of the divine arts. Even though he suspected the Patriarch was involved in his sacrifice, did the actions of one man warrant the condemnation of his entire clan? Could he really abandon the people he had once called family? He thought of his only childhood friend, Shana, who was probably going to be forced into a marriage for the good of the clan. The sight of his grandfather, grief-filled and haggard as he left the Patriarch's tent, flashed across his thoughts. Lastly, he recalled the oath he'd made long ago under the Sacred Vas tree. The answer was obvious.

He got to his feet as he came to a decision. There was an important question he needed to be answered. He asked, "Elder, apologies, but I don't think I can take your advice about my homeland. You said it was possible to heal a damaged spirit if the damage wasn't extensive. If someone uses techniques regularly while their spirit is underdeveloped, how long do they have until the damage is too extensive to heal?"

In response to his question, Elder Onki said, "It depends on the talent of the individual. A truly talented divine artist might be able to avoid serious damage when using a technique through pure skill and intuition, but they would still inflict some amount of strain on their spirit. In such cases, they might last a decade or two before the damage was bad enough to cause spiritual deficiencies. For most though, they'd have perhaps a few years before the damage reached that point. In either case, once the damage has gotten severe enough to seriously hamper the spirit, it is usually too late."

Enkai nodded cataloging that information. He had expected as much based on the Elder's earlier comments. Next, he said, "You say it is too late once they reach that point, but I've seen the Apostles. Elder Jagan showed me incredible things in the Well of the Dreamer. Surely there must be some way to heal divine artists whose spirits are severely damaged."

Elder Onki sat in silence for nearly a minute. He stared off into the darkness of the cavern, seemingly lost in thought. Even when he turned his gaze back to Enkai, his eyes were distant. He asked, "Are you sure this is what you want? There may be a way, but it won't be easy nor is it for the faint of heart."

Enkai wasted no time reassuring his master. "I am. I may have been away from them for all these years, but my clan is still my family and the Maro Province was my home. The people there don't even know what they are doing to themselves. If I do nothing, I'm abandoning them. Even if I returned with the knowledge I have now, no doubt they wouldn't believe me and most of their spirits are probably beyond the point of no return. In my clan, divine artists start learning techniques as soon as their spirits are awakened. Little thought is given to cycling aside from cultivation and anima control and only the clan warriors train their bodies with any regularity. I want to find a way to heal them, so they can at least have a chance."

Sighing, Elder Onki closed his eyes. When he opened them once more, his gaze weighed heavily on Enkai and made the severity of his next words clear. "Then listen well, En. Throughout the world, there are places of great power, items capable of enacting miracles, and individuals who wield more power than the three Apostles of the Green Mother combined. I don't know of a way to cure deep spiritual damage, but there are others who have a deeper understanding of such matters. If you truly wish to find an answer, then I suggest you seek them."

"Who? Who should I seek out?" Enkai asked.

"There are many places you could go, but I suggest seeking out Sages of the West, East, and South. They are great beasts known for their great power and wisdom. They sometimes aid humans who seek their counsel. One of them may have the answers that I don't. When you leave, I will have Jagan provide you with a map with their locations. I am sure she'd have one in that old city of hers."

Enkai sat back down in a cross-legged position as his mind churned through all the new information he was receiving. After Elder Onki finished speaking, he asked, "Wait, is there not a Sage of the North?"

Elder Onki didn't answer. He only held Enkai's gaze as the silence between them grew. Enkai frowned as the lull began to make him uncomfortable. He caught a twinkle of amusement in Onki's eyes. Then, it hit him and he blurted out, "Wait, you're the Sage of the North?!"

Elder Onki chuckled. "I have not laid claim to that title in centuries. I prefer my isolation. The world beyond the forest is full of politics, power struggles, and other nonsense. It gives me a headache just thinking about that. If you do seek out the other Sages, tell them you are my disciple. They should be willing to at least hear you out."

Getting to his feet, Elder Onki smiled at Enkai. The expression stretched the leathery skin that covered his craggy features and gave him the look of a snake eyeing its unsuspecting prey. Matching the motion, Enkai returned the smile. The moment passed and Elder Onki adopted a serious expression once more.

He said, "If you are determined to leave the forest, there is something I must tell you about your core."

Enkai nodded giving the Sage of the North his full attention. He had wondered about his core in the past, but Elder Onki had assured him multiple times that there was nothing wrong with it. His master said, "You are not a normal divine artist by modern standards. As I once told you, you are a Primal or, to put it simply, a human born with the core of a great beast. Many centuries ago, those like you were plentiful. However, after the great war that felled the heavens, Primals were condemned by those who ruled the heavens. Not many have memories long enough to remember the truth of your core, but anyone who takes more than a surface look at your spirit will recognize you as abnormal. I can offer you a method to hide the true nature of your core from others, but it won't work if you are cultivating or fighting. If anyone recognizes that you have a Primal core, they'll try to capture or kill you without fail, assuming someone doesn't attempt to do so because you're a Deviant. Your path won't be an easy one and the outside world will not be kind. Do you still wish to leave?"

"Yes, but I do have one question," Enkai said without hesitation. Though he was surprised to hear that he had the same type of core as a great beast: he didn't know what to think of that. Other than great beasts being born with naturally stronger bodies, he wasn't sure there was much of a difference at all. Still, there was no harm in making sure. "Will my core hinder my ability to advance in the divine arts?"

"No, you'll hardly notice a difference until you advance beyond the Gold Realm," Elder Onki answered. Enkai's smile broadened at the thought of becoming Gold. He understood that the heights of the divine arts went beyond Gold, but the idea of reaching such a milestone still excited him.

Out of curiosity, he asked, "What is beyond the Gold Realm exactly?"

His master chuckled though he didn't answer. Instead, he said, "That is a discussion for later. For now, go rest. Tomorrow, meet me at the summit and we shall start the next phase of your training. Before you leave, I must ensure you can at least defend yourself. As you are now, you assuredly wouldn't survive the journey through the forest. We've spent the past five years developing your foundation, but now I think it is time you took your first steps toward advancing your spirit. Before that though, you'll need a breathing exercise for cultivation. I shall teach you to breathe as the mountain does."

Bowing deeply, Enkai thanked his master. Filled with thoughts of his new purpose and the coming training, he turned away from Elder Onki and jogged toward the tunnel that led to Nin's burrow. Before he took more than a few steps, Elder Onki called out to him. "Make sure you talk to Nin. She deserves to know your intentions."

The thought of breaking the news to Nin put a bit of a damper on his excitement. He wasn't sure how she would react, but his enthusiasm would not be deterred. With his heart beating excitedly, he raced through the cavern. Without even thinking, he began cycling anima through his limbs Enhancing them as he jumped from boulder to boulder and into the winding tunnels of Old Omen.

Chapter 18

Dreams of blood and death haunted Jagan as she slept. Claws rent flesh amidst shifting shadows. Ash and smoke choked the red sky. Blood flowed over broken bones as primal cries filled the air. Heaven and earth trembled as they were thrown into chaos by a lone titan awakened after an age at rest.

Jagan, Daughter of Somn. I summon you ...

Jagan jerked from her fitful slumber. She trembled as the words filled her body and soul. She had been summoned. She spread her massive wings and leapt from her perch atop the crystal chandelier in the main audience chamber. Activating one of her Aspects, her third eye flared to life cloaking her entire body in ethereal purple mist. She dove beak-first into the floor of the chamber and passed through it like a phantom. She rapidly navigated through the complex by using her third eye to see through the solid material between her and her destination. In less than a few seconds, she reached it — the Hall of Remembrance.

Deactivating her Aspect, she stepped onto the cold tiles. Her talons clacked loudly as she walked through the wide hall. Torches of dream fire gave the hall a somber atmosphere. Throughout the hall, mementos of a lost age sat on display. Small alcoves carved into the walls every dozen feet held preserved natural treasures fit for kings. In-between each alcove, portraits of divine artists in varying degrees of finery from worn disheveled robes to attire fit for royalty lined the walls. Beyond the portraits, where the hall ended, a massive black iron door three times as tall as Jagan dominated the back wall.

Jagan pushed the heavy metal door open. As soon as she stepped through it, she felt the hum of concentrated dream essence against her consciousness. Purple light suffused the entirety of the large circular chamber which was barren but for a grand circular mosaic that spanned exactly half the room's floor.

The mosaic depicted countless images that shifted like a living entity as the tiles continuously changed in color. The glass-like material shimmered with otherworldly light and thin mist rose from it. Overtop the mosaic, thousands of dream wisps traveled in a set of three connected spirals each feeding into the other.

Jagan initiated her breathing exercise. Extending her will toward the mosaic, she fed a trickle of her power into it. The Dream Essence Fountain responded to her call and a chime rang through the chamber. The glow of the mosaic intensified as she fed more power into it. Finally, a second chime echoed throughout the chamber. She stepped forward.

Once both her feet touched the mosaic, the world around her fluctuated as though she were moving through hundreds of different scenes at the same time. The effect would have overwhelmed a lesser mind, but she shrugged it off. Eventually, she found herself standing, or rather floating, within a landscape thick with fog and distant lights. She knew this place well. It was the place of her birth; the Sphere of Dreams.

Dropping her breathing exercise, she let her spirit unfold within the immediate area and waited. In her mind, she held tight to one hope.

Mistress…

A figure comprised of deep purple mist materialized from the fog. The figure lacked definition and blended into the surrounding fog as if it had no clear beginning or end. Jagan's heart fluttered in anxious anticipation. As a dream beast, she recognized the border between dream and reality. How many times had she dreamed of a moment like this? Yet, this was no dream. Before her eyes, the specter gained definition slowly shaping itself into the form of a lithe woman.

A beautiful face smiled at her framed by flowing crimson hair that swept past the shoulders and down the back. Glowing indigo eyes watched her in silence while the head tilted slightly to the side. The faint traces of amusement glittered along her features. Then, she spoke.

"You've grown, Jagan."

Hearing her gentle voice filled Jagan's heart with joy. It was the same as she remembered. *How many times have I yearned to hear that voice again?*

Still, she needed to make sure. She had seen the ruler of Somn die with her own eyes, so this could be some type of trick. For now, she would play along until she could confirm the woman's identity. She swept one wing out and inclined her head.

"This humble servant greets you, my lady," she said. Her voice wavered as she spoke. Though it was restored while within the Sphere of Dreams, her feelings were also amplified. The pain, loneliness, and sorrow of the last millennium swelled threatening to seize hold of her. However, her resolve held firm. With the form of her former mistress in front of her, she could not allow herself to waver. "Do you remember the last thing you said to me?"

The woman's indigo eyes widened, her mouth parted in apparent disbelief, perhaps because she could sense the underlying skepticism. Silence ensued as Jagan waited for her to answer, hoping with every fiber of her being that she'd hear *those* words, the same words that were spoken to her by the ruler of Somn before she confronted the Usurper. When the pause ended, the woman walked forward. Time slowed. Every step caused the woman's features to become more distinct. Fine indigo robes materialized around her figure covering smooth alabaster skin. A golden circlet set with amethysts and heart-jade gems materialized on her brow. The powerful aura emanating from it was unmistakable.

The Crown of Somn?! Jagan's eyes widened in disbelief. The Crown of Somn was one of the most powerful divine treasures to ever exist; producing a fake would've been nigh impossible. Her heart seized. Now in front of her, the woman reached upward and placed a hand against Jagan's neck as she smiled up at her.

268

Jagan unconsciously leaned into her hand staring into the glowing eyes that evoked so many long-dormant memories. It wasn't until she spoke that Jagan's heart began to beat once more.

"Little one, I release you from your vow of service. Only I must face the consequences of my failures. Go. Flee and be free. Live life without war and despair," she said.

The mist around them flashed in response to memories of that fateful day which flooded Jagan's mind. The landscape changed mimicking the day of Somn's fall. Geysers of liquid fire burst through the ground igniting those not fast enough to dodge them. The heavens burned as Old Omen spewed burning earth and poisonous gases into the air. Divine artists rushed through the streets gathering anything they could of their lives in order to escape from the Usurper's Edict. Kneeling in the main audience chamber before the dais, her mistress stroked Jagan's bristling feathers and smiled at the young phantasmal owl who barely came up to her knee.

Jagan remembered her feelings that day: her frustration at being helpless to assist her beloved mistress, the sorrow of knowing her mistress would die, and the horror of watching her home burn. Caught within the emotion of the moment, Jagan had responded.

"Mistress, come with me. With your abilities, they'll never be able to find us. You can't stay here! If you go, we can ..." her voice broke unable to finish the statement, as if not saying it made her fear any less real. With each word Jagan spoke, the scene became more and more real. Both parties knew it was simply the power of the Sphere of Dreams reacting to their emotions and memories, but that didn't matter. Like two actors in a play, they spoke their lines, too engrossed in the last moment they'd shared together.

"I know how you must feel, little one, but I cannot leave. It's *me* he wants. If I run, I'd be leaving my people to suffer his wrath. He won't stop until he finds me even if it means chasing down every surviving citizen of Somn in order to draw me out," responded the ruler of Somn as she caressed Jagan's feathered face. Jagan knew the truth of her mistress's words, yet it only made her pain that much worse. Her own selfishness insisted that she accompany her mistress to the end. Death was preferable to life as a member of the losing side. She had no desire to see the heroes of Somn become the villains in the Usurper's new world order.

"I will—" she started to say, but her mistress interrupted her.

"Hush, I have released you and you are no longer bound to serve. I'll not have you throw your life away. Now go!" she declared with all the force of an empress issuing an imperial decree. Deep within her spirit, the familiar bond between woman and beast was severed. Jagan let loose a pealing cry. Her spirit ached from the loss of her bond. She took wing, spurred by her mistress's wishes Amidst the hurt and confusion, she heard her mistress speak one more time.

"Hold me close in your dreams, little one, and I will always be with you."

All at once, the vision dispersed. She looked into the eyes of the woman before her and tentatively extended her spiritual perception. For a brief moment, their spirits connected giving each a small look into the other. It was all Jagan needed.

She remembered the feeling of her mistress's spirit with such clarity that it pained her. She recalled the vastness, the calm, and the warmth within. There was much more power and depth than even she remembered, yet, at the same time, it was the same. This was no imposter. Her mistress was home.

"Lady Evaniel, how can this be? I saw the Usurper strike you down, body and soul. I felt your presence torn from existence by his foul weapon," Jagan wept, full of joy. She buried her head into her mistress's shoulder which would have knocked most humans over, but Evaniel returned the embrace squeezing Jagan fiercely. They stood there for several long moments each relishing the comfort of a long-lost companion. However, it did not last. Evaniel stepped back and gave Jagan a look that said more than words could.

"You and all who witnessed my *death* saw what I *willed* be seen."

Jagan's eyes nearly popped out of her head as she mentally reeled at the implications of her mistress's words. She started to ask for an explanation, but Evaniel held up a hand to forestall her request.

"I know you must have questions, but I cannot answer them at this moment. I risk much just by coming here to speak to you," Evaniel said somberly. Jagan immediately understood. The Usurper still ruled the heavens. If Evaniel was discovered, the consequences would be cataclysmic. Despite her disappointment, Jagan gave Evaniel her full attention, determined to be of assistance. "As much as I wish I could say I came for our reunion, I did not." She turned around and beckoned to the area behind her. "Chun, come here."

From the mist, another woman stepped forward cloaked in a green robe with silver lining and the symbol of a silver leaf emblazoned upon its breast. Jagan glanced between Evaniel and the newcomer. Chun appeared to barely qualify as middle-aged though Jagan knew well enough that divine artists extended their longevity using medicinal elixirs or simply ceased aging when they reached the higher stages of cultivation. Despite that, Jagan suspected Chun was not very old. She stood behind Evaniel, wide-eyed and silent like a frightened doe.

"Jagan, this is my daughter. Without her, I would not be standing here right now. She has been instrumental in my plans to right the wrongs of the past age," Evaniel said. Her voice grew low and cold as she continued, "That being said, I would very much like to know who attempted to scry her using the Well of the Dreamer."

Jagan blinked slowly as she took in Chun once more. The realization crashed into her thoughts like a roaring tide. She had seen a woman bearing a striking resemblance to Chun and wearing the exact same robes just the previous night.

Without thinking, she blurted, "It's you! You're the one he was looking for!"

Chun flinched away from Jagan, startled by her outburst. She clearly hadn't expected Jagan to address her directly. Evaniel frowned — a chilling expression with her otherworldly beauty.

"Jagan, *who* was looking for her?"

"Young Enkai, he—" Jagan started to say but stopped when she saw their reactions. Chun displayed an entire myriad of emotions, all within quick succession starting with surprise and ending with tears that began to form before she hurriedly brushed them away. Evaniel donning a blank mask hiding her reaction with experienced ease though her posture softened after a glance at Chun. When she looked back at Jagan, her eyes betrayed the concern beneath her stoicism.

"Please continue," Evaniel said. To Jagan, it sounded more like a command than a request.

Eager to assuage the sudden tension in the air, Jagan said, "He is a young boy barely over a decade old. Six summers ago, he was adopted by Ninsa, a moon rabbit under the charge of Onki, the Sage of the North. He still lives on Old Omen to the east of Somn as he did when you ruled. Young Enkai came to use the Well of the Dreamer at Onki's request though he also wished to use the Well in order to check in on his family and ..."

Jagan hesitated, then looked at Chun. Evaniel's brow furrowed as though she had already guessed Jagan's words. Seeing no other way around it, Jagan finished, "And to find the woman who killed his father."

Chun physically recoiled as though someone had smacked her. She sputtered, "W-what? Does he think *I* killed Kai? How does he know about that? More importantly, how is he even alive?" The words gushed out of her like a switch had been flipped. She leveled an accusatory glance at Evaniel, "You said the Sacred Vas tree would kill him! How is this possible?"

Now, it was Jagan's turn to recoil. Her mistress had used a *Sacred Vas tree*?! Jagan had heard rumors of those mythical trees; however, she'd never believed the legends. Sacred Vas trees were said to be born from seeds first sown by the Silent

Father during the birth of the world. Even as the greatest city of learning and knowledge in the world, Somn had contained only unverified accounts of Sacred Vas trees and those accounts had been ancient even in Somn's prime. The fruits harvested from a Sacred Vas tree were treasures beyond measure. However, the mythical natural treasure came at a great cost if the legends were to be believed. Jagan asked, "Did you obtain a Sacred Vas fruit?"

For her part, Evaniel seemed to have contracted a sudden migraine. She turned to Chun. "It should have. The tree should have sapped the life from him when it tasted his blood. He must have died; else the fruit would not have blossomed. Not to mention, Du Kai stabbed him in the heart. He can't have survived both."

Sensing an opportunity to clarify, Jagan added, "When we scryed his family, we observed a meeting. The names Du Kai and Makai were mentioned. Three of the four men in the meeting also wore red and yellow robes."

"Makai? That's the name of Enkai's grandfather. Red and yellow are the Du clan colors! It has to be him!" Chun exclaimed. Jagan nodded seeking to be helpful. Evaniel looked troubled. Jagan recognized the expression and it scared her. Powerful dream artists often had the ability to glimpse the strands of fate through their dreams and Evaniel was the greatest dream artist to have ever lived. The last time she had been surprised, Somn fell and the Usurper took control of the heavens.

Abruptly, Evaniel asked, "How did he come to live with Onki?"

"I'm not sure about the details, Lady Evaniel, but Ninsa told me a powerful great beast brought him to her. I assumed he was a child from one of the tribes that live in the human lands bordering Onki's territory," replied Jagan. Unfortunately, Evaniel didn't seem to get what she was looking for from her answer, so her mistress launched in a series of additional questions.

"And the boy? Have you noticed anything unusual about him? What of his spirit?"

"He is very well mannered for a boy growing up among beasts. As far as his spirit goes, he is only Lead, but he has some exceptional attributes like being the most stable Deviant I've ever seen and—"

"*What?!*" Evaniel hissed. Both Chun and Jagan flinched. Neither had expected such a reaction from Evaniel. The blatant surprise or her face and tension in her voice made Jagan's heart race. Her very human reaction starkly contrasted with her godly demeanor. Evaniel seemed to realize what happened and recovered her composure although when she next spoke, it was strained, "Are you certain he is a Deviant?"

"Y-yes, mistress," Jagan stammered.

"What is a Deviant?" Chun asked, bewildered. She glanced back and forth between Jagan and Evaniel, then added, "Is he some kind of criminal?"

How does she not know what Sin is? Jagan stared at Chun in disbelief. Chun noticed Jagan's look and blushed with embarrassment. Evaniel pinched the bridge of her nose. Taking a deep breath, she closed her eyes and exhaled. The tension bled from her. Jagan felt calm settle upon her and noticed that even Chun visibly relaxed. Opening her eyes and meeting Chun's gaze, Evaniel smiled.

"They are unfortunate individuals burdened with a curse called Sin that warps and twists the body and spirit. Most die or become twisted monstrosities called demons within hours of corruption, but Deviants are the exception. Their Sin is dormant which allows them to function and even use the Sin as long as it doesn't take control," Evaniel said. "While his being alive is an interesting development, it would be best to dispatch him especially since—"

"No!" Chun shouted interrupting Evaniel and startling Jagan. Chun stood her ground as the two stared at her. Lowering her voice, she said, "You can't just kill him after everything he's been through."

"Oh?" Evaniel said arching an eyebrow. Before Chun could answer, Evaniel cut her off. "While I understand you still bear guilt over what happened, we both know it was necessary. He poses a significant danger to our mission."

Chun scowled. "How could he possibly be a threat to us?"

Smiling still, Evaniel answered her daughter with the tone of a parent explaining something simple to a child, "Because he knows who you are. On top of that, he is the first child with a Primal core to be born on Genesis in centuries. He will attract attention. I shouldn't need to remind you that our enemies have hunted divine artists with Primal cores into near extinction. The term Forsaken is not exclusive to the Maro Province. If he ventures into the outside world, someone will recognize him as Forsaken and his life will be forfeit, but before he dies, he may tell someone of your existence. But that's not all. Let us assume he manages to hide his presence, he will continue pursuing a means to find you. If he seeks aid from one of our enemies and they learn what he knows, everything we've done will have been for naught."

As Chun responded, Jagan watched the exchange with intense fascination. Despite her past relationship with Evaniel, she had never seen her mistress act the way she did with her daughter. While her regal demeanor was still present, she moved and expressed herself much more freely than at any point when she'd ruled Somn. The two women went back and forth a couple more times before Chun looked away from her mother.

In a soft voice, Chun said, "Mother, please…"

The former ruler of Somn looked weary. She stepped closer to her daughter and stroked her hair while whispering in a comforting voice.

Jagan chose that moment to interrupt since she had pertinent information if they were going to decide young Enkai's fate. If at all possible, Jagan preferred young Enkai to live. He was the first Primal child in centuries, after all. As a great beast, she was naturally closer to him than she was with other humans. While not powerful, the connection between Primals and great beasts had been enough for Jagan, a member of an extremely elusive and solitary species, to become Evaniel's familiar over a thousand years ago. Moreover, Jagan's dreams suggested there was more to Enkai's destiny than death.

"Mistress, I may be able to be of assistance regarding young Enkai," she said catching the attention of both women. Chun looked suspicious while Evaniel gestured for her to continue. "I have dreamt about young Enkai since his arrival at Old Omen."

Evaniel let go of her daughter and turned her full attention to Jagan. She said, "Tell me of these dreams."

Jagan jumped into a description of her dreams. She started with her earliest dreams. She told of a heavenly storm passing a solitary mountain. The storm smashed against the mountain face, but the mountain did not yield. Next, she spoke of a boy, battered and alone, standing between a great flame of purity and a tide of chaos. In his hands, he held his heart. Finally, she explained her most recent dream, the one she'd dreamt just before Evaniel summoned her. A nightmarish hellscape stretched across the land. Smoke and ash shrouded the bleeding sky. Then, primal chaos shook heaven and earth laying bare the secrets of the past.

By the time she finished, Evaniel was pacing in front of her, brow furrowed. Jagan didn't interrupt. She knew her mistress was pondering the meaning of the dreams. Though the dreams of dream artists were sometimes prophetic, they were usually vague and open to interpretation. Most of the time, key details were missing from the dreams, or aspects of the dream were misleading. While Jagan was no amateur, she couldn't hold a candle to the former ruler of Somn. Men and great beasts once referred to Evaniel as the Lady of Dreams for good reason. Suddenly, Evaniel stopped midstride and whirled on Jagan.

"When did he become a Deviant?" Evaniel asked urgently.

"According to Ninsa, he's been a Deviant since he arrived," Jagan said immediately though her answer only seemed to make Evaniel more anxious. She started pacing again. Jagan didn't know what concerned her, but she knew it had to be serious for Evaniel to appear so distressed.

Stopping again, Evaniel asked, "What can you tell me about the great beast this Ninsa mentioned?"

"Nothing, my lady. She avoided most of my questions about it. I only asked about it a few times out of respect for Onki, and I was admittedly more interested in young Enkai's dream wisp familiar," she answered.

"His what?" her mistress said, eyes widening.

Jagan's heart constricted in dread. "When he arrived, he was bonded to a dream wisp. It was here with him last night though it spent the entire time here in the Essence Fountain, so I—"

Lady Evaniel gasped startling Jagan yet again. In a burst of movement, she grabbed Chun who recoiled in surprise. Next, she looked to Jagan and said with all the force of a ruler, "Jagan, find Enkai. Find him and sever his bond with that creature!"

Jagan who was confused by the gravity in her mistress's voice asked, "The wisp?"

"It's not a wisp! Go before it's too la—" Evaniel exclaimed before a soul-piercing hiss cut across the expanse of fog and lights.

A chilling voice echoed around them sending shivers down Jagan's spine. Next to Evaniel, Chun paled. *It is already too late.*

Evaniel exchanged a fleeting glance with Jagan before she disappeared along with Chun. Jagan activated the full force of her spirit and flung herself out of the Sphere of Dreams back into the heart of Somn. She took wing and activated her Aspect to become insubstantial. Behind her, *something* laughed. The beautiful hues of purple dream essence distorted and changed rapidly. By the time she was flying through the ceiling of the chamber, the entire room was filled with violent scarlet light.

Chapter 19

Silence blanketed the burrow when Enkai arrived. Shadows played along the back wall as moonlight streamed in through the entrance. His siblings were both curled up next to each other a few feet away from his usual resting place. In the dim light, Enkai noticed Nin's equipment was missing. A quick search of the burrow revealed she wasn't present. For a moment, he wrestled with the impulse to save their discussion for the morning but decided against it. After his discussion with Elder Onki, he felt invigorated because he had a clear view of what his future held.

Thankfully, a glance at the moon told Enkai exactly where Nin had gone. Whenever the moon was nearly full, Nin spent the night brewing and refining elixirs at the summit of Old Omen. Enkai didn't know exactly why she did that, but she'd implied a few times that her anima had some relation to the phases of the moon. Since elixirs used the alchemist's anima as a catalyst, he reasoned that her anima must be more potent when the moon was at its height.

Unfortunately, the journey up Old Omen would take at least a few hours even while cycling to Enhance himself. He began the hike in a relatively normal fashion climbing up the moonlight-strewn ridges and trails that made up the majority of Old Omen's rough face. The cool winds of the mountain were refreshing in the mid-summer weather. Below him, the Forbidden Forest rested peacefully under a curtain of moonlight. Somewhere beyond the green expanse, the five clans went about their usual business on the Maro Province struggling to attain a goal they could never reach. The thought spurred him to climb faster and increased his determination to accomplish his goal. He would find a way to restore the damaged spirits of his people and then return to his homeland. He doubted it would be so easy, but that didn't matter to him.

After about an hour of climbing, he got an idea. Similar to how he'd first attempted the Strike technique, he directed his anima to pool into his legs. Unlike what he'd done with the Strike, he kept the amount of anima tightly regulated to avoid overexerting his spirit. The process took a few minutes away from his climb as he tweaked the flow of anima to his liking.

Mentally preparing himself, Enkai kicked off with his Enhanced legs. He covered nearly five feet in a single step and tripped over a loose rock. His arms shot out to catch him before he kissed the hard stone. In order to avoid any unfortunate accidents, he spent several minutes practicing in order to get used to the strength of his Enhanced legs. Once he was sure he wouldn't accidentally launch himself down the mountain, he took off.

Enkai sped up the mountainside. With his legs empowered, he moved much faster than usual while cycling. He climbed the steep paths and jumped over the uneven ridges with ease. The wind rushed against him growing colder as he ascended. The feeling of moving so quickly was amazing. Since the technique thinned the amount of anima focused in his upper body, it wouldn't be as useful as full-body Enhancement in combat, but that didn't stop him from imagining how he could use such speed in a fight. High in the sky, the nearly-full moon illuminated his journey up the mountain. When he crested the lip at the summit of the volcano, he suspected the climb had only taken about half his usual time.

He stood on the lip for a moment looking out at the night sky. Stars painted the dark tapestry of the heavens with countless patterns of light. Below him, the world expanded outward until the earth met the sky. Beyond the horizon, the unknown called to him. In that moment, Enkai brimmed with anticipation. When he left the Forbidden Forest, he would be the first clansman from the Maro Province to explore the outside world since the Fall of Heaven. Over the past two days, he'd learned so much about the world beyond the forest. It contained wondrous sites, powerful great beasts, and so much more. The world of the divine arts waited for him.

"En?" a familiar voice called from behind him. Enkai turned around to face Nin. She looked up at him, head tilted and eyes questioning. He smiled down at her with the moon at his back. Despite his smile, Nin looked a bit concerned. Enkai realized that he probably looked a bit disturbed as stood at the edge of the mountaintop smiling like a madman in the moonlight. She asked, "Is everything alright?"

"Everything's okay, better than okay in actual fact. I've never felt this good in my life," he said perhaps more excitedly than he intended. The concern in her eyes wavered a bit and she smiled as well. Looking over her shoulder, she checked the stone basin she used for creating elixirs. The basin contained a pale orange mixture that slowly swirled as though it were mixing itself. Nin appeared satisfied with whatever she saw because she hopped up onto the lip of the volcano to stand next to Enkai.

"I assume your lesson with Elder Onki went well?" she asked, and they sat down next to each other.

"You could say that but...," he said. His smile faded slightly. Nin didn't miss the change, but she waited for him to continue. Taking a deep breath, he said, "I've decided to leave the forest."

Her nose started twitching which immediately gave away her distress. Enkai braced himself for the coming torrent of emotion, but it never came. She turned away from him to face the moon. For over a minute, she gazed at the lunar body in silence. Her ears drooped down to her shoulders and she sighed. Enkai nearly apologized on reflex.

Her voice was gentle on the night wind when she said, "Have I ever told you about the day you arrived here on Old Omen?"

"A little bit, but you've always avoided around the subject, so I assumed Elder Onki asked you not to talk about it," Enkai said nonchalantly.

Nin's eyes widened in astonishment, then she chuckled. She said, "I always forget how perceptive children are."

"I don't know if I would say that. I think it's more that you're bad at keeping secrets," he said. She wrinkled her face in mock outrage and pushed him just hard enough that he had to reach out a hand to steady himself. He chuckled as he righted himself.

"It's rude to point out those kinds of things, En," she retorted which earned her a cheeky grin. She huffed before she steered the conversation back on topic. The moon's light glimmered in her jade-green eyes as she collected her thoughts. The sight reminded Enkai of how different his life was compared to how it had been in the Maro Province. After years spent living with his new family, Enkai felt at home within the Forbidden Forest. He could remember a time when merely the thought of entering the forest had terrified him. Next to him, Nin finished her musings and said, "Elder Onki told me to keep the circumstances of your arrival a secret in order to protect you."

While he'd expected something along those lines, he still wondered exactly what about his arrival had warranted the need for secrecy. Doubtless, the reason centered around the great beast that had brought him to Old Omen. A few days after his arrival, Nin had given him a very abbreviated version of the event though she had dodged his attempts to obtain more information about his rescuer. He eventually dropped the subject as adapting to his new life became his primary concern. However, he occasionally caught himself daydreaming about the mysterious creature and each time, his visions of it became more outlandish and fantastical. So, when Nin began her retelling of the event, he listened with keen interest.

"The day you arrived was one of the worst days of my life," she began. Enkai suppressed the urge to comment deciding that his desire to know the truth was greater than his need to make quippy remarks. "Brem and I were collecting natural treasures for an experimental recipe I'd created. Brem was barely a year old at the time, but I let her come because I couldn't leave her alone with Elder Onki" She smiled as she recalled the story and Enkai chuckled at the thought of a miniature Brem mouthing off to Elder Onki. She continued, "Even then, she seemed to always get herself into trouble. On that day, she wandered away from me while I was extracting the roots of an herb. I heard her cry out and rushed over to see she had been bitten by a darkleaf viper."

Enkai winced. While not particularly large or fearsome, darkleaf vipers were incredibly venomous. A single bite could kill a great beast several times their size in less than a minute. Frankly, Enkai was a bit skeptical. "How did she even survive that?"

"She nearly didn't," Nin said. "When I got to her, she was on death's door. Thankfully, it was late and there was a full moon in the sky. I was able to keep Brem stable by channeling healing anima into her until we got back to Old Omen. There I gave her an elixir meant to fight off toxins, but it didn't work as well as it should have. I had to make a new elixir specifically to counteract the darkleaf viper's venom, so I carried her up here and got to work. The two hours it took for the elixir

to brew were the longest two hours of my life. I was so afraid I would lose her..."
She looked down on the sea of treetops lit by the moonlight. "Thankfully, Brem survived until the elixir was finished and made a recovery. When I was cleaning up, the Silent Father appeared."

She went silent for a moment. When she continued, her voice was full of intense reverence that Enkai had never heard from her. "It's strange. I remember the entire experience so vividly. He appeared out of nowhere like some sort of spirit, but the moment I laid eyes on him, I felt like I had known him my entire life. No, it was even stronger than that. It was almost like my own mother had come back from death to greet me. I felt so happy just being near him. He carried you between his teeth by the collar of your robes like you were one of his children. Somehow, I knew exactly what he wanted from me when I looked into his eyes. I'm sure he brought you to me knowing you would need a home."

Captivated by her story, Enkai visualized the events as he sat just a short distance from where they'd occurred. Seeking to make his visual more whole, he asked, "Who is the Silent Father? What did he look like? Is he powerful?"

"Slow down, En," she laughed. "Elder Orki said he is one of the Primordials. The stories say that the Primordials helped the gods create the world at the beginning of all things. Based on what I've been told, they rarely show themselves and when they do, many see their appearance as a great omen. The stories about the Silent Father say he breathed life into the very first creatures to walk our world. It all made me extremely nervous. There was far too much excitement for me — but after what he showed me, I never once thought of turning you away."

Though Enkai's mind was ablaze with curiosity about the Silent Father, her last words caught his attention. He asked, "What did he show you?"

Nin said nothing. She just looked at him for a long moment. Her expression changed from being reminiscent to being conflicted.

"He showed me what had happened before he found you," she said. Enkai froze, but his eyes widened and his heart raced. Nin gave him a worried looked when she saw his reaction. She added, "He showed me a man, your father I'm guessing, stab you in the heart underneath a tree that shone with more vital essence than I'd ever seen. I saw that man die at the hands of a woman with purple eyes. I felt your pain, loss, and sadness as the life bled from you. It was all a bit confusing at first, but I understood that you needed somewhere safe to recover. After you got settled, I decided not to mention it until you brought it up. I didn't want to force you to re-live such painful memories, though I questioned my decision every time you woke crying and screaming from your nightmares."

It was Enkai's turn to be silent. He couldn't believe Nin knew about his father's betrayal. She had seen what happened at the Sacred Vas tree. While he'd thought he bore the burden of trauma from that event all alone, she had known the entire time. He couldn't decide if he was angry, relieved, or both. He asked, "Does Elder Onki know?"

She nodded. Her tone was apologetic when she said. "I told him when I took you to him. If I was going to keep you, I needed his permission. I know it wasn't my place to tell him and I'm sorry for doing so."

Enkai pressed his face into his hands as he processed this revelation. Of course, Elder Onki knew. He had raised Nin and she frequently spent time with him. Their relationship made Enkai think of his grandfather often. As a child, there was nothing he wouldn't tell his grandfather. He may have been tough on Enkai, but his grandfather always listened and had even offered occasional advice. With that in mind, he couldn't blame her. After all, who else would she turn to when a supposedly ancient and powerful creature appeared out of nowhere with a mysterious child for her to care for?

"You don't need to apologize," Enkai sighed. "I should have told you both a long time ago. I just … I think I just didn't want to deal with it. Living here on Old Omen is so peaceful. I always felt so tense with my clan and I didn't know why. It wasn't until after my first few months here that I started to realize what the feeling was. In my clan, I lived under my father's shadow constantly. When I made a mistake, people talked about how my father did it better at my age. If I did something well, they said it was just because I was my father's son. On top of that, my admiration and respect for him made it all feel worse. Here though? Here I was just another child for you to care for. I could do what I wanted and no one would judge me. Even when I started feeling impatient about Elder Onki's training, I sometimes ignored those feelings because I liked the way things were."

"Then why don't you stay?" she asked. Her voice cracked just enough for Enkai to turn and face her. She met his gaze. Despite the sadness in her eyes, Enkai saw the determination to hear his reason which she more than deserved after everything she'd done for him. He ran his hand through his hair. A cold wind blasted past them kicking up ash within the bowl-shaped crater below the lip.

"Because my clan needs me," he said. "When I first arrived here, everything was so strange. On top of having no idea where I was, all the great beasts around us seemed so strong, especially Elder Onki. At first, I just explained it away as unfamiliarity with great beasts, but the more I saw, the more I felt like there was something I was missing. Yesterday, I learned the truth. Compared to what's beyond the Maro Province, my clansmen are weak. As if that isn't enough, I found out today that the understanding of the divine arts I learned from my clan is not only wrong: it's actually harmful." A bit of the bitterness he'd previously felt resurfaced. "My clansmen are sabotaging themselves and they don't even know. I have to find a way to help them."

"Why would you go to such lengths for people who threw you away?" Nin asked. Enkai was left speechless for a moment. "If there was so much focus on your father, someone must have known his intentions. Why didn't they stop him?"

Enkai had to admit they were good questions. Questions he had wondered about even as he'd climbed the mountain to tell Nin of his plans to leave. Knowing she deserved honesty, he shared his thoughts with her. "You're right. Someone did know. I heard the Du Patriarch talking about it with my father the day we left. It's how I learned that I was Forsaken. I was so afraid when I found out. I learned later from Elder Onki that the Forsaken are humans born with the same cores as great beasts and that people would want to hurt me if they found out. I think that's why my father tried to kill me. If I'm right, my clan might not welcome me back even if I am successful, but I'm still going to try. They're still my family and they need my help."

"But *we're* your family," she said. Enkai mentally kicked himself. He knew Nin would be upset about his departure; however, it had never occurred to him that she might view his journey in such a way. He'd be leaving her and his siblings behind. In a way, he was abandoning one family to help another.

He reached out and drew Nin into a hug. She didn't resist; instead, she rested her head against his shoulder and they both gazed out at the moon. After a few moments, he said, "Of course you're all just as much family as my clan. In a lot of ways, you guys are the family I always wish I'd had. I never knew my mother. My father almost never talked about her, but I found out eventually that she died during childbirth. So, I never really knew what it was like to have a mother. Then, I met you." He sighed. He felt very awkward talking about this, especially as he typically kept his feelings on the inside. When he looked down at Nin, their eyes met and he decided she needed to hear his words as much as he needed to say them. "I couldn't have asked for a better mother. No matter what, that won't change. Just like Jak and Brem will always be my brother and sister."

Without a word, Nin wrapped her arms around his midsection and buried her face in his chest. She seemed so small in that moment. When she let him go, she said, "So is there no talking you out of it?"

"Not a chance," he said, grinning.

"Then, I have no choice but to accept your decision," she said. Abruptly, she hopped down into the mouth and walked over to the basin. The pale orange mixture had turned white as winter snow during their talk.

Over the next few minutes, Enkai watched as Nin refined the mixture until only a small pool remained at the bottom of the basin. Enkai had never seen Nin refine a mixture so quickly. Using a spoon-like tool, she carefully gathered the mixture into a small clay tube, then stoppered it. She beckoned for him and he quickly made his way over to her. Once there, she presented the clay tube to him.

"If you are going to leave, you'll need to advance to have a chance at defending yourself," she said. "It's nothing special. I focused mainly on concentrating the vital anima to increase its potency so it doesn't have any unique properties, but it should contain enough anima to get you to the peak of Bronze, maybe even Silver with Elder Onki's help."

Enkai froze. His breath grew shaky and his eyes widened. When he reached out to take the tube, his hands were trembling. He collected the clay tube with both hands and gripped it like his life depended on it. Very carefully, he placed it securely within his robes. That done, he knelt down and scooped Nin into a fierce embrace.

"Thank you," he said. He didn't bother with anything more. There was no point. He could never repay Nin for everything she had done. If she was right, he might reach Silver before the year was out. It would probably take time for his core to process such high potency vital anima, but he wasn't daunted. He would easily trade a few weeks of rigorous cultivation for Silver. His thoughts raced and a broad grin spread across his face. *I'll be the youngest Silver from the Du clan in centuries!*

Nin's laughter got the better of him and he spun her in a circle mid-embrace. When he put her down, she grabbed the ironwood staff she usually used for mixing her elixirs from the basin. Enkai noticed she looked a bit tired, but she waved his concern aside.

"Don't worry. Refining always takes a bit of out of me and I refined the Orlang elixir further than I usually do," she said. She began to gather her tools into her bag. "If you have time to worry, then you can help me clean up."

They cleaned up quickly. Enkai was used to the routine since he'd often assisted Nin with her alchemy. As they packed the last of the tools away, Nin donned her woven leaf backpack and smiled at Enkai.

"Alright, let's get back home. I could use some sleep," she said. When they reached the edge, they climbed up onto the lip and began making their way down from the summit. They took their time since Nin was a bit tired from the creation of the Orlang elixir. After they reached the main trail down the mountain, the ground trembled.

They stopped and exchanged puzzled looks. In the six years that Enkai had lived on Old Omen, he had never experienced such a thing. Even in the Maro Province, the ground had never trembled. Such things only happened in stories. He made to ask Nin what was happening when the earth shook again. This time, it didn't tremble. It quaked. Above them, a thunderous crack echoed from the summit. Nin's face contorted in horror. Enkai's heart raced once more.

Abruptly, Nin grabbed Enkai forcefully pulling him down the path. Silvery-blue anima trailed from her as she activated her Enhancement technique. With no care for his dignity, she lifted him in her arms like some damsel and sped down the mountain. He cried out trying to get her to stop, but she seemed purely focused on getting back to the burrow. The ground quaked several more times as Nin blitzed down the mountain faster than Enkai had ever seen her move. The wind blasted his hair out of the loose ponytail he typically wore. As her feet touched the ground after jumping a ridge, the ground heaved violently causing the entire mountain to buck. Nin lost her footing and Enkai crashed onto the ground. He quickly recovered.

Within his spirit, he felt a familiar presence awaken. His familiar, the dream wisp, erupted from his chest and darted off to the east faster than he'd ever seen it move. He called out to it through the link attempting to draw it back but to no avail. Eventually, he gave up. There was no time to ponder the wisp's strange behavior as of late. He turned to Nin.

"Are you okay?" he asked her while ignoring the abrasions where his arms had met the rough stone. Nin didn't respond. Instead, she stared at the night sky, eyes wide and body trembling. Enkai saw true fear in her eyes. His heart pounding so hard he could feel it in his head, Enkai looked up. In the night sky, he spotted the source of Nin's fear. Something was very *wrong* with the moon.

It was red. Red as Sin.

Chapter 20

Sethara stepped through space after making her usual rounds through the other sectors. Normally, she only bore responsibility for Sector 1 which held the highest number of worlds including Genesis, the most important one of all. However, after her incidental discovery of a 7th magnitude anomaly several Genesis-years ago, her father had charged her with doing regular sweeps of all sectors.

Internally, she sighed. These sweeps were growing tiresome. On top of her normal duties, the responsibility of sweeping the other sectors stretched her thin. The Antediluvians, nine of the most powerful members of Eden, oversaw the nine sectors. Sethara managed Sector 1 while the other eight Antediluvians each governed another sector. Each Antediluvian was responsible for the maintenance, security, and administration of their respective sector. Over the past several Genesis-years, anomalies had started appearing at an unprecedented rate. A single anomaly was of little consequence to an Antediluvian, yet some of these new anomalies were much harder to detect or they matured much faster than normal. In some cases, like the 7th magnitude anomaly that started all this, it was both. These special cases were the reason Sethara had been tasked with doing routine sweeps. Though technically one of the weakest Antediluvians in terms of combat strength, Sethara possessed the highest synchronization rate with the Emanation, which among other things gave her an acute sense for locating anomalies. Unfortunately, the sweeps were beginning to interfere with her ability to manage her own sector.

She completed her transition into Sector 1. Typically, she started her sweeps from the outer sectors which were the most at risk of anomaly spawns, then worked her way back to Sector 1. Her Providence flared to life behind her like a newborn star. With only a slight mental nudge, she initiated the sector-wide scan, eager to be done with her sweep. Golden tendrils extended from her Providence and fed her information as they alighted on her body.

[COMMENCING SECTOR SCAN: SCAN LOCATION; Sector 1, Zones 1

through 9]

Scanning for Anomalies ...

Number of Anomalies: 0

Scanning World Record ...

Unusual World Activity detected in Zone 7 of Section 1

Scanning for Irregularities in the Emanation...

Unauthorized Access detected in Zone 7 of Section 1

[SCAN COMPLETE: Would you like additional information?]

Sethara resisted the urge to dismiss her Providence. She hadn't expected to find anything amiss in her own sector. Typically, the inner sectors almost never had issues. In the millennium since she'd been charged with overseeing Sector 1, there had been only a handful of matters that needed her direct intervention. For the most part, she dedicated her time to monitoring the plethora of inhabited worlds under her care. While unusual world activity wasn't inherently bad since she had multiple advanced worlds in her sector, the unusual activity raised a red flag when paired with unauthorized access. Such a combination likely meant an individual had ascended into the Transcendent Realm without proper authorization. Preparing herself, she commanded her Providence to provide additional information.

Visions streamed into her mind of the incidents in question. Her Providence provided information on the unusual world activity first. Images of men in powered armor patrolling a gigantic crater flashed through her mind. The surroundings indicated that some sort of battle had taken place. Pits in the ground and fires yet to be doused decorated the background along with corpses and broken machinery. Nearby, a commander stood atop a platform speaking to a group of soldiers. He leaned heavily on the haft of a great battle-ax whose blade glowed with the dim light of a dying fire. His armor was riddled with dents and cuts, but he appeared relatively healthy considering the amount of damage present. The soldiers listened to him speak with rapt attention and even the men patrolling the crater were listening. Sethara recognized the world though her attention was drawn to the crater. A clear view of the crater presented itself at her behest. Carefully, she inspected it while her Providence delivered its report.

[COMMENCING REPORT: TOPIC; Status of World CXCIX of Sector 1]

Records show a rapid deterioration of world matter independent of native life-form activity.

Abnormal gravitational fluctuations detected.

Minor signs of distortion in the Emanation detected.

All signs point to the manifestation of an anomaly.

Scanning for anomalies …

Number of anomalies: 0

[REPORT COMPLETE: Would you like to continue to the next topic?]

With a single step, Sethara moved through her sector and arrived at the world in question. The prospect of an anomaly appearing in Sector 1 was horrifying. Anomalies by their very nature caused destabilization and ruin where they spawned. Each anomaly weathered a small hole in the Emanation opening a pathway for the horrors that lurked beyond. Antediluvians had the ability to destroy the horrors and seal the openings in permanent stasis; however, they couldn't close them. Each opening destabilized the Emanation in the local area. Even sealed in stasis, the anomaly would increase the likelihood of other anomalies spawning nearby. If anomalies were beginning to appear in Sector 1, the problem was far worse than anyone in Eden realized.

She took manual control of her Providence which heightened her already divine senses to their limits. She scanned over World CXCIX and its surroundings looking for any possible signs of interference. Countless streams of information flew through her mind which processed and cataloged in relation to her search. Augmented by her Providence, she sensed the exact point of unauthorized access in less than a second. Before she investigated further, a white light flashed throughout her body as she activated her defenses. She couldn't be sure what or who was behind the unauthorized activity, so she erred on the side of caution.

Carefully, she connected to the Emanation through her Providence and threaded her consciousness into the point of access. Her perception of time slowed as her focus narrowed to include only World CXCIX. With a thought, she started the process of reviewing the recent access records. She dismissed the first few records because they depicted her arrival and scans of her sector. However, the next couple of access records caught her attention. Shortly before her arrival, someone had accessed the Emanation. The access had been very clumsy which meant the culprit had only recently ascended to the Transcendent Realm. Further investigation showed the culprit had created a temporary stasis, but she couldn't tell who the culprit was. When she attempted to access the next record, her Providence faltered.

[Unable to read record.]

Sethara blinked several times in surprise. She'd never encountered such a response in all her time as an Antediluvian. Unhappy with her Providence's response, she engaged a search for other instances of an inability to read a record.

[No records found. Would you like to contact The Garden for assistance?]

Unconsciously, Sethara frowned at the thought of reporting another unique problem to The Garden. If she did so without any other information, she would end up tasked with investigating the incident further anyway, since the problem was in her sector. Dismissing the prompt, she reviewed the last few records and found nothing of note. The next few moments were spent isolating the two offending records for closer examination. Her Providence failed to read the record once more, but when it attempted to move on to the next record, she stopped it. The stream of information froze which allowed her to access the information without her Providence.

Like the other records, the information passed through her mind as she attempted to read it, however, the attempt resulted in a pang of pain followed swiftly by a headache. Oddly, the pain wasn't caused by an attack that would have triggered her defenses. Instead, her mind had simply failed to process the information provided by the record which had resulted in mental feedback. Dispelling the headache with a thought, she took a different approach. She examined the record detailing the creation of the temporary stasis. Unlike the previous one, Sethara easily accessed the record, however, the individual who enacted the temporary stasis remained a mystery. In an attempt to identify the offender, she initiated a scan for recent entries into the Transcendent Realm.

[No new entries found.]

She frowned and muttered under her breath. "That makes no sense. If there haven't been any recent ascensions, then who erected such a haphazard stasis?"

Closer examination of the record didn't help either. Frustratingly, whenever she attempted to identify the individual in the record, she received another dose of mental feedback similar to the one for the unreadable record. Something was amiss, though exactly what it was eluded her. Someone had enacted an unauthorized temporary stasis, but she found no record of new entries into the Transcendent Realm which meant the perpetrator was from Eden, or the world itself had advanced far enough to access limited temporal control. Either way, she would need to conduct a thorough investigation. Then, there was the mysterious unreadable record of unusual world activity which could potentially be related to an anomaly. She didn't know where to begin unraveling that particular conundrum. For now, her best bet was to collect samples from the site for her Providence to analyze. If she found any leftover anomalous material, she might be able to piece together what she was missing.

As she mulled over her plan of action, a slight fluctuation in the Emanation caught her attention. It was distant and had her perception not been enhanced from manually controlling her Providence, she wouldn't have picked up on it. A quick inspection of the fluctuation told her it was coming from Genesis which immediately worried her. Fluctuations weren't supposed to happen on Genesis. Frowning down at World CXCIX, she decided to revisit the problematic records after she saw to Genesis.

"I wonder if I'll ever know peace again?" she mused, as she missed the tranquil period before she discovered the 7th magnitude anomaly. Permanently isolating the records for later examination, she stepped through space-time, Genesis-bound.

Chapter 21

Jagan broke through the roof of the citadel. She flew high into the night sky, pausing with the moon at her back. Her mind was racing and her heart hammered in her chest. She needed to calm herself. *Something* had spoken to her beneath the citadel. Merely hearing its voice had nearly thrown her into a panic. Her third eye flashed with power resonating with the dream essence all around her. Her mind refocused and her heartbeat slowed. Once calm, she surveyed her surroundings.

As her Aspect enabled her to move through solids, her third eye allowed her to see through almost any material. Its sight wasn't perfect. It was like gazing into a thin fog, that was not quite capable of masking anything close to her but obscured the further reaches of her sight. The situation was not good.

Tremors shook the earth. While she completed her assessment, she could sense the tremors growing fiercer. Small trees and some of the more fragile buildings in Somn collapsed filling the air with dust and dirt clouds. Beneath the citadel, a mass of red energy writhed rapidly toward the surface. She recognized the sickening feel of the energy immediately. The tide of Sin felt volatile and *hungry* in her spiritual perception. She had less than a minute before it broke through.

My dream ... she thought horrified. She needed to find Enkai. He clearly had a part to play in what was to come. She turned toward Old Omen and activated her Aspect once more. Her body became insubstantial to eliminate the wind resistance, as she shot through the sky like an arrow in flight. Using her will, she called out to Onki, but he didn't answer.

The moment she left the city boundaries of Somn, a great thundering boom echoed across the forest below her. She looked back fearing the worst and saw her nightmares made reality. Hundreds of creatures composed of Sin burst through the ground into the streets of Somn. They were a chaotic mass with features ranging from the beautiful to the horrific. Jagan realized they reminded her of Eidolons which often took shapes reminiscent of their s in life. However, unlike Eidolons, they radiated chaos and hostility.

The ground shook more violently. The wind swept into a frenzied tempest of fearsome gusts and howling gales. Storm clouds forming directly over Somn rapidly expanded as more creatures broke through the surface. Along the ground, cracks formed and expanded rapidly until they covered the entirety of Somn. Each crack released the same violent red essence, like fissures releasing toxicity into the world from deep within the earth.

Much to Jagan's horror, the chaos didn't stop there. The creatures moved as soon as they reached the surface. Jagan longed for the ability to scream — she wanted to warn the denizens of the forest. Countless great beasts called the forest their home. If these creatures below flooded into the forest, those great beasts would be caught unaware. The forest she loved would become a warzone and a spawning ground for demons. She couldn't let that happen.

She stopped mid-flight and turned back to Somn. The ancient city swarmed with embodiments of Sin, all pushing toward the forest. With a massive surge of her spirit, Jagan poured an incredible amount of anima into a single technique. Around the city floating high above the writhing spirits of Sin, the remaining dream wisps of Somn heeded her call. Amidst the rumbling, thundering, and screeching, a single pure note rang across the city. At the borders, walls of forged dream essence formed, each one curving upward toward the center of the Somn. Several of the wisps winked out of existence and Jagan felt the strain on her spirit for the first time in centuries, but she successfully constructed a protective dome over the entire city.

The earliest Sin creatures to emerge smashed against the barrier with dogged fury and more of the malevolent spirits rushed forward to attack the barrier. They crashed against it like a scarlet wave. Jagan knew it wouldn't hold forever, but it would buy her time to get to Enkai and give the great beasts of the forest time to figure out what was happening. Though the barrier stopped the creatures, the fissures continued to spread through the earth. Hopefully, the other Elders sensed the Sin before it was too late.

She continued her flight toward Old Omen without further delay. When she passed the river that divided her territory from Onki's, pain lanced through her spirit. She tumbled downward hundreds of feet before she recovered. Dazed, she flew back up only to be assaulted once more with excruciating spiritual pain. She recovered much faster the second time. After erecting several layers of defense, she ascended and braced for the next assault. When it came, she was ready.

What hit her could only be categorized as spiritual malice. In her opinion, it shouldn't even have qualified as an attack — it was pure spiritual pressure. To attack her in such a way, the assailant had to be leagues more powerful than her. Beneath the calm of her mind, she could feel the ancient tethers of her primitive bloodline calling for her to flee as quickly as possible. She ignored them. After all, she was no common beast driven by instinct. Her mistress had told her to find Enkai. Her dreams and Evaniel's words told her that the boy was pivotal.

She steeled her resolve and pushed back against the pressure. She brought the full might of her spirit and will to bear against the assailing force. With a great mental shout, she repelled the assault which gave herself room to breathe. She expected another attack, so she prepared her defenses again. And this time, she laid a trap. Whatever was attacking her was powerful, but even the mightiest of creatures could be bested if caught unaware.

The trap was simple but effective. When the attacker launched another onslaught on her spirit, it would be assaulted in kind with an attack of her own, a Phantasm, a creation of the mind made real through pure force of will. It was the deadliest form of attack a dream artist or beast could muster. Only truly skilled dream artists could manifest one. Because she was a phantasmal owl, Jagan had a natural talent for such attacks. She poured her will into the Phantasm and crafted a vicious attack that would break the mind of her assailant. She wove it into the foundation of her defenses so it would react the moment they were triggered.

The fourth attack came just as she finished preparing. The force of the pressure was twice as powerful and nearly overwhelmed her defenses in the first breath. Thankfully, her trap went off at that moment. The Phantasm launched, almost undetectable to any spiritual senses but her own, and completely undetectable by mundane means. One of the traits that made Phantasms so deadly was their subtlety. Not all were as insidious as Jagan's attack, but all inherited the elusive nature of dream anima.

Jagan felt her attack connect and the pressure ceased immediately. Following her spiritual senses, she descended closer to the forest floor in search of her assailant. Even if her attack didn't incapacitate her opponent, it would leave them vulnerable. She needed to finish this before her foe recovered.

A magnificent attack. A chilling voice echoed directly into her mind. Jagan abruptly pulled her descent short. She recognized the voice. It belonged to the very same creature that had spoken in the Sphere of Dreams. But how could it be speaking to her? It should be trapped within her barrier in Somn with the Sin creatures at the very least. Her thoughts were disrupted as the voice spoke once more. *Let's see how well you handle it.*

Jagan barely had time to realize what the voice meant before the Phantasm hit her. Her strained defenses didn't stand a chance against its insidious destructive force. In the brief moments of resistance that she managed, Jagan recognized that the attack was a more powerful mirror of her own. Then, it ripped through her mind. Since she had created it, she knew she couldn't repel the Phantasm once it took root, especially in its empowered state. So, Jagan guarded the inner reaches of her consciousness and formed a bastion around her most powerful memories in an effort to save the most important parts of her mind from the attack. In those desperate moments of salvage, she was undone by the very attack she had wrought.

Mentally unable to command her body, she plummeted hundreds of feet crashing to the earth like a meteor from the stormy sky. She vaguely registered the pain of her broken body from her sanctuary deep within her mind. She had landed directly on top of a fissure that emitted Sin essence. She could feel the Sin as it probed at the edges of her tattered unprotected spirit. Once inside, the foul energy would warp her body and spirit into that of a demon. If she were able, she would have shattered her core right then and there. She would rather die than be transformed into a mindless monstrosity.

Despite her condition, she was already beginning to recover. Her decision to protect the innermost parts of her mind paid off. Within her mental sanctuary, she began the agonizing process of reconstructing her ravaged mind. Her consciousness was severely dulled, she didn't notice the spirit that watched her from several feet away. She barely registered its presence as it floated over to her battered body. It was small and hardly of note. Only the familiar feeling of dream anima caught her attention.

A single dream wisp floated above her. Seeking assistance, she reached out to it. If she could use the dream wisp as an anchoring point, then she could mend her broken mind much faster. She made contact with the wisp, yet instead of the mist-like feel of dream anima, she experienced a shock of chaotic malice. In her vulnerable state, she panicked and tried to pull away from the contact; however, no matter how hard she struggled, she couldn't break free. The *wisp* held her mind firmly in its will — which should have been impossible. Wisps didn't have wills of their own. Even in her impaired state, Jagan should have been able to easily break her connection with the wisp. There was only one way it could hold her. One of the memories she held onto triggered. Her mistress was saying something, but the words were unclear. She stopped struggling and attempted to focus on the memory. The vision clarified and Evaniel's warning echoed in her mind.

"It's not a wisp!"

When she realized the truth, her still recovering mind screamed in primal terror. The *wisp* which had simply been holding her mind in its grasp chuckled. She watched in horror as the dream wisp transformed. The purple mist of its body changed into a ball of writhing scarlet energy. Tendrils of barely restrained Sin sprouted from the wisp and latched onto her body. The voice of her nightmares spoke once more.

How unfortunate. The loyal servant abandoned by her mistress, it said within her mind. Jagan mentally curled into a ball seeking some escape from her circumstance. Shame and fear ruled her thoughts. She was cognizant enough to know she should do something, but not whole enough to do anything. She was powerless. From within the mass of red tendrils, two serpentine eyes gazed down at her. *It's a shame that you chose to put up that barrier. Had you not, I might have let you be, but you chose to become an obstacle.*

Jagan barely understood what the voice was saying. Her mind still struggled to comprehend anything in its debilitated state. Because the entity held her hostage within its will, she couldn't recover and her subconscious flooded her with fear that destroyed any attempt at focus. She abandoned all pretense of resistance and retreated deeper into her sanctuary. The feelings there were warm and hopeful, in utter contrast to her current situation. She simply wanted to serve her mistress. It was all she'd ever wanted — to serve the woman she loved and admired.

Ah, so you wish to serve? Without any defenses, her spirit stood no chance against the creature. Sin poured into her anima channels and burrowed toward her core. Jagan understood what was happening and she wept. The voice consoled her in a hushed tone. *Don't worry. You will serve your purpose well.*

Pain and chaos followed. The Sin consumed everything it touched. Once it had compromised her anima channels, it split toward her mind and core. Futilely, she tried to fight back, but it utilized the power of her own spirit against her. Then, it reached her mind. She called forth the full force of her shattered will to drive it away from her sanctuary. Sadly, no matter what she did, the Sin progressed ever closer. When it breached her mental sanctum, her will to fight broke. She begged and she pleaded, but it was deaf to her cries. It consumed and it changed her. When the Sin finally settled, she was Jagan no longer.

Chapter 22

Enkai and Nin raced down the crumbling ridges and treacherous trails of Old Omen. The very earth beneath their feet shook with a terrible fury. The effect on Old Omen made moving down the mountain dangerous. Enkai had already almost died when the hard stone beneath his feet had collapsed and sent him tumbling downward. Only Nin's fast reflexes had saved him. Without at least a Silver body, there was no chance he'd have survived the fall.

She had composed herself shortly after Enkai's familiar darted off. However, she continued to steal troubled glances toward the peak of Old Omen. Enkai couldn't blame her. The earthquakes were loud, but they didn't compare to the cacophony unfolding at the summit. Thunderous cracks echoed every few seconds from above that made Enkai concerned the mountain might collapse from the top down. Even worse, he understood the natural state of a volcano after seeing the one guarded by

Daughter of Fire. If Old Omen woke from its long slumber, he couldn't even imagine the devastation it might bring to the Forbidden Forest.

Moving quickly, they arrived at the burrow within a few minutes of their initial departure from the summit. Enkai could never have moved so fast on his own, but Nin carried him most of the way. He cared little for his dignity given the situation, so he didn't complain especially not after his near demise.

"Brem! Jak!" Nin called frantically as they arrived at the burrow entrance. A cursory glance inside told Enkai that the burrow was empty. Nin quickly realized the same thing because she whirled on Enkai in a near panic. "Where could they be?!"

Before Enkai could answer, a man of stone emerged from the ground within the burrow. Enkai immediately recognized it as one of Elder Onki's puppets. It quickly jogged up to them.

"Nin," the puppet said with Elder Onki's voice. "Brem and Jak are safe. Come, I will explain while we move."

"Wait!" Enkai said. He dashed into the burrow. Once inside, he located the woven leaf backpack Nin had made for him years before along with a medium-sized wooden box. Shoving the box into the bag, Enkai darted back outside where Nin and the puppet waited. The entire affair had taken less than half a minute.

Neither bothered asking what he had retrieved, and they moved the moment he emerged. Since the burrow was closer to the base of Old Omen, the terrain proved a bit tamer than on their descent from the summit. As such, Enkai traveled on foot alongside Nin and Onki's puppet. They set a ruthless pace, but Enkai made sure to keep pace by occasionally Enhancing his legs as he'd done on his initial climb. During their rush, Elder Onki relayed the situation.

"These earthquakes are waking Old Omen. When we reach the base, you must take the children and head south," he said to Nin.

"But if we head south, we'll be leaving the forest. We'll be heading right into human territory," she said glancing worriedly at Enkai. "Enkai will become a target if we do that. It won't be safe for any of us."

"I know," Elder Onki said. His voice was strained and heavy as though he carried a great burden. "But you cannot remain here. Something is *wrong* within the forest. I sense Sin. Far too much of it. Even if I succeed in calming the volcano before it wakes, you will not be safe in the forest and I cannot spare the power to protect you. I'm already at my limit."

Nin huffed. The expression on her face spoke volumes on how she felt about leaving the forest, but she didn't protest. Even Enkai heard the gravity in his master's voice. There was no other option.

When Nin didn't respond, Elder Onki said, "Hopefully, it will only be temporary, little rabbit. However, just in case it is not, I left a black iron amulet with my puppet at the base of the mountain. Use it to hide Enkai. Take him to the Sage of the West who lives on the Black Isles. She will aid you."

Elder Onki's words placed the seeds of real fear into Enkai's heart. Sure, he'd been afraid when the quakes started, however, his master's words contained a dreadful sense of finality. Enkai could hear *acceptance* in the ancient sage's words. Acceptance of what? What would happen to the Sage of the North?

While he had been anxious during his descent, he'd never really believed he was in danger. Elder Onki was like a mountain in his own right: unbending, reliable, and more powerful than anything Enkai had ever imagined before meeting him. If he was truly at his limit, it meant whatever was happening was *really* bad.

One glance up at the Sin-red moon reminded him that he should be alert. Oddly, during this entire ordeal, his Sin had been quiet even when he'd nearly fallen down the mountain. Usually, he could at least feel it stirring when he was in distress. Now though, it was disturbingly tranquil.

As if he could read Enkai's thoughts, Onki's puppet looked back at Enkai though it continued moving easily. Through the puppet, Elder Onki asked, "En, how do you feel?"

"I'm okay. I can go faster, by the way," Enkai said.

"I'm sure you could. I see you've been experimenting. Focusing anima into your legs to run and jump faster? Keep up that type of initiative and you'll have no problem developing your own techniques when you're ready," his master said. Enkai swelled with pride. "That said, you must conserve your strength. You'll need to move quickly once we get to the base and Nin can't carry you all."

They were silent for the rest of their journey to the base of the mountain. When they arrived, Brem and Jak emerged from behind a nearby tree along with another stone puppet. Both rushed up to Nin nuzzling her and asking dozens of questions all at once. Nin did her best to calm them, but her relief showed just as much as theirs. The moment she saw them, most of the tension in her body dissipated.

Enkai smiled while observing the affectionate display and said, "Hey guys, I'm perfectly fine too. Thanks for asking."

Jak who was currently squeezed between Nin and Brem in a three-part embrace said, "We were worried about you too, En! Brem even wanted to go looking for you when the rumbles started."

Brem broke free of the embrace. Her tail puffed up as she scowled at Jak. Enkai laughed, and to Brem, he said, "Sounds like you really were worried."

"I was only worried cause you're so weak. So fragile you could've stumbled and died for all I knew. Anybody would be worried," Brem retorted. She huffed and dug her paw into the ground in a show of annoyance. Enkai just laughed again. Brem's ears flattened against her head and a tiny growl started in her throat. "What's so funny?!"

"You're right. I am pretty weak," Enkai said kneeling down beside Brem. He patted her on the head. Brem looked up at him suspiciously but didn't object. "Lucky for me, I've got a great family looking out for me.'

Brem met his gaze and her tail wagged a bit, though as soon as she noticed it, she pulled away from Enkai. "Well, don't get too used to it. You'll have to pull your weight eventually."

Enkai smirked at his sister's words. Brem was always like this. The little umbral fox couldn't comfortably display emotion to anyone except Nin. Enkai didn't know why, but he'd never asked. He only knew it had something to do with what had happened before Brem came under Nin's care. Besides, the knowledge wouldn't change anything. Brem was his sister and that's all that mattered. They each had their own ways of showing affection. Off to the side, Jak had a large grin plastered across his face, while Nin looked close to tearing up.

"While this is touching, we have more pressing matters at hand," Elder Onki said. Just as Enkai got to his feet, another earthquake rocked the land and nearly knocked him back to the ground. One of the puppets caught him with a steadying hand. As Enkai made to step away, the puppet held his arm firmly. He gave the puppet a questioning look. "You all need to get moving, but before that, I must speak with Enkai." With that, the puppet nodded to Nin and pulled Enkai a few feet away from the rest of the group.

Enkai asked, "Is this about my Sin?"

"Partially, you need to be on your guard once you begin moving through the forest," he said. Enkai opened his mouth to assure Elder Onki that he would be alert, but he was interrupted immediately. "Do not speak, just listen. I have much to tell you and we are running short on time." Another earthquake rattled their surroundings punctuating his remarks. A darker, more humorous part of Enkai wondered if Elder Onki was creating the earthquakes to be dramatic. "First, put this on once you leave the forest and do not take it off in the presence of other humans."

The puppet extended its closed fist then opened it to reveal a tiny ball of lumpy black metal with a translucent silk cord threaded through it. Enkai took the amulet and immediately felt the effects. His spirit quieted the moment the black metal touched his flesh until it was dull and muted. He grimaced in distaste. Reluctantly, he placed the amulet within his robes.

"Black iron. It disrupts anima and essence; however, it will also stop others from being able to perceive your spirit and serve as minor protection against spiritual attacks. While you wear it, you won't be able to use techniques and your spiritual senses will be dulled, so it's far from ideal, but it is the best solution I can offer you for now," Elder Onki said.

Once again, a quake shook the earth though this time the sound of several trees falling echoed in the distance. Thunder cracked across the sky and rain fell from dark clouds. Tiny fissures began forming at the base of Old Omen. A few feet away, Nin hugged his siblings and whispered reassurances to them while they all waited anxiously for Enkai and Elder Onki to finish speaking. Enkai wanted to go to them, but Elder Onki wouldn't have delayed them if it weren't important.

When Elder Onki continued, his voice was even more strained than before. "I cannot maintain these puppets much longer. Old Omen grows restless. Listen carefully, En." Enkai pulled his focus back to Elder Onki. "There is much I had hoped to teach you and hopefully, I will have the chance, but if I do not, Nin will at least be able to set you on the right path. I meant what I said earlier. You are ready to move forward on your journey through the divine arts. Your foundation is solid as a mountain. All you need is anima to fuel the advancement and you should reach Bronze, then Silver without issue. However, you must be wary! The stronger you become, the more powerful your Sin will grow and the harder it will be to control. En, do *not* underestimate Sin or it *will* consume you."

Enkai felt as though time had stopped, while his heart continued beating. He recognized the feeling — adrenaline. He became acutely aware of the weight of the elixir within his robes. According to Nin, all he needed to do was drink it and he'd have enough anima to break through to Bronze and, possibly, Silver.

Eagerly, he pulled out the clay tube and gazed at it. The puppet gazed at the vial for a moment before shaking its head slowly. With one hand, it grabbed Enkai's shoulder and with the other, it pushed the hand gripping the vial back into Enkai's robes.

"I assume Nin made that from the Orlang fruit Jak found," Elder Onki said. It didn't surprise Enkai that the ancient tortoise knew about the fruit, but he was surprised his master could ascertain the nature of the elixir by looking through a puppet. Enkai hoped to one day have such amazing spiritual senses. He reluctantly replaced the elixir in one of his inner pockets. The puppet nodded approvingly. "Advancing may be simple, but don't drink that until you are in a safe location. You won't be able to process it all at once anyway and such a large influx of anima could excite your Sin or disrupt your ability to Enhance yourself."

Enkai bowed and said, "Thank you for your wisdom, master. I will wait."

"Good. Now go," he said. Enkai ran over to his family who immediately began to move. As they entered the tree line, Elder Onki called out, "Nin, I—"

Enkai couldn't hear the last few words over the roar of thunder above. Next to him, Nin's ears twitched. She stopped to look back causing them all to halt as they waited for her. When she turned back to them, her expression was pained, and she swiped a hand across her eyes. The rain came down in torrents and soaked them all even through the heavy canopy. In the direction of Elder Jagan's territory, Enkai saw a red light that filled him with a terrible sense of foreboding. One last time, Enkai glanced back at the puppets created by Onki. He wished he could have seen the old great beast one more time. An earthquake pulsed through the earth and the puppets crumbled into mud that was swept away in rain. As Enkai ran deeper into the forest with his family, he wondered if he would ever see his master again.

Chapter 23

Red moonlight played among the dancing shadows beneath the canopy as Enkai and his family fled. The sky churned violently like a feral beast roused from its slumber. A din of cracking stone and shifting earth sounded from the direction of Old Omen. They were moving quickly. Nin led the way carrying Jak who was the slowest of the three siblings. Meanwhile, Enkai ran behind her with Brem by his side. Though Enkai was Enhancing his movement by channeling anima into his legs, Brem kept pace simply by virtue of her bloodline. Like the umbral wolves that his father had killed on their way to the Sacred Vas tree so many years ago, Brem became stronger and faster while moving under the cover of darkness and shadow.

They traveled in silence. Initially, Enkai and his siblings had thrown questions at Nin, some of which she answered. When the cries of great beasts started echoing through the forest, they had gone quiet. The night's events weighed heavily on each of them. They were running from their home without any guarantee that they would be able to return. Nin had tried to reassure them, but they all heard the uncertainty in her voice. All the while, the ominous Sin-red moon hung in the sky. Nin constantly glanced back at Enkai with concern in her eyes and Elder Onki's warning was fresh in his mind. Despite all the apprehension around it, his Sin remained eerily calm even though Enkai himself was undeniably very anxious. Normally, the scarlet anima showed some kind of reaction when he experienced stress. Enkai simply hoped he wasn't experiencing the calm before the storm.

The group moved south parallel to the river that divided the territories of Elder Onki and Elder Jagan. Unfortunately, they couldn't seek refuge with Elder Jagan or any of the other Elders because if Old Omen erupted the destruction would spread for miles. To make matters worse, Nin sensed several hostile presences from near the river which meant they had to avoid getting too close.

Eventually, the terrain became more and more uneven as the elevation steadily decreased. If they'd been traveling along the riverbank, they would have seen the rapids that rushed through the forest until the terrain finally evened out at the lowest elevation. Torrents of rain washed over them and made traversing the sloping landscape even more dangerous. Once the ground turned into a treacherous mix of mud and rain-slicked stone, Nin relaxed their pace. Due to difficult terrain and quakes that constantly threatened to throw them from their feet, their progress slowed to a grueling crawl. Midway down, Jak stopped piggybacking with Nin in order to help Brem and Enkai move through the terrain. Jak seemed to have much less trouble moving around which Enkai attributed to his brother being an earth great beast. Much to his embarrassment, Enkai needed more help than Brem. Even while Enhancing his legs, he still struggled to move at all without falling over. He felt like a toddler taking his first steps, especially with Jak reaching out to steady him when he started to lose his footing occasionally.

During their descent, lightning flashed overhead followed by the crack of thunder. Enkai saw a bolt strike a tree about a hundred feet below where the terrain leveled out. While unlikely, the idea of being struck by lightning only increased his trepidation. All the while, his muscles burned from the exertion required just to continue moving in these conditions even while cycling. He gained a new appreciation of his physical training over the past half-decade. When he'd first trekked through the wilderness years ago with his father on their way to the Sacred Vas tree, the hike had routinely exhausted him so much so that they had been forced to take frequent breaks and that was with good weather. At that time, he could never have imagined himself traveling for over an hour in such perilous conditions. On the plus side, Enkai noticed his left elbow no longer pained him. He didn't remember when he stopped feeling the dull ache, but he wasn't going to complain.

Near the end of their descent, Nin stopped at a cluster of trees. She used the trunk of a tree to anchor herself against the continuous flow of rain and mud washing down the slope. Enkai and his siblings latched onto the same tree which despite growing on uneven terrain felt quite sturdy. All three siblings were panting and appreciated the break. Though his nerves kept his mind alert, his spirit ached from the strain of the last day. Just last night, he had exhausted himself fighting Elder

Onki's puppets. His spirit had yet to fully recover even if his body had. If spiritual strain rendered him incapable of cycling, he would certainly collapse of exhaustion without the anima to sustain him. He sorely wished he knew a breathing exercise to help replenish his spirit faster.

Meanwhile, they all noticed Nin's heavy breathing and bowed posture. Jak and Brem exchanged concerned looks since she should've been the last of them to get tired. Though she never talked about her cultivation rank, Enkai suspected she was at least Silver though now he wondered if she was within the Gold Realm. Elder Jagan's statement about beasts being able to change their bodies as they got more powerful lent some credence to his suspicions. Nin spent most of her time in a humanoid form that allowed her to easily walk on two legs and handle alchemical tools.

For his part, Enkai couldn't help but feel partly responsible for Nin's condition. It was for his benefit that she had refined the Orlang elixir which had drained a good deal of her anima, not to mention all the energy she'd burned carrying him down the mountainside once the quakes started.

Abruptly, Nin went rigid. Her ears perked up and her nose twitched. She gazed to the east which reminded Enkai that their trek paralleled the journey he and Nin had taken the night before on their way to Elder Jagan. In fact, if Enkai remembered correctly, Nin's creepy spider friend lived not too far from where they were. He thought to himself, *I hope we don't run into him.*

No more than ten seconds after this thought, Nin tackled Enkai to the ground in a burst of sudden speed. Enkai cried out in surprise then groaned as the wooden box in his backpack jammed into his spine. With rain and mud washing over him, he choked while trying to gain his bearing. Immediately after he hit the ground, Nin's body weight disappeared. He got to his feet and was nearly blinded by a bright flash of moonlight which was followed by a mind-piercing screech that nearly sent him stumbling back to the ground.

Once the spots cleared from his eyes, Enkai saw Nin looking up at the branches of the tree. Behind her, Jak and Brem whimpered while also looking upward. Enkai activated his Spirit-sight. When he saw what hung from the tree, his heart skipped a beat.

Anansi, Nin's giant spider friend, loomed ominously over their group. Something was horribly wrong with him. His already terrifying arachnid features had been warped into a horrific visage. His fangs, which had been small compared to the rest of his body, curved nearly half a foot from his jaw like wicked daggers. From the tip of each fang, opaque liquid coalesced before dripping onto the ground where it hissed and bubbled in the mud and stone. His forelegs had been similarly sharpened to deadly points. The four long legs that supported his body were bent at odd angles making Enkai wonder if Anansi was even capable of walking anymore. The hairs covering his body vibrated in a strange pattern that distorted his image. Finally, each of his eight eyes shimmered with the baleful spark of Sin. One word sprung to Enkai's mind when he beheld Anansi's twisted form.

"Demon," he said taking a trembling step back. The moment he spoke, Anansi's Sin-filled eyes all swiveled to focus on him. From all around them, a warbling gargle echoed. It reminded Enkai of Anansi's voice, but there were no words, only cacophony. If he concentrated, he felt like he might have been able to hear the signs of something more. Unfortunately for him, he had very little time to think about the noise.

His spirit erupted with pain. He gasped in agony and nearly collapsed. Panic threatened to take hold, but Enkai focused his mind. Old habits kicked in and he tried to suppress his fear with a few calming breaths. A quick glance inward told him nothing was wrong with his spirit on the surface; however, the pain radiated from deeper within. Before he could probe any further, a burst of wracking agony shot through him.

He screamed.

Nin glanced back at him, her face strained with worry and stress, while his brother and sister froze in horror. The moment Nin turned away from Anansi, he pounced. Brem called out a warning and Nin reacted just in time. Instead of avoiding the attack, she summoned a ball of blue moonlight in her palm and faced her former friend. When they collided, Anansi attempted to snare Nin with his warped forelegs. Nin twisted her body at the last second and slid underneath the demon spider. Mid-slide, she thrust her palm upward into the underside of Anansi's head. Her blow exploded in a radiant burst of moonlight that lit up the surrounding area. Anansi was sent airborne, but one of his legs whipped out catching Nin in the side of the head.

Enkai watched the entire exchange feeling completely helpless. The pain brought him to the ground where he sucked in heaving breaths on all fours like a dying beast. Nearby, Brem had gone into full combat mode. She snarled at Anansi and shot dozens of shadow needles from her tail at the airborne arachnid. Jak, on the other hand, was approaching Enkai hesitantly. Even in his addled state, he could tell his little brother wanted to help but didn't know how to do so. He tried to speak though no words came, only a strained groan which increased the anxiety on Jak's face. He moved to put a hand on Enkai's shoulder.

Unfortunately, the moment his brother came within a foot of him, his suspiciously dormant Sin reacted. The scarlet anima went from tranquil to rabid in less than a second. It was like it had been waiting for its moment to strike. The agony increased one hundred-fold nearly knocking him unconscious. The cords of Sin coiled around his anima channels constricted and then expanded burning every inch of his spirit they touched. The closer Jak got, the more crazed his Sin became. A thought, both foreign and familiar, uncoiled in the depths of Enkai's mind. *Food.*

Deep spiritual hunger rocked through him. For a moment, his brother was no longer his brother. Enkai didn't see Jak, but easy prey full of rich earth anima. Once he got close enough, he would enhance both his arms and quickly snap the monkey's neck. Then, he could...

Enkai snapped out of it as his conscious mind reeled in disgust and horror at the idea of harming his brother. When his brother was no more than a few inches from him, he Enhanced himself then leapt backward startling Jak. Though he didn't realize it at the time due to the pain and horror, the jump carried him nearly a dozen feet backward which was far longer than he intended or should've been able to jump.

"Jak, stay away from me!" he shouted. As soon as he landed, he dug his hands and feet into the earth to stop his momentum from carrying him downhill. Just creating distance between himself and the group helped enormously. The pain subsided along with the hunger and the movements of his Sin slowed to a crawl. While not comfortable, it was much more manageable With his head free from the fog of pain and unwelcome thoughts, he surveyed the area. Jak stood at the same spot Enkai had left him before leaping away. He was staring at Enkai with a mix of confusion, hurt, and concern. Several feet behind Jak, Nin battled Anansi while Brem supported her with sporadic barrages of shadow needles. He immediately moved to assist Nin, however, the pain grew with each step he took and dark whispers echoed in the depths of his mind. After three steps, he stopped, unsure of what to do.

Jak, who was watching him the entire time, called out, "En, what's wrong?"

"I don't know. Don't worry about me though, help Nin," he said raising his voice to be heard over the rain, thunder, and sounds of battle. With one more anxious glance at him, Jak turned to help in the fight.

Stepping up next to Brem, Jak grabbed a fistful of mud and chucked it at Anansi as soon as he got a clear shot. In his Spirit-sight, Enkai saw the telltale yellow glow of earth anima infused into the mud that Jak threw. The anima-infused projectile smashed into Nin's opponent like hard stone The attack didn't do much damage from the looks of it, but it did distract Anansi for just a moment which was all Nin needed. Pale moonlight flashed through the area causing all three siblings to shield their eyes. The flash was followed by a mental screech of pain that echoed through the area and was then followed by silence. When the light faded, Nin stood over Anansi's corpse which bore several burn marks along with a smoking hole in the center of his body.

Jak and Brem rushed over to Nin who had suffered several cuts along her body from her former friend's sharp appendages along with a deep gouge on her brow. Enkai couldn't tell if any of the injuries were serious, but her jade-green fur was matted with blood. His siblings gently nuzzled her despite the injuries and she embraced them in kind. The embrace lasted a few seconds before she focused on Enkai. She released Brem and Jak then started walking toward him. Enkai noticed her movements were shaky which told him that either her exhaustion was getting the better of her or her injuries were as bad as they looked. Despite his desire to run to her, he felt the pain in his spirit increase as she drew closer. His Sin also grew more active with each step she took.

"Stop," he said holding up his hand and attempting to remain calm. She stopped. Her spirit brushed his once more probing for the problem. Oddly, the sensation carried with it much more feeling than it ever had. He felt her exhaustion and worry as well as her silent grief over Anansi's fate. Anansi had been her friend, yet he had died by her hand crazed and corrupted by Sin. Lastly, the emotion that overpowered all the others was love. Her motherly love was like a healing balm on his ailing spirit. As quickly as it came, her touch was gone.

After withdrawing her spirit, a look of despair passed through her eyes. He guessed it was probably in response to his Sin being active. Nin and Elder Onki had warned him since his arrival about the dangers of Sin. She gave him a reassuring smile, but he knew it was fake. She took another step forward causing the pain and Sin to react in kind. After seeing first hand the effects of her approach, she backed away a few steps. By the end of it, they stood ten feet apart staring at each other, yet to Enkai the distance felt much greater. From the look on Nin's face, he could tell she felt the same way.

"What's wrong with En?" Brem asked Nin as she and Jak walked over to stand next to her. Despite the fact that Enkai was sure both of his siblings had never seen a demon, they were holding up fairly well. Both of them were covered in mud and looked miserable. However, the fact that they'd managed to stand and fight as well as hold themselves together afterward spoke volumes of their mental tenacity.

Nin didn't answer immediately, so Enkai did. He said, "My Sin isn't dormant anymore. When you guys get closer, my spirit hurts and my Sin gets worked up. It started when Anansi showed up." He said no more, unwilling to voice the thoughts that had tainted his mind when Jak had tried to help him.

Brem and Jak exchanged confused looks which made sense since neither knew much about Sin or demons. Throughout his entire stay on Old Omen, his Sin had never caused any major issues, so there had been no reason for them to worry about it. Jak, ever-inquisitive, asked, "Are you going to be okay?"

Enkai wanted to reassure his little brother, but he couldn't bring himself to lie. He was exhausted, emotionally, physically, and spiritually. So, he said with a shrug, "I'm not sure. In truth, it's probably not safe for me to be around you guys. I might become a threat and hurt you."

"Enkai, that's not ... ," Nin started to say, but he interrupted her.

"I think you guys should go," he said. A long silence punctuated by the crack of thunder overtook the group. Though he hated it, Enkai would rather die alone than endanger his family. He watched his words take hold of each member of his family. He couldn't look Nin in the eye. Based on her expression, someone might as well have stabbed her in the heart. Jak trembled on the edge of tears as he kept his eyes on the ground with his hands balled into fists at his sides. In contrast, Brem looked as though she might bite Enkai.

"Don't be stupid!" Brem shouted startling him. "We can't leave you! We have to all make it out of this okay!" She pawed the ground aggressively as though she might charge. "If you say that again, I'll hate you forever!"

His sister's explosive response took Enkai completely off guard. He snapped out of the melancholy that had settled over him then clenched his fists in frustration. He didn't want this, but what else could he do? He worked up the courage to glance at Nin. Though he intended it to be a fleeting glance, she held his gaze with eyes filled with hardened resolve.

"We will never leave you, En," she said. Each word carried the fearsome authority only a mother could wield. Beside her, Jak wiped tears from his eyes and nodded fervently. Any resolve he had to leave his family shattered and blew away in the howling wind. Of course, he didn't want to leave them. He just didn't know what to do, and the fear of his Sin putting his family in danger hung heavily over his heart. Tears formed at the corners of his eyes. In a gentle voice that carried over the chaos around them, Nin said, "It's going to be okay, En."

He wiped the tears from his eyes smearing his face with dirt and nodded. He wanted to believe her more than anything, but a horrible dread anchored itself in his heart. Even so, he smiled. Wishing to change the subject quickly, Enkai took off his backpack and fished out the wooden box he'd retrieved from the burrow.

"Jak, catch!" he called as he threw the box underhand to his brother. Jak caught the box easily and his eyes widened. Nin's eyes brightened the moment she saw it while her posture eased significantly. She glanced at Enkai and he smiled, this time genuinely.

With Jak holding it, Nin opened the box to reveal two rows of six clay tubes similar to the one nestled within Enkai's robes. Each of the tubes was marked by colored paint which denoted the contents. The case contained Nin's personal elixir supply. In her haste to get to Brem and Jak, she must have forgotten about it, but Enkai had figured it would be useful. Before taking anything out, she asked Brem and Jak how they were feeling. Both said they were fine. With one quick glance at

Enkai, she carefully pulled three of the tubes from the box, two marked with green and another marked with pale blue.

"En," she called. With a pinpoint toss, she threw one of the green marked tubes at him which he caught with an outstretched hand. He unstoppered the tube and downed its contents in one gulp. He knew exactly what this elixir did. It was Nin's personal recipe for easing physical fatigue and rejuvenating strained muscles. He started feeling the effects almost immediately. The aches echoing throughout his body faded gradually until only the dull throb in his back remained from when the box had jammed into his spine. Nin drank the other two elixirs. Enkai knew that the pale blue tube contained some kind of healing elixir since Nin marked all her healing elixirs with pale blue to match the color of moonlight and her own anima. Stowing the elixir case in her bag, she leaned against the tree near Anansi's corpse for nearly a minute while the elixirs took effect. In that time, most of the cuts on her body healed completely while the others either closed or started to scab over. With the pouring rain washing away the blood in her fur, she appeared almost as good as new.

"Let's get moving," she said eyeing Anansi's corpse with a mixture of fear and grief. The three siblings raised no objections. Enkai had no wish to see what a demonic Eidolon looked like.

Their trek continued albeit a little awkwardly. Enkai had to keep his distance, so he followed behind them about a dozen feet which led to several pauses as they waited for him to navigate difficult stretches of the slope. He also fell several times. The first time he fell, Jak rushed to help him only to send Enkai into a fit of agony.

After that incident, their pace slowed even more than it had before their stop. Despite their abysmal pace, the family eventually made it to the end of the difficult terrain, but sadly, they didn't find any solace there.

All around them, malicious red light waited in the distance. They had nowhere to go. Every direction except for backward hinted of Sin. Nin stopped them to think of a plan. Meanwhile, she sent Jak to climb one of the trees in order to get a better look at their surroundings. Enkai rested a short distance away within sight of the others.

In order to keep his mind off the dull pain in his spirit, Enkai went through his belongings. He had a spare set of the green robes Nin made for him in the backpack along with a set of alchemy tools he'd made himself under Nin's supervision. Other than that, he only had the Orlang elixir, which he considered drinking for a full minute before replacing it in his robes, and the black iron amulet. With nothing better to do, Enkai fished the amulet out of his robes. Shockingly, his pain disappeared the moment his fingers brushed the cold metal. Quickly pulling the black iron lump out, he stared at it for a moment. With his other hand, he grabbed the thread tied around the dark metal and lifted it out of his palm. As soon as the black iron lifted from his skin, the pain returned. His eyes widened.

"Of course ...," he whispered to himself. Elder Onki had told him that black iron disrupted anima and essence. Since Sin was a type of anima, it made sense that the black iron would disrupt its activity. Just to make sure, he repeated his experiment once more touching the black iron to his skin while observing his spirit. Though the black iron made his spirit feel dull and unfocused, he could still see it if he concentrated hard enough. Once the black iron settled in his palm, his entire spirit stilled. The Sin stopped slowly coiling around his anima channels and settled into a position similar to its dormant state. Unfortunately, even though it was still, he could sense it pulsing with latent volatility like a rabid beast straining against its restraints.

After a few more tests, he sighed. The black iron definitely had a canceling effect on his Sin and made the pain in his spirit vanish. The fact that his pain vanished when the Sin calmed meant the two were related even though the pain had started before his Sin began causing trouble. He needed to talk to Nin about this. He didn't want to wear the black iron amulet while they traveled through the forest. It would render him incapable of defending himself as well as significantly hinder his ability to keep up with the group. At the very least, he had a starting point on how to manage his Sin. He added it to the long list of problems he had to deal with.

Holding the amulet by the thread to avoid contact, he prepared to call Nin. Unexpectedly, he felt something pull at him from within his spirit. He recognized the feeling immediately. It was the exact same feeling he got when he summoned his familiar, except the pull wasn't coming from his end of the bond. Instead, it felt like his familiar was calling to him. This had never happened before. Without even thinking, he tapped into his bond with the minor spirit. As soon as he did so, he felt an alien presence touch his mind. Before he could wonder what was happening, a familiar voice spoke through the bond.

Young Enkai, the voice said. Enkai immediately felt a surge of relief when he heard it.

Elder Jagan, he said through the bond. *How are you speaking to me right now?*

It's a long story, however, the short of it is that I used a technique that harnessed the power of all dream wisps after I was attacked in my home. Surprisingly, even your dream wisp responded to my technique. I am using it as a means to contact you, she said. Understanding dawned on him. Her story explained why his wisp had unexpectedly darted off when everything started. In truth, he hadn't even thought about his familiar since leaving Old Omen, as everything had happened so fast.

The news that Elder Jagan had been attacked also concerned him. He asked, *Are you all right? Who attacked you?*

I was injured, but it is nothing serious. I think you are familiar with at least one of my attackers, she said.

Through the bond, an image flowed into his mind. Two women stood before him in a world of fog and light. Though he vaguely recognized surroundings, his attention focused squarely on the women. The first was the most beautiful woman Enkai had ever seen. She wore flowing indigo robes that emitted faint traces of something greater. Her face was like a sculpture of perfect beauty which simultaneously made her hauntingly mesmerizing and distinctly alien. Her eyes were wells of power that bore directly into his soul. Lastly, crimson locks spilled over her shoulders and back framing her abnormally beautiful face. As shocking as seeing the first woman was, Enkai's heart nearly stopped when he saw the second.

Lin Chun hadn't changed much since the last time he'd seen her. She even still wore the matriarchal robes of the Lin clan as she had on their journey to the Sacred Vas tree. Unlike the last time he had seen her, she lacked any sort of authority. She seemed almost nervous from what he could tell and she was looking at the first woman expectantly. Additionally, Enkai noticed that both women had the same exact shade of crimson hair.

Before he had time to fully process the image, Elder Jagan continued: *Those women came to me asking questions about you. When I refused to tell them where you were, they attacked me. Although I defended myself, they were too powerful. I managed to escape, but they summoned demons to pursue me. That's when I used the technique that attracted your wisp. When I couldn't contact Onki, I tried reaching out to you.*

Enkai balked at the overflow of information. While he found it hard to believe that he was at the center this chaos, her story made sense to him. In addition, he had a chilling thought — had this all happened because he tried to scry Lin Chun? As far as he knew, Lin Chun was a powerful dream artist and from the looks of the other woman, so was she. Had they sensed his scrying attempt and tracked it back to Elder Jagan? After all, she had been the one to perform the scrying through the Well, not him. His stomach dropped at the thought that this might all be his fault.

Another thing that bothered him was the claim that Lin Chun and the mysterious woman had called forth the demons. How did they relate to Sin and how were they able to summon demons? Dozens of questions raced through his mind. He reached through the bond and said, *Elder Jagan, where are you? I have a lot of questions, but I'm with my family. We need to get out of the forest especially if what you say is true.*

I see. I'll send you my location. Be safe, young Enkai, she said and then sent him a series of images depicting where he needed to go.

Wasting no time, he grasped the black iron in his hand. If he was right, he would be able to approach his family while touching the amulet. His hunch was right. Nin regarded him with wide eyes when he came closer and backed up several steps as he approached.

"En, what are—" she said before stopping. She stared at him for a moment in concentration and he realized she must be trying to look at his spirit. Understanding dawned on her face. "Are you wearing the amulet Onki gave you?"

He nodded and explained, "I just realized that when I'm wearing it, I don't feel any pain and my Sin calms down." The news had a massively positive effect on her mood and alleviated some of her concerns. Before she could ask any more questions, he continued, "I have some other good news. Elder Jagan contacted me."

Nin's ears perked up. She took a few steps forward. Nearby, Brem noticed Enkai and made her way over hesitantly followed by Jak who had returned from his climb up the tree. Enkai glanced over each member of his family and resisted the urge to sweep them all into a fierce embrace. Instead, he told them what he had learned.

Chapter 24

Along with his family, Enkai raced to the location Elder Jagan had shown him. Since Enkai wore the black iron amulet, they moved at a slower pace, though he maintained a brisk jog thanks to the effects of Nin's rejuvenating elixir. He led the way. Thankfully, they made good time since the terrain flattened out which left only the occasional thick patch of shrubbery and muddy forest floor as obstacles in their path. While they traveled, Enkai noticed his family's mood had improved dramatically. He heard them chatting behind him. He caught the tail end of a conversation when they drew close to their destination.

"Are you sure we can trust her?" Brem asked. "She said she would eat me last time I saw her."

Behind him, Enkai heard Nin laugh. She said, "As I told you before, she was only teasing because you were being rude."

"She started it! I told her to not read my thoughts then she called me weak!" Brem shot back.

Nin sighed. "She said your will was too under-developed, so she was overhearing your thoughts, not that you were weak."

From somewhere next to Brem, Enkai heard Jak say, "You also said her core and head were full of feathers." Even though he wasn't looking, Enkai sensed the glare he knew Brem was giving Jak after that comment. Enkai had been on the receiving end of more than a few similar glares throughout the years. Jak continued, "I'm just saying, it wasn't unprovoked. Besides, I don't like her either. She creeps me out, but I'd rather we were with her next time a monster attacks us. And, she's an Elder, so she'll know what to do."

Enkai chuckled. Despite being the youngest, Jak often sounded like the most mature of the three siblings. While Enkai liked to think he could claim that title, he sometimes let his emotions get the better of him. He smiled slightly and thought, *Maybe I should take notes from Jak.*

Once Enkai notified his family that they were close, Nin hushed his brother and sister. Minutes later, they arrived at their destination in silence. A glade opened up amidst the trees. Enkai crept up to a bush bordering the glade to investigate. While he didn't suspect any issues, he wanted to be sure the location was safe. He glanced around the glade in search of any telltale signs of Sin or an ambush. He saw nothing. Nin sidled up next to him and peeked as well.

"It looks clear," she said. "But, isn't Elder Jagan supposed to be waiting for us?"

As the words left her mouth, Elder Jagan's voice echoed around them. *I am here. The glade is Shrouded. Come...*

Enkai mentally kicked himself for not realizing that sooner. Based on her sheepish smile, Nin had had similar thoughts. Elder Jagan was a powerful dream beast, so they should have expected their meeting place to be masked in some way. Otherwise, any creature prowling the forest might stumble across it. With a nod to his family, Enkai stepped into the glade.

The air shimmered around him as he stepped forward. Instantly, Enkai sensed something was wrong. Looking around, he noticed several things simultaneously. Firstly, his spirit quaked even though he wore the black iron amulet. He felt the amulet shudder against his skin beneath his robes. Then, the dark metal started to radiate heat. At the same time, all noise except his own footsteps and breathing vanished the moment he stepped into the glade. The rain made no sound as it continued to fall. Not even roaring thunder, howling winds, or rumbling earth disrupted the glade. It was as if Enkai had stepped into a completely different world, separated from the chaos around it. Somehow, he instinctively knew there was more than a Shroud at play. The feeling reminded him of the Sacred Vas tree's glade. Finally, his eyes locked onto the two creatures at the center of the clearing.

Floating in the very center of the glade, a ball of Sin similar in shape to a wisp watched him. It was a writhing mass of coiling tendrils that reminded him all too much of the Sin nested within him. In the center of the tendrils, two serpentine eyes stared directly at him. While thoroughly creepy, Enkai's attention lingered for barely a moment on the Sin wisp. The second creature demanded all of his attention and filled his heart with despair.

Elder Jagan stood slightly to the side and behind the Sin wisp, like some kind of bodyguard. At a glance, Enkai might not have noticed how *wrong* she looked. Her red-tipped indigo feathers shone in the red light of the moon while her third eye blazed like a beacon above her eyes. However, it was the smaller details that unnerved and hinted at the truth. Along her body, white tips of bones poked through her feathers glinting horridly in the light. Small dark stains dotted the brighter feathers of her breast. Given that a few bones poked through some of the stains, Enkai suspected the dark spots were bloodstains. Then, there were her eyes. The previously golden orbs now regarded him through a veil as red as Sin. When he met her gaze, he truly felt despair because he understood that the creature standing before him was no longer the Elder Jagan he knew. And to make matters worse, he'd led his family right to her.

He noticed all this within a few seconds as adrenaline sharpened his senses to a razor edge. He whirled around to warn his family, but he was too late. They'd stepped into the glade. Nin immediately noticed his expression, then her eyes were drawn to the Sin wisp and Elder Jagan. Enkai saw the realization strike her as her ears went rigid, her eyes narrowed, and the fur of her tail flared up. Before either of them could react, the Sin wisp spoke with a voice that sent chills slithering through every bone in Enkai's body. Based on the responses of his family, they heard it too.

"At last, we can finally speak once more, little light", it said. When he heard the voice, a wave of memories came flooding back. The memory of his dying mind descending into fog and light surged to the forefront of his mind. The previously obscure memory played out in vivid detail right up into the moment something pierced his spirit. Understanding stuck Enkai full on and left him in stunned silence. The strange creature laughed. Enkai felt its mirth through his familiar link and paled. "That's right, little light! I've awaited this meeting eagerly since our deal and you've played your part marvelously. I do hope you can forgive me that I muddled your memory a bit. Didn't want you telling anyone about our deal."

Enkai didn't understand how this was possible. How could something like that be tied to his spirit and he hadn't noticed? What did it mean it muddled his memories? Is that why he hadn't remembered the world of fog and lights until just now? A memory of a dream surfaced from his past. He saw an empty vastness as he slept. He couldn't remember why he slept, but he yearned to reach out for the lights in the distance, then a little light had appeared. Suddenly, his strange sense of familiarity when he'd gone to visit Elder Jagan.

"I've been with you since the beginning. Were it not for me, you would have died under that tree. Be thankful, little light," it said. Enkai suppressed a shiver. Did the creature just read his mind? He felt amusement from his familiar link. The voice spoke again, but this time only he could hear it. *A wonderful question! Perhaps I am reading your thoughts? We are so intimately connected, you and I.*

Enkai felt his breath came quicker. Nin stepped forward as she broke out of her own stupor. Her eyes lingered on Elder Jagan. She said, "Elder Jagan? I know you're in there. You have to fight it. We need your help."

Elder Jagan's head swiveled so that her eyes fell on Nin. Enkai knew the futility of Nin's plea and he was certain she did too, yet he still hoped in his heart it would work. The massive owl regarded Nin coldly for a moment. Enkai saw nothing in her eyes but predatory hunger. The voice chuckled.

"I'm afraid you won't find her so responsive. But I wouldn't worry too much, as she's doing well under my care," the Sin wisp said. Enkai saw no immediate response from Nin, however, his heart sank. While he had no reason to believe this creature, its words only confirmed his suspicions. Even if it were lying, Elder Jagan certainly didn't look like she'd be of any help in their current situation.

"What are you?" Nin asked, voice edged with fear and anger. She glanced briefly behind her at Brem and Jak who were huddled together as if to make sure they were still there. Both siblings seemed to instinctively stay quiet, not wanting to draw attention to themselves. Enkai noticed Nin shift in order to put herself directly between the Sin wisp and his siblings. Subtly, Enkai matched her movement.

"Ah, I suppose I cannot blame you for not recognizing me in this form," it said. In front of their eyes, the Sin wisp changed. The tendrils retracted becoming misty while its color shifted from harsh red to soft purple. Tiny vapors drifted off it fading into nothingness as they separated from its body. When the transformation finished, Nin stared at the creature in silent shock. Enkai felt like he might throw up.

346

"En, is that your familiar?" Jak asked hesitantly. Enkai didn't respond because he was too busy feeling sick to his stomach. Even while wearing the black iron amulet, Enkai could feel the connection between himself and the creature. Mentally, he sensed its mocking amusement. He'd unwittingly placed his family in peril.

"I see you all recognize me now." The wisp bobbed up and down playfully. To only Enkai, it said, *It's a shame Onki isn't here. I would've liked for the entire family to witness my return. Alas, it seems the earthquakes caused by my children are keeping him occupied. I suppose I should thank him if he survives since without his efforts you would have been buried under a tide of lava and ash by now and I would have been robbed of this wonderful reunion.*

Enkai stepped in front of his family. Fear gripped his heart as the full weight of his situation settled on his shoulders. The creature had implied earlier that it had been responsible for Elder Jagan's condition. On top of that, it had just said its *children* were behind the earthquakes that had awakened Old Omen. If this creature was even half as powerful as it was insinuating, Enkai was certain they stood no chance against it. Thankfully, the creature didn't appear to be hostile though Enkai had little hope it would stay that way.

Seeking to keep the creature talking, he asked, "If you've been with me all these years, why wait till now? And why do all of this? What's the point?"

"As I've said, I simply wish to return to the Prime Sphere. I'm not even really responsible for it all. Reality is just such a fragile construct. And my timing was simply a matter of utilizing the opportunities presented," the creature said, shifting back to its previous Sin wisp form. "You see, I'm not really here. This form you see now is merely a conduit of sorts to facilitate my return to the Prime Sphere — one of many pieces of my essence disguised and scattered throughout the world after I'd hidden away in the Sphere of Dreams. When you took this conduit to Somn, all I had to do was find the Essence Fountain where the barrier between the two Spheres was thin and follow its light. Once I knew where to go, I sent my little beacon back to you to avoid suspicion. Of course, Jagan never suspected a thing. Why would she question a dream wisp's attraction to a Dream Essence Fountain?"

Prime Sphere? Sphere of Dreams? Somn? Enkai struggled to piece together the creature's meaning. He remembered the way his familiar had rushed toward the Essence Fountain beneath Elder Jagan's home. He guessed Somn was either the name of the citadel or the city. However, he couldn't even begin to understand the other two terms, while his mind churned as it attempted to find an avenue out of this situation. To make matters worse, he had no idea how much of his thoughts the creature could read, so any plan he came up with needed to assume that his intentions were already known. He needed more information.

"Why me?" Enkai asked, partially to buy time and partially because he honestly wanted to know.

"Coincidence," it said. When it didn't say more, Enkai's frown deepened. Perhaps sensing his discontent, the creature added, "Are you expecting me to say that I handpicked you from birth to serve as my deliverer into the Prime Sphere?" Harsh laughter echoed throughout the glade sending waves of fear through Enkai and his family. Instinctually, they all huddled closer together though Enkai kept his eyes on the creature. "No. As I said, I had many contingencies. It was mere coincidence that you formed a connection with a piece of me. It could have been anyone, but I am glad it was you. After all, not only were you connected to the Lady of Dreams, but even one of my kin took an interest in you."

"The Lady of Dreams?" Enkai asked, remembering the vision he'd seen through his familiar link. He'd wanted to ask about it, so he welcomed the opportunity. "You mean Lin Chun?"

The harsh laughter returned causing Enkai to involuntarily take a step back. His hip brushed Nin's shoulder as he did. Without a word, she reached up to hold his hand.

"There is so much you don't know," it said. Enkai glared at the Sin wisp. The casual way it mocked his ignorance filled him with anger. His Sin strained harder against the black iron's effects and he grimaced. Out of habit, he shoved his anger down into his subconscious. Though he couldn't control all his emotions, he had long learned to temper his anger. Surprisingly, Enkai sensed a pang of displeasure from his familiar link. The Sin wisp met his gaze evenly and added, "I see that like many, you too squander the gift I have given you."

In an instant, dozens of tendrils erupted from the Sin wisp and wrapped around Enkai in a blur of motion. None of them even realized what had occurred until the tendrils yanked him away from his family and lifted him several feet into the air.

"Let me go," Enkai shouted struggling against the tendrils. They held fast like bands of steel around his torso pinning his arms to his sides.

"I think not. Instead, I will show you how to use my gift," the creature said. Against his collarbone, the black iron amulet went from warm to scorching hot in an instant. He cried out in pain and shock as the smell of burning flesh hit his nostrils. The Sin within his spirit expanded and slithered up and down his anima channels moving closer and closer to his core despite the black iron. Enkai gritted his teeth and fought against it, but his spirit felt sluggish and unresponsive while he wore the amulet. The black iron burned a hole through his robes and rain turned to steam as it hit the metal.

A ball of moonlight-blue light streaked past him and exploded into the Sin wisp. It was quickly followed by two more along with a spray of shadow needles and a ball of hardened mud. Enkai glanced backward to see his family in a V formation with Nin at the head and his siblings at her sides. Their eyes were fierce and resolute.

"Let my son go!" Nin said, her voice filled with steel. Somewhere overhead, a silent bolt of lightning flashed across the sky illuminating them all for a brief moment. Despite all the attacks, the creature looked unharmed. The eyes in the center of the Sin wisp turned to regard Nin and his siblings.

"You know, my gift flourishes in conflict. The most powerful of its recipients are forged by a life of hardship and battle," it said. Its tone was thoughtful; however, Enkai sensed the flow of calculating murderous intent through his familiar link. Dread and pain caught in his throat. He thrashed wildly against the bonds knowing the creature planned to attack his family. Once again, the creature regarded him. "I believe I know how to best help you reach your full potential."

In the blink of an eye, the tendrils released him and lashed out. He screamed Nin's name in warning just before he hit the ground hard. His head smacked against the earth covering his face in mud and dazing him. He groaned through gritted teeth and pushed himself onto his hands and knees. Even though adrenaline pumped through his body, he took precious seconds to recover. He found it hard to focus through the pain of the amulet burning him and the ringing in his head. When he finally managed to get his feet under him, he looked for his family.

He followed the tendrils of Sin which extended past him like blades. When his eyes reached their ends, something inside him shattered. Tendrils ran through each member of his family. His brother and sister were slumped against each other as their lifeblood flowed freely into the muddy earth. Nin, on the other hand, was suspended by dozens of tendrils. She had tried to intercept the attack in order to protect Brem and Jak, but the tendrils had simply pierced through her body into his siblings despite her efforts. With a terrible sucking noise, all the tendrils withdrew dropping Nin into a heap on top of Brem and Jak.

Enkai rushed over to them. His hands were instantly coated in blood as he grabbed Nin gathering her into his arms.

"It's going to be alright. I can fix this," he choked out. His mind raced and his hands trembled so hard, he could barely move his fingers. Only one thing mattered at that moment. He needed to heal them.

Tears streaked down his dirt-covered cheeks as he wrestled the elixir case out of Nin's bag, almost dropping it in the process. The case was riddled with holes from the attack. Disregarding its condition, he hurriedly pulled the lid free and looked inside. Most of the elixirs had been destroyed. Their clay tubes were punctured spilling the contents on the inside of the case. However, one elixir marked with moonlight-blue was unharmed. He pulled the cork off with his teeth and poured it into Nin's mouth which hung slightly agape. Frustratingly, some of the liquid spilled down her cheeks, but he managed to get the majority of the healing draught down her throat. He waited in horrid suspense for several seconds for some sign that the elixir was taking effect. Nothing happened. His breath came in heaving sobs as he tried to stay calm. He needed to be calm. He had to think.

"They're dead," the creature said behind him. A torrent of rage exploded from within him. He was so angry his vision swam with red. He heard his heartbeat hammering in his ears. The Sin within his spirit broke into his anima channels. It devoured the vital anima in them growing larger and faster by the second. The creature chuckled. "That's it. Accept who you are. Stop hiding from yourself and embrace your potential."

His rage grew into a murderous frenzy that spurred the Sin on even further. He wanted to kill this mysterious creature that had attacked his family. He wished all the curses of earth and heaven upon it. He wished it had a corporeal form so he could wring the life from it with his own hands. He looked long and hard at each member of his murdered family. Each corpse amplified his anger until his eyes rested on

Brem. Just as the Sin pushed against his core, Brem's words flashed through his anger-filled mind.

We all have to make it out of this okay!

Enkai struggled against his emotions by trying to grab hold of the words. They offered him a moment of clarity in the haze of rage and hatred. He gazed down at Nin again. Mercilessly, her eyes were closed. The elixir still hadn't taken effect. Carefully, he pulled the Orlang elixir from his robes. Vital anima had natural healing qualities. An elixir of refined vital anima wouldn't be as powerful as an elixir made specifically for healing; however, Enkai prayed the increased potency of the Orlang elixir would make up the difference. Reaching over to them, he first gave a portion of the elixir to Jak followed quickly by Brem. Just as he poured the last of the Orlang elixir down Nin's throat, the creature spoke again.

"Enough clinging to the past, little light. Your future awaits you."

Enkai whirled on the creature with a curse born of his wrath fresh on his lips, and then there was a metallic pop. He winced as a sharp stab of pain lanced through the area below his collar bone. In the fraction of a second, some part of his mind that was still keeping track of his situation cried out. The black iron amulet had shattered. Before his conscious mind could truly register the significance of that event, pain swallowed his mind as the unrestrained Sin punctured his core. Scarlet anima flowed through his spirit devouring everything it touched. When it threatened to consumed even his life essence, a seed buried long ago bloomed in a magnificent blaze of silver-white.

***

In a forest of redwood trees with silver-white leaves, the Silent Father slept. Around it, mighty creatures milled about grazing peacefully on leaves and grass. The sheer variety of creatures in the wood would have astonished even the denizens of the Kazoan Jungle. With each breath the Silent Father took, a pulse of vital energy flowed through the woodland affecting each of the creatures in a unique way. The mightiest of them slept close to the Silent Father and guarded it against a threat that would probably never come.

Without warning, the Silent Father's Semblance ignited around its antlers and shoulders. The mantle of silver-white flames roared with power that attracted the attention of every creature within the wood. They all looked at their master waiting for it to wake, yet nothing happened. The Silent Father continued to sleep. Its breath was peaceful and measured while its human face remained tranquil. The creatures looked at each other in confusion then resumed their activity. Only the creatures closest to the Silent Father saw the smile spread across its human face.

Chapter 25

After the Sin pierced his core, the world changed. The earth and sky became as red as Sin. The terrain vanished and the rain stopped which left only the malevolent red in all directions. It was like being at the bottom of a sea of Sin, so deep that no trace of the world he once knew remained. The Sin permeated the very air around him crushing his body and spirit. For an eternity, Enkai experienced only pain and grief. The ravenous anima tore away at his spirit piece by piece until only the tiny spark of his life essence kept him whole. The image of his dead family dominated his mind superimposed over a backdrop of regrets. However, his strained will raged against the onslaught, despite being long past its limit. By all rights, his spirit should have crumbled under the assault. Yet no matter how much the Sin devoured, his life essence never wavered – a silver-white flame adrift in a red sea.

At some point, grief gave way to anger which then turned to blame. He blamed the strange creature that had saved his life and murdered his family. He blamed Elder

Onki for not being there to protect Nin and his siblings. He blamed his family for refusing to leave him instead of saving themselves. He blamed his father and Lin Chun for betraying him and starting all this. But most of all, he blamed himself. In the end, he was the problem. If he had never come to Old Omen, Nin, Brem, and Jak would still be alive. None of the events that led to this point would have occurred.

"You're right, boy, this is all your fault."

A figure emerged from the red. It towered over Enkai casting a great shadow on his already diminished spirit. When he peered into the face of the new arrival, he saw the cold grey eyes of his father. Du Kai stood before Enkai. He looked the same as he had on that fateful day down to the wear and tear on his red and yellow robes from their trek through the Forbidden Forest. He regarded Enkai for a long time. He didn't look angry, just tired and disappointed.

"I'm sorry," Enkai choked out after finding his voice. "I tried, I—"

"Failed," Kai said. His hard voice overpowered Enkai silencing him. "I had such high hopes for you as did the entire clan. Now, look at you, a disappointment until the end."

Enkai bowed his head in shame. Some quiet part of him remembered his father's death, but the memory drowned beneath the mire of regrets and broken dreams. He knelt in the shadow of his father and wept at the magnitude of his own failings. His father dwarfed him in every way. Even if he'd been weak in the grand scheme of things, Enkai knew his father would have excelled if he'd been given the same opportunities he'd had. His father had flourished in infertile soil while Enkai had barely made any progress after years under the tutelage of one of the most powerful great beasts in the land.

"That's right, boy. I'd have led our clan into a new age of prosperity. Now because of you, they scrape for an alliance with the Hu clan," his father said gripping him by the hair and lifting him so that their eyes were level. Enkai didn't fight him. When Kai continued his voice rumbled with fury. "You couldn't even die properly! Instead, you survived and hid within the forest. Six years, boy! Did you enjoy your respite while our clan struggled? Did the oath you swore mean nothing to you!?"

Kai threw him to the ground. The titan of a man held his right hand out calling forth a blade of solid Graywind anima and thrust the blade through Enkai's shoulder in one smooth motion. Enkai screamed and scrambled backward, away from his father. His arm went limp as the blade tore free. His sobs became rasping gasps as the pain of the wound added to his suffering.

"Father, what are you—" he started to ask only to be interrupted as the blade sliced toward his head. He ducked, narrowly avoiding the blow. A blast of wind emitted from the blade knocked him on his back. He gritted his teeth as he looked up at his father's menacing form. When his father raised the Graywind forged blade again, anger coursed through him. Pressure built within his chest, as he remembered his father's betrayal.

"This is your fault," he whispered. Within him, the pressure became unbearable. Enkai locked eyes with his father who met his glare with his own. Du Kai scowled down at him. He shook his head the same way one might when dealing with a particularly petulant child.

"Pathetic," Kai said. The word resonated through the sea of Sin echoing a thousand times. His father's scowl deepened and his eyes grew colder. "It pains me that your mother died giving birth to you. You bring nothing but shame to her memory."

"Shut up," Enkai said under his breath. The pressure increased again making Enkai tremble as it begged to be released. Kai ignored him and continued.

"Was her death not good enough? Is that why you led the family that took care of you to their deaths? Perhaps it's for the best. Filthy beasts are no replacement for your clan. It was time you were reminded of that."

"I said shut up!" Enkai shouted as he surged to his feet. Rage burned within him until he could feel his blood boiling. His body temperature soared to inhuman levels. His vision swam, but it didn't matter. His anger called to the Sin and the Sin answered. It filled him with power. He jumped backward barely reacting in time as his father aimed a thrust at his heart.

His father faced him, blade in hand. Enkai needed a weapon, so the Sin provided one. His body flared in pain as his muscles bulged with strength. His fingernails extended and hardened into razor-sharp claws. His teeth became fangs while the muscles in his jaw ached with the need to rip into his prey. Full of bloodlust, Enkai pounced.

Kai waited for him calmly. His stance was relaxed with his Graywind-forged blade at his side. At the last possible second, razor-sharp wind whipped around Kai slicing into Enkai. He powered through the wind enduring dozens of cuts by summoning more Sin to repair the wounds. Kai sidestepped his first attack and cut upward across Enkai's torso with a flick of his wrist. Enkai barely managed not to bisect himself on his father's blade by twisting mid-air which sent him tumbling past Kai. He recovered instantly and launched into a series of swipes with his claws, which his father dodged gracefully.

"Is that the best you can manage, boy?"

Enkai drew deeper from an unending ocean of Sin. The ravenous anima reacted to his will and bestowed more power in exchange for another piece of his waning spirit. Enkai gave himself willingly — he needed more power. Some part of him cautioned against using the Sin, but he ignored it. If he could overcome his father, it would be worth it. He was done being trapped in the shadow of a man who would sacrifice his own son.

Cycling the Sin through his body, Enkai crouched and prepared to lunge at his father. His muscles bulged with latent strength straining against his skin with the promise of explosive violence. His claws and fangs elongated while his enlarged muscles tore through his robes.

Like the calm before the storm, son and father faced off against each other, each waiting for the other to make the first move. Enkai decided to break the standoff. With the power coursing through every inch of his body, he erupted into a storm of claws and teeth. Dozens of blows with enough power to rend flesh and bone rained down on his father. However, Du Kai hadn't held the title of Head Warrior in the Du clan for nothing.

For each blow Enkai launched, his father responded with a counterattack of steel and wind. They clashed over and over in a savage dance of blade and claw. While it became clear that Enkai reigned supreme in speed and power, Kai dwarfed him in combat skill and experience. A lesser opponent would have crumbled in the face of Enkai's onslaught, but the former Head Warrior of the Du clan was undaunted. Kai wove through Enkai's attacks sporadically initiating his own assault that forced Enkai on the defensive. Kai's impenetrable defenses fanned the flames of his rage. For his wrath, the Sin gifted inspiration.

After swaying back to avoid a deadly thrust that would've pierced his heart, Enkai let himself fall back to the ground. He landed on his back in a precarious position though he made sure he was ready to strike. His father slashed downward to take his unprotected head. Just as Enkai had hoped he would. With all his might, he kicked up and slammed both his heels into his father's abdomen. The blow connected while Kai was mid-swing which interrupted his attack and sent him several feet backward. He recovered quickly, but the blow had done some damage.

The father-son pair clashed again, but this time Enkai changed his strategy. He made a conscious effort to keep his attacks erratic and unpredictable. The more Sin he cycled the easier it became to change his rhythm on the fly. The effect was almost immediate. Kai's defense went from effortless to pitched, as he was forced to find new ways to avoid Enkai's ever-expanding angles of attack. Enkai learned quickly that he wasn't constrained by normal limitations anymore. He attacked from all sides contorting and straining his body as he danced on the edge of chaos. The rush was intoxicating.

Then came his moment. In a dazzling display of agility, he blitzed his father and initiated half a dozen feints in a single rush. Instead of backing off, Kai called his bluff by launching into a series of rapid slashes at Enkai meant to force him back or slice him to bits. Enkai wove through the first two attacks avoiding them by a hair's breadth. When the third bit into his shoulder, the forged Graywind anima struggled to cut through Sin-Enhanced muscle and bone. Enkai seized his chance. With the arm of his injured shoulder, he grabbed Kai's wrist biting through the pain as the motion disrupted the blade. Kai pulled against his grip but Enkai's superior strength was too great. Before his father could do anything more, he raked the claws of his free hand across his father's torso. Unlike the Graywind blade, his claws tore through flesh and bone like paper. The telltale crack of Kai's ribs echoed through the red sea. Kai coughed as blood spilled from his mouth. Staring his father in the eye, he yanked the Graywind blade from his shoulder and stepped back ignoring the burning sting of his wounds which his Sin was already repairing.

Kai met his gaze, but his strength failed him and he fell backward onto the ground with a dull thud. His only response was a grunt of pain upon impact followed by several bloody coughs. Enkai crouched down next to his sword arm. Still looking his father in the eye, he ground his heel into Kai's wrist in an attempt to force him to release his grip on the blade. For a few seconds, they glared at each other as his father refused to succumb while Enkai increased the pressure bit by bit. Surprisingly, Enkai enjoyed this little contest. He liked seeing his father struggle pitifully to hold onto the very manifestation of the divine arts he'd chosen over his own child. For the great Du Kai, nothing was more important than his pursuit of the divine arts. With that in mind, he smiled when something cracked and his father groaned in pain finally releasing his grip on the blade which vanished almost immediately.

"Now who's pathetic?" Enkai asked looking down at his father, Du Kai opened and closed his mouth several times in an attempt to say something, though only rasping breath and wet coughs emerged. Watching his father's broken and bloodied form struggle to speak, Enkai began to hear a soft droning around him. He ignored it and leaned over his father. He put a hand to his ear tauntingly. "Speak up, father. I can't quite hear you. Was it this hard to hear me call out to you when you stabbed me in the heart!?"

By the end, he was yelling in his father's face. After a moment, a few broken words escaped his father's lips: "You... worthless... child..."

His anger spiked filling him with power as the Sin responded in kind. Channeling Sin was becoming incredibly easy. Its power rested at his fingertips. With just a thought, he could gain even more power. However, his anger had evolved over the course of the fight. As his father lay defeated before him, the heat of his rage died leaving only cold wrath.

"Even now, you can't bring yourself to admit you were wrong," he said then chuckled darkly. The soft droning in the background grew louder and his ears started to hurt. The droning penetrated his thoughts disrupting his anger. In response, the Sin coursing through his body flared up and filled him with incredible power. Once again, he basked in the intoxicating flow of strength. If he just pushed a little further, he would have the power to do whatever he pleased. No one would ever take anything from him again. He knew what he had to do. "I've always lived my life thinking of how I could be more like you, but I realize now that you are nothing. I am so much more than you ever were." Kai mumbled a few words incoherently, yet Enkai didn't care to hear them. His father's words meant nothing to him any longer. "Goodbye, Du Kai. In the end, you were as much of a failure in the divine arts as you were as a father."

He raised his clawed hand over his father's heart. Taking one last look at the man, he struck downward, claws pointed to pierce the heart. The droning reached a crescendo in his ears, becoming unbearably loud. He stopped the strike just above Kai's already broken ribcage as his wrath faltered once again. Like last time, the Sin responded, but this time no matter how much power the violent anima granted him, the haze hanging over his mind became thinner and thinner. Then, he heard a voice among the droning.

"En, please ... Please, come back," the voice said. At first, he couldn't recognize the speaker. For some reason, the words sounded distorted in his ears.

He reached up to inspect his ear for possible injuries that might impede his hearing, but when he touched his ear, he accidentally scratched the side of his head and winced. A warm line of blood trickled down onto his fingers. Numbly, he looked at his hands. They were monstrous and covered in blood. The skin on his hands had grown taunt and leathery against the muscles beneath and the bones jutted out along the back of each hand creating bloody bone spurs. Each finger ended in a wicked black claw as deadly as any blade. He stared at his hands in shock. While he had expected the claws, the rest confused him. When had his hands transformed so much? They didn't look human at all instead they looked more like the hands of a

...

Demon. The word echoed through his mind like a shockwave blasting away the fog of his anger and leaving only horror and disgust. He recoiled as if he had been physically attacked. As he hit the ground, he glimpsed his arms and legs. Dark leathery skin stretched over unnaturally dense muscles that corded together along each of his limbs. Bones poked through the skin at irregular intervals forming grisly spikes. His feet had changed in a similar way to his hands though they lacked claws in favor of more bone spurs. Once the reality of his transformation settled on his clear mind, he lost the contents of his stomach. Even as he retched pitifully, his tongue touched teeth which had become pointed. While he trembled from the horrible realization, the voice strange voice spoke again. This time, Enkai recognized it.

"En, please ... Brem and Jak need you," Nin called. "Please, come back."

Nin's words stopped the flow of Sin around him. His father faded away into Sin before his eyes. Enkai rose unsteadily to his feet, then looked for Nin. He didn't see her. Her voice echoed all around him. His unhinged emotions clamored like storms of chaos in his mind. The dam he'd held over the years had shattered leaving his feelings free to wreak havoc in his conscious mind. As he failed to find Nin, his anger, sadness, and fear threatened to overwhelm him. The Sin quivered around him, eager for the chance flow freely once again. He kept it at bay by sheer force of will by using Nin's voice as his anchor.

"I can't find you! Where are you?' he shouted into the vast expanse of Sin.

"I'm here, En," she replied. He looked around once more. When he found nothing, his anxiety spiked. "Concentrate, En. Follow my voice."

He took a few shaky breaths to center himself. Out of habit, he turned his senses inward glancing at the state of his spirit but something strange happened. Instead of going inward like normal, his awareness expanded outward ballooning until he could see the whole of his spirit. A maelstrom of Sin thrashing through his anima channels. In his core, a battle raged between vital anima and Sin. The two types of anima swirled back and forth warring for supremacy. From the looks of it, the silver-white anima was losing.

Enkai pulled back and his perspective shrank until he was once again within the scarlet sea of Sin. Before he could focus on the strange phenomenon, Nin called out again. This time, Enkai focused on the direction of her voice instead of her words. While concentrating, he realized the sound wasn't really echoing around him. That was the Sin replicating her words. He wouldn't let it win. The Sin was trying to manipulate him again. It had succeeded by creating an apparition of his father. He should've seen through that trick, as he'd known his father had died years ago, but he'd let his emotions get the better of him. Looking down at his clawed hands, he hoped the cost of his failure wouldn't be his humanity. After figuring out the Sin's trick, he tuned out the reproductions and honed in on the original source. Seconds later, he took off in the true direction of his foster mother.

Moving through the Sin was like trying to swim in honey. Every step he took was more difficult than the last. His strength was waning. After a few steps, he saw a faint silvery-blue light. The closer he drew to it, the brighter it became until it took the shape of a large rabbit that had to be Nin. He pushed forward with all his might careful not to accidentally summon more Sin for strength since he instinctively knew it would only drag him further from his goal.

As he progressed, the sea of Sin began to change. Small dots of silver-white light floated past him. Each one that passed him granted his waning body a small bit of strength to keep going. The further he went, the more lights appeared. Like a drowning man struggling to the surface for air, Enkai strained every fiber of his being to reach Nin. In his core, he felt the tide of the battle gradually began to change along with his environment. As more dots of silver-white light appeared, his vital anima flared brighter and forced back the tide of Sin.

Finally, he arrived. With one mighty push, he reached his deformed hand toward Nin. As soon as he touched her, his perspective changed. The expanse of Sin ended.

Starting from Nin, an ocean of silver-white spread across his line of sight, though unfortunately, the area behind him stayed Sin-red and continued to restrain him. No matter how hard he struggled, he couldn't move completely out of the Sin. Its hold on him felt absolute. He stopped struggling once he realized it was futile.

Nin said nothing at first. When he touched her, she held his hand in her paws. Unlike her usual form, she didn't look remotely humanoid. As she was, she appeared completely bestial and glowed the color of radiant moonlight. While the glow wasn't blinding, it did obscure her features making it difficult to make out anything except her general shape and the color of her eyes. Enkai guessed the more bestial shape was her original form even though he'd never seen it before, and he suspected the glow had something to do with the strange environment they found themselves in. The two locked eyes with each other for a brief moment. However, Enkai averted his gaze after he realized she was seeing his twisted body. The shame of succumbing to the Sin even after all the warnings he'd been given weighed as heavily on his spirit as the Sin itself. A few moments passed while he choked on his shame, but still, she said nothing. Only after he chanced a glance at her reaction did she speak.

"I'm so sorry, En," she said. Her words carried only sadness and regret. Her jade eyes searched his as though she were looking for something. Enkai's heart wrenched. The idea of Nin apologizing for anything that had happened seemed preposterous. She'd done everything she could. She deserved none of the blame.

In an attempt to make her feel better, he said, "I'm fine. You have nothing to apologize for. You saved me from the Sin. If you hadn't called for me, I would've ..." He trailed off, unable to finish.

Nin smiled. The expression lit up her face and filled Enkai with a sense of hope and reassurance that he desperately craved. Sadly, it didn't last. Her smile dimmed and her eyes grew sad once more as she said, "En, your brother and sister are dying."

Enkai felt his spirit shudder as a flood of negative emotions threatened to pull him away from Nin and back into the virulent sea of scarlet behind him. Despite the pull of the accursed anima, Nin held fast to his hand giving him the anchor he needed to resist. When the tide passed, he said, "So the Orlang elixir didn't work for them? Is there anything I can do?"

"The Orlang elixir stabilized their spirits, but they got swept up in the massive influx of anima," she said. Some of the guilt on his shoulders lifted upon learning the Orlang elixir had helped his family. However, he was confused by her other statement.

"What do you mean by 'influx of anima'?" he asked suspecting it had something to do with their surroundings.

"There's a war going on inside you Enkai," she said which didn't surprise him given the state of his core. Although, it surprised him that she knew about it since he didn't feel the telltale shiver that told him she was looking at his spirit. "There's so much anima I can't even fathom it. I'm not sure what happened after I died, but—

"

"What …?" Enkai asked interrupting her, though he trailed off as his mind went blank from the shock of her words. "Died? But you said …"

His voice faded out again as she averted her eyes. The realization came crashing down on him with the force of an avalanche. The signs were all there in plain sight. The fact that she wasn't in her humanoid form, the strange glow that matched the color of her anima, the fact that she hadn't included herself when talking about the effects of the Orlang elixir, and her unfocused features. Nin wasn't alive. He was talking to a spirit. An Eidolon.

"No, you can't be …" he said trailing off once more. His face twisted with sorrow and grief when Nin finally met his gaze and he saw the truth in her eyes. He felt himself begin to crumble, but before anything happened, Nin pulled him down into an embrace. It was awkward since she was no longer humanoid though Enkai didn't care. Perhaps because he was in direct contact with her spirit, his negative emotions washed away. He felt her love for her children wash away all else.

"En, I know you're hurting right now, but your brother and sister need you. It took me a while to reach you through all that Sin, so we don't have much time. My spirit was strong enough to anchor itself in the flow of vital anima, but theirs weren't. I'm here with you and I always will be, I promise," she whispered giving him one final squeeze before she let go. Enkai nodded though he kept hold of her paw for fear that she might fade away if he let go. Part of him knew it was childish, but he held on nonetheless.

"This place," she said gesturing all around them, "is a manifestation of what is going on within your core. Your mind must've retreated into your spirit because of shock." Enkai remembered the strange occurrence when he'd attempted to scan his spirit. The experience of expanding outward made sense if his will was already within his spirit. He gazed out into the tranquil silver-white void then behind him into the turbulent sea of Sin. Both appeared never-ending. If this was truly a manifestation of his core, Enkai wondered how such vastness could be possible. His core was still in the Lead stage which meant there was no way it could contain such boundless amounts of anima. When Nin saw his confusion, she continued, "I can't be sure how this has happened, but I'm guessing the creature that attacked us has something to do with all that Sin behind you, while I can feel the Silent Father's influence in all this vital anima. In any case, you're the only one who can help Brem and Jak. Vast amounts of anima or not, this is still your spirit."

"But how do I help them?" he said. While he wanted to help his siblings, he had no idea where to start. In fact, the sheer amount of anima flowing within his core beggared his imagination. He felt small and insignificant in the face of it. However, Nin's expression was one of determination, so he knew she must have a plan of some kind.

"As I said before, our spirits were swept into your core when the anima flooded it, but even with my help, you'd never be able to find Brem and Jak in all this anima. We don't have much time before their spirits destabilize either. You'll have to expel all this excess anima from your core in order to find them, but even that won't be enough. Their bodies suffered a lot of damage from that creature's attack, The Orlang elixir stabilized their life essence so they haven't become Eidolons, but their bodies are too damaged to serve as vessels for their souls."

"How do I expel all this when I don't have a breathing exercise?" Enkai asked. He hated having to ask questions like this. A breathing exercise was one of the most basic foundations of the divine arts. The fact that he didn't know one frustrated him. It was even worse considering he had been only a day away from being taught one by Elder Onki. In order to cultivate his spirit, he needed to absorb essence from his surroundings to create anima. Breathing exercises were the primary method of gathering essence for both man and beast. They also allowed those who practiced the divine arts to expel unwanted elements from the body and spirit. Enkai's father, for example, used to cultivate Graywind anima, a type of hybrid anima created from wind and blade essence, however, if he cultivated during a storm, he might also have gathered water essence which needed to be expelled before he could begin creating Graywind anima. Unfortunately, without a breathing exercise, Enkai couldn't hope to accomplish what Nin asked.

"You may not have a breathing exercise, but I do. The same one Onki would have taught you," she said smiling.

"Huh?" Enkai asked, confused. As far as he knew, Nin couldn't expel the excess anima for him. If she could, why wouldn't she have already done so? He caught another hint of sadness in her eyes before she responded giving him the impression, he wouldn't like what she said next.

"En, I'm a spirit trapped by all this anima within your core now. Even if I get out, I'll either be consumed by a great beast or I'll fade away slowly until nothing but essence remains. If I'm to choose, I'd rather my spirit be put to use by someone I love."

Though she didn't go any further, more than just her words passed between Enkai and his foster mother. He knew exactly what she was implying. In the Maro Province, the death of a clan member meant more than just the loss of a loved one. It signaled a passing of the torch from the deceased individual to their children or their next of kin. After the Eidolon spawned from the deceased clansman, the clan warriors subdued it. Then, the clan leader and elders prepared the Eidolon to be absorbed by the family member or loved one. In doing so, the clans ensured that the knowledge and power of their ancestors helped keep the clan strong even after their deaths. Enkai couldn't absorb Nin's entire spirit since he had no affinity for light anima, but he could absorb her remnants of life essence which would pass on some of her memories and experience.

However, the thought of absorbing Nin horrified Enkai. While her body might be dead, the Eidolon contained all her emotions, memories, and knowledge. As she was now, he could still talk to her and she could still comfort him. Once the Eidolon was gone, he would have to face the reality of her death at the hands of the creature he'd unwittingly aided.

Nin must have recognized at least some of his apprehension because she said, "En, I know I'm asking a lot from you, but only because I know you can do it. I want to do this. You, Brem, and Jak are…" She stopped and reached out to place a paw on his chest while she held his gaze. "I … I can't describe how much joy our family gave me. If I have to choose between saving my children or saving myself, there isn't even a choice. Please, En." For the first time since he found her, Enkai saw the true toll Nin had endured. In her eyes, he saw the sadness, grief, pain, and heartache she struggled to keep at bay for his sake. Even in death, she was staying composed so she could best help her children. For all her strength and love, she had been powerless when her children needed her.

"Alright," Enkai whispered, barely keeping himself together. When he accepted her proposal, a weight lifted from her shoulders. He saw genuine happiness and hope in her eyes that bolstered his own waning heart. At the very least, he took comfort in knowing he was doing his part in giving his foster mother peace after death.

"Thank you," she said and embraced him once more. The hug ended far too soon, but he didn't complain. He understood that they had limited time. "After you absorb my spirit, you'll need to do three things. First, you'll have to advance to Silver so you can use my breathing exercise. There's plenty of anima in your core to fuel the advancement. With luck, reaching Silver will also reverse some of the changes caused by the Sin when your body is reforged. Speaking of which: be careful of the Sin during the process. Even if you don't use it, it will probably attempt to compromise your advancement." She wore a dire expression as she continued, "Once you hit Silver, don't try to advance any further. You aren't ready for Gold and you'd tear your spirit apart trying. It might be tempting, but you mustn't do it.

The Gold Realm requires much more than just anima to reach it and a failed attempt would cost you dearly and doom your brother and sister."

Enkai nodded. He couldn't deny that the thought had crossed his mind. With all this anima in his core, how far would he be able to advance if he tried? Despite his desire for power, he trusted Nin and couldn't risk his siblings. He would wait.

"Second, use my breathing technique to expel all this anima then find your brother and sister. They should be easy to locate once it's all gone. The third task will be the most difficult, but it's also the most important. Once you have hold of their spirits, you must form a covenant by linking your life essence to theirs. A covenant is like a familiar bond except the connection runs much deeper. The covenant will allow their spirits to use your body as a vessel, but it does have one major drawback."

She hesitated before continuing. Nin's words were heavy with severity which told him that whatever drawback covenants imposed was not to be taken lightly. "Because the covenant links the life essence of those involved, members of a covenant are bound to each other in the most intimate way possible. The bond will strengthen you, but it will also change you. Each covenant affects those involved differently so I can't say what kind of changes will happen. And unlike a familiar bond, a covenant cannot be broken once enacted. Normally, I'd never ask you to do something like this, but that Sin wisp seems to want you alive and it plainly cares nothing for Brem and Jak. If you form a covenant with them, their lives will be tied to yours and the three of you can figure out what to do from there."

Enkai said nothing in response to her explanation. Instead, he focused on digesting all its information. He recognized her reasoning for the covenant.

For some reason, the strange Sin wisp had an interest in him. Enkai knew the creature had avoided hurting him for some reason. It referred to Sin as its gift and undoubtedly wanted to see Enkai consumed by the scarlet anima. But did it save him just to see him turned into a mindless demon? Enkai wasn't so sure. While under the influence of Sin, he hadn't felt mindless. He'd been savage and wrathful, but he'd always felt in control. He thought back to the joy he felt watching his father suffer and it sickened him. Even after all his father had done, such cruelty was beyond him. At least, he had thought so. Elder Jagan had said he would become something worse than a demon if he fell to Sin. What had he almost become? At that moment, Enkai promised himself that he'd never let his Sin overtake him again, especially not with his brother and sister tethered to his soul.

"Okay, I understand," he said. He took a shaky breath, then realized there was something major that needed to be addressed. "Wait, once the covenant is complete, what then? What'll happen to Brem and Jak? Even if they use me as a vessel, won't they be affected since they can't return to their bodies?"

Nin looked less certain as she answered, "I'm not totally sure what'll happen, but without the covenant, their life essences destabilize and they'll become Eidolons like me. Don't worry though. As long as their life essences survive, you should be able to, at the very least, find new vessels for them or, possibly even, restore their bodies somehow when you become powerful enough."

Enkai wished she had a more concrete answer for him though he couldn't blame her given the circumstances. He satisfied himself with the knowledge that he would at least be able to save Brem and Jak. As Nin said: they could figure the rest out once they were safe.

"Oh, and one last thing, En. Promise me that you won't blame yourself for this and that you'll look after your brother and sister," Nin said sounding nearly on the verge of tears. For his part, Enkai failed at keeping his tears at bay.

"I promise," he said, voice cracking.

Smiling encouragingly at him, she asked, "Are you ready?"

Enkai didn't answer for another breath. It was a small act of defiance on his part against the forces that conspired to take his family away from him. Memories flashed through him about his families, both beast and man. Memories of dinner with his grandfather and training with his father played alongside memories of running the forest with his siblings and harvesting natural treasures with Nin. One memory superseded all the rest. It was just before the Ritual of Waking on that fateful day so many years ago.

He stood in the center of the front room in his home. His grandfather had just stepped out to attend to his duties as a clan elder. Enkai busied himself with making sure his ceremonial robes were properly adjusted since he didn't want to embarrass his father by appearing untidy. In order to avoid mistakes, he used the polished silver emblem given to his father as a gift for advancing to Silver as a mirror.

Technically, the decorative piece was meant to act as a symbol of his father's status, but Du Kai cared little for such things so the family had found a practical use for it.

Just as he got everything into place, the door opened as Kai pushed his way in. Thanks to his father's status, their home was larger than most so Kai could stand at his full height. Without a word, Kai walked over to Enkai and looked him over. Enkai stood straight with his shoulders back and chin up as his father inspected his attire. Instead of speaking, Kai knelt in front of him and adjusted the sash that ran from Enkai's shoulder to his hip then tightened the belt around his waist so that the robes pulled closer to his form. After the adjustments, his father put his hands-on Enkai's shoulders and looked him over once more. All the while, Enkai was enjoying the attention. His father almost never fussed over his clothing the way the parents of other clan children did.

Kai caught his gaze and held it for several moments. Enkai didn't dare look away for fear of appearing weak to his father. Eventually, he smiled and Enkai's eyes went wide. His father never smiled. The expression passed quickly, but Enkai felt a surge of triumph. He hoped he could make his father smile more in the future.

"Once you step out there, you'll be taking your first steps in the world of the divine arts," his father said. They were close enough that Enkai could feel deep vibrations in the air from his father's voice. Excitement bubbled up inside him. Today, he would awaken his spirit; he was certain. After the ritual, he would officially be considered a divine artist. Kai squeezed his shoulders then Kai asked, "Are you ready, boy?"

Looking down at Nin, Enkai took one long steadying breath the way he'd been taught so many years ago. With his purpose clear in his mind, he smiled at Nin and said, "Yes, I'm ready."

Even in the face of such dire circumstances, their smiles reflected unhindered love. They smiled in unspoken agreement that their last memories of each other should be happy. Facing a world seemingly filled with hardship, Enkai burned the tender moment into his memory.

"Remember, I'll always be with you," Nin said. Then, her smiling face disappeared in a flash of moonlight. Swiftly, Enkai found himself free of the Sin's grasp as the two oceans of anima parted leaving only a small space between where Nin's spirit waited for him. Without hesitation, Enkai stepped into the light.

Chapter 26

Sethara warped into Genesis's local space and looked down on the world. While she wondered about the nature of the fluctuation she'd felt, she remembered a personal matter. Though she wasn't technically allowed to directly interfere with the events on Genesis unless they pertained to her duties as an Antediluvian, she still occasionally employed the use of third parties to nudge matters in a direction she found favorable. Unfortunately, her sweeps for anomalies took her away from Sector 1 regularly which meant she'd been forced to neglect her own personal interests. Despite all her power, she still bowed to the authority of time in the grand scheme of things. Resolving to check in with her personal matter later, she focused her attention on the task at hand.

Another quick jump brought her to the epicenter of the fluctuation. When she realized where she was, unpleasant memories resurfaced from long ago. She stared down at the ruins of Somn, the accursed city of the Traitor who'd rebelled against the heavens. Although she'd been too young to fight at the time, she knew plenty about the Traitor's uprising. In her younger days, she'd considered visiting the ruins in moments of weakness, but she'd never done so. Even as she stared down at the ruined city swarming with Sinspawn, she wondered why her father had never wiped the place off the face of Genesis.

The area surrounding Somn looked as if it was in the midst of an apocalypse. Violent storm clouds obscured the sky raining down lightning and torrents of water onto the terrain below. Earthquakes split the ground in several locations, and trees in the forest and buildings in Somn collapsed. Off in the distance, a lone volcano trembled on the cusp of an eruption, ready to shower fire and ash upon the landscape for miles. Sethara recalled that several powerful great beasts called the forest their home including the Sage of the North, Onki. Their wellbeing didn't concern her overmuch though she made a note to check on Onki before she wrapped up her business here. While she didn't care about the fates of beasts, for the most part, the death of a Sage was something to note.

She descended a few hundred feet to get a better look at the situation. None of the Sinspawn responded to her presence which was to be expected. Only those who had advanced into the Transcendent Realm could see her if she did not wish to be seen. Hostile spirits infested Somn like a plague. Many streamed out of the ruined city into the dark forest surrounding it. Somewhere within Somn, something was causing fluctuations in the Emanation and she needed to find out what.

Fluctuations in the Emanation only occurred during an event of world-altering magnitude. Fluctuations, even minor ones, marked a change in the flow of fate. Though they weren't inherently bad, such an event could cause worldwide instability and unstable worlds produced anomalies. Other factors played into the manifestation of anomalies, so normally Sethara wouldn't be too concerned, however, her experiences over the last several Genesis-years had been anything but normal.

She accessed the Emanation through her Providence and scanned for the source of the fluctuations in the city below. A fraction of a second after she started, another fluctuation rippled across the Emanation. With ease, she pinpointed its exact location. She eyed the citadel within the central district of Somn. She recognized the place from the reports she'd read long ago. It was the Traitor's former seat of power.

Is it possible she left some kind of trap after all this time? Sethara thought then ruled it improbable. After the Traitor's death, her seat of power had been investigated by Eden for additional threats, yet nothing of note was found. Somn itself was razed by the Order in the aftermath of the conflict. Even so, paranoia won out and she erred on the side of caution. Imposing her will on the Emanation, she enacted a temporary stasis on Genesis.

One moment, the earth was quaking and the sky was thundering and the next, everything stopped. Falling trees ceased their descent. The earth halted its motions. The sky became a tapestry of dark silence with streaks of lightning and rainfall painted between heaven and earth. The Sinspawn below froze, their twisted forms caught in various states of motion. Satisfied with her work, Sethara descended. Although she could simply step through space to the location, curiosity got the better of her. She wanted to see the Traitor's home despite what she told herself. Unfortunately, she never got the chance.

Her temporary stasis shattered. The backlash dazed her briefly, as the event had caught her completely off guard. All activity resumed and a cacophony echoed from earth and sky. Lightning flashed followed by a heavenly cry of thunder across the land. As one, all the Sinspawn and several demons who emerged from the forest turned their heads to the sky and released primal cries that echoed for miles. Recovering, Sethara erected her defenses as she sensed power erupt from the source of the fluctuations. Her Providence blared out a warning in her mind.

[Warning: Primordial Activity Detected. Searching records ...]

As her Providence spoke, a great crash shook earth and sky. The vibrations affected even Sethara in her lofty position. She searched her memory accounting for each Primordial. There were only seven that she knew of. Additionally, each Primordial corresponded to a different type of anima, so their presence elicited a massive influx of anima and essence into the surrounding area depending on the Primordial in question. Other than the Sinspawn, she noticed Sin essence flowing through the fissures in the earth, however, she couldn't fathom the possibility of a Primordial of Sin. After all, though technically anima, Sin was a malady of the spirit and, by extension, the Emanation from which spiritual energies were born.

Primordials were literal incarnations of the fundamental forces involved in the creation of Genesis. Her mind churned trying to think of another possibility.

[Records found. Access Denied. Would you like to request access from The Garden?]

Sethara paused as her churning thoughts changed to confusion. She had been denied access to a record? Only two individuals in the whole of Eden with the ability to withhold access from her and they were both members of her immediate family. *Why would they restrict my access?*

Before she could dwell on this quandary, a surge of power blasted into the sky followed quickly by a beam of Sin that pierced the storm clouds above. The sky turned red and scarlet lightning flashed across the heavens. With another surge of power, the beam expanded into a massive pillar connecting heaven and earth, Sethara barely stepped back in time to avoid getting hit by the influx of virulent anima. The ground around the Traitor's former home collapsed in on itself as the complex was swallowed by Sin.

Quickly, Sethara accessed the Emanation. Her Providence began a slow rotation in preparation for combat. The white disk thrummed with power while the two pillars to the left and right moved up to flank Sethara, ready to intercept any incoming attack. While she was faced with the unknown, she decided against retreating or calling The Garden for assistance. Although many of the Primordials had fought with the Traitor against her father, Eden had had a non-aggression pact with them since the conflict. If the creature behind the Sin was truly a Primordial, then it should honor the pact.

"I'm surprised," something said from within the pillar. Two dark eyes pierced the glow of the vibrant Sin. In the back of her mind, Sethara thought she heard the sound of snakes hissing her name. "Not many would remain so calm in my presence." The pillar of Sin dispersed and revealed the creature's true form.

Sethara resisted the urge to flee as the small part of her that was still human recoiled instinctively at the creature's appearance. Fortunately, Sethara had transcended the fragility of humanity long ago. The creature's umber eyes locked onto her, seemingly unimpressed with her divine soul. She met its gaze evenly, refusing to be intimidated. Its head was level with her while its serpentine body extended out of the earth for hundreds of feet. Scarlet scales scintillated in the light of the raging storm above. Sparks flew from the scales as lightning struck them over and over. The creature didn't seem to notice.

"You'll find the members of Eden are not so easily cowed, serpent," Sethara said. Though internally she was in turmoil, her face remained impassive as ever.

"Eden? Is that what the Usurper is calling his nest of lies?" the Serpent laughed.

"I would watch your tongue," Sethara said. If it truly represented Sin, then she doubted she could trust it. Sin by its very nature is destructive, antagonistic and hostile. A Primordial of Sin would exemplify all those qualities. Raising her chin, she continued, "Only by his grace do your kind enjoy the protection of the non-aggression pact. Some have not forgotten the role the Primordials played in the Traitor's rebellion."

Though said in response to the creature's taunt, her words were true. After the conflict, some of her father's forces wished to hunt down the Primordials who'd supported the Traitor; however, the ruler of Eden forbade it. Sethara couldn't blame him. Not only were many lives lost in the conflict, but Genesis also suffered scars that still marred its face. Additionally, Sethara couldn't imagine what the death of a Primordial would do to the stability of the Emanation. The ancient creatures were as much a part of the Emanation as they were individual entities.

"Ah, is that so?" the Serpent said. Its head snaked up so it was mere inches from Sethara. Waves of hostility rolled off it. Despite her instincts telling her to defend herself. She let the malicious intent wash over her like rain on a mountain. She smiled when the creature withdrew its head. It frowned as it took her in once more and its serpentine features showed surprise which Sethara found pleasing. However, as she was about to respond, its smile returned. "You don't know who I am. The Usurper didn't tell you, did he? Poor dear, kept in the dark by your own father."

The Serpent laughed and shook the very earth with its mirth. Off in the distance, the lone volcano quivered. A series of thunderous cracks echoed from the volcano before it went silent. Abruptly, a deluge of ash and lava spewed from the massive mountain. The flow sputtered immediately after it started until it slowed from a violent torrent to a gradual flow. It was almost as if something had held the eruption back. Though she didn't pay much mind to the eruption, the volcano mirrored the state of her own mind. Sethara was already thoroughly frustrated given recent events, so she didn't have much patience for the Primordial's provocations. She kept calm by reminding herself that she had a purpose.

Obviously, this Primordial had been the source of the fluctuations. Most of them hid away in their own Spheres or in isolated areas of Genesis. When they revealed themselves, it meant something significant was happening. No less than five Primordials had appeared in the conflict between the Traitor's forces and Eden. Since then, their contact with humanity had been almost nonexistent. She needed to ascertain what the creature's motives were before it caused some kind of turmoil on Genesis.

"I tire of your taunts, Primordial. Identify yourself and state your business," she said. The serpent continued smiling, undaunted by her commanding tone. She considered channeling her Providence into her voice to unleash her Divinity, but she decided to wait. Despite everything, she didn't want to provoke a Primordial if she could avoid it.

"I could tell you what you want to know, but don't you want to know what father dearest is hiding?" it asked. Its eyes bore into her. Even though Sethara did, in fact, want to know, she didn't see how the creature could grant her such information.

"What game are you playing?" she asked, frowning.

"Why not try scanning me with that Providence of yours once more?"

She crossed her arms, her skepticism plain on her face. She wasn't surprised the Serpent knew she had scanned it. After all, she had to access the Emanation in order to do so and, as a Primordial, the creature must've noticed. She decided to humor it for the moment. With a thought, she erected several more subtle layers of defense against every conceivable form of attack as well as a fail-safe that would shield her from any feedback she might receive if something interrupted the scan. She raised a hand toward the creature and thousands of golden strings flowed from her Providence. The strings touched along its snout and neck. Technically, the strings were unnecessary for the scan, but she wanted to gauge the creature's reaction. If it were willing to put itself at a disadvantage by being in contact with her Providence, she might be inclined to believe what it was saying. Despite the invasive nature of the scan, the Serpent didn't resist. It just smiled and watched her with its eerie umber eyes.

[Record Found. Accessing ... Access granted.]

Subject: Primordial of Sin

Aliases: Serpent of Discord, The Drifting Chaos, Daystar of Bedlam, World Eater, Progenitor of Calamity

Threat Level: Extreme

Most Recent Instance: Last appeared on the eve of the Battle of Somn and was destroyed by the Antediluvian Primarch and the Voice of Eden.

[Importing additional details ...]

Information flooded her mind imparting knowledge of various appearances of the Primordial of Sin. She witnessed the creature's destruction at the hands of Abelard, her brother and the Antediluvian Primarch, and her father, the Voice of

Eden. She experienced the unfathomable power of the weapon her father wielded as he struck the blow, the very same weapon used to execute the Traitor. Several other events streamed through her mind which detailed the creature's known abilities and its interactions with Eden and the gods that came before them. When the process concluded, it left her confused and alarmed.

"How ...?" Sethara asked, but she trailed off as she failed to find the right words. Not only did her sudden access to the record make little sense, but the creature's very existence was also an enigma. Based on the information she'd been given, the Serpent's capabilities were unbelievable. Moreover, she couldn't believe the creature had survived her father's attack. After seeing the infamous weapon her father had wielded during the war in action, she couldn't believe any entity capable of surviving its wrath. Yet here was the Primordial of Sin, right in front of her. Another mystery was the why of the matter. Why had her father and brother attacked the creature? If they were so willing to bring down Primordials, then why had her father been so adamant about forming a non-aggression pact with them? More questions than she could count flitted through her mind and she didn't know where to start.

The Serpent chuckled. It turned to the west and its eyes widened though its smile remained. Still facing away from her, it said, "Rules are made to be broken. You'll find those imposed by your Eden are no different from any others. If you wish, I can show you more."

Though she should have felt angry at the creature's arrogance, the knowledge she had now gave her pause. She wondered whether the creature's statement was meant as a provocation or if it was simply stating the truth. In her moment of contemplation, her Providence prompted her.

[Warning: Inaccuracy found in the Primordial of Sin record. Automated update failed. Would you like to manually update the record with current information?]

This must be this creature's doing. Sethara hesitated. Updating the record would immediately notify Abelard of her activity since technically she wasn't authorized to view said record. While she preferred to deal with her issues solo, she accepted that she probably couldn't handle the creature in front of her in direct combat. Furthermore, given her new insights into the creature's past, she was certain that trusting it would be ill-advised. Nevertheless, she disliked the idea of being left out of the loop. Her family ruled over Eden, yet they still felt it necessary to hide things from her. After all that she had done for them, she found the secrecy insulting especially from her father. The Voice of Eden constantly spoke of devotion to duty, virtue, and staying true to Eden's cause. Apparently, that included hiding important information from his own daughter. With that in mind, she chose to ignore the prompt for the moment, though she didn't dismiss it.

"What do you mean?" she asked, resuming her impassive demeanor.

The creature looked back at her and its eyes narrowed in amusement. "Come see for yourself," it said. Space shifted as the Serpent disappeared from her sight. Below, the citadel collapsed without the creature's bulk to support the broken foundation. At first, Sethara thought the creature had just fooled her to make its escape yet a quick glance to the west revealed that it had simply moved several miles away. The Serpent of Discord appeared to be observing something on the ground. Sethara shifted through space so that she stood next to the creature's lowered head. One of its umber eyes locked onto her before turning to a small glade below. Curious about what the Primordial found so interesting, she directed her attention to the scene in the glade.

Only one thing in the glade warranted her attention. At the edge of the clearing, a raging vortex of anima spun with barely restrained force. Though its sphere was only roughly ten feet in diameter, it contained an absurd amount of anima densely packed inside it. Vital anima and Sin vied for dominance. Meanwhile, something pulsed from within the sphere and essence from the surroundings flowed into it in great waves. The effect made the sphere looked like a planet of swirling silver-white and scarlet red with its own gravitational pull drawing in the elements around it. Upon closer inspection, Sethara sensed something strange prompting another message from her Providence.

[Warning: Primordial Activity Detected. Searching records ...]

[Records Found. Accessing... Access Granted]

Subject: Primordial of Vitality

Aliases: The Silent Father, Firstborn of the Emanation, The All-Soul

Threat Level: Low

Most Recent Instance: Brief encounter with Antediluvian Xisuthras after the Battle of Somn

[Importing additional details ...]

Sethara pushed the information away as it began to flow. She was familiar with the Primordial of Vitality and knew that the record wouldn't tell her anything new. Her senses told her that the Silent Father wasn't in the area, so she suspected the creature was linked to whatever moved inside the sphere of anima.

Beside her, the Primordial of Sin said, "He's broken our connection. I'm not sure if I should take offense." It chuckled again. Sethara began to understand that the creature found everything amusing in one way or another. "I cannot wait to see what he will do with my gift."

Suppressing the urge to scowl, Sethara peered into the ball of churning energy. The sheer density of anima would have blinded any mortal, but her divine senses pierced through the layers of anima. Her eyes widened and she asked, "Is that a child?"

The Serpent glanced over at her and, impossibly, its smile widened once more. "Not just any child."

When the creature didn't elaborate, she focused on the boy again with her divine senses. Once she did, she peered into his body and spirit for several seconds in silence. As soon as she'd confirmed her suspicions, her demeanor changed completely.

"Do you take me for a fool?" she said channeling the force of her Divinity. The pressure of her words ruptured the very fabric of the land, shattering trees into splinters and turning stone to dust. If not for the sheer amount of anima surrounding him, the boy's body and soul would have crumbled as well. For its part, the Serpent appeared unperturbed. She pointed a finger at the sphere. At the tip of her finger, white energy gathered condensing itself into a singular point that would shear through anything once unleashed. **"Have you and your kin decided to test the might of Eden? It seems you have mistaken our kindness for weakness to be exploited."**

The boy was a Primal, a divine artist with a Primal core. Over a millennium ago, Primals had waged war against Eden under the banner of the Traitor. After the war, the Voice of Eden issued an Edict condemning all Primals. Rightfully so, Sethara believed, since their kind had supported the Traitor's actions. With his power, her father used the Emanation to rewrite fate which curbed the number of Primals born each year until humanity was cleansed of their kind. Although none had been born in centuries to her knowledge, some still remained from the previous age and were hunted by Eden's agents on Genesis.

The fact that this Primal child sat below her within the grasp of not one, but two Primordials carried extreme significance. The Primordials may as well have declared war on Eden. Perhaps if it were only the Serpent of Discord, she could overlook the situation after dealing with the boy. However, the Silent Father had also staked a claim. History showed that when the Silent Father acted the other

Primordials followed suit. If they didn't already know about it, the remaining Primordials would either support the Silent Father or refuse to interfere with his plans. Sethara prepared to update the Primordial's record in order to notify Abelard, certain she would need backup.

"I'm not your enemy, Daughter of Eden, and neither are any of my kin," the Serpent said, not taking its eyes off the boy. "Moreover, this wasn't meant as a provocation or declaration, but rather as a sign of goodwill. After all, I know you could have notified your superiors about my return, yet you haven't done so. Why?" The creature turned its head to face her fully. "Because you are no fool. Your intuition tells you there's something off, but you don't have the information you need to find the truth. Now, you're wondering if I have the answers you seek."

She channeled all her Divinity into her next words. Primordial or no, if the creature answered her falsely, she would know. Face impassive, she asked, "**Do you?**"

It didn't answer immediately. Instead, it met her gaze and held it for a short while. The creature's eyes were alien to her and masked any sign of the certainty she sought with the unknown. Finally, it said, "The game being played eclipses both you and me and there are things even I do not know. However, there is someone who can give you the answers you seek."

Sethara received no indication that the creature was attempting to mislead her. She lowered her finger dispersing the attack meant to kill the Primal boy. "**Who?**"

Before it spoke, a chill ran down her spine as a sparkle of glee glinted in the creature's eye. "Your mother."

For the first time in a millennium, Sethara's resolve faltered. Old wounds threatened to tear themselves open as thoughts of her father played through her mind. Despite herself, she had always wondered about the truth behind the loss she experienced that day. Composing herself, her gaze drifted to the crumbling ruins of Somn and said, **"The Traitor is dead, serpent."**

Its next words made her mind go blank. "Evaniel lives, daughter of Eden. What's more, I know where you can find her."

Chapter 27

Enkai glided through the primary events of Nin's life. Guided by her dying will, her memories streamed into his mind as her Eidolon merged with his spirit. It was like passing through a tunnel where scenes from Nin's life played along the walls. Many were vague or unremarkable fading away as they passed no doubt never to be remembered. Others produced vibrant sights and clear sounds that hinted at their inherent significance. However, Nin's lingering will pulled him toward a very specific memory.

The experience reminded him of his walk through Elder Jagan's home filled with dream essence and illusions. A pang of sadness gripped his heart when he remembered the ancient owl's fate, so he banished those thoughts. He needed to stay focused or he would fail.

Although no longer bound by it, Enkai still felt the Sin fighting for control of his spirit; however, he also felt the cleansing warmth of vital anima which kept it at bay.

In addition to these two sensations, Nin's spiritual essence enveloped him in a protective cocoon. Though he perceived the events within this strange plane of anima as real, his mind understood that they were in fact manifestations created by his subconscious, so his will could navigate the events unfolding in his spirit. He owed Nin for that understanding. During his struggle with the Sin in his core, he had truly believed he was fighting his father even though his semi-conscious mind recognized it as impossible. Once he'd heard Nin's voice, it was like being roused from a waking dream. Enkai knew that once he learned Nin's breathing exercise, he would need to utilize vital anima to advance while simultaneously containing the volatile Sin which no doubt would attempt to influence him again. The burden of the coming task weighed heavily on him as drew closer to his destination.

A moment later, he reached the event Nin wanted him to see. As soon as the memory began, Nin's presence disappeared. From that moment onward, he was on his own. Instead of dwelling on that terrifying reality, Enkai focused all of his attention on the memory with the intention of absorbing every detail. Time wasn't on his side. A single mistake on his part would unequivocally cost the lives of his siblings and his sanity. Even worse, his failure would mean that Nin's sacrifice had been for nothing. In more ways than one, the fate of his family rested in hands. With steeled resolve, he immersed himself in the scene.

***

"What is this place?" Nin asked looking up at Onki's puppet beside her. She stood in a cavern located some distance below Onki's lair. The space was too small for the ancient tortoise's massive bulk, so he had sent one of his puppets to accompany her. The cavern itself reminded her of Onki's lair. Holes of all sizes riddled its ceiling which occasionally emitted a haunting drone as wind flowed through the openings from somewhere else on the mountain. The floor of the cavern was unlike most places on Old Omen. It was primarily composed of dark soil that smelled of fertile earth. In the center of the cavern, a small pool of bubbling water released plumes of steam that filled the air with warm moisture. Along the walls, bioluminescent fungi lit up the otherwise dark space with soft green light. At the edges of the cavern, shadows danced where the steam caught the light from the fungi creating a ring of shifting darkness around the chamber.

The puppet walked forward to stand at the edge of the pool beckoning Nin to follow. After a moment, Onki said, "The last time this mountain unleashed its fury on the world, the eruption was so violent that fissures formed throughout the mountain. Molten rock ate through the bones of the mountain and flowed not only through the mouth, but from these fissures as well. When the mountain was finally silent, the end result eventually became the tunnel system that runs through the mountain. In some places, caverns like this were formed."

Nin listened with rapt attention. She loved it when Onki told stories, so much so she had to stop herself from sitting down to listen as she normally did.

"This place is special though. Its location is unique compared to others like it. It is a confluence of elements that formed over the centuries. Water from spring storms and melting winter snow are filtered through the mountain's bones to end up here.

Hot gases from the magma chamber below heat the water. The steam produced carries moisture to the fungi and soil while they draw nutrients from the mountain's core. All the while, wind feeds fresh air through the cracks and tunnels. It is a balance born of coincidence in the wake of the eruption."

Nin glanced around at the various aspects of the cavern. Excitedly, she opened her Spirit-sight. The atmosphere in the cavern changed. Several elements of essence wove together in a slow and complex balance that only nature could weave. The display was beautiful. However, Nin didn't know why Onki had brought her here, so she asked, "Why did you bring me here?"

"Patience, little rabbit," he said. "Do you know what the wise men of old called the mountains of the land?"

Nin shook her head. Onki often told her stories about the humans, but she couldn't remember anything about wise men or mountains.

"In the time before the gods descended from the heavens to wage war in the mortal realm, humans strove for divinity in any way they could. Some built faiths to be worshiped as gods among men. Some accumulated power through battle and war, so that none could challenge their strength. Others still sought vast amounts of wealth that could provide any wish they desired. However, it was the wise men of old that sought divinity not through faith, wealth, or power, but through isolation. They became known as hermits who kept to the wilderness away from their fellow man. Many of these hermits lived completely alone on the highest mountaintops, some of which even pierced the clouds. These mountain men believed that mountains were not just titans of the earth, but bridges that connected to the very heavens."

Her heartbeat sped up a little bit. She asked, "Were they right? Are mountains really connected to the heavens?"

The puppet smirked which looked strange on its stone visage. It clasped its hand behind its back and turned to face Nin. "Who is to say? I have lived on this mountain for thousands of years. I've seen the earth change and the heavens fall, yet there are still things even I do not know. When the gods descended, some say they descended from the mountaintops. I'm afraid Old Omen was not one of them. True or not though, the mountain represents an unmistakable link between earth and sky. Only such a link could create a place like this," Onki said gesturing around the chamber with the puppet. "Even Old Omen has this connection and this place is the heart of that link, where elements of both domains intertwine in harmony." He paused for a moment staring into the pool as if it held some secret Nin couldn't perceive. Finally, his gaze fell on her. Even though Onki wasn't physically with her, Nin felt the ancient weight of his gaze as she met the puppet's cold stone eyes. "It is here that I discovered my greatest achievement. A breathing exercise built to embody the connection between earth and sky."

"I don't understand. I already have a breathing exercise," Nin said frowning. She understood the concept of mountains being bridges where the elements meet. However, she didn't understand how that could translate into a breathing technique. She also didn't understand why she needed to know about it. Nin already had a breathing exercise that she'd inherited from her bloodline. Like most great beasts, the breath of the divine arts was as instinctual for her as normal breath. For great beasts, the divine arts were an extension of the natural world in which they dwelt. As a result, most great beasts were not taught the divine arts so much, as it was already a part of them.

"In the divine arts, all things start with breath. While you can use very basic techniques and train your body before learning a breathing exercise, you cannot cultivate without breath. Breathing exercises allow man and beast to connect with the world. This connection begets the exchange of essence into anima and vice versa. Breathing exercises come in many forms bearing distinct benefits and weaknesses, but all share one weakness. They rely on the act of breathing. If a creature cannot breathe, it cannot cultivate. Additionally, few are able to use their breathing exercises in combat because the rigors of battle often strain the body's ability to breath. Our bodies are the vessels that stop our spirits from fading away as Eidolons and unbound spirits do, however, they are also barriers that separate our spirits from the essence around us. Breathing exercises are the bridges we form to overcome that divide."

The puppet began pacing at the edge of the pool which signaled to Nin that Onki was in deep contemplation. It always surprised her how expressive he seemed to be with his puppets while his actual form seemed so dour. It made her wonder what he would be like if he ever took on a human form. She was certain he was powerful enough to do so, but not all beasts wished to change their bodies in such a way. Nin for one looked forward to the day when she could shift her own body. She loved stories of humans in particular and couldn't wait to see what it felt like to be one. Sadly, she would have to wait until she reached the peak of the Gold Realm to completely shift her form. Her attention was pulled away from idle daydreams when Onki continued.

"I sought a way to overcome the limits of breath. I found my answer in the Old Omen and the beliefs of dead wise men. If you think about it, this chamber is like our cores. A cauldron where elements, both internal and external, mix to form something new and unique. Old Omen is a bridge between earth and sky which gives rise to this phenomenon, yet at the same time, it is also the *vessel*. There I had my answer. So, I created a breathing exercise unlike any other. A breathing exercise that relies not on breath but the body itself to act as the bridge between the spirit and the essence of the world."

Her eyes went so wide she thought they might pop out. She couldn't believe what he was saying. It sounded crazy. "How can you have a breathing exercise that uses your body but not breath? It isn't like you can breathe through your skin."

The sound of a chuckle emanated from the puppet. Its stone visage smiled at her and Onki replied, "Are you so sure?" Upon seeing her uncertainty, the smile widened. "I understand your skepticism. Such a concept is not intuitive, but I assure it is possible."

"What's it called?" Nin asked. Despite herself, she couldn't keep the bubbly excitement out of her voice when asking.

"The Heart of Earth and Sky. My crowning achievement I pass on to you," Onki declared. The puppet stepped forward and placed a hand on Nin's brow. Before she could respond, her anima resonated with the essence around her. Her Spirit-sight became awash with color and she saw more nuances in the essence than ever before. Then, her skull flared with pain as knowledge passed from Onki to her.

***

The memory faded in Enkai's mind. The knowledge of the Heart of Earth and Sky filled his thoughts. Even after all he'd seen, the breathing exercise developed by his master still stretched the limits of credulity. He lamented not being able to talk with Elder Onki at that moment. The knowledge imparted from Nin to him framed his master in a completely different light. Until that moment, the title of Sage meant little to him given his limited experience, but now he knew. His master had been a true Sage, wise and possessing of an understanding far beyond his comprehension. Without being told, Enkai understood that the Heart of Earth and Sky was a treasure any divine artist would covet.

Following the memory of the Heart of Earth and Sky, more information presented itself to him as Nin's Eidolon merged fully with his spirit. Unlike before, there were no accompanying memories, just the sudden knowledge of things he hadn't known before. New insights on covenants, alchemy, and natural treasures flowed into his mind. The last bits of guidance Nin could impart to him before her spirit merged with his own.

Focused on the task at hand, he ignored everything except for the knowledge about covenants. After the information settled, he had learned the method of enacting a covenant.

Without further delay, Enkai started his daunting mission of advancing, mending his soul, and rescuing his siblings. First, he searched his spirit for the link with his "familiar". With more force than was necessary, he destroyed the connection between himself and the creature that had used him since childhood. The ease of the break surprised him. One moment it was there, the next it wasn't. All it had taken was a thought. The darker part of himself he'd yet to confront mused that he could've easily prevented so much death and suffering had he not clung to his past like a lost child. He dismissed those thoughts swiftly, not willing to break his promise to Nin so soon after her sacrifice. Instead, he turned his attention to his core.

After a brief moment of hesitation, he cultivated for the first time in his life. Despite his inexperience, his spirit knew what to do like the lungs knew how to draw breath. His core churned with power that begged to be harvested. Enkai tapped into the wellspring of vital anima battling against the Sin in his spirit. His core quickly consumed the vital anima and funneled the spiritual energy into the rest of his spirit. A flood of silver-white washed away the scarlet stain within his anima channels. Unfortunately, the Sin didn't sit quietly. The virulent anima burrowed deeper into his spirit resisting the cleansing tide of vital anima.

Enkai strained his will, and sensation returned to his body. As vital anima replaced Sin, he became aware of his physical condition once more. The numbness the Sin provided was replaced with biting cold and exhausted weakness throughout his body along with the smell of blood, mud, and rain. A quick test revealed he couldn't move, yet he didn't let that bother him. Instead, he focused on completing his advancement.

He took in the condition of his spirit. With the support of his will, the vital anima had successfully purged his anima channels of Sin; however, the cords of Sin coiled around them had remained. They wound around his anima channels throughout his body. Much to his dismay, each cord of Sin now fed from his core in the same way his anima channels did. In fact, it appeared almost as though he had two sets of anima channels, one, an intricate network of silver-white and the other, a mess of coiling scarlet cords. He continued to cultivate while he surveyed his spirit.

Astonishingly, his overfull core pulsed several times and released large amounts of vital anima. His anima channels swelled with each pulse of his core. Strength suffused his muscles. He was able to move his fingers and toes. The chill from his surroundings overwhelmed every nerve in his body and sharp pinpricks of pain danced along his arms and legs. His fingers and toes felt like they would fall off. After one final pulse from his core, he drew breath. He hadn't even realized he wasn't breathing before that moment. For the next few moments, he lost his concentration as he cycled between choking coughs to expel mud from his nose and mouth followed shortly by rasping gasps that pulled in as much air as he could manage. He realized two things midway through this episode. He was lying on his back with most of his body submerged in mud, and his body was still twisted from the Sin. He had hoped the transformation had only been within the landscape created by his subconscious. Sadly, that wasn't the case.

Eerie silence still hung over the glade though Enkai could feel the occasional quakes that rumbled through the earth beneath him as well as the rushing wind on his cold-soaked body. Another test of his strength revealed he still couldn't get up though he managed to pull his face partially from the thick mud so that he could breathe normally. Once his breathing steadied, he resumed his cultivation.

Immediately, Enkai noticed a slight difference in his spirit. The anima in his core which had previously appeared opaque and cloudy now looked clearer and more vibrant. The core itself had gone from being a cloudy black orb to a slightly less cloudy black orb. His anima channels had grown thicker and more substantial though the cords of Sin had as well.

Did I just advance to Bronze? Enkai thought. The pulses must have been his core advancing. He suppressed a pang of guilt as he thought of Brem then pushed onward.

Again, his anima channels swelled with the vital anima which slowly revitalized his weakened body. More bodily function returned though he ignored his body as he focused entirely on cultivating his spirit. Cracks began to form along his anima channels as they continued to grow in size. Although alarmed, he didn't stop for a moment. In time, his channels became so saturated with vital anima that small amounts of the silver-white spiritual energy bled through the newly formed cracks. The anima that emerged from his channels soaked into his flesh and his entire body trembled violently. Involuntarily, he gouged furrows into the earth with his claws.

Still, he continued to cultivate more and more anima with his core. The cracks in his anima channels elongated and widened allowing more vital anima to bleed outward into his body. The tremors grew worse and a low growl emanated from his throat. Pain spiked through his exhausted frame highlighting each ache and sore in agonizing detail. Eventually, he was blinded once again to all but the events of his soul. The process appeared to be going well until the vital anima spilling from his anima channels collided with the cords of Sin.

Like a broken dam, the cords split open and discharged a deluge of Sin into his body. Enkai bent the full force of his will against the rush of Sin but the scarlet anima tore through his hold. Panic flitted at the edges of his consciousness. However, he remained steadfast and changed his tactics to meet the shifting tide of Sin. Abandoning any attempt to restrain it, Enkai forcibly increased the size of the cracks throughout his anima channels while he simultaneously pushed his spirit to cultivate faster. Unfortunately, no matter how hard he pushed, the vital anima couldn't match the Sin's pace. At the rate the Sin was going, it would overtake him once more.

In an act of desperation, Enkai tapped into the Sin in his core which acted as a source for the cords running through his spirit. The Sin answered eagerly and smoothly flowed into his grasp. As soon as Enkai drew from the Sin in his core, the streams of vital anima flowing from his anima channels and the cords of Sin halted. For a few breaths, his tumultuous spirit experienced stillness for the first time in what felt like years. Enkai clutched both vital anima and Sin within his core, each ready to be cultivated. Enkai knew that the Sin would become aggressive once more as soon as he started cultivating vital anima again. At the same time, he couldn't cultivate Sin since doing so would continue his demonic transformation and cost him his humanity.

Unsure of what to do, Enkai observed the Sin and vital anima in his grasp in the hopes of gaining some insight from the spiritual energies. The vital anima rested peacefully within his grip emanating steady warmth. As he focused on the silver-white energy, he experienced feelings of perseverance and resilience. On the other hand, the Sin shifted, continuously emitting fluctuating temperatures as if it couldn't decide whether it wanted to be hot or cold. Enkai also felt nothing but chaos and craving from the scarlet anima. He wracked his brain for any missing details that could solve his current predicament. As his mind caught between defeat and inaction churned, a whisper of madness crossed his thoughts.

Could I mix them? he thought as he peered at the two masses of anima in the core of his soul.

The only thing he knew about hybrid anima was that it was created by mixing two types of anima during the cultivation process and he only knew that because of his father. He remembered his father stating that the creation of Graywind anima was possible because blade and wind anima shared a synergistic bond. Years ago, Elder Onki had told him that vital anima existed within all living creatures. During the vision shown to him by Elder Jagan, he had witnessed the terrifying demon horde of the Sin Wastes. Though twisted and crazed, the demons appeared to be living creatures. Despite how insane the prospect sounded, Enkai saw no other choice available to him. In his heart, the decision was already made. He would rather doom himself by taking a risk than allow himself to be eaten away in a futile contest with his Sin.

Without hesitation, Enkai smashed the primal forces of Sin and Vitality together within his core.

**

Power, unlike anything Enkai had ever experienced, coursed through him. He shivered, not from the cold but from the changes occurring in his body and soul. Mixing vital anima and Sin had created something that had transformed the very landscape of his spirit. In the center of his core, between the oceans of Sin and vital anima, a seed of power shone like a flawless garnet in the noonday sun. The garnet-colored anima filled his spirit with a sense of wholeness. It pulsed with possibility as though he could achieve anything so long as he held it in his grasp. Once he allowed the hybrid anima of Sin and vitality to flow from his core, the transformation was swift and astonishing.

He lay amidst the muck of the earth, still numb to the raging storm, quakes, and howling creatures that ravaged the forest, and watched the events within his spirit in shock.

As soon as the garnet anima came into contact with his anima channels and the cords of Sin coiled around them, it absorbed the battling energies, consumed them, then began reproducing itself of its own accord. Much like the Sin, this new anima seemed to move of its own volition as though driven by an internal desire. Thankfully, unlike the Sin, the new anima rested firmly within his control. This hybrid anima was his original creation and obeyed his will. With just a thought, he halted its advance, then let it begin again.

When the process finished, his anima channels pulsed with the latent power of the strange new anima. The cords of Sin had transformed straightening and reorganizing themselves into a parallel mirror of his anima channels; although, they still bore the scarlet hue of Sin. Aside from their color, Enkai couldn't tell the difference between the two.

He felt his body changing even as he marveled at the changes in his spirit. The hybrid anima he'd created flowed from the cracks in his anima channels, both new and old. The Sin in his core was oddly well-behaved as it merged with the vital anima it'd previously battled.

In truth, the changes inflicted unimaginable pain as the new anima seeped into his flesh and bones transforming and reinforcing them. He felt his bones shift, snap, repair and thicken themselves all throughout his body. His skin tightened, stretched, and crawled as a result. As far as Enkai knew, attaining a Silver body usually wasn't so gruesome; however, his partial demonic transformation made his advancement more complicated. He hoped the changes caused by the Sin would be reverted especially since any human or beast he encountered in the world beyond the forest would attack him on sight with such a monstrous appearance. As he was, he had no idea what was happening to his body, since the pain and tremors caused by cracking bones and tearing muscle demanded his full attention.

After what seemed like an eternity, Enkai sat up and opened his eyes. The first thing he noticed was that he was alone. Elder Jagan's Sin-twisted form was gone and he saw no sign of the Sin wisp. Next, the smell of sulfur and bile flooded his nostrils. Foul-smelling sludge covered his body from head to toe. While disgustedly wiping it from his face and arms, he discovered the sludge was a mix of mud and a slimy black substance. When he saw it, his breath caught in his throat. He'd seen something similar before when his father had advanced to Silver. Once a divine artist reached Silver, his or her body was baptized by anima which reinforced his or her physique and removed any impurities. These impurities often took the form of foul-smelling black material secreted from the skin during the process. Interestingly, there was much more of the slimy substance than he remembered from his father's advancement to Silver.

Enkai sat in the pouring rain for a few seconds in a daze as the truth dawned on him. He was Silver. His excitement died prematurely as a spike of pain shot through his spirit. Unfortunately, he didn't have time to celebrate the accomplishment. He felt the swirling forces of vital anima and Sin straining against the boundaries of his core. Even at Silver, the amount of energy was far too immense for his spirit to handle. He either had to cultivate the spiritual energy or expel it. Despite his promise to Nin, he considered using the anima for cultivation. After all, Nin hadn't known about the garnet anima. Nearly all of it had been consumed during his advancement, though a small garnet seed within his core remained. If he cultivated the vital anima and Sin, he could create more of the hybrid anima and possibly advance further. The possibility tempted him more than he cared to admit; however, he abandoned the notion in the end. Kneeling under the scarlet moon, Enkai prepared to expel the foreign anima.

He dropped into a trance after excising all breath from his lungs and initiated the Heart of Earth and Sky. His time slowed as the breathing exercise took effect. His skin alighted with sensations he'd never experienced. Closing his eyes, he visualized his spirit housed within his body as an entity unto itself. He concentrated on the first hints of burning pain from his lungs and imagined his spirit struggling for breath as his body did. Once the image was firmly in his mind, he drew a single slow breath while he simultaneously pictured his spirit doing the same. He repeated this process three times. On the third breath, the breathing exercised bloomed into full effect.

Using the breathing exercise came naturally to him thanks to the insight inherited from Nin. When he expelled the third breath, he pushed the first wave of vital anima and Sin from his core. The anima passed through his skin in a rush and swirled around him as it was displaced. His fourth breath refreshed both body and spirit as his spirit learned to sustain not only itself but the body as well. His fifth breath was silent for his nose and mouth drew no breath.

A spiral of crimson and silver-white surrounded his body as Enkai cleansed his spirit. Each breath of the Heart of Earth and Sky sent waves of anima out of his core. As expected, the Sin didn't go quietly. Once he stopped cultivating it and began expelling it, the virulent anima resisted him every step along the way, however, the vital anima continued its benevolent assistance. The expelled silver-white anima interposed itself between Enkai and the expelled Sin which lashed out at him in an attempt to force its way back into his spirit. The result was a sphere of swirling spiritual energy so dense he could see it without his Spirit-sight. The two aspects of anima battled for supremacy with Enkai at their center which blinded him to the glade and forest beyond. Though he stayed focused on expelling all the anima, Enkai marveled at how alive the anima acted. Based on the night's events and Nin's words, he suspected there were forces beyond his comprehension at work.

As his core emptied, Enkai noticed two small pearls of anima floating within his core. They were foreign to his spirit, yet he immediately recognized their spiritual energies. The first pearl emitted no light but instead appeared like a shadowy hole in his spirit while the second radiated soft yellow light. Once he spotted them, Enkai redoubled his efforts. In his deep concentration, Enkai barely perceived anything other than the events of his spirit. He allocated any attention not being focused on expelling anima to monitoring the state of his brother and sister.

In the midst of expunging the anima from his core, another quake, larger than the others, shook the ground and a moment later, Enkai experienced an extreme sense of unease. Shivers ran down his spine reminding him of the feeling of having his spirit scanned, but more sinister. For a moment, he feared that the strange Sin-wisp had returned, however, he kept calm by maintaining the Heart of Earth and Sky which afforded him a welcome sense of clarity. Even if something was out there, he could do nothing about it at that moment. He needed to remain focused on the task at hand. Once he completely expelled the foreign anima nesting in his spirit and successfully anchored the spirits of his siblings to his own, he could address any potential threats. With that in mind, he banished his fear and continued.

By the end, exhaustion set in once more, yet this time it was just his spirit. It was a strange sensation being spiritually fatigued while his body was fresh from his advancement to Silver. Thankfully, he knew that spending some time refilling his spirit with the Heart of Earth and Sky would relieve some of the strain, but sadly, he had no time for that.

He gently gathered up the pearls of shadow and earth anima that represented his siblings. As soon as his will touched them, he felt their pain, fear, and weariness. He also experienced the emotions they'd held in their last moments. Jak had been afraid for Enkai's safety in the hands of the Sin wisp. Brem, on the other hand, had been angry at herself for being too weak to protect her family. Her frustration struck a chord with Enkai. He too knew the pain of helplessness. Thankfully, their spirits appeared unharmed though a bit weak.

Enkai grasped a sliver of his own life essence which served as the fire that gave him life. Immediately, his fatigue increased twofold and he nearly passed out. He carefully connected the sliver to his siblings' spirits. Once the connection was complete, he began the final step of the covenant.

Chapter 28

A short time later, Sethara furrowed her brow glancing askance at the Serpent of Discord. It appeared to be riveted to the child cultivating below. For her own part, Sethara digested the information the Serpent had given her— a location along with a story she found hard to believe. Nevertheless, she discerned no attempt at deception through her divine senses. Despite the assurances that her Divinity afforded her, she couldn't shake her distrust of the creature before her.

"Why should I trust your words?" she asked gazing down at the swirling ball of spiritual energy.

"Your divine senses tell you as much, do they not?" the Serpent asked right back. Although she wasn't looking at the creature, she could hear the amusement in its voice which only irritated her further. If the creature was, in fact, capable of deceiving her, then it could have simply offered reassurances to give her a false sense of security. Instead, the loathsome creature chose to shift the focus onto the integrity of her own senses as opposed to its words. If she pressed further, she might get the answer she desired, but she would be admitting that she didn't trust the power of her own Divinity, a power that was the manifestation of her own will and spirit. Its question forced her to make a choice between doubting her own abilities or trusting the Primordial's words. In so doing, the Serpent had turned her decision to channel her Divinity against her. All the while, the creature continued gazing down at the Primal child as though it were some great spectacle.

She decided against pressing further and chose instead to trust her own power. When she didn't answer immediately, the Serpent chuckled and turned to look her in the eye. The motion caused the scarlet moonlight to glint off its rain-slick scales as they shifted.

"If there is nothing else, Daughter of Eden, then it is time I bid you farewell," the Serpent of Discord said.

In different company, Sethara might have admitted that there was no longer a need to channel her Divinity into her words, however, she continued to do so for no other reason than that she disliked the creature's attitude. With barely masked annoyance, Sethara replied, **"Do you think I will just let you leave unmolested? With a Primal child no less?"**

"We both know that if you truly wished to stop me, you would have done so already," it said. Once more, it glanced downward at the cultivating child. "Besides, I won't be taking him with me."

Sethara hid her surprise behind a mask of impassivity. **"You expect me to believe you would just leave him here after you've shown such interest?"**

The Serpent smirked, an expression that highlighted its unsettling eyes, and said, "I do not claim divinity, so I expect belief from no one."

Tiring of the creature's games, she said, **"Speak plainly, Primordial."**

If a serpent could shrug, Sethara imagined the Primordial would have done so. Instead of replying, it lowered its head to the ground directly above the swirling mass of spiritual energy that contained the Primal in question. Its serpentine eyes leered down at the child like a predator eyeing its unsuspecting prey. After a moment, it returned to face her at eye level.

"It's true that I have a vested interest in the fate of this particular child, however, you do as well," it said. Sethara crossed her arms and the beginnings of a scowl peeked at the edge of her lips. She couldn't wait to hear what nonsense the creature would spew. "His name is Enkai and he happens to be of interest to Evaniel. He comes from the very same region where she hid from the eyes of Eden. In fact, she sacrificed him to a Sacred Vas tree. He would have died had yours truly not gotten involved."

Despite herself, Sethara had to admit her interest was piqued. Sacred Vas trees were relics of an age long before the Traitor's rebellion. Such relics were kept under close watch, so she should have been aware of any Sacred Vas trees being used, especially since they required the lifeblood of a Primal to produce their legendary fruit. Still, she showed little interest outwardly. She said, **"I could simply retrieve**

the information I need and dispose of him. If the Traitor truly lives, it would be foolish of me to let him live to become her tool."

"He harbors a wound in his heart inflicted by her. She betrayed his trust, fooled his father into sacrificing him, then killed the man. And these are the only the crimes he knows of. I doubt he will be so eager to serve her interests."

Sethara frowned. She'd found herself doing that often recently. **"The Traitor has turned those with greater animosity to her cause."**

"Then make him your own," the Serpent said. "If you kill him, you might eliminate a potential problem, but you might also incur the ire of myself and my kin. However, should you let him live, he becomes indebted to you, and in the times to come you gain a potential asset who holds the favor of the Primordials. Most importantly, he could serve as a bargaining chip when you find your mother and, perhaps, she'll be more inclined to speak honestly with you if you've shown a Primal mercy."

Despite the Serpent's ominous tone and the implied threat in its words, Sethara considered its appeal seriously. It helped that she had already thought of a few scenarios in which having the Primal alive would be advantageous. The true problem was that by sparing him she was directly disobeying her father, the Voice of Eden, a crime with consequences from which not even their shared blood would spare her. In truth, a few Primals still walked the face of Genesis, but they were either hunted by her agents or deemed too innocuous to be a concern; however, they were known elements. The Primal before her was not only of interest to several powerful entities, he was also a Deviant which meant he would be unpredictable at best. At the same time, she realized that if she truly wished to travel down the path before her and find the answers she sought, it would be best to keep him alive.

"Very well, I will keep him alive for now," she said as she dropped the divine power from her voice. She saw no reason to continue using it. The Serpent nodded then glanced at the sky. With that settled, she asked the question that bothered her most about the serpent, "Why did your record require such high authorization?"

The question seemed to catch the Serpent by surprise, though this only appeared to amuse it further. "Fear, Daughter of Eden."

"The Voice of Eden fears you? You may be dangerous, creature, but he has bested you before and he could do it again."

The Serpent chuckled darkly. It said, "The mighty Usurper fears the nature of my gift, so he tried to make me disappear. I do not blame him. Those who ruled before him feared it as well. Even the name they gave it, Sin, was born of their fear."

"Your 'gift'?" she asked. "The corrosive nature of Sin is of no threat to any member of Eden. You speak nonsense."

The Serpent snorted derisively. Its next words were spoken with the tone of an elder correcting a child. "My gift is not corrosive in nature."

She laughed, but it was the dry amusement of one who hears the absurd. Gesturing at the chaos around them, she said, "Ah, I suppose the beasts being corrupted by your Sinspawn are mistaken. Shall I inform the divine artists twisted into monstrosities and driven mad by your gift that they've got it all wrong?"

Before responding, its eyes flashed and the Sinspawn vanished, the sky cleared, and the earth stilled. In the eerie silence that followed, Sethara caught sight of the moon which resumed its normal hue. When it turned to meet her gaze, she looked into the eyes of a creature far older than she could fathom.

"My gift comes at a price, not all who accept it are able to pay"

"Then what is the nature of your gift?" Sethara asked, her impatience with the creature clear. The Serpent didn't answer immediately instead it gazed down at the Primal boy then off into the distance as if searching for something just beyond sight.

"Change," it said. Then, its smile became practically impish. In her heart, Sethara wondered if she had made a terrible mistake by not calling Abelard.

In an instant, the atmosphere of ancient mystery surrounding the creature vanished. "I've enjoyed our talk, Daughter of Eden. I wish you well, as next time we meet matters will be much less simple."

Faster than she could react, the Serpent vanished. She didn't even feel the shift in the Emanation. One moment the creature was there, then nothing. The display unnerved her more than she was willing to admit. In the back of her mind, she wondered what other tricks the Serpent hid.

After a moment lost in thought, she lowered herself to stand before the Primal boy. She mumbled to herself, "What is simple about this situation?"

She took another look at the boy familiarizing herself with her charge. At present, he was weeping as he knelt in a pool of mud and his own impurities. Around him, three great beasts lay dead amidst the filth with puncture wounds all over their bodies. It was truly a piteous sight.

He wore a tattered robe made from green fabric and bore a simple backpack made of the same material. He carried an impressive physique that showed signs of thorough conditioning and a good bone structure. His tanned skin bore the rough texture of one who had lived their life outdoors. Beneath the muck, his face had the hard-defined lines of a rugged man offset by the soft features of a child still maturing. His golden blonde hair hung like a rag from his head, covered in mud and grit. His beautiful jade eyes held a strange air of gentleness that contrasted with his other more animalistic features. At the end of each finger, he had dark fingernails that were as sharp as a lion's claws. His canines extended into sharp points and were slightly larger than normal.

Spiritually, he was a mess. His spirit bore the marks of severe strain unmistakably due in part to the anima that surrounded him. Even if the Primordials responsible were careful, the boy was lucky the influx of spiritual energy hadn't torn him apart. A glance at his core revealed he had recently advanced to Silver. In all honesty, she wondered how he'd managed to expel such a large amount of anima while still in the Foundation Realm though she would doubtless find out shortly. On that note, she commenced a basic scan using her Providence.

[Scanning ... Commencing report.]

Subject: Du Enkai of the Du clan

Birthplace: The Maro Province

Cultivation Level: Silver

[Importing additional details ...]

[Warning: Subject identified as a Primal. According to the 7th Edict issued by the Voice of Eden, all Primals are to be eliminated.

Would you like to notify the nearest Shofet?]

Dismissing the prompt, she allowed the additional information to flow. Events played through her mind detailing the boy's life from his birth to present. She recognized his birthplace, the Maro Province. It had been the refuge of deserters and cowards from the conflict between her father and the Traitor. The descendants of those deserters lived in isolation and practiced the flawed divine arts of their ancestors which had embedded their errors over the course of a millennium. In short, she had deemed the location to be of little interest. However, it seemed she'd been made the fool. The most wanted criminal in all the sectors had been right under her nose, yet she had failed to notice.

As for the boy's life, he'd had a troubled past though hardly the worst she had witnessed. There were only three things of note to her. The first was two visions shown to him by the Serpent of Discord, so she wasn't sure how reliable they were. The first vision was of a woman known as Lin Chun killing the child's father several years prior. Based on the second vision, she surmised that Lin Chun shared a connection with the Traitor since the two of them had been shown together. Interestingly, Lin Chun had deep crimson hair; the very same hair color Sethara had inherited from the Traitor.

Unsurprisingly, the boy knew nothing about the serpent's true identity. Sethara noted that the creature had killed the boy's adoptive family in an effort to force synchronization with his Sin, which had actually worked. Deviants who utilized their Sin were dangerous and those that merged it with their own anima were even more so. In the future, she might be able to use the Primal against the Serpent. He would never be a real threat to the Primordial, but he could still serve as an inconvenience.

The second point of note was the boy's training. The Sage of the North had trained him which explained his impressive foundation. Additionally, through an odd set of circumstances, he had inherited the ancient beast's breathing exercise, the Heart of Earth and Sky. The breathing exercise explained how such an inexperienced child had managed to expel such large amounts of anima from his spirit. His growth had been slow, yet if he could survive the outside world, he might prove to be a powerful asset in his own right. Lastly and most surprisingly, the boy had formed a covenant with the spirits of two young great beasts whom he considered family.

She pinched the bridge of her nose, an old habit from her life before ascending. Her life had become infinitely more complicated over the course of a few hours. After mulling the matter over for a few minutes, she thought of the perfect use for the Primal that would cultivate his talent while also ensuring he stayed in line. She waved her hand and dispersed the sphere of anima.

Chapter 29

After sealing the covenant, Enkai cried as the events of the night caught up with him. He could feel his siblings slumbering within him much like his *familiar* had once done. They floated like two moons around his core. However, the connection he had with his siblings was so much more than the link he'd shared with the false dream wisp. In order to complete the covenant, each member had to open themselves up completely to the other members while the link sealed. It was a strange and frightening type of vulnerability to have oneself completely exposed to another even for only a moment. In that moment of exposure, Enkai hadn't been able to hide the pain of Nin's death from them. Even in their slumber, he felt their fitful anguish at the truth he had unwittingly visited upon their dreaming minds. He dreaded the moment when they woke to find their bodies gone and their mother dead.

He held Nin's body in his arms. If he kept his gaze above her neck, she appeared to be sleeping, yet the sight of her blood matted fur had already burned itself into his memory. It was a small mercy that the bodies of his siblings had been largely unmarred aside from the puncture wound where the tendrils had pierced their hearts. The vision of his family impaled by razor-sharp tendrils of Sin flashed through his mind.

Fury nested in his heart, yet it didn't burn like normal anger. Frustration, grief, and hopelessness vied for dominance in his thoughts, but the anger was quiet. It had been pushed beyond the fiery passion he'd felt while fighting the apparition of his father in his mindscape. It had become barely a whisper: a promise of violence made in the depths of his soul. So, the rage waited patiently because while other emotions ruled his thoughts, the fury would have its turn once he found the right target.

Eventually, he collected himself. The cool-headedness taught to him by both his father and Elder Onki took control. He didn't know what to do going forward. He'd decided that he would eventually leave the forest, but he'd imagined doing so after finishing his training and learning about the outside world from Elder Onki and Elder Jagan. Now, Elder Jagan had become a demon and he had no idea what had become of Elder Onki. He had no knowledge of the world beyond the forest and still had no clear notion of how to progress in the divine arts. He somehow had to survive his journey, restore his siblings' bodies, find a way to save the people of the Maro Province from themselves, and track down Lin Chun and the creature that had killed Nin. The weight of his tasks seeded doubt in his heart. They seemed impossible feats yet one glance at Nin's face in its final rest pushed him to his feet. When all was said and done, he didn't have the luxury of wallowing in his own self-pity and helplessness. Nin had sacrificed everything in order to give him another chance. He owed it to her and his siblings to succeed.

Once on his feet, he didn't bother wiping his eyes for fear of getting blood and mud in them. He peered closely at the anima swirling surrounding him. Before he could move on, the expelled anima needed to disperse. He didn't want to find out what would happen if he crossed through the battling energies.

In the meantime, he examined his body. To his extraordinary relief, the demonic transformation had been reversed. The bone ridges, sharpened teeth, and wicked claws were gone. However, he was still far from normal. He still had claws or, at least, he thought he did. His fingernails were black curving into a sharp point a quarter of an inch above each fingertip. His teeth were flat once more, yet his canines had become more developed. He pulled off his soiled robes to get a better look at how his body had developed. Once he managed to get the robes off, he noticed his hair had gone from chestnut brown to golden blonde. He didn't need to look at Jak's body to know that his hair was the same color as Jak's fur. He glanced at his nails again and realized that they were the same color as Brem's claws. He wondered if these were side effects of the covenant.

After pulling off the robes, something fell out of them and hit his foot. Bending down, he saw two jagged pieces of twisted grey metal. He picked one up and discovered that it was warm to the touch. Taking a closer look, he realized what they were. It was the black iron amulet Elder Onki had given to him. Unfortunately, the amulet seemed to have lost all its power. Sighing, he dropped the drained metal. It was yet another setback that would make his journey more difficult.

Standing there over his family, Enkai resolved to bury them. He took the lid of Nin's elixir case and started digging. Only moments after he started, the anima swirling around abruptly dispersed and revealed an otherworldly beauty who stood a couple of feet away from him. He stopped digging and gawked at her. Suddenly aware that he was completely naked, Enkai moved the wooden lid over his exposed member.

The mysterious woman was adorned in a skin-tight bodysuit that looked like it was woven from starlight. Floating behind her, a white disk spun lazily while two brilliant pillars floated either side of it. Goosebumps rose on his arms and neck as he met the woman's seafoam green eyes which shone like stars reflected on a calm ocean tide. His wonder waned when he noticed her crimson hair. It was the same shade as Lin Chun's. Upon closer inspection, she bore a striking resemblance to Lin Chun's companion in Elder Jagan's vision. She took him in with an impassive expression while he regarded her with open suspicion. He had no idea if this otherworldly beauty was related to Lin Chun, but he was beginning to distrust red-headed women. No matter how irrational, they'd only brought him misery.

"Who are you? Where are Elder Jagan and that creature?" Enkai asked more forcefully than he intended. The woman raised an eyebrow at his tone and he immediately felt the urge to apologize. Instead of capitulating to that impulse, he squared his shoulders and held her gaze. It was a small act of rebellion against his own powerlessness in the grand scheme.

Surprisingly, the ghost of a smirk showed itself on her perfect features. She said, "The Primordial is no longer here. I assume the demon you knew as Jagan was sent elsewhere, but I do not know."

She extended her hand and a long shaft of white light extended from her closed fist. At one end, a curved flat blade formed creating a spade-like shape. She tossed the spade of hardened light at him. He caught it and held the sparkling implement awkwardly then shot her a confused look.

"Finish honoring your family, then we shall speak." she said. The gesture took Enkai off guard and caused him to tear up.

He blinked the tears away, gave her a nod, and started digging. Enkai worked in silence while the mysterious woman waited patiently. Burying his family took the better part of an hour. He buried them under one of the trees at the edge of the glade so their bodies would serve as nutrients for new life. During the process, he continuously checked on Brem and Jak, partially to make sure their spirits were alright and partially to remind himself that he wasn't alone. While digging, he thought about the strange woman's words. She had called the creature a Primordial. Nin had mentioned that Primordials helped the gods create the world at the beginning of all things. How was it possible he'd somehow ended up bonded to something like that? He doubted the woman was referring to the Silent Father which meant that he had been involved with not one but two Primordials. The scope of that realization made Enkai miss his simple days wandering Old Omen with his siblings.

When he finished, Enkai looked up into the now clear sky as the first rays of sunlight peeked over the canopy. Even though it would be another few hours before the sun rose to its full height, the sunlight gave Enka new hope. It was a relief to see that even after a night of hopelessness and despair, the sun would still rise to meet the dawn. He was alive. His siblings, though disembodied, were alive. As long as they survived, a new day would come to banish the night.

He bowed deeply in front of the grave and Nin's smiling face flashed through his mind. No words seemed appropriate, so he said with all his heart, "Thank you for everything!"

Once he'd made his peace, Enkai opened his backpack and pulled out his spare robes. They were soaked through but the leaf-green garments had been spared the muck. He quickly donned the robes and discovered that they were much snugger than they should have been. The fabric wrapped tightly around his biceps and chest while the hem rested a few inches above his ankles. Advancing to Silver must have affected him in more ways than he'd initially thought.

Turning toward the mysterious woman, he walked over to stand before her. She regarded his approach coolly taking in his tight-fitting robes and dirt-smeared appearance with her soul-piercing eyes. He handed the spade of hardened light back to her. Even after digging through the earth, the instrument was somehow immaculate. The moment the instrument left his grasp it scattered into a shower of sparks that dissipated before they hit the ground.

"Thank you for your kindness," he said then bowed his head. Despite his suspicion, the woman had shown him unexpected compassion and he was no boar.

"No need for thanks, it was common decency," she said waving her hand dismissively. "Besides, you may not be so thankful once our business is concluded."

"What do you mean?" Enkai asked. His muscles tensed slightly from suspicion though he kept his expression neutral.

"I am Sethara, Watcher and Guardian of this world," she said dispassionately. Enkai noticed her feet didn't touch the ground, as she levitated an inch or two above the ruined earth. Enkai took in her appearance once more: her unnaturally perfect beauty, her wondrous attire, the strange disk flanked by two pillars floating behind her back, her shining eyes, and her otherworldly essence.

On a hunch, he opened his Spirit-sight. Since he was now Silver, he could see the spirits of other divine artists and great beasts. The act nearly knocked him unconscious! He didn't even manage to look directly at her. He *couldn't*.

"I wouldn't recommend doing that," he heard her say.

The stories of the Fall of Heaven slipped into the forefront of his mind. Stories of divine beings descending from the heavens to wage war in the mortal realm. His heart rate sped up.

"Are you a goddess?" he asked, voice full of astonishment.

She didn't answer his question. She just smiled and extended her hand. Hesitantly, he took it. As soon as their hands touched, a soft white light enveloped his body and they drifted upwards.

"Do you know the fate of individuals such as yourself? Divine artists born with the core of a great beast?" she asked as they ascended.

Enkai tried to remain composed as the ground retreated further and further away. He had been at great heights before, yet in those circumstances, he'd had the benefit of solid earth beneath his feet. The sight of nothing but open air to break his fall should this strange woman choose to drop him was unsettling.

"I was told that people would try to hurt me if they found out. That I had to keep it a secret," he answered quickly, not wanting to give her a reason to drop him.

She nodded and stared off into the distance. They were hundreds of feet above the tree line overlooking miles of forest. Enkai turned his gaze in the same direction as the woman and noticed that the tree line broke several miles from their current location and gave way to a vast wasteland of strange terrain and multicolored clouds.

"The Grave of the Fallen is home to twelve tribes each with a lineage spanning back to the event you know as the Fall of Heaven. Several of those tribes still have records from the period before the Fall of Heaven. If you were to make contact with any of those tribes, their Elders might be capable of identifying you. If you weren't captured immediately, word would eventually make its way to a Shofet and you'd be hunted down, your memories would be searched to ascertain if you knew the location of any others like you, then you would be executed. If you somehow managed to evade detection in the wasteland and make it to the civilized territories beyond, you'd doubtlessly be recognized by one of the Seven Orders and promptly handed over to one of the Shofetim before you managed to make any progress toward any of your goals."

"How do you—" he started to ask before a brief glance from Sethara silenced him. He mentally kicked himself. Of course, the goddess knew what he wanted, why wouldn't she? He chewed over her words. Despite the severity of the fate she described, Enkai considered his options. Elder Onki had said he could find aid with the Sage of the West. If Enkai made it to that Sage, he could enlist her help. Perhaps, with the Sage's aid, he might be able to achieve his goals. The problem was he had no idea how to get to the Black Isles where the Sage was. Nin might've known, but she was gone and Enkai hadn't seen that information in her memories. Unfortunately, the more he considered it, the slimmer his chances seemed.

"Why are you telling me this?" he asked. He recalled the truth Elder Onki had told him. Forsaken weren't people who couldn't practice the divine arts, they were divine artists born with the same core as great beasts. As a goddess, Sethara must have known that as well. So, his real question was why a goddess such as herself was speaking to a Forsaken instead of smiting him on the spot? Why bother telling him about all the terrible things he should expect in the outside world? After all, it had been the gods that declared his kind as Forsaken in the first place.

"Because there can be error even in divinity," she said turning to meet his gaze.

"Ah," he answered dumbly. What else could he say? Enkai hardly considered himself qualified to comment on the wrongness or rightness of the gods. Then again, he had asked and even though he didn't understand it, she had given him an answer. So, he asked the only question he could think of at that moment, "What does that mean for me?"

"It means you have a choice, Du Enkai," she said. "By Divine Law, I am obligated to execute you here and now, but I have chosen to not do so for reasons I cannot divulge at this time. That said, I am directly disobeying Divine Law by allowing you to live which means I cannot simply allow you to wander the world freely. If you remain here within the forest, it would be simple to hide your existence. I've checked on the Sage of the North and he lives, however, extreme spiritual exertion has left him in a deep slumber. He'll not wake for a year or so given the circumstances."

Enkai shook his head and said, "I have to leave the forest. I don't care how dangerous it is or what I must do. There are people depending on me." In truth, Enkai wished he could stay in the forest, but he couldn't imagine life on Old Omen without Nin. Although he was relieved that Elder Onki was alive, it simply wouldn't be the same even once his master woke from his slumber. Besides, he'd made the decision to leave before his world fell apart, and he planned on following through even if his circumstances had become far more complicated.

"Then, perhaps, we can help each other," Sethara replied. A slight smile peeked across her face. "If you agree to undertake a quest, I will allow you to journey beyond the forest."

Enkai nodded. If he wished to restore his siblings and save the people of the Maro Province from themselves, the choice was clear. "Will this quest get in the way of my journey?"

"It may slow you down, but I doubt you will be deterred."

"Then I accept," he said without hesitation.

Once more, her eyebrow arched in amusement and a smirk snuck onto the corner of her lips. She said, "Don't you want to know the nature of the quest before you agree?"

"If I can leave the forest and it isn't going to stop me, then it doesn't matter what I have to do," he replied. He smacked his closed fist against his chest. "I have people who are relying on me, so tell me what you need done and I'll add it to the list."

She considered him as if she were seeing him for the first time. The force in his voice even surprised Enkai, yet it had come out so naturally. The garnet anima in his core filled him with confidence and strengthened his resolve making his words heavier as they left him. Enkai might have been imagining it, too, but his voice sounded deeper. He wondered if that was another side effect of his advancement to Silver.

"Very well, your quest is simple. There is a child not unlike yourself, touched by powers that have shaped his life since birth. Even now, forces plot to control or harm him. I have a vested interest in that child's future, but I'm forbidden from directly interfering in this world's affairs. This," she said gesturing around at the cracked earth, toppled trees and dead plant life, "was an exception. Additionally, all my other agents will be indisposed handling other tasks so you will handle this matter for me."

"How? Do you want me to guard him?" Enkai asked. As the Head Warrior, his father had occasionally guarded the Du Patriarch during his visits to other clans. Even though he had advanced to Silver, Enkai wondered how effective he would be as a guard in the outside world especially since there were people like Kartuk and the Daughter of Fire out there.

Much to Enkai's shock, Sethara chuckled. Her response was even more surprising. "In a way, I suppose. Your objective will be to accompany him on his journeys. His life will only get harder as he grows older, a truth that I am sure will pertain to you as well. There will be no shortage of sycophants and troublemakers seeking to worm their way into his confidence. More than anything, he will need someone he can trust in his company. You will be that person."

"What if he doesn't want me around?" Enkai asked. It felt like a childish question, but it was worth asking. After all, it had been years since he'd had any human interaction. Elder Onki and Nin had seen to his basic education on the divine arts and alchemy, but outside of that, he had very little knowledge of matters in the outside world. Not to mention, he suspected his social etiquette was truly horrendous. His family had been wonderful, but they were still great beasts at the end of the day.

Sethara gifted him with a genuine smile that stole the breath for his lungs. She said, "That's a great question. I would recommend making a good first impression lest you have to find an answer for it."

Enkai shook his head in wonderment. Was she serious or was he being teased by a goddess? "Alright, I understand."

Instantaneously, the white disk hovering behind her thrummed with power. Her eyes shone like newly born stars. The radiance burned his eyes, yet Enkai found himself unable to look away. Pain shot through the arm holding Sethara's hand and arrested his heart. His mind blanked as his spirit shrank from her power which left him completely at the goddess's mercy. The pain increased severalfold along his chest as though hot irons were being pressed into his flesh.

Then, she spoke and his very being threatened to unravel under the power of her voice. **"I, Sethara, bestow upon thee, Enkai of the Du clan, a Divine Quest. From here on, thy fate art entwined with Gilmes, heir of the Stormthrone and head of the Kuru family. Thy Word has been given, thy vow pledged. So long as it holds, I grant thee the protection of my Shroud. Let this accord be marked for all to witness."**

The burning along his chest intensified then all the pain vanished abruptly. In a moment of recoil, Enkai yanked his hand from her grasp. He realized immediately how stupid the action was when he looked down at the tree line hundreds of feet below him. Thankfully, he didn't plummet to his death. He simply stood on thin air just as Sethara did. Sethara favored him with a raised eyebrow as he grabbed ahold of her hand once more. Even though he didn't fall, he couldn't convince himself that it wouldn't happen. If he was holding onto Sethara, he would at least have someone to hang onto if she released the power holding him aloft.

Sethara laughed which startled Enkai. "Don't worry, I don't plan on dropping you," she said. She pointed to his chest and smiled again. "You are now one of my servants, after all."

Curious what she meant, he pulled open the cross-section that formed the collar of his robes. A white tattoo contrasted against the tanned skin above his heart. The mark was identical to the white disk flanked by twin pillars floating behind Sethara.

"What is this?" he asked running a finger over the mark. It was warm despite the cold air. "What did you do?"

"You are now one of my Godmarked. The mark is spirit-deep. Focus on it and it will lead you to Gilmes," she said.

She stepped forward pulling him with her. The landscape changed instantly, then they once again stood on solid earth. An uneven wasteland stretched out before them. They stood on a hill and Enkai spied a large collection of buildings a mile or so away. In the distance past the buildings, multicolored storm clouds churned ominously. Behind them, an enormous chasm split the earth for miles Enkai gapped at the sudden change in scenery. Beyond the chasm, the wasteland continued. It was both disconcerting and exciting how different the new landscape was from the places he had known.

"This is the border of the Grave of the Fallen and the Tempest Dominion. Tread carefully here and follow the mark." She let go of his hand and took a step away from him.

He recognized that she intended to simply leave. In a moment of near-panic fueled by proximity to the unknown, he asked. "Are you just going to leave me here?!" His question conveyed far more of his fear than he would have liked. She raised an eyebrow but said nothing.

I... I just..." he stammered. He stopped, feeling stupid for his own insecurities especially after being so confident beforehand.

Before he could formulate a proper response, Sethara pointed to the collection of buildings. "Gilmes will arrive in that town along with a small retinue of guards in a week's time. I suggest you clean yourself up and formulate a plan of action before then. Or do you think you'll be unable to make good on your word?"

He blinked several times as though dazed He opened his mouth to reply then closed it when nothing came to mind. For half a minute, she eyed him as he fidgeted awkwardly. Finally, he met her gaze and she said, "Good, I expect great things from you Du Enkai. Until next time."

Without even a glance backward, she turned away from him and vanished in a single step. Just like that, Enkai was alone far away from any home he'd ever known. The morning was still young so the rays of light from the sun barely illuminated the strange landscape. A chilling north wind swept through the wasteland and pierced the folds of his still damp robes. For a moment, fear and doubt pulled at his heartstrings, so he took a calming breath to settle his nerves. He had no time for doubt and fear of the unknown. There was nowhere to go but forward. Nin was gone, Elder Onki was incapacitated for a year or longer, and as far as the Du clan knew he had been dead for over half a decade.

After briefly checking on his siblings, Enkai focused on the Godmark. He quickly discovered that the mark was more than it initially appeared to be. In addition to the physical tattoo, it appeared within his spirit amongst the web of his anima channels. It radiated blinding white light that obscured the finer details of his spirit. Thankfully, he found that he could ignore the obfuscation of his spirit by concentrating. Finally, he sent his will into the Godmark.

A teenage boy appeared in his mind. He looked every bit like a prince out of a story, High cheekbones and a square jaw were the first thing Enkai saw. He was smiling which showed off pristine white teeth and appeared to be talking with someone though Enkai couldn't see who it was. His dark skin was pristine and bore no marks of hardship while his clothing belied his status as someone of great importance. He wore fine blue robes with golden trim that billowed in some unseen wind. The cuffs and hem featured a flowing white design that reminded Enkai of clouds. Emblazoned on the right breast of the robes was a dark storm cloud with lightning bolts shooting out of it in every direction. Above his right shoulder, an engraved shaft bearing similar storm-related themes extended into a spearhead made of a strange blue metal whose surface rippled with currents of crackling purple energy. On each hand, he wore blue gloves with white inlay threaded along the fingers and back.

Abruptly, the boy turned to look directly at Enkai and Enkai stared into his storm-grey eyes. At first, Enkai thought he was looking at something beyond his sight, however, the young man asked, "Who are you?"

Startled, Enkai's focus shattered and his connection with the Godmark broke. He glanced at the mark on his chest. In the back of his mind, he felt the tug of the Godmark urging him to head south. *That must be where he is.*

"Kuru Gilmes," Enkai said, feeling out the name. Gilmes was definitely the most grandiose person Enkai had ever seen. Even the Du Patriarch's ceremonial robes paled in comparison to Gilmes' attire. He was struck with a pang of self-consciousness as he looked over his unkempt visage from his muck-covered feet to his dirt strewn face. Before he found Gilmes, he needed to find a way to make himself presentable.

With that in mind, Enkai gazed southward to the town. The strange landscape was full of new and exciting possibilities. Wondering what the future would hold, he took his first step forward, weary yet hopeful.

Epilogue

Deep in the heart of the Grave of the Fallen where trees grew thick and the bounty was plentiful, Zan, chieftain of the Asher tribe, and several Asher elders rushed toward the sacred grove. It had been late when the earthquakes had started. By the time Zan got the elders together and ready to aid his people, three of their longhouses had collapsed from the quakes.

Another quake shook the ground beneath their feet, but this time, they were forced to stop as all the elders lost their footing. Zan barely remained standing. A moment later, they recovered and increased their pace to the grove.

The Cedar Grove was a sacred site for their people. It was the site where their founder, Asher, had died in service to the gods during the Fall of Heaven. Since that day, the grove had been a symbol of their tribe's favor with the gods above. For Asher's sacrifice, the heavens gifted blessings of fortune and strength to his descendants.

Zan dashed into the grove, his Gold-sense active and scanning for disturbances. He needn't have bothered. In the center of the grove, the altar dedicated to Asher had been sundered. Directly behind it, a great monolith rose from the ground casting a long shadow over Zan and the elders.

"What is this?!" Zan asked Abira, the oldest of his elders.

Like the rest of them, she'd gone pale at the sight of the ruined Asher altar, but she looked to him with wide eyes then cast a fearful glance at the monolith. "I ... I do not know. It looks like some kind of tower." She glanced once more at the Asher altar then went silent.

Zan shook his head. She was being of no help, so he approached the tower. It was massive measuring a few hundred feet around, at least, and several times that in height. As Zan drew closer, one of the elders called out to him but he ignored them all. Nine rings of intricate runes circled the structure from top to bottom. As soon as Zan drew close enough to touch the tower, the first ring of runes flared with power and the sound of stone grinding against stone filled the grove. Zan watched in fascination as a large section of the tower wall in front of him slid into the ground revealing a dark passage into the tower. Above him, light bloomed. He stepped back and looked up to see the top of the tower was glowing like a beacon in the night.

Then, the essence hit him. Like a tidal wave, it flooded out of the dark passage and washed over him. He started into the dark interior of the tower. Tentatively, he extended his Gold-sense into the passage. When he felt what was within, his eyes widened and a smile curled its way onto his lips.

He glanced at the ruined Asher altar, then to his shaken companions. "Rejoice, my brethren. It would seem the gods have once again shown us their favor."

***

Deep underground in the depths of Old Omen, Onki slept. His spirit was drained and his body ached as it never had. Miraculously, only a few miles of forest had been affected by Old Omen's eruption. He had successfully stemmed the tide.

However, Onki felt regret and defeat. He did not know that he'd been forced to contend with the power of a Primordial. If he had known, perhaps, he would not have been so wracked with guilt. In his unconscious state, he dreamed of the family he'd failed to protect. He hoped with all his heart that they had made it to safety.

His last words to Nin echoed in his dreams.

"Nin, I'm sorry I could not do more. Tell the Sage of the West, I expect her to take good care of my daughter and grandchildren."

***

Throughout the Spheres, the Primordials felt one of the Serpent of Discord move for the first time in an age.

In the depths of the Kazoan Jungle, the Ancestor Trees quivered and the jungle went silent. From all over the jungle, the Favored raised their enormous trunks to the sky in unison and released a primal call that echoed for miles beyond the jungle's borders. Atop the oldest of the Favored, Kartuk raised his Kazoan spear to the sky and joined their call. At the center of the jungle, the followers of the Green Faith bowed before a tree that pierced the heavens.

Somewhere beneath the ocean's surface, something shifted and the oceans grew restless. Sea dragons and leviathans woke from ancient slumbers, hungry from centuries of rest.

In the Sphere of Fire, the First Flame flared to life for a breath and the Fire Essence Fountains around Genesis birthed thousands cf fire wisps.

Hurricanes and tornadoes washed over the eastern continent as the Breath of the World exhaled. In his throne room, Sky King An reacted out and silenced the wind with the force of his will.

Like the Silent Father, the Blind Tapestry continued to sleep and weave the threads of fate.

In its prison, the World Breaker flexed against its restraints. They did not give, but it worried not. Soon, it would be free.

Glossary

Terms of Cultivation

Affinity: The natural talent of a creature for the various elements of anima. Very few divine artists or great beasts cultivate anima outside of their affinity.

Anima: Internal spiritual energy used for cultivation of the divine arts

Anima Channels: The network of spiritual pathways run through the body from the core.

Breathing Exercise: A special breath technique that allows a divine artists and great beast to take in essence from their surrounding for the cultivation of anima.

Essence: External spiritual energy used for certain techniques and creating anima.

Essence Fountain: A font of potentially limitless essence

Core: The center of a creature's spirit and the place where essence is refined into anima and anima is cultivated for the divine arts.

Eidolon: The remains of an awakened spirit that lingers after the death of a divine artist or great beast

Divine Arts: A gift given by the gods to all living things in a time long past

Divine Artist: a practitioner of the divine arts. Nearly all humans are capable of practicing the divine arts though not all awaken to that potential.

Great Beast: A beast capable of utilizing anima and essence. Most beasts fall within this category though there are still mundane creatures.

Foundation Realm: The first realm of cultivation achievable after awakening the spirit. Contains Lead, Bronze, and Silver

Natural Treasures: naturally occurring objects infused with spiritual energy or linked to spiritual phenomena

Rank: The cultivation level of a divine artist or great beast. The more advanced the cultivation level the stronger the practitioner.

Realms of Cultivation: The stages of cultivation that denote the maturity and nature of an awakened spirit. Each realm contains three ranks of cultivation.

Sin: A dangerous and volatile type of anima that adheres to the spirit.

Technique: A specific utilization of anima or essence that produces an effect correlating to the practitioner's spirit.

Characters

Brem: An adolescent umbral fox and Enkai's younger adoptive sister

Daughter of Fire: Apostle of the Green Mother who protects the Fire Essence Fountain of the Kazoan Jungle

Du Enkai: A young boy forced to leave the Maro Province after the Ritual of Waking and later adopted by Nin and Elder Onki.

Du Kai: Enkai's father

Du Makai: Enkai's grandfather

Du Ba Kou: The Du Patriarch

Du Ba Ren: Son of the current Du Patriarch

Du Shana: Enkai's only childhood friend and granddaughter of the current Du Patriarch

Elder Jagan: An ancient phantasmal owl who guards the lost city of Somn

Elder Onki: A black tortoise who rules over Old Omen

Elder Win: An elder and advisor of the Lin clan

Evaniel: An ancient divine artist recently reborn thanks to the efforts of Lin Chun

Jak: A young yellow monkey and Enkai's younger adoptive brother

Kartuk: Apostle of the Green Mother who shepherds the Kazoan Behemoths

Lin Chun: the former Lin Matriarch who aided in the rebirth of Evaniel

Lin Fa: The current Lin Matriarch and daughter of Lin Chun

Lin Feng: A veteran Lin warrior who gave Enkai the wisp lantern

Nin: Adoptive mother of Brem, Enkai, and Jak and adopted daughter of Elder Onki

Purifier: Apostle of the Green Mother who guards the border of the Kazoan Jungle from demonic incursions

Sethara: Antediluvian of the 1ˢᵗ Sector and overseer of Genesis

The Serpent: One of the Primordials

The Silent Father: One of the Primordials

www.ingramcontent.com/pod-product-compliance
Lightning Source LLC
Chambersburg PA
CBHW051509250626
47156CB00001B/27